# ATTACK SURFACE

*The Complete Idiot's Guide to Publishing Science Fiction*
(with Karl Schroeder)

*Essential Blogging*
(with Rael Dornfest, J. Scott Johnson, Shelley Powers,
Benjamin Trott, and Mena G. Trott)

*Down and Out in the Magic Kingdom*

*A Place So Foreign and Eight More*

*Eastern Standard Tribe*

*Someone Comes to Town, Someone Leaves Town*

*Overclocked: Stories of the Future Present*

*Little Brother*

*Content: Selected Essays on Technology, Creativity, Copyright,
and the Future of the Future*

*Makers*

*For the Win*

*With a Little Help*

*Context: Further Selected Essays on Productivity, Creativity, Parenting,
and Politics in the 21st Century*

*The Great Big Beautiful Tomorrow*

*The Rapture of the Nerds* (with Charles Stross)

*Pirate Cinema*

*Homeland*

*Walkaway*

*Radicalized*

# ATTACK SURFACE

## CORY DOCTOROW

**TOR**

A TOM DOHERTY ASSOCIATES BOOK
NEW YORK

This is a work of fiction. All of the characters, organizations, and events portrayed in this novel are either products of the author's imagination or are used fictitiously.

ATTACK SURFACE

A Tor Book
Published by Tom Doherty Associates
120 Broadway
New York, NY 10271

www.tor-forge.com

Tor® is a registered trademark of Macmillan Publishing Group, LLC.

The Library of Congress Cataloging-in-Publication Data is available upon request.

ISBN 978-1-250-75753-1 (hardcover)
ISBN 978-1-250-75752-4 (ebook)

Our books may be purchased in bulk for promotional, educational, or business use. Please contact your local bookseller or the Macmillan Corporate and Premium Sales Department at 1-800-221-7945, extension 5442, or by email at MacmillanSpecialMarkets@macmillan.com.

First Edition: October 2020

Printed in the United States of America

0  9  8  7  6  5  4  3  2  1

To the whistleblowers, who listened to the voice of their conscience and spoke the truth: Daniel Ellsberg, Thomas Drake, Chelsea Manning, Bill Binney, Edward Snowden, Alexander Nikitin, and the Panama Papers' John Doe, and all the others. Society owes you a debt of gratitude. You risked your freedom, your fortunes, and even your lives to bring us the truth.

And to the reporters who helped them reveal the truth, especially Daphne Caruana Galizia, who was murdered for doing her job. Rest in peace.

May we be inspired by your example, and find the bravery to reveal corruption wherever we find it.

My sole motive is to inform the public as to that which is done in their name and that which is done against them.

—Edward Snowden

# ATTACK SURFACE

# CHAPTER 1

That was why I loved technology: if you use it right, it gives you power—and takes away other peoples' privacy. I was on my sixteenth straight hour at the main telcoms data-center for Bltz, the capital of Slovstakia. Those are both aliases, obviously. Unlike certain persons I could name, I keep my secrets.

Sixteen hours, for what my boss had assured the client—the Slovstakian Interior Ministry—would be a three-hour job. You don't get as high as she did in the Stasi without knowing how to be a tactical asshole when the situation demands it.

I just wish she'd let me recon the data-center before she handed down the work estimate. The thing is, the communications infrastructure of Slovstakia was built long before the Berlin Wall fell, and it consisted of copper wires wrapped in newspaper and dipped in gutta-percha. After the Wall came down, responsibility for the telcoms had been transferred to the loving hands of Anton Tkachi, who had once been a top spook in Soviet Slovstakia. There are a lot of decades in which it would suck to have your telcoms run by an incompetent, greedy kleptocrat, but the 1990s represented a particularly poorly chosen decade to have sat out the normal cycle of telcoms upgrades. Because internet.

After Tkachi was purged—imprisoned 2005, hospitalized with "mental illness" in 2006, dead in 2007—the Slovstakian Ministry of Communications cycled through a succession of contract operators—Swisscom, T-Mob, Vodaphone, Orange (God help us all)—each of which billed the country for some of the jankiest telcoms gear you've ever seen, the thrice-brewed teabags of the telecommunications world, stuff that had been in *war zones,* leaving each layer of gear half-configured, half-secured, and half-documented.

The internet in Slovstakia sucked monkey shit.

Anyway, my boss, Ilsa, She-Wolf of the SS, promised the Interior Ministry that I would only need three hours, and the Interior Ministry had called up the telcoms ministry and given them orders to be nice to the Americanski lady who was coming over to do top-secret work for them, and give her everything she needed. I can tell that they laid it on thick, because when I first arrived at the country's main data-center, a big old brutalist pile that I had to stop and take a picture of for my collection of Soviet Brutalist Buildings That They Used to Shoot You for Taking Pictures Of—hashtags are for losers who voluntarily submit to 280-character straitjackets (and sentences can too a preposition end with)—the guy on the desk sent me straight to the director of telcoms security.

His name was Litvinchuk and he was *tightly wound.* You could tell because he had his own force of telcoms cops dressed like RoboCop standing guard outside his door with guns longer than their legs, reeking of garlic sausage and the sweat of a thousand layers of Kevlar. Litvinchuk welcomed me cordially, gave me a long-ass speech about how excited he was to have some fresh foreign contractors in his data-center (again) and especially ones from a company as expensive as Xoth Intelligence.

"Wait, that's not right word," he said, in a broad Yakov Smirnoff accent (he had a master's from the London School of Economics and I'd watched him do a TEDx talk where he sounded like a BBC World Service newsreader). "Exclusive? Illustrious?" He looked to me—specifically, to my tits, which was where every Slovstakian official I'd met addressed his remarks. I didn't cross my arms.

"Infamous," I said.

He smirked. "I'm sure. Miss Maximow"—he pronounced the *w* as a *v,* as they always did as soon as I got east of France—"we are all very excited to have you at our premises. However, I'm sure you understand that we must be careful to keep records of which contractors work on our sensitive systems." He slid a paperclipped form across his desk to me. I counted to seven—more efficient and just as effective as ten—and picked it up. Nine pages, smudgily photocopied, full of questions like "List all NGOs and charitable organizations to which you have contributed, directly or indirectly."

"No," I said.

He gave me his best fish-face, which I'm sure was super-effective against the farm boys cosplaying Judge Dredd in the hallway. But I'd been glared at by Ilsa, She-Wolf of the etc., etc., and had been inured to even the hairiest of eyeballs.

"I must insist," he said.

"I don't fill in this kind of form," I said. "Company policy. Xoth has negotiated blanket permission to access your premises from the Interior Ministry for all its personnel." This was true. I hated paperwork, and this kind of paperwork the most—the kind that asked you questions you could never fully or honestly answer, so that there'd always be an official crime to pin on you if you stepped on the wrong toes. Lucky for me, Xoth had a no-exceptions policy that techs were not allowed to fill in any official documentation at client sites. I'd take notes on my own work, but they'd go up the chain to my boss—Ilsa, She-Wolf etc.—who'd sanitize them and pass them back to the Interior Ministry for their own logs, omitting key details so that we would be able to bill them for any future maintenance.

I did my best to look bored—not hard, I was so bored my eyeballs ached—and stared at this post-Soviet phone commissar.

"I will fill it out for you," he said.

I shrugged.

He worked quickly, pen dancing over the paper. Not his first paper-pushing rodeo. He passed it back to me. "Sign." He smiled. It wasn't a nice smile.

I looked down. It was all in Cyrillic.

"Nope," I said.

He switched off the smile. "Madam." He made it sound like *missy*. I could tell we weren't going to get along. "You will not get into my data-center until we have gathered basic information. That is our protocol."

He stared at me, fish-face plus plus, clearly waiting for me to lose my cool. Long before Ilsa began her regime of hard-core stoicism training, I had mastered situations like this. You don't get far in the DHS if you don't know how to bureaucracy. I turned boredom up by a notch. I tried to project the sense that I had more time to burn than he did.

He held out his hand. I'd assumed he'd be a short-fingered vulgarian, but he had pianist's fingers, and a hell of a manicure, the kind of thing that made me feel self-conscious about my lack of girly cred. "ID."

Xoth gives us fancy ID cards to wear on client sites, with RFIDs and sapphire-coated smart chips and holograms, props for impressing rubes. I could knock one up in an afternoon. I unclipped mine from my lanyard and handed it over.

The pen danced again at the bottom of the form, and he turned the paper to show me. He'd added "signed, per, Masha Maximow" to the signature line. *Good for you, Boris. You made a funny.* What an asshole.

"We done?"

He carefully made a xerox on a desktop printer/scanner/copier—one that I knew five different exploits for, and could use to take over his whole network, if I wanted to—and handed it to me. "For your records."

I folded it into quarters and stuck it in my back pocket. "Which way?"

He said something in Russki and one of the Stormtroopers struggled in under the weight of his body armor and escorted me to the data-center. I took one look at the racks and racks of hardware, zipped up my fleece against the icy wind of the chillers, and got to work. It was going to be a long three hours.

B y the time I finally finished, I was freezing and swearing. My hoodie was totally inadequate and I suspected that my long-fingered vulgarian had ordered one of his Armored Borises to turn the thermostat down to sub-Arctic.

But it was done, and the test-cases ran, and so I got up off the folding chair I'd been hauling around the data-center's corridors as I moved from one rack to another, tracing wires, untangling the hairball of grifty IT contractor short-cuts and fat-fingering.

Surveying my work, I had a deep feeling of . . . Well, to be honest, a deep feeling of pointlessness. I'd labored for sixteen hours—fifteen if you subtract meals and pee breaks—getting the Xoth Sectec network appliance installed, and all I had to show for my trouble was an inconspicuous black one-unit-high server box, mounted on the bottom shelf of the furthest rack (this was

Xoth policy—put our gear in the most out-of-way place, just in case barbarian hordes topple our dictator clients and storm the gates, looking for mediagenic evidence of collaboration with evil surveillance contractors) (that would be me).

But now I got to celebrate. I looked over my shoulder and made sure I was alone—the RoboCops had made a point of standing behind me, watching my ass, as I dragged my chair around—bent down and touched my toes, feeling the awesome stretch in my hamstrings and the unkinking of my neck and shoulders as my hair brushed the ground. Then I stood, cracked my knuckles, plugged my laptop into my phone, and tunneled out to a network box I'd left in my hotel room that morning, making sure it was all charged up and successfully connected to the hotel's wifi, which (see above) sucked monkey shit. I fired up a virtual machine on my laptop, choosing a container with a fully patched version of the latest freebie version of Windows, and used its browser to connect to Facebook.

The Slovstakian uprising hadn't figured out that the only real use for Facebook in a revolution was as a place to teach people how to use something *more secure than Facebook*. All their communications was in a couple of groups that they accessed over Facebook's Tor Hidden Service, good old https:// facebookcorewwwi.onion, which was pretty good operational security (if I did say so myself).

Their problem was that they were way, way outgunned—as of now, they were facing down the best Xoth had to offer (at least, the best Xoth had to offer in its middle-upper pricing tier). Things were about to get very, very bad for the plucky demonstrators of Slovstakia.

The virtual Windows box in my virtual machine connected through the hotel's network to Tor—The Onion Router, a system that bounced network connections all over the world, separately encrypting each hop, making it much harder to trace, intercept, or modify its users' packets—and to Facebook's hidden service, a darknet site based in a much nicer data-center than this one, in an out-of-the-way corner of Oregon with remarkably low year-round temperatures (ambient chilling is the number one money-saver when it comes to running a building full of superheated computers).

I alt-tabbed into my monitor for the Sectec box beside me, using an untunneled interface on my phone's native network connection. That Sectec box could handle ten million simultaneous connections, combing through all their packet-streams using machine-learning models originally developed to recognize cancer cells on a microscope slide (fun fact!). Sure enough, it registered the existence of a stock Windows laptop in the Sofitel Bltz, communicating over Tor. It profiled the machine by fingerprinting its packets, did a quick lookup in Xoth's customer-facing API to find a viable exploit against that configuration, and injected a redirect to the virtual machine on my laptop. I pinned the monitor window to the top of my desktop and flipped back to the VM, watching as the browser's location bar flickered to an innocuous-seeming error message, and by flipping to a diagnostic view of the VM, I could see the payload strike home.

It used a 0-day for Tor Browser—always based on a slightly out-of-date version of Firefox and thus conveniently vulnerable to yesterday's exploits—to bust out of the browser's sandbox and into the OS. Then it deployed a higher-value exploit, one that attacked Windows, and inserted some persistent code that could bypass the bootloader's integrity check, hooking into a module that loaded later in the process. In less than five seconds, it was done: the virtual machine was fully compromised, and it was already trying to hook into my webcam and mic; scouring my hard drive for interesting files; snaffling up saved password files from my browser, and loading its keylogger. Since all that was happening in a virtual machine—not an actual computer, just a piece of software pretending to be a computer—none of that stuff really happened, thankfully.

Now it was time to really test it. Sectec has a mode where it can scour all the traffic in and out of the network for specific email addresses and usernames, to locate specific people. I gave it Litvinchuk's email address, and waited for his computer to make itself known. Took less than a minute—he was polling the ministry's mail server every sixty seconds. Two minutes later, I controlled his computer and I was cataloguing his porn habits and downloading his search history. I have a useful script for this; it locates anything in my targets' computers that make mention of *me*, because I am a nosy bitch and they should know better, really.

Litvinchuk was into some predictably gross porn—why is it *always* being peed on?!—and had googled the shit out of me. He also had a covert agent who'd searched my room; they had put a location logger on my phone using a crufty network appliance I'd already discovered in my epic debugging session in the data-center. I could have fed that logger false data, but I turned it off because fuck him sideways. I downloaded half a gig of videos of Litvinchuk in full-bore German heavy latex, gleaming with piss, then stood, stretched again, and shut my lid.

I'd started my adventure at 4 p.m. the day before. Now it was 8 a.m. and that meant that the demonstrations in the main square would be down to skeleton crews. Anyone interesting only came out after suppertime and worked the barricades in the dark, when the bad stuff always kicked off. That's when the provocateurs and neofascists came out—often the same people—and the hard-core protesters had to work extra hard.

I called the Sofitel on the way back and ordered room service. All they had was breakfast and I wanted dinner, so I ordered triple, and gave up on explaining that I only needed one set of cutlery.

I arrived at the room's door at the same time as the confused waiter. I waved at him and carded the door open, then followed him and his cart in. He was one of those order guys you saw around the hotel, someone who'd once had a job in Soviet brute-force heavy industry but ended up pushing room service trolleys when it all went to China. Those guys never spoke English, not like their strapping sons, who spoke gamer-international, the language of Let's Play videos and image boards. "Dobre," I said, "Pajalsta," and took the folio from him and added a ten-euro tip—everything at the Sofitel was denominated in euros, ever since the local currency had collapsed. I hadn't even bothered to change any cash on this trip, but I had bought a 10,000,000,000-dinar note from an enterprising street seller who'd been targeting the tourist trade. I liked the engraving of the opera house on the back, but the Boris on the front was a unibrowed thick-fingered vulgarian straight out of central casting. I kept forgetting to google him, but I was pretty sure he was being celebrated for something suitably terrible, purging Armenians or collaborating with Stalin.

My alarm went off four hours later. I found my bathing suit and underwater MP3 player and the hotel robe, made sure all my devices were powered down with their USB ports covered, and headed for the pool.

Swimming—even with loud tunes—always churns my subconscious, boredom forcing it to look inward at its neglected corners. So somewhere around the fiftieth lap (it was a small pool), I remembered what was happening that day. I did the time zone calculation in my head and realized there was still time to do something about it. *Fucketty shitbuckets.* I hauled myself out of the pool and toward a towel.

I perched, dripping, on the room's desk chair and powered up my phone for a quick peek at the pictures of the screw-heads on my laptop. I had covered all the screws with glitter nail polish and shot clear pics of each one, with a little label beside it, so that I could easily verify whether someone had unscrewed my laptop lid and done something sneaky, like inserting a hardware keylogger or, you know, some Semtex and packing nails. I used an open-source astronomy package designed to match pictures with known constellations to verify two of the seven screws. The glitter patterns had become old friends by this point, since I checked them every time I'd been out of sight of my computer before powering it up again.

I booted it, pulled the towel over my head (to defeat hidden cameras), and keyed in my passphrase while going "AAAAH" medium-loud, just to defeat anyone trying to guess my passphrase from the sounds of my fingers on the keys. Xoth had an airgap room for really sensitive stuff, walls shielded with a Faraday cage, full of computers that undercover Xoth techs bought by walking into consumer electronics stores and buying computers off the shelf without ever letting them out of their sight. After being flashed with a Xoth version of Tails, a paranoid Linux distro, and having their wifi cards and Bluetooth radios ripped out with pliers, their USB ports were covered with 3-D printed snaps that couldn't be removed without shattering them. You brought your encrypted data in on a thumb drive, requisitioned a machine, broke the seal, plugged in your USB stick and read the data, then handed the machine back to a tech to be flashed and resealed. Compared to that shit, I wasn't all that paranoid.

Litvinchuk had been a busy Boris: my computer downloaded and sorted his own wiretap orders as he took the Sectec out for a spin. I looked through the list, and yup, I already knew a lot of those names. They were the people I was planning to meet for drinks in a few hours. I made a few quick revisions to my Cryptoparty slides.

It was getting to be time for lunch-ish or dinner-esque, whatever you call a 3 p.m. meal. I was about to phone down for room service when my phone alarmed me, which isn't something it does often, because I've turned off every notifier.

When that chirp goes off it is a pure sphincter-tightener.

"Wedding of Marcus Yallow and Ange Carvelli" and a shortened URL. Because livestreaming. Because Marcus. Because exhibitionist attention-whore. Because shithead.

God, he drove me crazy. I fired up the livestream. They'd made everyone they loved fly to Boston for the wedding, because of the girl's grad school schedule, and they'd filled the hall with robots they borrowed from the MIT Media Lab to give it some nerd cred. Of course she didn't wear white. Her dress was ribbed with EL wire that pulsed in time with the music, and Marcus's suit—Beatles black, with a narrow tie and drainpipe pants that made his legs look even scrawnier than usual—was also wired up, but it only pulsed when they touched, moving bands of light across its surface from the point of contact.

Okay, that *was* pretty cool.

The officiant was a prominent Cambridge hacker, one of the ones they'd hauled in when they were after Chelsea Manning. She'd been a kid then, but now she looked older, her wife holding their kids on her lap off to one side. She wore a colander on her head, because she was ordained in the Church of the Flying Spaghetti Monster, which was frankly too much.

Marcus and his girlie exchanged vows. Marcus promised to make her coffee, rub her feet (ugh), review her code, and say sorry and mean it; she promised to back down when she was wrong, forgive him when he apologized, and love him "until the wheels come off" (double ugh). They kissed and received their applause. I gave it three minutes, making sure that the ceremony was well and truly done and the reception about to start. I'm not a monster.

Here's the thing about Cambridge: they have drone delivery there. For a little extra, you can time the delivery to the minute. I checked the time in the corner of the screen. There was a big window right behind the officiant with a view of the Charles River and the snow and the tracks of students' boots. I checked the time again.

The drone came right up to the window and rapped on it politely. It had four big rotors and a sensor package that fed me all kinds of telemetry on the activity in the room, from Bluetooth device IDs to lidar outlines of all the humans in the space. The wedding livestream showed it tapping on the window from the bride and groom's POV (the stream ran off about a dozen cameras and was smart enough to switch between them based on which one was capturing the most action); the stream from the drone showed me the opposite view, Marcus and his girl and all their nice nerdly friends and family gaping at the fisheye camera.

Marcus broke the tableau by opening the window, and the drone daintily coasted into the room and deployed its box into his hands. He pulled the ripstrip on the plasticky wrapping and revealed the gift-wrapped box within. She took the card out of the envelope and read it. I admit it gave me a shiver to hear her say my name.

When Marcus heard it, his face did a funny. *That* gave me a shiver too—a different kind. He and I have a complicated history. I rubbed my fingers, the ones he'd broken when I was only sixteen. He did it in order to steal my phone, because I had a video that exonerated him of being a terrorist. Complicated. Those fingers hurt whenever I thought of him.

He looked at the drone's sensor package. "Thank you, Masha," he said. "Wherever you are." The usual was for this to be a recording that you could watch later, but if you were a creepy stalker chick (ahem), you could watch it in real time. I emojied the drone and it bobbled a curtsey and gave me five seconds to commit another $50 to hold on to it for five more minutes, because it had other packages to deliver. I released it and its feed died.

On the livestream, I watched them unwrap my gift. I'd almost sent them a bag of kopi luwak, which is a kind of coffee bean that's fed raw to a civet cat, then harvested from its poop and roasted, but then I'd read an animal welfare article about the treatment of civet cats. So I'd given them a Raspi Altair 8080: that is, a 1974 "personal computer" that you controlled with a row of faceplate switches and read using peanut-bulb blinkenlights, which had been painstakingly restored with a Raspberry Pi open-source CPU inside it, giving it approximately eight bazillion times the computing power. Most of the interior was left empty by the refit, and the craftswoman who'd sold it to me had filled the empty space with a bunch of carved wooden automata that cranked a set of irregular gears around in whirring circles while the computer was operating, which you could see if you swapped in the optional transparent case.

Marcus knew exactly what it was (because I'd found it through his Twitter feed) and how much it cost (because he'd moaned about never being able to afford it, not in a million years), and he had a look of profoundly satisfying shock on his face. He told his girlie all about it in that spittle-flecked hyperactive mode he slipped into when he was really, really excited. The expression that crossed her face was even more satisfying: a mix of jealousy and appreciation that I reveled in like the petty, terrible person I am.

I felt like the fairy who curses Sleeping Beauty out of spite when she thinks she hasn't been invited to her christening, except that this was a wedding and not a christening. Oh, and they invited me, of course.

But I had work to do. Hey, I'd sent a thoughtful gift, even if I totally upstaged their stupid nerd chic wedding. Shoulda had a nerdier wedding, if they didn't want to get upstaged.

I was still hungry and now it was getting to be time to head out to the square. Room service at the Sofitel sucked anyway. I'd get a doner kebab. Hell, I'd get a sack of them and bring them along.

The vegan café where my pet revolutionary cell met was called the Danube Bar Resto, and they could always be found there before the night's action, because fuck opsec, why not just make it easy for the secret police to round you all up somewhere far from a crowd? I despair.

Kriztina was already there, chowing down on something that had never had the chance to breathe and live and run and play. I cracked open the crumpled top on my sack of kebab and let her smell the meaty perfume. "Save room," I said.

She laugh-choked and gave me a mouth-full thumbs-up as I sat down next to her. There were eight of them in Kriztina's little cell, a couple of graphic designers, two webmonkeys, a poet (seriously), and the rest didn't even pretend to be employed. Few under-thirties in Slovstakia were, after all.

"You want drink?" Oksana always had spending money. I'd pegged her as a snitch when I first met her, but it turned out she just made good money working for a law firm that did a lot of western business and didn't mind having a trans girl for a paralegal. Once I'd satisfied myself that she didn't appear anywhere in Litvinchuk's master lists of turncoats, I'd come to like her. She reminded me of some of the women I'd known in the Middle East, brave fuckers who'd managed to look like a million bucks even as their cities were being pounded to gravel around their pretty shoulders, fearless beneath their hijabs and glamorous even when they were covered in dust and blood.

"Sure." It would be something with wheatgrass and live microbes and probably twigs, but mostly orange juice and mango pulp. The guy who ran the place liked to talk about how the chlorophyll "oxygenated" your blood—of course chlorophyll only makes oxygen in the presence of sunlight, and if you've got sunlight in your colon, you've got big problems. Even if you could get grass to fill your back passage with oxygen, it's not like your asshole has any way to absorb it. I get my oxygen the old-fashioned way: I breathe.

"Tonight—" Kriztina started. I held up a hand.

"Batteries or bags," I said. Everyone looked embarrassed. Those of us whose phones had removable batteries removed them. The rest of them put their phones into the Faraday bags I'd handed out when I first started hanging out with these amateurs.

"Before we talk about tonight, I want to walk you through some new precautions." They groaned. I was such a buzzkill. "First: running Paranoid Android is no longer optional. You have to get the nightly build, every night, and you have to check the signatures, every single time." The groans were louder. "I'm not fucking around, people. The Interior Ministry now has a network appliance that gets a fresh load of exploits three times a day. If you're not fresh, you're meat.

"Second, make sure your IMSI-catcher countermeasures are up to date. They just bought an update package for their fake cell towers and they'll be capturing the unique IDs of every phone that answers a ping from them. The app your phone used last week to tell a fake tower from a real one? Useless now. Update, update, update. Check every signature, too.

"Third, make sure your smart-meters aren't sneaking back online. After Minsk, the Interior Ministry's really looking for a chance to pull the same trick, turn off heat in the middle of February for anyone they suspect of demonstrations.

"Finally, everyone has to wear dazzle, no exceptions." Again with the groans, but I got the tubes out of my bag and passed them around. The dazzle was super-reflective in visible light and infrared and anyone who tried to take a picture of someone wearing it would just get a lens flare and jitter from their camera's overloaded sensors. It had been developed for paparazzi-haunted celebs, but the smell of the stuff and the greasy feel it left on your skin—not to mention persistent rumors that it was a powerful carcinogen—had doomed it to an existence as a novelty item used only by teenagers on class picture day and surveillance-haunted weirdos.

I slurped the green juice Oksana had just handed me and was pleasantly surprised to discover that it tanged unmistakably of tequila. She winked at me. Oh, Oksana, you are a hero.

"Get to it," I said. "Update before we leave. Remember, opsec is a team sport. Your mistake exposes all your friends."

They got to it. Kriztina and Oksana and I checked everyone else's work, and then each other's. Friends don't let friends leak data. We also smeared each other with dazzle, and they made jokes in Boris about the smell, which I could almost follow, though my Boris was a lot worse than everyone else's English.

"Nazis tonight," Kriztina said, looking at her phone. She knew people who knew people, because Slovstakia was so small that everyone was someone's cousin. That meant that when someone's idiot skinhead cousin and his friends started boozing and heil-ing and getting all suited and booted, which meant telescoping steel rods (the must-have neo-Nazi fashion accessory of the season) and brass knucks. The neo-Nazis were someone's useful idiots; they'd come out to the demonstrations and shout about bringing down the government, and then they'd start giving those one-armed salutes and charging the police lines.

It wasn't that they lacked sincerity—they really did hate immigrants, especially refugees, especially brown ones; as well as Russians, Jews, Muslims, queers, vegans, the European parliament, and every single member of the national congress, personally. They may have even come by those views organically, by dint of their own intolerant knuckleheaded generalized re-sentment. But these characters also had money, a clubhouse, a source for those nifty telescoping batons, and someone had given them workshops on how to make a really effective Molotov, without which they would surely have re-moved themselves from the gene pool already.

I'd been inside Litvinchuk's network for a month, ever since I landed in-country to backstop the sales team that was working him, feeding them URLs of pastebins where hackers dumped sensitive data they'd pulled out of his data-centers, data we also trickled to his political rivals, making him look worse and worse and making the case to give us a shitpile of reserve-currency dollars better and better.

So I knew what his theory was on the skinheads: he blamed the Kremlin. He blamed the Kremlin for *everything*. It wasn't a bad strategy—Moscow cer-tainly did like to meddle in the affairs of its former satellite states. But I had figured out which personal accounts his own senior staff were using, and done some digging there, and *I* thought that maybe the skinheads were actually un-witting skirmishers in the civil service empire-building that Borises excelled at. Which didn't necessarily mean the Kremlin had clean hands; maybe they were backing one of Litvinchuk's lieutenants in the hopes of destabilizing things and replacing their canny adversary with someone dumber and more biddable.

"What do we do about it?"

Kriztina and her cell exchanged looks, then muttered phrases in Boris that I couldn't follow. This turned into an argument that got quieter—not louder—as it intensified, dropping to hisses and whispers that were every bit as attention-grabbing as any shouting match. It was lucky for them that the Danube Bar Resto's other customers weren't snitches (I was pretty sure, anyway).

"Pawel says we should back out when they show up. Oksana says we should go to the other side of the square, and move if they go where we are."

"What do you think?"

Kriztina made a face. "I hear that they're going to go in hard tonight. Maybe the big one. It's bad. If we're in the background when they go over the barricades—"

I nodded. "You don't want everyone in the world to associate you with a bunch of thugs who crack heads with the cops."

"Yes, but also, we don't want to sit by and let cops bust our heads to prove we're not with them."

"That's sensible."

Oksana shook her head. "We must protect ourselves," she said. "Helmets, masks."

"Masks don't stop bullets," Pawel said.

"I agree. Masks don't stop bullets. If they start shooting, you'll have to shelter or run. Nothing's going to change that."

He made a sour face.

The tension was palpable. Kriztina's pretty face looked sad. Her little cell had been good friends before they'd been "dangerous radicals." I didn't have that problem because I didn't have friends.

"It's true that you can't survive bullets and it's true that the pinheads are going to try to provoke something terrible if they can. It's true that the cops on the other side are scared shitless and haven't been paid in a month. There are some factors you can control, and some you can't. Wishing things were different won't make them different. It's okay to call it a night and try again later. Maybe the cops and the Nazis will cancel each other out."

All of them shook their heads in unison and started talking. Even the bystander vegans couldn't ignore the racket. Kriztina flushed and waved her hands like a conductor and they quieted down. The staring vegans pretended to stop staring.

"Maybe we can win them over," Kriztina said, quietly. Everyone groaned. This was Kriztina's go-to fantasy. None of us had even been alive in 1993 when the tanks rolled in Moscow to put down Yeltsin's ragtag band of radicals, but of course they all knew the story of how his young, idealistic supporters had spoken to the soldiers about the justice of their cause and then the tank drivers had refused to roll over the revolutionaries. Then there had been borscht and vodka for all the Borises, and the big Boris, Boris Yeltsin, had led the USSR to a peaceful transition.

Pawel broke the tension. "You first." We all laughed.

I knew what to say next. "It's been an honor to serve for you. We will drink together tomorrow, here or in Valhalla." Wrong mythos, but there isn't a Boris alive who can resist a good Viking benediction.

We paid the bill and I chugged down my wheatgrass margarita, and Oksana linked arms with me as we left the Bar Resto, while Kriztina expertly relieved me of the bag of doners and handed them around. We ate as we walked. I pulled out my phone at a red light, one last slot-machine pull at my social-media feeds, and saw Marcus and his girlie, smiling radiantly as they got on a tandem recumbent bike to ride off to their honeymoon, looking so sweetly in love I nearly tossed my kebab.

Kriztina saw something in my face, and let her hand touch mine. She gave me one of her pretty, youthful sisterly smiles and I smiled back. Once, I'd had female friends who'd been there when some stupid boy did some stupid thing, and even though I didn't have that anymore, Kriztina let me pretend I did, sometimes.

As we got closer to the main square, we ran into other groups heading the same way. A month ago, the nightly demonstrations had been the exclusive purview of hard-core street fighters in his-'n'-hers Black Bloc/Pussy Riot masks. But after an initial rush of head-beating that rose, briefly, to the notice of people outside of this corner of the world, the police had fallen back and the numbers of babushkas and families with kids went up. There were even theme nights, like the potluck night where everyone had brought a covered dish and shared it with the other protesters and some of the cops and soldiers.

Then the neo-Nazis started crashing the police lines and the cops stopped accepting free chow from the likes of us. Now, nightly skirmishes were standard issue and the families were staying home in growing numbers. But the night was a relatively warm one—warm enough to walk without gloves, at least for a few hundred meters—and there were more kids than I'd seen in at least a week. The older ones bounced alongside their parents, the younger ones were in their arms, dozing or watching videos on phones. Of course the idents of those phones were being sucked out of them by the fake cell towers cutting right through their defenseless devices' perimeters.

The square buzzed with good energy. There was a line of grannies who had brought out pots and wooden spoons and were whanging away at them, chanting something in Boris that made everyone understand. Kriztina tried to translate but it was all tangled up with some Baba Yaga story that every Slovstakian learned with their mother's borscht recipe.

We stopped by a barrel fire and distributed the last couple kebabs to the people there. A girl I'd seen around emerged from the crowd and stole Kriztina away to hold a muttered conference that I followed by watching the body language out of the corner of my eye. I decided some of Kriztina's contacts had someone on the inside of the neo-Nazi camp, and judging from her reaction, the news was very bad.

"What?" I asked. She shook her head. "*What?*"

"Ten p.m.," she said, "they charge. Supposedly some of the cops will go over to their side. There's been money changing hands."

That was one of the problems with putting your cops on half pay: someone might pay the other half. The Slovstakian police had developed a keen instinct for staying one jump ahead of purges and turnovers—the ones that didn't develop that instinct ended up in their own cells, or dead at their own colleagues' hands.

"How many?"

Borises are world-class shruggers, even adorable pixies like Kriztina. If the English have two hundred words for "passive aggressive" and the Inuit have two hundred words for "snow," then Borises can convey two hundred gradations of emotions with their shoulders. I read this one as "Some, enough, too many—we're fucked."

"No martyrs, Kriztina. If it's that bad, we can come back another night."

"If it's that bad, there may not be another night."

That fatalism.

"Fine," I said. "Then we do something about it."

"Like what?"

"Like you get me a place to sit and keep everyone else away from me for an hour."

The crash barricades around the square had been long colonized by tarps and turned into shelters where protesters could get away from the lines when they needed a break. Kriztina returned after a few minutes to lead me to an empty corner of the warren. It smelled of BO and cabbage farts, but was in the lee of the wind and private enough. Doubling my long coat's tails under my butt for insulation, I sat down cross-legged and tethered my laptop. A few minutes later, I was staring at Litvinchuk's email spool. I had remote desktop on his computer and could have used his own webmail interface, but it was faster to just slither into his mail server itself. Thankfully, one of his first edicts on taking over the ministry had been to migrate everyone off Gmail—which was secured by 24/7 ninja hackers who'd eat me for breakfast—and onto a hosted mail server in the same data-center I'd spent sixteen hours in, which was secured by wishful thinking, bubblegum, and spit. That meant that if the US State Department wanted to pwn the Slovstakian government, it would have to engage in a trivial hack against that machine, rather than facing Google's notoriously vicious lawyers.

The guiding light of Boris politics was "trust no one." Which meant that they had to do it all for themselves.

Litvinchuk's cell-site simulators all fed into a big analytics system that mapped social graphs and compiled dossiers. He'd demanded that the chiefs of the police and military gather the identifiers of all their personnel so that they could be white-listed in the system—it wouldn't do to have every riot cop placed under suspicion because they were present at every riot. The file was in his saved email.

I tabbed over to a different interface, tunneled into the Xoth appliance. It quickly digested the file and spat out all the SMS messages sent to or from any cop since I'd switched it on. I called Kriztina over. She hunkered down next to me, passed me a thermos of coffee she'd acquired somewhere. It was terrible, and reminded me of Marcus. Marcus and his precious coffee—he wouldn't last ten hours in a real radical uprising, because he wouldn't be able to find artisanal coffee roasters in the melee.

"Kriztina, help me search these for texts about letting the Nazis get past the lines."

She looked at my screen, the long scrolling list of texts from cops' phones. "What is that?"

"It's what it looks like. Every message sent from or to a cop's phone in the past ten hours or so. I can't read it, though, which is why I need your help."

She boggled, all cheekbones and tilted eyes and sensuous lips. Then she started mousing the scroll up and down to read through them. "Holy shit," she said in Slovstakian, which was one of the few phrases I knew. Then, to her credit, she seemed to get past her surprise and dug into the messages themselves. "How do I search?"

"Here." I opened up a search dialogue. "Let me know if you need help with wildcards."

Kriztina wasn't a hacker, but I'd taught her a little regular expressions-fu to help her with an earlier project. Regexps are one of the secret weapons of hackerdom: compact search strings that parse through huge files for incredibly specific patterns. If you didn't fuck them up, which most people did.

She tried a few tentative searches. "Am I looking for names? Passwords?"

"Something that would freak out the Interior Ministry. We're going to forward a bunch of these to them."

She stopped and stared at me, all eyelashes. "It's a joke?"

"It won't look like it came from us. It'll look like it came from a source inside the ministry."

She stared some more, the hamsters running around on their wheels behind her eyes. "Masha, how do you do this?"

"We had a deal. I'd help you and you wouldn't ask me questions." I'd struck that deal with her after our first night on the barricades together, when I'd showed her how to flash her phone with Paranoid Android and we'd watched the Stingrays bounce off it as she moved around the square. She "knew" I did something for an American security contractor and had googled my connection with "M1k3y," whom she worshipped (naturally). I'd read the messages she'd sent to her cell's chat channel sticking up for me as a trustworthy sidekick to their Americanski Hero. A couple of the others had wisely (and almost correctly) assumed I was a police informant. It looked like maybe she was regretting not listening to them.

I waited. Talking first would surrender the initiative, make me look weak.

"If we can't trust you, we're already dead," she said, finally.

"That's true. Luckily, you can trust me. Search."

We worked through some queries together, and I showed her how to use wildcards to expand her searches without having them spill over the whole mountain of short messages. It would have gone faster if I could read the Cyrillic characters, but I had to rely on Kriztina for that.

When we had a good representative sample—a round hundred, enough to be convincing, not so many that Litvinchuk wouldn't be able to digest them—I composed an email to him in English. This wasn't as weird as it might seem: he had recruited senior staff from all over Europe and a couple of South African merc types, and they used a kind of pidgin English among themselves, with generous pastings from google Translate, because opsec, right?

Fractured English was a lot easier to fake than native speech. Even so, I wasn't going to leave this to chance. I grabbed a couple thousand emails from the mid-level bureaucrat I was planning on impersonating and threw them into a cloud machine where I kept a fork of Anonymouth, a plagiarism detector that used "stylometry" to profile the grammar, syntax, and vocabulary from a training set, then evaluated new texts to see if they seemed to be by the same author. I'd trained my Anonymouth on several thousand individual profiles from journalists and bloggers to every one of my bosses, which was sometimes handy in figuring out when someone was using a ghostwriter or had delegated to a subordinate. Mainly, I used it for my own impersonations.

I'm sure that other people have thought about using stylometry to fine-tune impersonations, but no one's talking about it that I can find. It didn't take much work for me to tweak Anonymouth to give me a ranked-order list of suggestions to make my own forgery *less detectable to Anonymouth*—shorten this sentence, find a synonym for that word, add a couple of commas. After a few passes through, my forgeries could fool humans *and* robots, every time.

I had a guy in mind for my whistleblower—one of the South Africans, Nicholas Van Dijk. I'd seen him in action in a bunch of flamewars with his Slovstakian counterparts, friction that would make him a believable rat. I played it up, giving Nicholas some thinly veiled grievances about how much dough his enemies were raking in for their treachery, and fishing for a little finder's fee for his being such a straight arrow. Verisimilitude. Litvinchuk would go predictably apeshit when he learned that his corps was riddled with traitors, but even he'd notice something was off if a dijkhead like Van Dijk were to narc out his teammates without trying to get something for himself in the deal.

A couple passes through Anonymouth and I had a candidate text, along with a URL for a pastebin that I'd put all the SMSes into. No one at the Interior Ministry used PGP for email, because no normal human does, and so it was simplicity itself to manufacture an email in Litvinchuk's inbox that was indistinguishable from the real thing. I even forged the headers, for the same reason that a dollhouse builder paints tiny titles on the spines of the books in the living room—even though no one will ever see them, there's professional pride in getting the details right.

Also, I had a script that did it for me.

"Now what?" Kriztina looked adorably worried, like I might grow fangs and tear her throat out.

"Now we give Litvinchuk fifteen minutes to check his email. If he hasn't by then, we text him from Van Dijk's phone. Which reminds me." Alt-tab, alt-tab, paste in the number, three clicks, and I'd disconnected Van Dijk's actual phone from the network, making sure that Litvinchuk couldn't reach him.

It was very dark now, and cold, and my ungloved fingers burned. Typing done for now, I tugged on my gloves, turning on the built-in warmers. I'd charged them all day, and they should be good for a full night on the barricades. Kriztina's gloves had cigarette burns on the fingers that must have let the cold in. Filthy habit. Served her right.

The square was more crowded now. Barrel fires burned, and in their flickering light and the last purple of the sunset, I saw a lot of flimsy homemade armor.

"You guys are in so much trouble."

"Why?"

I pointed at a young dude who was handing out painter's masks. "Because those masks won't do shit against tear gas or pepper spray."

"I know." She did fatalistic really well.

"Well?"

She shrugged in Boris. "It makes them feel like they're doing something."

"Feeling isn't enough," I said. "Maybe in the past, in the Vaclav Havel days or whatever. Back then you had these basket-case Borises who ran their secret police on vodka and purges and relied on their own engineering talent to make listening devices the size of refrigerators that needed hourly repairs and oil changes. Now, spooks like Litvinchuk can fly to DC every couple years for the Snooper's Ball trade show, where the best-capitalized surveillance companies in the world lay out their wares for anyone to buy. Sure, they're all backdoored by the Russians, the Chinese, or the Americans, but they're still about a million times better than anything Slovstakia is going to produce on its own, and they will peel you and your friends like oranges.

"Not just surveillance, either—you should see the brochures from the less-lethals industry these days. Melt-your-face pain rays, pepper spray and nerve gas aerostats, sound weapons to make you shit your pants—"

"I know, I know. You tell me this all the time. What do you want me to do? I try to be smarter, try to make my friends smarter, but what can I do about all these people—"

I could feel the heat rising through my body. "The fact that you don't have a solution doesn't mean that you don't need to find one and it doesn't mean that one can't be found. You and your seven friends aren't going to change shit, you need all these people, and you know something they don't know, and until they know it, they are going to get creamed." My hands shook. I stuffed them in my pockets. I shook my head, cleared out the screams ringing in my ears, screams from another place and another time. "You need to be better because this is serious and if you're not better, you'll die. You understand that? You can run from these jokers, hide with Paranoid Android and Faraday pouches, but you will make mistakes and the computers they run will catch those mistakes, and when they do—"

There was doner kebab coming up my gullet, and I couldn't talk anymore without puking, or maybe sobbing, and I couldn't tell you which would be worse. I'm not an idiot: I was talking to myself more than I was talking to her. Having a day job where you help repressive regimes spy on their dissidents and a hobby where you help those dissidents evade detection is self-destructive.

I get that.

But tell me that *you* don't do anything self-contradictory. Tell me that you don't find yourself dissociating, doing something you know you'll regret later, something you know is wrong, and doing it anyway, like you're watching yourself do it.

I just have a more dramatic version is all.

Kriztina must have seen something in my face, which I hated. It wasn't her business what was going on in my heart or my head.

But she took me in a big hug, which Borises also specialize in. It was a good hug. I snuffled the snot back in, willed my tears away, and hugged her back. She was tiny underneath all those layers.

"It's okay," she said. "We know you're only trying to keep us safe. We will do our best."

*Your best won't be good enough,* I didn't say. I took her hand. "Let's stroll."

The protest crowd was big now, throngs, really, and some of them were singing folk songs in rounds, deep voices and then the high, sweet ones.

Kriztina sang along under her breath. The song floated across the square and it changed the rhythm of the night, made people stamp their feet in time with it, made them lift their heads to the police lines. Some of those cops nodded along with the singers. I wondered if they were the same guys who'd agreed to let the neo-Nazis get through their lines and smash the parliament.

"What do the words mean?"

Kriztina's eyes were warm when she turned to me. "Most of it is nonsense, you know, 'Slovstakia, our mother, on your bosom we were fed,' but the good parts are very good, I think, 'all of us together, different though we are, will work together always, strong through understanding, invincible unless we forget who we are and attack our brothers—'"

"No way."

"Seriously. The words were written by a poet in the seventeenth century after a terrible civil war. I modernized it a little in the translation, but—" She shrugged. "It's our old problem, this kind of infighting. Always someone who wants to build himself a little empire, have ten cars and five mansions, and always the rest of us in the square, fighting about it. Spending blood. But from what you say, maybe this time we lose, no matter how much blood."

I looked at the police lines, the milling crowds. It was full dark now and there were huge steam clouds sweeping the square, pouring off the barrel fires, lit by the huge LED banks that shone out from behind the cops, putting them in shadow and the protesters in full, photographable glare. Their support poles glittered with unblinking CCTV eyes. The police vans ringing the square sported small forests of weird antennas, ingesting all the invisible communications flying around the square, raiding phones for virtual identity papers at the speed of thought.

"You guys are pretty much fucked," I said.

Kriztina grinned. "You sound like a Slovstakian."

"Ha ha. The truth is that it's a lot harder to defend than it is to attack. If you make one mistake, Litvinchuk and his goons will have you. You have to be perfect. They need to find one imperfection."

"You make it sound like we should be attacking."

I stopped walking. Yeah, of course that was what we should be doing. Not just playing around at the edges, pitting one adversary against another with false-flag emails—we should be doing a full-court disruption to their whole network, shutting down their comms when they needed it the most, infecting their phones and servers with malware, making a copy of everything they said and did and siphoning it off to a leaks site on the darknet that we'd unveil at the worst possible moment.

I checked my phone. Nearly fifteen minutes had gone by.

"I think you should," I said. "But once you do, the game will change. Once they know that you're completely inside their network, they'll have two choices: turn and run or crush you like bugs. I think they'll go for option two."

"Masha." My name sounded weird and natural at the same time when she said it. It was a Russian name, once upon a time, and there were Borises in my ancestry stretching back to the Ashkenaz diaspora. Not just Jews, either: in the old photos, my grandmother looked like a Cossack in drag. Cheekbones like snowplows, eyes tilted like a Tolkien elf. I turned to stare at her. "Masha, we are not inside their network. *You* are."

Oh.

"Oh." It was true, of course. I'd taught them a little ("teach a woman to phish . . .") but if I packed up and left, as I was scheduled to do in two weeks, they'd be sitting ducks.

"I could provide remote support," I said. "We'll encrypt emails, I'll send you the best stuff."

She shook her head. "You can't be our savior, Masha. We need to save ourselves. Look at them," she said, and pointed.

It was the painters, the Colorful Revolutionaries, who took their inspiration from those nuts in Macedonia who'd gone around splashing all the public monuments and government buildings with brightly colored paint. Long after the "revolutionaries" had been chased away or arrested, the paint remained. It had built up a lot of hope (and made a ton of money for Chinese power-washer manufacturers). In Macedonia, "vandalism" was a misdemeanor and the worst they could do to you is give you a ticket for it. Slovstakia's parliament hadn't hesitated to make vandalism a felony, of course. They'd watched Macedonia just as closely as their citizens had.

Slovstakia's painters had perfected the color wars, loading their slings with cheap latex balloons filled with different colors of long-lasting paint, swollen eggs they whirled in a blur over their heads before releasing them in flight, arcing toward their targets. It was like Jackson Pollock versus Goliath.

Like all the radical cells, they did their own thing, separate from Kriztina and her group. No one was sure where they'd show up or what they'd do when they got there. Litvinchuk had a fat file on known and suspected members, and I'd toyed with joining them when I got to Slovstakia, before deciding that they were too low-tech for me to work with. You couldn't deny that they were effective: they'd been working their way along the top row of windows, egging each other on with feats of breathtaking long-distance accuracy, bull's-eyeing each window in succession from left to right. The cops below them on the line, behind their shields and faceplates, flinched every time one of those bright balloons arced over their heads. The floodlights caught the colored mist that spread out from each bursting bladder, and I imagined that it was powder-coating the cops underneath in a rainbow of paint and glitter. Glitter was the pubic lice of the Colorful Revolutionaries, spreading inexorably through even the slightest glancing contact, impossible to be rid of.

The cops. I checked the time on my phone again. It had been sixteen minutes since I'd sent that email to Litvinchuk and there was no sign of the chaos that was supposed to ensue. Shit.

"I think we've got to find a place to sit down and plug in my laptop again," I said, tilting my head at the cops.

"Shit."

"Yeah."

We looked around for a place to sit. There'd been benches in the square, two administrations ago. Then the first wave of protests hit, mild ones by day, that involved thousands of people sitting politely in the square on every single bench, eating ice cream. There was no law against eating ice cream, and you're not loitering if you're sitting in a designated sitting zone. The last act of the old prime minister—long since deposed after a no-confidence vote and a midnight flight in the presidential jet loaded with bales of paper euros, so much of it that they burned out six bill-counting machines before giving up and weighing it by the ton to estimate its value—had been to remove all the benches and replace them with waist-high "leaning benches" that tilted at a seventy-degree angle. That'll teach those ice-cream-eating motherfuckers!

But there wasn't anywhere to sit, so that naughty old Boris had the last laugh, I guess.

"Here," Kriztina said, taking off her coat, leaving her in nothing but an oversized sweater that made her look even tinier and younger and more vulnerable. She folded the coat and set it down on a clean-ish patch of asphalt.

"You're such a martyr." I settled down onto it and dug in my bag for my phone. "And thank you." Before I had my lid up, there was a commotion from the police line. A flying squad in Vader-chic riot gear had emerged from the parliament building with guns at the ready, and they now stood behind the line of rank-and-file cops, barking orders. "Holy shit." I put my laptop away and Kriztina pulled me and her coat from the ground. Everyone in the crowd was holding up a phone to capture the commotion; the clever ones had the phones mounted backward on long, telescoping selfie sticks that towered over the crowd.

"I guess Litvinchuk got the email, huh?"

People were streaming past in all directions now, jostling us. The guns the new goons were pointing at their police colleagues were also pointed into the crowd. Any shots that missed (or pierced, I suppose) those cops would be headed straight at us. The crowd was sorting itself into a giant V shape with a clear space behind the police line, protesters crammed in on the side, selfie sticks and phones going like crazy.

We were also crammed in with the crowd, because Kriztina had all but lifted me off my feet and dragged me out of the potential line of fire.

It was a tense standoff. The cops were shouting at the goons, the goons were shouting at the cops, gun muzzles were out. One of the Colorful Revolutionaries stepped out into the empty V of space, a girl barely five feet tall, with that telling coltishness of early adolescence, and fitted a paint balloon to the pocket of her sling. She began to spin. The crowd held its breath, then someone shouted something that I semi-translated as "Don't do it, you idiot," in a voice that was half-hysterical twitter. The girl's eyes were narrowed in concentration and the sling whirled around her head, its whistle cutting through the crowd noise, and she bared her teeth and grunted like a shot-putter as she let it fly, and it flew true, the crowd turning as one to watch it arc through the cold air and the harsh LED light to spatter, perfect dead center, on the ass of one of the riot cops. She pumped her fist and dove for the safety of the crowd as the cop spun with a yelp and instinctively reached for his besplattered ass—then brought his hands unbelieving to his eyes, the banana-yellow glitter paint sparkling on his Kevlar gloves. The goons behind him had, as one, aimed their guns at him and I swear I could see their fingers tightening on the triggers—but miraculously, none of them shot this dumb Boris fuck in the back and sent his lungs sailing over the square. When the paint-spattered cop went for *his* gun, his comrade had the presence of mind to slap it out of his hand, and it skated across the icy square toward the crowd, skittering and then gliding, revolving slowly.

There followed one of those don't-know-whether-to-shit-or-go-blind silences as everyone—protesters, cops, elite goons, and let's not forget the neo-Nazi skinheads—contemplated their next course of action.

The leader of Litvinchuk's goons was faster than the rest of us. He barked an order and his boys all settled their muzzles back into an even distribution across the police lines, and the cops re-formed themselves back into an uneasy line, facing them. The chief goon barked out names—the names we'd provided—and pulled officers out of their line, one at a time, cuffed them, and led them away.

When the first one went, the crowd's curiosity, already close to peak, blew through all its limits. But then as more and more were led away, that curiosity and the insistent buzz of people narrating the action into their phones reached a feverish intensity.

By the time it was done, half the cops on the line were gone. A few of the goons moved to fill in the empty spaces, standing shoulder to shoulder with the cops they'd just been pointing their guns at. The remaining cops were more freaked out than the crowd. I looked around for the neo-Nazis, easy enough to spot—skinhead uniforms, always clumped together, always glaring at anyone who glanced their way, always with cans of beer—and couldn't spot them at first. Ah, there they were, way at the back, talking urgently among themselves, waving their hands, even shoving each other. They must have been in a fury: ready to rush the lines, keyed up for serious out-of-control violence, now trying to master all that psycho energy. Some were doubtless considering the short numbers on the police line and wondering if they could break through even without turncoats ready to help them with it; the others likely remembering the savage reputation of Litvinchuk's private enforcers, the country's most fearsome torturers and disappearers of political enemies, the only force whose pay was never delayed, let alone cut.

Alcohol is a hell of a drug. The pinhead who broke free of his friends was so drunk he was practically horizontal, not so much running as failing to completely fall, but his klaxon was working and he opened his big dumb mouth wide enough to let out all the drunksound that was begging to be free. His war-yodel drew the attention of everyone in the square, and he had that nice, big open V-shaped empty space to charge through, holding his piece of rebar up in one hand like a villager with a pitchfork, heading straight for the gun that had gone skittering away.

The leader of the goon squad shouted an instruction at him, just once, loud enough to be heard over the drunkspeak. Then, goon-prime tipped a finger at one of his men, who raised his rifle, aimed, and blew the Nazi's head off with an expanding round that sent bone fragments and chunks of brain out in a fan behind him.

One thousand camera-phone eyes captured the scene from every angle.

The first scream—a dude, somewhere behind me—was quickly joined by more. Someone jostled me, then again, harder, and then hard enough that I went down on one knee, Kriztina hauling me back up to my feet with her tiny, strong hands. "Thanks," I managed, before we were swept up by more running bodies, having to run and push ourselves just to keep from being trampled.

Then we couldn't hear the screaming anymore, not over the sound-weapons that the cops had switched on. These sonic cannons combined very loud sound with very low sounds with gut-twisting efficacy, literally making you feel like you were about to shit yourself even as your ears shut down. The crowd was virtually immobilized as people froze and twisted and covered their ears. After a pitiless interval, the cannons finally switched off, leaving a post-concert whine ringing behind them, the death throes of our inner ear hairs.

I couldn't see the cops anymore—too many bodies, the neat V erased by a tangle of people, many weeping or holding their torsos or heads. A loud pronouncement, too distorted to make out.

"What did he say?" I said to Kriztina, making sure she could see my face, read my lips.

"He wants us to go." Her voice sounded like it was coming from the bottom of a well.

"I want to go," I said.

She nodded. We looked around for the rest of our group, but it was hopeless. People were milling about aimlessly, crying or searching for their friends. I pulled out my phone. No signal. In situations like this, the cops are always trying to strike a delicate balance between keeping the internet service turned on (and spying on everyone) and turning it off (and preventing everyone from coordinating). I guessed that they'd decided they had all the data they needed on the protesters to find them later, so now it was time to get rid of them. There were some who weren't going to be moving under their own power—people who had been hurt in the stampede and were lying on the frozen cobblestones, either alone or, if they were lucky, in the arms of someone. I remembered all those families I'd seen, all those kids.

Some people get overwhelmed by situations like that. I've seen it happen and I understand it. I'm not one of those people, though. My limbic system— the fight-or-flight response—and I are on speaking terms, but we've got an arrangement: it doesn't bother me and I won't bother it. So what I felt was urgency to get gone, but not fear. I felt for the people lying on the ground, but a foreigner who couldn't speak their language was going to be less than useless compared to someone who knew where the hospital was and how to talk to the paramedics, and that someone would reach them soon enough.

Kriztina, though, was in rough shape. Her face was so bloodless it was almost green, and her teeth were chattering. Probably a little shock, plus the temperature had dropped another ten degrees. "Come on." I pulled her toward the ring road around the square, toward a road I recognized as leading toward my hotel. It would be safe.

Kriztina let me lead her along for a few minutes, at first with a big group of crying and scared (former) protesters, then in a thinner and thinner crowd as we moved toward the business district and the Sofitel.

Look: I'm a compartmentalizer. It's my superpower. Part of me had just watched a guy get killed, sorta-kinda because of me, and had been in a stampede. Part of me knew that I'd done something insanely risky that night, something that could cost me my job and worse. Part of me, though, was thinking about the fact that I was responsible for this little sidekick-slash-sister of mine, a hobby that had metastasized into a moral duty, and that she was as keyed up and adrenalized as I was. Neither of our phones was working, and if Litvinchuk held true to form, they'd stay dead for hours, meaning that no one could get through to us or vice versa for the foreseeable, which meant I'd have to keep her out of trouble. I had a hotel room of my own and the turn-down service would have left us chocolates to replenish our blood sugar after that intense experience, which was good first-aid protocol, so it was practically medical advice that said we would have to go into my hotel room and get the fuck away from all that danger that she doubtless wanted to drag me back into.

I took her hand in mine as we turned into the Sofitel's road, and I felt her trembling. I hoped that was cold, or excitement, because trauma was going to be a pain in the ass. The Sofitel had two big Borises out front with semiautos and body armor. They glared at us as we approached. I glared back. Glaring isn't personal with Borises: they see smiling as a sign of insincerity.

I held out my room key. One of them took it from me without a word and touched it to an NFC reader on his belt. It lit up green. He nodded. "Welcome."

I began to lead Kriztina through the door, but Boris #2 put a hand on her shoulder and held a hand out, presumably for a key, though I'm guessing a bribe would have worked just as well. "She's with me," I said. Boris 2 pretended he didn't understand. I took the liberty of moving his hand—I'm no black belt, but I've always found jujitsu more relaxing than yoga—and yanking Kriztina into the hotel. I wasn't in the mood for this. The guard shouted at us and followed us in, slinging his gun and reaching for me. I was *not* in the mood for this. I sent him sprawling on his ass, and by this time, the check-in clerk had come out from behind her desk. She and I had already crossed swords when I'd checked in and they hadn't wanted to bill the room to the corporate booker, demanding a credit card from me. I don't do reimbursement, and so I'd just flipped down the seat attachment on my suitcase and opened my laptop and started answering email, studiously ignoring her until such time as her boss's boss had spoken to my boss and sorted things out. Sitting on the suitcase's cool little seat instead of one of the lobby sofas weirded out everyone who came in or out of the lobby, as intended, and kept things moving along.

She recognized me right away and, I'm sure, realized that I would be the world's biggest pain in the ass if she got in my way.

"My friend is coming with me."

"She must be on the register."

"No," I said, and dragged Kriztina past her to the elevators.

She dogged our heels. "I'm sorry, madam, but all guests have to be on the register, it is a regulation."

"I'll add her to the register later, when I check out."

She followed us into the elevator. "Madam—"

"Does the regulation say when guests have to be added to the register?"

"Madam, it's our policy—"

"Good, we can discuss the policy in the morning. Good night."

I felt her eyes burning into my back from the closing elevator doors as I dragged Kriztina toward my room door. She wasn't going to evict me in the middle of the night, not with all the cops busy somewhere else. I was willing to bet that if I were a dude coming back to the Sofitel late at night with a couple of underage hookers, no one would bat an eye, state of emergency or no state of emergency. But let a lady try and show some sisterly solidarity, and suddenly it was ENFORCE ALL THE POLICIES. Fuck that.

Speaking of which.

In the room, door closed, I kicked my shoes, coat, hat, and gloves into a pile at the bottom of the closet, then peeled out of my thermal tights down to the regular tights underneath them. Kriztina stood in the doorway, leaning against the hotel-room door. She was stare-y and shaking. Mild shock. I got her a cola out of the minibar, wrapped her hand around it.

"Drink, then get some layers off. It's been an intense night." I waited until she'd swigged, then took the can from her, set it down, and helped her get her coat off. "Boots, too, don't want slush on my carpet." She bent and took them off because her mama raised her right. I sat her on the end of the bed and put the can back into her hand. "Let's see what Litvinchuk made of all that, shall we?" I got my laptop out of my bag and sat next to her, turning my body to block her view when I typed my passwords. Litvinchuk's emails were a mix of English and Boris and I speed-read them with Kriztina over my shoulder. They'd taken forty-one cops into custody, and there had been more than fifty arrests of demonstrators as we left the square. The IMSI catchers had conducted a census of all the phones in the neighborhood that night and the back-end had opened tickets with the Ministry of Communications to pull all the calling records to produce a social graph and mark out highly connected nodes, then run an information-cascade analysis: that was a cute machine-learning trick that tried to identify leaders—formal or informal—by looking at people whose communications produced "cascades" of activity: Alice calls Bob, who then calls Carol and Dan and Eve and Faith, so Alice is the boss and Bob is her lieutenant and love-slave.

The best part of these information cascades was that they produced "actionable intelligence"—go and round up all these Alices and you'll seriously disrupt your adversaries. And since Alice may not even know that she's the boss—she might just be a "highly connected thought leader" whose words inspired her minions without her having formal authority, you could never prove that you had the wrong gal, which meant you could assume you had the right gal, which meant that companies like Xoth could show that they were adding value to your little authoritarian basket-case republic.

I searched through the records for my number, Kriztina's, and then the numbers for her radical cell. The anti-Stingray wares we were running should have been able to spoof the IMSI catchers and send back random identities that passed checksum verification so that software wouldn't be able to tell straight off that the idents were faked. It seemed to have worked: the countermeasure gave a random IMSI to anything it thought was a spoofer, and generated new random numbers for each interaction. Of the tens of thousands of numbers the cops had captured that night, hundreds would be fake.

I paged through the arrest records quickly, letting Kriztina scan the names. She sucked air between her teeth a few times, as she recognized some of her pals who'd be rotting in police dungeons by now, or maybe getting a cattle-prod enema, this being a favored tactic of Litvinchuk's human intelligence specialists. It was a rough world out there—the sooner young Kriztina learned to compartmentalize, the better.

I resolved to give her some training.

I folded down my laptop and stuck it on the desk, then turned to face her.

"Kriztina, your side could have been slaughtered tonight. You know that, right?"

She looked away.

"Come on, kid, stay with me. That could have been a bloodbath. You said it yourself, without me you won't be inside their networks anymore."

She glared at me, an angry Slavic elf. "So what do you want? I can't become a superhacker in two weeks."

"No, you absolutely can't. That's why you and your little group need to stand down."

"What the fuck are you talking about?" When she was upset, her accent got stronger. "Fuck" became "fahkh" with a throat-rasp at the end.

"I'm talking about facing reality. The reality is that Litvinchuk and his friends there are in a dangerous state. On the one hand, a single good push could knock them over, you saw that tonight. On the other hand, they know how close they are to collapse and they're not fucking around. The struggle doesn't need you. Find somewhere to go, deep underground, another country, I don't care. Wait—six months, a year—and the government will fall of its own accord."

She went from confused to furious in an instant and started shivering harder than she had out there in the cold.

"And who will push it over?"

"Someone else."

"What will become of them?"

I shrugged, feeling like a Boris. "If they're lucky, they'll survive."

"Why them and not me?"

"Because you're smarter than that."

She glared at me and then slowly, deliberately, stood and began to dress, putting on her layers.

"Where are you going?"

"My friends are out there. They need help. When someone needs help, I go to them. I don't run away."

I wasn't going to beg. *Go ahead,* I thought. Not my trouble. I put her in a compartment.

The door closed behind her.

The phone rang.

I yanked it out of the wall. It would be the desk clerk, pissed off about Kriztina still, and she could go fuck herself.

My phone rang.

It was in do-not-disturb mode, but there was a small number of phone numbers it was programmed to override on. Embarrassingly, one of those was Marcus Yallow's. But it wasn't him, of course. He didn't even have that number (but if I ever gave it to him, I wanted to make sure he could get through, because I'm an idiot).

"Masha, we have to talk. Lobby in five minutes. A car is coming."

Ilsa, She-Wolf of the SS, can turn on the ice water on demand.

I ran a washcloth under the tap and did a bits-and-pits wipe-down worthy of any Frenchwoman, yanked out the drawer where I'd stuffed all my clothes and dumped it onto the bed, found underwear, a clean T-shirt from a tech conference in Qatar, jeans. My thermal tights were too gross to bother with and I was pretty sure I wouldn't be logging any outdoor hours.

I compartmentalize, but that doesn't mean I wasn't aware that something terrible was about to happen. Truth be told, I'd been expecting that call for months, since the first time I'd done a surveillance appliance installment and then walked straight to the first group of dissidents I could find and explained how to defeat it. Quoting *1984* in my line of work is a ridiculous cliché, but George Orwell always got me with this line, "You know what is in Room 101, Winston. Everyone knows what is in Room 101." I'd known since day one that it would end with someone like Ilsa, over something like this.

Orwell named names, you know that? He fell in love with a British spy, much younger than him, while he was dying of TB and bitter over the Reds who'd betrayed his faction during the Spanish Civil War and shot him in the throat, so he made a list of all the people who trusted him, but whom he didn't trust, wrote it on a piece of paper in his own handwriting, and gave it to this spook lady. As far as anyone can tell, she never acted on it.

Orwell must have been one hell of a compartmentalizer, is what I'm saying.

In the elevator, I made sure my phone and laptop were powered down with their encrypted drives unmounted. Then I checked my hair in the mirror—it looked, basically, like I'd just been drinking my face off—and remembered that I'd forgotten to put on any eye makeup. Ilsa always looked like she'd come from a salon, and wore these severe suit-y numbers that looked like they'd been made in East Germany and then tailored in Hong Kong by a master couturier. I liked the contrast. My *Mr. Robot* hoodie/jeans drag made a statement: I am not a lifer, I am the talent, I can't be easily replaced, and so I can wear whatever I want.

She was in the lobby, standing by the bar, looking at her phone. She slipped it inside her handbag—Faraday fabric; I'd snuck a feel once when we were going through airport security together—and zipped it.

"Ms. Maximow."

"Ms. Netzke." Ilsa's real (ish) name: Herthe Netzke (that was what her ID said, anyway).

"Come."

The car was waiting out front. No driver. She drove. Better opsec, no need to trust someone not to repeat what they overheard.

"Ms. Maximow."

"Yes?"

She pulled the car over. We'd only gone a couple blocks. It was very cold out and weird colors swirled through the fog as the bubble-lights of the police checkpoints a few blocks away filtered back to us.

She looked at me. She never Botoxed, I can tell you that. Years in the hard-smoking Soviet era had bequeathed her with a set of wrinkles of magnificent fracticality, wrinkles in the wrinkles, which she finished off with a short, severe iron-gray haircut like Judi Dench as a Marine commander. She had one of those German noses that looked like a ski jump, and hazel eyes that were big and wide-set, eyebrows full and expressive. Her dangling old-lady lobes were pierced, but I never saw her wear anything in them.

She had the terrible gift of fixing her attention, cobra-style, pinning you under it. Even with the lights off inside the car, I felt her stare. She was waiting for me to talk. I would outwait her. This game was easy, and I'd already learned to play. I was better than her at it.

"It was very foolish."

*Foolish* was about as emphatic as she got, and it was reserved for monumental fuckups.

I shrugged. My heart thudded. I kept my face cool. I'd been slapped around before, and even worse, but this was scarier in its own weird way. Maybe knowing that Ilsa had overseen so many executions, so many nights in numberless cells . . . All the bad dudes I'd ever met were just boys LARPing GI Joe: she was the real deal. Far as I could tell, there was nothing underneath Ilsa but more Ilsa. It was amazing. I wanted to be like that someday. In one of my compartments, anyway. In another compartment, I hated her and myself for that.

"You realize that you're compromised now."

I shrugged. Compromised is only a few letters away from compartmentalized. "You're overreacting. You think that the next autocrat looking to hire Xoth is going to call Litvinchuk for a reference?"

"Why wouldn't he?"

I hadn't really thought about that. It's not like there was a LinkedIn for dictators where they all hung out and traded notes on cyberwar contractors—as far as I knew, anyway.

"Well, for one thing, I think there's a pretty good chance he'll be dead in a ditch."

She considered it with Teutonic cool. "Even so. His own people, his contractors, they will get out. There's also the chance that a reporter will publish—"

"No there isn't." There hadn't been a functional press in Slovstakia in eight years. They rated a part-time stringer from RT who reported on a neighboring basket-case republic, a dissident who published anonymously on Global Voices, and the state broadcaster, the sole TV Slovstakian channel on the air, rebranded as "The Choice." Borises are not without humor.

"Probably not. But it's not a domestic story. If anyone knew about this, it would be news in many countries. Everywhere Xoth operates, and then some."

"Better make sure I don't tell it, then."

Boy, was that the wrong thing to say. "Masha, you're out."

"Come on, I was just—"

"You can't unsay that. This was going to be a disciplinary meeting. Now it's a termination. You made your choice." She was not without tenderness.

"I'm sorry."

"I'm sure you are. I wish you the best in your future endeavors. Needless to say, there will be no references."

My stupid tears welled up in my stupid eyes. I put them in their own compartment, but they were slippery. "Herthe—"

If it wasn't sympathy in her eyes, it was a perfect fake. The wrinkles gave her a lot of expressive range. I think she practiced with them in front of a mirror. "Masha, I know you. I used to be you. The things you're doing, you're trying to destroy yourself. It's not that you threatened Xoth, it's that the threat shows how far gone you are. If you're going to crash and burn, my job is to make sure you do it far from Xoth and the rest of us."

"Herthe, I swear, it was just a smartass response. I haven't been sleeping so well. Why don't I get a few hours' sleep, why don't we *both* get a good night, and start over?"

"Disbelief, denial, bargaining. Guilt and anger are next. Then depression and hope. Good luck, Masha." She popped the locks.

She was good at this. I was about to leave the car when I thought to ask, "Severance? Notice?"

"This kind of job doesn't fall under those sorts of rules. Besides, you're being terminated with cause. You may keep your equipment and we will pay your hotel bill for the night. You have your outbound plane ticket."

I did. Xoth's travel agent always booked full/flexible fares and seemed to get stellar deals on them, the kind of thing you need an IATA membership and a backdoor password to get normally. Hell, I could probably even cash it in at the airport ticket desk for euros, dollars, or Swiss francs.

I shivered on the street as Herthe's car pulled away.

I grasped for a landmark to orient myself, and found a familiar church spire. I was only steps from the Danube Bar Resto. It was 2:30 in the morning, which meant that the bar would just be closing, unless it already had.

I hugged myself and pulled my hood up. I still had my dazzle makeup on and it made my face itch. I could taste it on my lips. I rounded the corner and slowed down. The Bar Resto still had its lights on, and I could see shadows moving behind its plate glass. I was about to hurry over when something stopped me, I wasn't sure what. I looked around again more carefully. There had been a kind of ambient state of emergency on the streets on the way over, the fog and night sky reflecting back the bubble-lights on the tops of the police cars and roadblock fences, a kind of diffuse light show.

Now the streets were dark. Apart from the Bar Resto's window, there was no light at all. Black against the dim, silhouettes moved within the parked cars lining the street.

I turned on my heel and ran, and heard opening car doors behind me, then shouts, then running feet, then the sirens and lights I'd been missing broke the night wide open. The noise was incredible and as I cornered and cornered again, I felt the between-the-shoulders itch of an inbound truncheon—or bullet.

I skidded to a halt down one of the tiny alleys that lined the old town, barely wider than my shoulders. I consciously slowed my breathing and peered down the alley to double-check that it wasn't a dead end, then used the shiny black screen of my phone as a mirror to peek around the corner. Not even a glimmer. I took a few more breaths, then eased out of the alley, listening intently.

Distant shouts and sirens, from the direction of Bar Resto. Nothing from nearby. I formulated a hypothesis: the people in the cars—secret police and a goon squad—hadn't been staking me out, they'd been staking out the Bar Resto; Litvinchuk or someone beneath him had decided that after tonight, they were going to clean house. I reversed my coat to the white side and detached the hood before walking purposefully back toward the Bar Resto, looking as much as possible like someone going somewhere.

The sounds grew louder—shouts and breaking glass. I stopped at the final corner, tucked my phone into my coat's breast pocket with the lens peeking out and recording, then stepped out onto the sidewalk and glanced quickly down the street, letting the camera get a good look, taking a good look myself.

Chaos, people struggling under cops, the window of the Bar Resto shattered and in shards. I kept my pace even as I crossed to the opposite corner, *someone going somewhere, someone, somewhere,* my shield of invisibility and respectability.

I didn't recognize anyone at this distance, at this speed, in this light. But statistically, I knew some of those people being dragged into the yawning maw of those white cargo vans, lined with steel benches and shackles.

I was almost to the other side when the blast hit. Before I knew it, I was on my belly with my hands over my head, feeling the deep-frozen street through the legs of my jeans and in my cheek. The night was white, then orange, then I felt and heard the sound, a *whump* that never gets easier, no matter how often you've felt it. It winded me, made me feel like a huge hand was squeezing me from every side, like the blood was being crushed out of my torso and up into my head, like the worst sinus headache ever. I think I blacked out, possibly more than once. The moment seemed to go on a lot longer than it had any business doing.

I came to my knees and barfed, trying to get it all up and out as quickly as I could, looking around, checking whether anyone was coming for me, ready to run from another explosion. The Bar Resto and the apartments over it were mostly rubble, except for a cross section that rose three and a half stories, like an architectural rendering: bathtub, stairwell, kitchen. It was so dark I couldn't tell if anyone was up there, or under the mounded rubble at its base.

I rose and my head spun and I just managed to turn my face before I barfed again, getting it on my boots instead of down my front. I took two steps toward the blast, then heard the sirens over the ringing in my ears, understood that the bouncing emergency lights on the fog were getting closer, and so I made myself walk—walk, dammit, Masha, not like a fucking drunk, come on—toward the hotel. I didn't think anyone was after me, personally, at this point. Ilsa wouldn't tell Litvinchuk that I was fired, because to do that she'd have to tell him *why*. It would all be very quiet. That's how Xoth did things. Discretion was their brand.

Emergencies are weird. Three blocks from the blast, it was as if none of it had happened. I tasted blood and realized I had a nosebleed, which I wiped at with my glove. Was I staggering? I was. Something not quite right with my inner ear just yet. Give it time.

Two more blocks and I saw the entrance of the Sofitel. The guards were there and they remembered me.

"Ma'am—"

"I am staying here."

"Yes, but—"

"I am a guest here."

"Ma'am."

"Get out of my way."

He looked at me.

"Please. I'm hurt and need to go to my room to clean up."

No one does stony-faced like a Boris.

"I'm checking out." I said this loud enough to attract the attention of the woman behind the counter. She didn't bother with stony, went straight to scowl. But she said something into the mic pinned to her lapel and the guard listened to his earpiece and let me through.

I didn't glance her way as I crossed the lobby but felt her eyeballs boring into my back the whole way.

The elevator mirror lied to me. No one could look that terrible. I unzipped the Faraday pocket in my coat and withdrew my room-key, touched in, zipped it back in as I opened the door.

Showering, I nearly fell in the tub, but caught myself. My legs and armpits needed a shave and I didn't have a razor. Fuck it. I got good at fast showers when I was doing my time in Central America with Zyz, but I'd had shorter hair then. I'd get it chopped as soon as I found a place to settle.

The Sofitel wasn't the only hotel in Blzt, but it was the nicest by far. Everything else was either a glorified youth hostel or a crumbling, ex-Soviet pile with an angry Boris sitting at a desk outside of each floor's elevator lobby, ostentatiously marking down the comings and goings of everyone who got in or out of the elevators.

I checked into the least-worst of these, the Kharkiv, and when the check-in clerk demanded my passport, I beckoned her close and slid her a hundred-dollar bill. It was faster than arguing. She gave me a long, considering look, then plucked a key off a board behind her and passed it over.

The eighth floor was nearly entirely derelict, with plywood permanently wedged into the doorways of nearly every room. The "concierge" behind the desk in the elevator lobby smirked at me as I wheeled my bag past him, waving my key at him. Room 809 was between two boarded-up rooms, which was fine with me—more privacy was always preferable.

In the room, I stripped the stained coverlet off the bed and dug my silk sleep-sack out of my bag before sitting down at the scratched desk to unpack my laptop and phones and collection of SIMs. I plugged in a prepaid SIM from a company that sold cheap data roaming to business travelers and checked that I could tether my laptop to it and fire up a VPN.

It was 7 a.m. and I was simultaneously exhausted and frantic, unable to stop replaying the night's events, unable to stop racing around a mental hamster wheel that made stops at my total savings (absurdly fat), and Kriztina's chances (terribly thin). I climbed into my sleep-sack and listened to the footsteps from the floor above me and the traffic noises from the street below leaking through the drafty window and the grimy drapes. I put my laptop and phone in my backpack and went down to the hotel's breakfast room and ate some stodgy porridge with pickled vegetables and salted meat, then went back to the room and lay back down again, trying to pay attention to the sound of my stomach gurgling while I put Kriztina and her friends into a purpose-built compartment.

I finally drifted off, waking up just after noon, feeling bloated and fraught, the sense of a powerful sorrow and danger just over my shoulder. I got into my VPN and did some careful work to verify that Xoth had indeed terminated my official access, including the backdoors I'd left for myself. Someone farther up the chain had been watching me. The undigested breakfast in my gut curdled a little more.

On the other hand. If I couldn't get into the Slovstakian state networks, then I didn't really have much to offer Kriztina anymore, did I? I'd given them the help I could, when I could, and I'd warned them to get away when it became clear that I wasn't going to be able to keep on offering that kind of help. It had been good advice and they were adults, capable of making their own decisions. The fact that they—and every other dissident—were likely to end up in the knucklebreakers' custody was a reality they would have to reconcile for themselves.

Aeroflot had been steadily cutting the flight schedules to Blzt as the protests had grown and grown and the number of business travelers had shelved off. There was still a daily Moscow flight, and a twice-weekly Berlin service. I could get that Berlin flight the day after next, visit the offices of my Swiss bank on the Ku'damm, take a fast train to a luxury spa in the countryside somewhere, and decompress for a week or two, far from conflict and responsibilities. A week of that, I'd be ready to think about what to do next. That was the advantage of being me: I *could* fight other peoples' battles—for money or for my own reasons—but I didn't *have to*.

I tried to go clothes shopping, slogging from heavily guarded mall to heavily guarded mall, stubbornly insisting that *somewhere* there must be a store selling a single, solitary garment I'd voluntarily wear. It was a comfortably pointless way to spend a few hours, and I ate a numb pizza at a Domino's and went back to the hotel. There was another protest planned for the square, and I had to detour around several police blockades. That was okay by me. The last thing I wanted was to involve myself with the protests. I'd be in Berlin in thirty-six hours. All I needed to do between now and then was nothing.

I shared the elevator to the eighth floor with a hooker and her client, all of us awkwardly looking away from one another. When the doors opened, the man behind the desk waved them through, then insisted on seeing my key and noting its number. I began to get the impression that the eighth floor was reserved for the most special guests at the hotel.

I set down my bag next to my bed, stripped off my underlayers, and then pulled on thermal tights and a sweatshirt—the room was freezing, presumably on the assumption that any tenants would be (a) short-term and (b) engaged in vigorous physical activity. I plugged my laptop into the wall charger and then zipped it into my bag, climbed into the sleep-sack, and closed my eyes. For a merciful change, I fell asleep quickly.

I woke to find myself in the dark room, with the sense that there had just been a loud noise. I sat up, looking around, reaching for my bag, shucking swiftly out of the sleep-sack, trying to remember where the light was, where I'd left my shoes.

Then I heard a scream from the street below, and a car horn, and then more screams, and then a terrible, rending crash. I stopped feeling for the light switch and went to the window, opening the blinds from the edge, looking down.

It was a bad crash, one of the city's Finecab subcompact autonomous taxis bent around an empty planter, and I reflexively snorted: the self-driving vehicles were an absurd source of national pride for Slovstakia, and if you've heard of Slovstakia, there's a pretty good chance that this is literally the only thing you know about it: "Oh, that's the country that was stupid enough to buy gen-one automatic taxis." The Finecabs were notorious for getting into fender benders, and had become a symbol of how easy it was for foreign companies to sell garbage tech to the country's ruling elite (see also: Xoth).

But this wasn't one of the customary comedy-crashes. From the sounds filtering up from the road, someone had been hurt. I saw someone in hotel livery rush to the car and decided it wasn't my problem anymore. I went back to bed.

I was just drifting off when I heard another crash, farther away, accompanied by blaring horns, then another, almost immediately after, and screams that didn't stop. I looked out the window and saw that others were doing the same, some of them holding their phones, and then they were shouting excitedly at each other in Boris. I retreated to my bed and got out my phone, tunneled out to the free world, and started looking for Slovstakia in the feeds.

Even though it was all in Cyrillic, it wasn't hard to figure out the night's news from the pictures: first the massive protests in the central square, then a baton charge from the cops and a countercharge, blood and tear gas, and then more gas, pepper spray, and the crowd broke and ran for it. That much I'd seen before, but what came next was anything but the usual.

At first, it was just photos of car wrecks, all involving Finecabs, many with injuries. Judging from the clothing of the injured, they were all protesters. I started to get a bad feeling. I kept scrolling. More injuries, more crashes— then, a shakicam video, racking up views like a broken odometer: an autonomous taxi speeding toward a crowd of protesters who were standing on an empty street corner. The protesters noticed the cab as it drew near to them and broke and ran, and then—*the cab chased one of them.* It was a woman, in a puffa jacket and snow boots, and as she ran, her friends screamed in horror. She turned a corner and the view from the camera started to jerk as whomever was holding it raced after it, rounding the corner just as the car sped off. The woman was lying motionless in the street.

That's the video you probably saw, if you saw any of them, but for me, it wasn't the worst. Compared to the videos taken from *inside* the taxis, by passengers who were hammering at the emergency stop buttons, that video was relatively benign. The screams from inside the cars as their victims' heads starred the windshields and left behind streaks of blood and hair were a thousand times more terrifying.

I knew I wouldn't be going back to bed that night. I logged in to Aeroflot and booked a ticket on the next flight out, to Moscow the next morning. It wasn't Berlin, but it didn't have to be. I could get to Berlin from there. I could get *anywhere* from there.

Where should I go? I felt alone and small, and ashamed to have been fired. I was good at being alone, and scared could go into a compartment, easy.

Apparently I wasn't the kind of person who worked for Xoth anymore. I didn't want to be that kind of person. Chances were pretty high that Xoth had sold Litvinchuk and pals the exploits to take over those cars. I'd been complicit in some pretty terrible shit before, sure, but what if Kriztina had been thrown over one of those little subcompacts, or crushed against a building by one, or run down and driven over?

I messaged her, just a quick encrypted check-in, and then, because I was going to be leaving soon, I packed my bag and synched my sensitive files to an encrypted cloud store, then securely erased them off my laptop. Now I could comply with an order to log in to my laptop and enter my hard drive's passphrase without turning over my most sensitive data.

Doing that took my mind off Kriztina, but it also focused my attention on what I was going to do after my flight landed in Moscow in a few hours. Reflexively, I looked at my calendar, though of course all my appointments related to a job I'd just been fired from with extreme prejudice. But looking also reminded me that it was Tanisha's birthday, or it was in Europe and would be shortly in San Francisco. The reminder was smart enough to include my address book entry for her and *that* was smart enough to include her last social post, a selfie of her in afro-puffs, grinning in front of a huge crowd of protesters somewhere else—Oakland, of course.

Seeing her smiling out of my laptop weaponized my loneliness, making it physical, an elephant on my chest, so that I gasped and gasped before my breath came back. Tanisha was a remnant of another life of mine, one without so many compartments and so many contradictions to stuff into them. It had been years since we'd been in regular contact, but still, she was one of the few people whose birthday was still in my calendar, and I never missed sending her a note.

> Happy birthday, Neesh! Thinking of you

That was truer than I meant it to be.

> hope you have a killer day. Stay safe, stay weird, stay you. XO Masha

That was all, a message whose mere existence—still thinking of you—carried as much meaning as the words inside it. I sent it and went back to looking at connections from Sheremetyevo.

Then my phone rang.

My screen showed TANISHA, and an older pic, which dated back to the last time I'd seen her, which was at Burning Man, with her in a silver bathing suit and her afro all crazy around her head, playing an upright bass in a jam band that we'd wandered into.

Tanisha was calling my old number—I mean, my OG number, the cell number I'd gotten at twelve—which forwarded to a cloud asterisk call-server that had a ton of rules that allowed a very small number of people to forward onto whatever phone I was using at the moment. I was religious about updating the forward, even though (or because) it meant my mom could reach me whenever she wanted to, which was both more often than I wanted to speak to her and less often than I wanted her to want to speak to me.

"Yo."

"Masha?"

"Hey, Neesh. Uh, happy birthday."

"That's tomorrow."

"Not where I am."

"Oh. Shit. Is it like three a.m. where you are or something?"

"Two a.m. Don't worry about it, I was up."

"Masha, tell me you're not still partying. You're too old for that."

I laughed. "I'm not too old for it, but no, I'm not partying." I looked around the terrible Soviet-era hotel room. "Packing for a flight." Then I wished I hadn't said that.

"Where are you flying?"

Maybe some part of me wanted to have this discussion with her. Otherwise, why would I have raised the subject?

"I'm still deciding that."

There was a pause on the other end. "Uh, okay. You must be hella far away, though, the call sounds terrible."

"I am, but I'm also putting the call through a bridge. Makes the logs harder to fingerprint."

She sang a few bars of the *Mission: Impossible* theme, which was her traditional way of telling me that she wasn't impressed with my paranoia. But she trailed off weakly. "Sorry, I'm in no position to be mocking you."

Oh. I tried not to pay much attention to US politics—after all, most of what I hated about present-day America was stuff I helped to invent. But of course a call out of the blue from Tanisha was more likely to be soliciting professional advice and not catching up on gossip.

"Tell me about it."

The long silence spoke volumes. I was sure she was thinking something like, *Can I even trust this phone connection?*

"Neesh, if you want to talk more *privately,* I can call you back. You still have that app?" We used to use Signal for phone conversations when I was in-country, and Tanisha said she was going to try to get her pals to use it too, but I knew that without active reminders of the threat model most people would default back to the standard way of talking.

"Uh," she said.

"Thought so. Reinstall it, and I'll call you in five."

"Can you hear me?" Signal calls were a lot more jittery than regular voice or even Skype, prone to drop into Dalek-sounding interference and voice-in-a-box-fan juddering, but my roaming SIM was pretty good and Tanisha had found a spot with good reception, so it was almost as good as a regular call—for now.

"I hear you." She sounded exhausted and it was only late afternoon on the West Coast.

"What's going on, Neesh?" I thought maybe the connection had been cut. "Neesh?"

"Sorry. Let me get my head straight. Just a sec."

This wasn't like her. Tanisha had the straightest head I knew—the Tanisha I knew was an iron woman.

"Okay, it's like this: I've been going out for the Black-Brown Alliance meetings and rallies, the big ones in Oakland. I took precautions, we all did—phones locked and in airplane mode when we were on-site, no fingerprint unlocking, all our cards in Faraday pouches. We only talk in person with phones off or using encrypted disappearing chat. But I always remembered what you told me—"

"There's a difference between mass surveillance and targeted surveillance."

"Right. So I've been extra careful. I use a burner for all that stuff, and I wear dazzle to the demos, watch out for kettles and get out fast when they start to form. But—"

"Come on, spit it out."

"You'll think I'm being paranoid."

"Neesh, trust me, I will never, ever think you're being too paranoid."

I heard her sigh and waited. With Neesh, sighs always came in pairs, it was something we used to tease her about. I hadn't thought of it in years, but my subconscious remembered. There it was.

"You were the one who taught me about binary transparency, right?"

"Yeah."

Binary transparency was an exciting idea, but also a complicated one that almost no one could actually understand. First, you had to understand what a hashing function is: that's a cryptographic algorithm that takes a long file (say, a computer program or an email or a software update) and generates a short "fingerprint" number from it that a human being can easily read aloud and compare with other fingerprints (for certain values of "easily"). If the hashing function is working well, it should be basically impossible to deliberately create two different files that have the same fingerprint, and likewise basically impossible to figure out what was in the original file just by looking at the fingerprint (for "basically impossible" think of all the hydrogen atoms being turned into computers that worked until the universe's heat-death to guess the answer, and still running out of both space and time).

Next you have to understand public-private cryptographic keypairs. The short explanation: whatever a public key scrambles, only the private key can unscramble, and vice versa. So everyone shares their public keys as widely as possible and guards the secrecy of their private keys with their lives. If you get something you can decrypt with my public key, you know it was encrypted with my private key (and only my private key). If you encrypt something with my public key, you know that only someone with my *private* key can decrypt it. If you want to send me something that only you and I can read, you encrypt it with *your* private key and *my* public key, and then I use *my* private key and *your* public key to decrypt it—and now I can be sure that only people with my private key can read the message, and only people with *your* private key could have sent it.

When you combine hashing and keypairs, it gets cool: you can first hash a file, then encrypt the hash with your private key, and I can use that hash to check whether you sent the file, and whether the file was changed between you and me.

Got all that? No? Join the club. Almost no one understands this stuff, which is a pity, because now we're about to get to binary transparency, which is awesome af, as the kids say.

Stay with me: hashing lets you create a short "fingerprint" of a file. If you have your own copy of the file, you can hash it again and make sure it matches the fingerprint. If it doesn't, someone has altered the file since it was hashed. Keypairs let you scramble a file—or a fingerprint—so that you can be sure who sent it, and also make sure it wasn't changed, and even make sure no one else can see what the file is.

Now let's talk about software updates and backdoors: all the software running on all the computers you rely on is, approximately speaking, total shit. That's because humans are imperfect, so they make errors, which is why every book you've ever read has typos in it. The difference is that you can usually figure out what the writer meant even if there's a few typos sprinkled around, while tiny mistakes made by computer programmers lead to crashes, data-loss, and, of course, the possibility that other computer programmers—let's call them "hackers"—break into the program, take over the computer, and destroy your life.

So we say "security is a process and not a product"—meaning that we're going to be discovering bugs in the software you're depending on forever, and we need a way to fix those bugs when we find them. That's why every computer you use bugs you all the time to update it with a patch from the people who made it.

Now, cryptography *works*. If a programmer does her job right and doesn't make mistakes, the messages that her program scrambles will resist brute-force attacks until the end of time and space (see above). When a government wants to access someone's secrets, they need to find a way to get at them without directly attacking the crypto. I mean, why burn resources and time attacking the part of the lock mathematically proven to be secure? There are so many other angles for a government to use.

Like, they could send someone to your house and put a tiny camera, the size of a pinhead, in a position that lets them see your screen. Or they could wait until you leave your laptop in a hotel room and send someone to break the—inevitably shitty—hotel-room door locks and take over your computer, with BadUSB or by sticking a hardware keylogger in it or some other method. But physical intrusion is so *pre-digital;* it lacks the elegance of a software-based attack.

Which brings us back to "security is a process." For software to be secure, it has to have a way to receive updates from the people who made it, because they're always finding bugs, and will always find bugs, and so security is a process and not a product.

What about forcing a company to update its software with something that *introduces* a bug, rather than fixing one? Companies are not happy about doing this, but maybe you can bribe a low-level employee, or you can get your attorney general to threaten to put the CEO in jail unless he orders a flunky to write some spyware and ship it to the target(s) in the guise of a security update. As a bonus, paranoid people worried about government surveillance are also the people who are most diligent about applying security patches.

That's where binary transparency comes in. Even if a company is willing to push spyware disguised as security, they probably don't want to send it to all their users, not least because the wider things are spread, the more likely it is that someone will spot the switcheroo and blow the whistle. The best way to ship a targeted backdoor is to *target* it—at a user, a city, a region, possibly a country, but ideally not everyone, because "everyone" includes "bored, obsessive grad students who decompile every update from every company looking for a thesis subject."

Which means that one way to spot a backdoor in your security update is to compare every update you receive with all the updates that everyone else receives. That's binary transparency: programs ship with binary transparency modules that automatically take a fingerprint of every update they receive, and send that to one or more transparency servers, possibly with a fingerprint of the program before and after the update's installation—sometimes there are different versions of programs based on language, so the English patch might not be the same as the Chinese patch because their error messages are in different languages. But when two Chinese users get two different patches, something might be going on.

Binary transparency is elegant and cool. It gets turned on *before* companies get deputized to spy on their users, which means that it's already in place when the G-men show up at your door. If they force you to push out a backdoor, binary transparency will reveal it. If they force you to push out an update for everyone that turns off binary transparency, everyone will notice and their paranoid targets will stop using it.

This means that a rational government agency won't even bother to ask for backdoors, because they'll never work. Because binary transparency takes backdoors off the table, it takes *asking for backdoors* off the table too.

That's the theory. But binary transparency is one of those things that's exciting in theory and really messy in practice. First of all, nearly every binary transparency alert is a false alarm: maybe the company sends different updates to different customers as a way of live-testing an experimental feature, or the update or its fingerprint gets changed in some minor way by an ISP that's doing deep packet inspection or some other dumb thing. Neither of these things happen very often, but they both happen a *lot* more often than binary transparency catching a real backdoor (in part because companies known to have binary transparency turned on understandably don't get as many backdoor demands from spies). So almost no one knows what binary transparency *is,* and if you do, chances are that all you know about it is that it's a thing that you can safely ignore because it only ever throws false alarms.

Which wouldn't be so bad if government agencies were rational, but spies are by definition total weirdos. Think for a second about the kid you knew growing up who always wanted to be a spy someday—the combination of grandiosity, authoritarianism, and paranoia. In the 1960s, the CIA tried surgically implanting cats with listening devices—and training them to spy on America's enemies. (This is real. Google "acoustic kitty.") Think about this for a second: not only did the CIA think the veterinarians who insisted you couldn't implant huge battery-operated recording devices in live cats were just not trying hard enough—they also thought you could *train cats.* Because when you give paranoid, grandiose authoritarians an unlimited budget and no oversight, things get *fucked up.*

So any assumption that the spies won't come knocking on a binary transparency shop because it'll only waste their time and yours drastically overestimates the extent to which spies are adverse to wasting their time and yours.

Which means some of those alerts from binary transparency checks aren't false alarms. They're just spooks betting on their ability to bull their way through stupid, uncooperative reality.

Binary transparency is still used, because it shows up on checklists of "things companies should do to resist spying," but in practice, everyone ignores it. Except Tanisha.

"It's Hushush. I got an update this morning and I was about to run it when I got a binary transparency error. I almost just tapped OK, but then I remembered you telling me about it, and how no one ever paid attention to it, which meant that bad guys might just try to chance it and backdoor stuff that has binary transparency turned on. But you know, I have things to do that don't involve being a technology person, like fighting white supremacy, and . . ."

"Yeah. That's how it goes for everyone. The radiologist who's scoping your tumor wants to know if you've got cancer, and if the only way to find that out is to plug in the network cable that's never supposed to be plugged in, then cancer wins one hundred percent of the time."

"Yeah."

Someone on my floor—maybe the commissar in the elevator lobby—let out a long, windy fart that was so loud I could hear it through the wall. I snorted.

"What was that?"

"You heard it?" Signal's sound-processing was getting better, evidently.

"Are you laughing at your own farts, Masha?"

"No, someone else's from the hotel here."

"'Here' is . . . ?"

"Blzt."

"Where?"

"In Slovstakia."

"Where?"

"It was part of the USSR. I wouldn't recommend it as a destination."

"Damn, girl, you are an international jet-setter."

"If you could see the dump I'm in, you'd be a lot less impressed. Are you going to tell me what happened next?"

"I'm working around to it. Impatient much? Okay. Well, that was a week ago. I was using it to stay on top of the Black-Brown Alliance, right? There are ten of us in my affinity group, all organizers from way back. Our target's been the expansion of the Oakland Fusion Center, which you'd think would be a soft target after the leaks, but they're *vicious,* because they're fighting for their lives and they know it."

I knew about the Oakland Fusion Center, of course—a war on terror boondoggle that absorbed tons of federal funding to help local cops coordinate all their surveillance gear with various feds, from the DEA to the NSA. And I half remembered that they'd had some kind of leaky scandal, but I couldn't remember what it had been all about.

"Remind me?"

Tanisha sighed and that took me back, because it was the special sigh she reserved for alleged white allies who managed to pay zero attention to something that every brown person they knew was talking about nonstop.

"The dump last month? Hello?"

"I've been on a different continent, Neesh. Cut me some slack, would you? How much do you know about the popular uprising in Slovstakia?"

"Wait, *that* Slovstakia? Shit, you were *there*? Did you see that Nazi kid get shot? Did you see the showdown?"

"You shame me. I suck. You know about all the struggles for justice in the world and I know about nothing that doesn't affect me and my personal bubble of privilege. Now, are you going to explain, or should I go read the Wikipedia entry and call you back in twenty minutes?"

Tanisha snorted. "Wikipedia? That dump's a whitewash. The redpill bros and the Blue Lives Matter folks have figured out that brigading Wikipedia gets them better bang for their buck than hitting social media. That's where all the lazy journalists go for their backgrounders. The tl;dr is that the Fusion Center got hacked and dumped, which they're blaming on Pakistan, of course, but everyone else says it's an inside job, because that's what the leaker said, you know, 'I got into this job to help people but I found myself hurting people, blah blah,' standard Snowdenisms.

"Anyway, the dump showed that the Oakland PD was dirtier than you could believe. Some of the narcs were running a protection racket and using the Fusion Center's feeds to watch their victims, make sure they weren't holding out, and these guys were sharing passwords and tips for erasing their traces in the logs. Another guy, a sergeant, was pimping underage girls and using the Fusion Center to track down his rivals and check out his johns to make sure they weren't undercovers. It just got worse and worse—cops having affairs with each other and talking about killing their wives and husbands, really deep and detailed plans, not just tossed-off jokes."

"Okay, this is ringing a bell."

"Yeah. I mean, at first everyone was like, ho ho, boys in blue will be boys, and this is Oakland PD after all, everyone knows how dirty they are. But as the dump got mined and analyzed, it just got worse until the feds had to come in and start making arrests. They said they were going to close down the Fusion Center and everyone was like ding-dong the witch is dead, but I was all, hold up, this was way too easy, there's something coming. I have burner accounts subscribed to fedbiz and the Federal Register, watching for sneaky procurement announcements and RFPs, and I spotted what looked a hell of a lot like a plan to make the Fusion Center *much* bigger, like ten-X, and I fed that through the Black-Brown Alliance to the Freedom of Information affinity group and they filed a bunch of public records requests, which all got denied, bringing in ACLU of Northern California. Then there was a leak—another dump, not as big as the first one—including a ton of the documents they were blocking us on, and then everyone could see that the cops and the contractors who'd built the center saw this as life-or-death, go big or get buried. Internally they called it a Super Fusion Center, with a whole unit dedicated just to hacking suspects' devices to gather evidence."

"Shit."

"Yeah." There was a long pause, that kind of phone silence you get with digitally compressed calls where small noises like breathing and shifting get edited out, leaving total flatline silence. "Masha, I never asked you too much about what you do, you made it clear that I wouldn't like the answers, but these memos, they were talking about cops secretly activating the cameras and mics of all the phones in a ZIP code and listening in for a perp's voice or a keyword."

"And?"

"And, I was like, come on, that's science fiction, it's some vendor overpromising to get a big contract. But . . ."

"But is it possible?"

"Yeah."

I shrugged, even though she couldn't see me. "Yeah, it's possible. Baseband radios, the chips that talk to the phone towers, they're garbage, no real security to speak of, and they can be used to man-in-the-middle all the traffic going in and out of the phone without the OS knowing thing one about it. If you had a trove of exploits for Android and iOS it wouldn't be impossible to use baseband attacks to take over all the phones connected to a given tower, though that exploit would probably be discovered pretty quickly, and even the feds are going to run out of zero-days eventually. But if all you cared about was compromising most phones—the ones with out-of-date operating systems—then yeah, that wouldn't be too hard at all. People might figure it out when their batteries started running down twenty-five percent faster, but shit, batteries suck anyway—"

"You're ratholing, Masha."

"Sorry, sorry. Yeah, it's possible."

"You said that."

"I meant it."

"Well, that was the thing that got everyone's ears up, got the city councilors starting to sweat, got the press involved. It's just such a special horror, the idea of your phone watching you, and it was like, everyone could imagine how the cops would take one look at this and say hell yes, we would like very much to turn every phone in the East Bay into a listening device, thank you very much. Once that got going, we were able to stage some really big protests, you know, not the usual pattern where a thousand people come on day one, and then five hundred and then fifty and then it's just five sad losers with hand-lettered signs. This was like Occupy was, back in the day, got bigger and bigger, people bringing their kids down and all, and it was like, Oakland PD was caught between a rock and a hard place, anything they did to crack down on the protests would just prove our point, so it looked like we were gonna win."

I needed to pee. I hit mute and sat on the toilet. I could guess where this was going.

"That's when things started to get sketchy. Email's always been a sewer of unreliability, but it got worse, and it sure felt like the messages we were sending to each other were going missing more than all the other messages. A bunch of people started organizing on Facebook because they are old, and then Facebook shut down their group for violating 'community standards' and yeah, that's happened before too, but the timing was spooky. Then came the traffic stops, and the weirdly specific minor drug busts, and anyone who was late on a parking ticket or a library book was liable to get a visit from OPD. We figured they were going after the leaders, the organizers, like Cointelpro 3.0, and so we started to really bear down on our opsec, and also to make sure we were clean as whistles, everyone's bills and fines paid up, no one leaves the house without ID, no one goes near anything bustable. One comrade went to a house party and it got raided fifteen minutes later, a hundred people arrested, and then we stopped going to house parties."

"Now you've got a binary transparency alert. What is it for?"

"Openstreetmaps."

I flopped back down on the sofa. Openstreetmaps was the fair-trade hippie-granola version of Google Maps, but it had the advantage of including static maps that were signed and mirrored all over the web, meaning that you could download a region's maps and then navigate with them without the phone company, the government, and Google knowing about it. Poisoning the maps you sent to a group of protesters wouldn't be that interesting—it's not like you could get them to walk into the ocean by drawing a road that wasn't there. But every protester would be downloading Openstreetmaps, and that meant that poisoning Openstreetmaps would be a good way to sneak onto protesters' phones.

"It's just you? Not any of your little gang?"

"My affinity group. No, just me. I called them before calling you."

"Huh."

"Masha."

"Okay, here's the worst-case scenario. They've looked at the encrypted communications going through your 'affinity group'"—I tried not to pronounce the finger quotes but I'm sure I failed, because being irritated by cutesy jargon is my superpower—"and though they can't see what you're all saying to each other, they *can* see that when *you* say something, other people start talking, or acting—"

"This is information cascades, right?"

"Uh . . . right."

"You explained it to me, girl. You were drunk as fuck, though. Kept talking about how you were the command-node for our little group, which is cute."

The last couple times I'd seen Tanisha, it was at parties or Burning Man, big, crowded places where we could lose ourselves dancing and not have to talk too much about what I was doing and who I was doing it to. I didn't like the idea that I'd gotten drunk enough to discuss tradecraft with her and then forget it had happened. I was accustomed to thinking of myself as more careful than that, or at least more compartmentalized.

"I guess I must have. Yeah, that's information cascades, and it's worst case because if they're going after you, it's because they figure that you're a leader and they're going to neutralize you."

"That was what I was afraid of. What's the best-case scenario?"

"*Best* case? Software error—no one's hacking anyone. But assuming you *are* being attacked, best case would be something like a drive-by, untargeted attack: someone's broken into the Openstreetmaps server and they're serving out malicious payload with every *n*th download, just to see what they got. Petty criminal dumdums, in other words—not sinister government forces."

"Let's hear it for petty criminal dumdums, then."

"Don't get your hopes up, Neesh. You should be treating this as a live fire exercise. If it turns out it's just dumdums, then you'll save yourself the embarrassment of being hacked by dumdums. If it turns out it's the law, you *definitely* don't want to wind up hacked, because they'll use you to nail everyone you trust and love."

"Including you, right? I mean, maybe they've already got me, right?"

"Even if they don't, you reached me by calling my private number and it's not hard to figure out who controls that. On the plus side, it's also not hard to figure out that I'm an old friend of yours who's been talking with you on and off since we were teenyboppers, so maybe the machine-learning system that's ingesting all your phone records will discount me."

"I hate this."

"You chose it."

Clearly the wrong thing to say. Long silence.

"Masha, don't be an asshole."

I knew exactly what she meant—*I* chose it, I'm the one who went to work building these systems, I'm the one who made them my life and filled my every waking hour with them. Choosing to be an activist wasn't choosing surveillance: choosing to make surveillance was choosing surveillance. I knew what she meant because we'd had this argument before, which is one of the advantages to talking with old friends, all that shared history, all those old conversations in the data-bank. It was also the crisis of talking to old friends, because it liberated the fragments that had been compartmentalized years ago, let them stretch and breathe and remind you of all the ways you had disappointed yourself and everyone whose opinion you ever cared about.

One of us was going to have to speak to break the silence. She was clearly trying to control her temper. I was trying to reassemble my compartments.

"I don't really think you're an asshole, Masha." Tanisha was a sentimentalist. A good friend. Someone who would back down. I wished I could be like her.

"I'm sorry too, Neesh. Let's reboot this. You're actually in pretty good shape, all things considered. If they're trying to hack you, it means they haven't hacked you yet. Plus, it's not one hundred percent certain you're being hacked by the cops themselves—maybe it's one of the contractors in line for fat payouts if the plan goes ahead."

"Why is that good news?"

"Because they won't have a warrant, so they have to be a lot more cautious about getting caught, meaning they can't be as aggressive. I think you should just make a lot of noise about this—the alternatives are to either ignore it and tighten up your opsec, or try to fake them out by letting them take over your device and then use that to feed them fake info, and I don't think you're sneaky enough to manage that."

"Gee, thanks."

"It's a compliment. Sneakiness isn't the same as smartness. To maintain the charade, you'd have to make zero mistakes, and they'd only have to find one mistake. But if you go public and make a noise, then people like you might be more careful about their own shit, which will help *you*, because if they can't get to you, the next step would be to get to the people you talk to and intercept the messages they exchange with you."

"And then what?"

"Then what what?"

"I go public and what happens next?"

"Next you'll probably get some of the academic security researchers asking to analyze the update, which is harmless. If you hear from Citizen Lab, you should totally go for it, those University of Toronto types run a tight ship. The bad guys keep on trying to pwn you—but they'd do that anyway. Maybe some of them will take it personally when you out them, but do you really care if the war criminals trying to take over your stuff are doing so because of a grudge?" I thought of some of my former co-workers, the kinds of things they got up to when they had a grudge. "Okay, grudges could make things worse, but Neesh, you're already plenty fucked."

"You're really good at pep talks, you know that?"

"Hey, join the club. I'm fucked, you're fucked, everyone we know is fucked. At least we know it and get to steer our canoes on the way over the falls."

"Are you drunk?"

I rewound what I'd just said. My compartments were breaking down. I was clearly overwrought and overtired. "Just dealing with my own shit. Sorry, Neesh, that wasn't nice. You're not fucked-fucked, just a little fucked. If it helps, you're only fucked because someone thinks you pose a threat. So you're doing something right?" I meant it as a statement, but it came out as a question, because in my line of work, if someone knows enough about you to consider you a threat, you're doing something wrong and potentially fatal. "I'm sorry, seriously."

"Yeah. Me too. But I'm not sorry I'm trying to do something." Which was supposed to sting, I think, because if I was doing anything these days, it was something bad. I thought about Kriztina and her merry band.

"I'm glad you're doing something, Neesh. Maybe I should come and join you."

Her voice got soft. "You'd be very welcome, you know that, right? I miss you, Masha. We all do."

I put that one in a compartment for later. "I miss you guys too. Uh, you know, I'm kind of thinking of heading back to the US sometime soon—"

"You'll stay at my place."

"Is that an invitation?"

"You don't need an invitation with me, ever. I don't know what you're doing there, but we could use you here." She swallowed audibly, a couple times. "It's getting hard around here, no joke. It's like every time things look like they're at a breaking point, they don't break, they just stretch, and we all get stretched out. Meanwhile, any time someone puts up any kind of fight, well, next thing we know that person's getting arrested for some bullshit—and everyone else is just that little bit less willing to fight. No one knows what's true, everyone might be an informer or an agent provocateur. You know how stuff works, you could make a real difference."

Kriztina and her friends. My compartments strained and buckled. "Knowing things isn't enough, Neesh. Trust me, I know. The reality is that you are outgunned and outflanked and outresourced. Sprinkling internet fairy dust on your political uprising isn't going to change that fundamental truth."

Another one of those total, compressed silences. It went on for so long I had to look at my phone's screen to make sure the call hadn't dropped.

"Hello?"

"I'm here, Masha."

"I don't want to discourage you—"

Her derisive snort was straight out of my teen years, a ghost from the past.

"What do you counsel, then, Masha? Should we use typewriters and couriers to organize our resistance?"

"Don't be stupid. Couriers are easy to intercept and a camera can take a long-range photo of your typewritten memo."

"Yeah, I figured that out for myself. So what *should* we do, Masha?"

This is where this discussion always broke down. We'd had versions of it for decades, and there was one time that it went so badly that we didn't speak to each other for a year.

"Neesh, just because I don't know how to solve your problem doesn't mean that I can't tell you that your solution isn't making it better. I may not know why you have a headache, but I can tell you that beating your head against that wall isn't helping any." Thinking: please don't give me *another* bunch of suicidal idealists to babysit while they destroy their own lives.

"I've heard you say that before, and I'll tell you what I think: it's bull-shit. Every single change in the world has come from people *trying* to change things. That includes all the long shots. Yeah, I don't know how we go from our little affinity groups and our protests to a better world, but I know that doing *nothing* sure won't help. There's every reason we could fail, but no reason we can't succeed."

When you compartmentalize really well, it can be like you're outside of your body, watching it react to the things around it. A long way away, I noticed that part of me reacted to this "every reason we could fail/no reason we can't succeed" with a surge of hope, wanting to rush home to Tanisha and join her at a barricade somewhere; another part of me wanted to shake Tanisha by the shoulders and say, *Wait a sec, surely you should pay a little attention to "every reason we could fail" before you put yourself at risk of a beating, life in prison, maybe being killed?*

That second part was *fierce,* flooding my body with adrenaline and making my hands shake. It was imagining Tanisha getting hit in the face with a tear-gas cannister and losing an eye, and right next to her, holding her limp and bleeding body, was me, eyes swollen and streaming from the gas. From far away, I heard myself breathing in my terrible hotel room, realized I was hyperventilating.

Somewhere, a computer was watching this call just as I was watching myself. Maybe neither of us had been compromised and all it could see was that Tanisha was talking to me and that I was talking to her, old friends linked by nothing more than shared history. Or maybe it had full access privileges to every word and every breath, ingesting feeds from our cameras and mics, rooting stealthily through our filesystems for stored credentials and logs.

This fact was something I had lived with on both sides, and I knew that the way to deal with it was to pretend it wasn't there—to act as though everything were fine and normal, like phones were things to let you talk to your friends, not to let anonymous strangers watch and judge you. You had to pretend this because otherwise you became a terrible person, paranoid and angry all the time, and you made your friends' lives terrible.

"I guess so, Neesh." That was the voice of normal. Reassuring. "I'm glad you're out there fighting. You're my hero. Seriously." It was a normal and good thing to say. Saying it made me a normal person, a good person. "There's a good chance I'll make it to California soonish, no reason not to. It'll be so good to see you. Stay safe, okay?"

"I will. You too, Masha. We're still your friends here, all of us. We love you. Any time you're in trouble, you can call on us."

I'd done that once, had them run interference for me while I did something stupid and no-reason-we-can't-succeed, trying to get away from all the spook stuff with Marcus Yallow as my insurance policy (which he fucked up). Tanisha and Becky had gotten away clean then, but no thanks to me. Pure chance. They could have ended up in a world of shit. If the computer listening to us knew that fact, it would be paying a *lot* of attention to this call, walking our social graphs and looking for people to add to the "targeted surveillance" list—people whose every byte would be scraped and stored forever, cleartext and ciphertext alike. The cleartext would give you insight into the ciphertext, because you could use the conversations on either side of the black box of encrypted stuff to infer what happened inside that black box (I email you and ask you if you know any good lawyers, you have an impenetrably encrypted conversation with a lawyer, then you email me back and suggest that I get in touch with your friend, the lawyer—it's a pretty good bet that the encrypted emails were about whether the lawyer would talk to me). Then there's the very real possibility that the crypto we're using has some kind of undiscovered flaw in it, and someday in the future that flaw will be revealed, and our black box will spring open.

I was ratholing again, deep-diving into my own paranoia.

"Thank you, Tanisha," I said. Then I blurted, "I love you," which isn't something I say very often, and hadn't planned on saying then.

The machine silence was unbearable. My armpits were suddenly slick. "I love you too, Masha. We all do."

"Bye." There was nothing else to say.

"Bye."

I kept the silent phone to my ear for some time, feeling the warmth it had generated encrypting and decrypting our conversation. The hotel room felt suddenly cold.

I realized I was holding my breath and let it out. Set down my phone and breathed in. A chime.

I had a new message. From Ilsa.

> *Take care of yourself.*

I dropped the phone. The timing of the message was no coincidence. Ilsa was letting me know that the watchers I'd imagined were there. She had first-hand knowledge of them, which meant that either Xoth was watching me for its own reasons (I could do the company some real PR damage) or they had a contract to do so—maybe Xoth itself wasn't worried about me blabbing, but one of its customers wanted to make sure I didn't out them for their domestic spying.

Another chime. I didn't want to pick it up, but I couldn't not look. The message came in over an encrypted chat app I'd used with Xoth, one that signed in with an identity that was separate from my phone number.

> *You can take care of your friends without exposing yourself, if you're careful.*

Did Ilsa know what Tanisha and I had talked about? Was she inside my phone? Or was this just a blanket warning? Had she done a quick check on Tanisha, seen the kind of shit she was into, and infer that Tanisha would have been calling me for opsec advice? This kind of analysis—figuring out who knew what and how they knew it and what else they'd be able to figure out shortly—had made me the rock star of Carrie Johnstone's operations. Since then, I'd reflexively used it to examine my own life and circumstances, and if it wasn't for the compartmentalization, I'd have a permanent case of the willies.

Go compartments!

I didn't answer Ilsa and I didn't block her either, because as much as that would have made me feel better, it wouldn't help me figure out her next move and mine. Realistically, Ilsa didn't want to hurt me—all she wanted was to ensure my silence. Of course she wasn't going to *buy* that silence, because that would mean rewarding me for my shenanigans, and as a matter of principle, she wouldn't do that.

Ilsa probably thought she was being friendly, doing me a favor. Because that's the kind of person she was, and that's what passed for a favor among people like her. People like me.

I was suddenly so, so tired. My eyes were scratchy and sore and when I stood to get a glass of water—every glass in the bathroom was dirty and the water ran so slowly it took a full minute to rinse and fill it—all my joints complained.

I needed to sleep. The flight to San Francisco from Moscow would take fourteen hours. I could have dinner, watch a movie, and snuggle down in a lie-flat bed and *still* get nine solid hours.

# CHAPTER 2

The Aeroflot lounge was shuttered for the duration, but there was a snack bar in the waiting room. I bought hard salami ciabattas and coffee.

Even with the protein and fat and carbs and caffeine, I was a wreck.

I am pretty good at sitting still and waiting. It's an important skill in my line of work. Impatience, not fear, is the mind-killer. I used to calculate Fibonaccis in my head, but eventually I found a way to get into that same no-thought space without the useless math. I rocked my head from side to side, then my hips, finding a neutral position that was easy on my joints, and then I mind-fully, slowly, checked in with every part of me, starting from the last joint of my right big toe, working my way up to the crown of my head, really paying attention until I was sure that I could feel exactly what was going on with each part, moving as little as possible.

I'd taken a pretty bad set of knocks that night, but I'd managed not to notice them—the Compartmentalizer, scourge of self-care!—until I went through this exercise. I had bruises on one elbow and both knees; scrapes on a shin and both palms; aching muscles in my shoulders and jaw, which I must have been hunching and clenching (respectively).

When I opened my eyes, I felt every one of those pains, but also a kind of calm that I needed. I was the only one. All my fellow waiting passengers had a tense, last-chopper-out-of-Saigon vibe. I carefully suppressed my irritation at them. One of the things I'm good at spotting in myself is the fundamental attribution error: that's when you assume that your own dumb mistakes are the result of normal, excusable human fallibility, while *other people's* mistakes are the result of their fundamental lack of character. As in, "When I forget to do the dishes, that's because no one's perfect. When *you* forget to do the dishes, it's because you're a selfish asshole."

I started to rehearse my Moscow game plan. The bank machines would be open when I landed and I could draw out dollars from my Swiss Visa, enough to see me through for a few days in San Francisco. I could spend the rest of the time tracking down people who might have a little contract work for me. Same as anyone laid off from a high-tech job, really, except that I'd be parachuting in to troubleshoot cyberweapons. Anything so long as it paid well and didn't involve sales support, I hated having to work with sales. The guys who closed deals for spyware were inevitably the kinds of colossal assholes you found in sales, but with even less conscience, if you can imagine such a thing.

I took Moscow on autopilot. When you know an airport well enough, you don't even have to think about it. Got cash, picked up a vending-machine SIM with euros, and found a seat in an Aeroflot business lounge close to my gate.

As I was settling in with two fingers of pre-lunch vodka, Signal chimed. A burner SIM meant that no one could phone me using a phone number, but this was coming over the lounge wifi by way of my VPN, and whoever was calling was on my trusted list.

HERTHE NETZKE was the name on my screen, and the picture was the lobby card from *Ilsa, She-Wolf of the SS,* Dyanne Thorne in her jodhpurs and knee-high boots. Thankfully, she'd never called my phone while in the same room as me. In my experience, ze Chermans are not so hot on the old Nazi jokes.

"Hello."

"Masha."

"Hello."

Herds of businessman Borises drifted by. The other people in the lounge fingered their phones and shuffled their possessions. I had a powerful urge to drink. I knocked back half of the vodka.

"You're all right?"

"Not really, no. Not after what happened last night."

A moment, then: "New tactics are shocking, so the chatter after their deployment will inevitably be out of proportion. A crude suicide bomb would have resulted in significantly more casualties, but that would not have inspired the same terror of this novel attack."

Ilsa always talked like that. I mentally called it *Rommelling*—waxing coldly theoretical about strategy when everyone else was hot and anxious. It was part of her ice-queen schtick. It wasn't a good look on her: fronting all tough was more Carrie Johnstone's style.

"Don't savvy me, Herthe." Meaning: don't try to make me think that none of the cool kids are worrying about this, so neither should I. "Friends of mine are missing."

"Your young Kriztina." Of course she knew about her.

"Is she safe?"

"She wasn't in the attack."

Even after a couple vodkas, I spotted the evasion. "That's not what I asked."

"She was in a cell when the attack came. The targets were fascists, not your friends, Masha. Litvinchuk is a smart man; he implements different tactics for different factions. This sort of thing scares Nazis right down to their tiny souls. Your crowd all dream of martyrdom, so this sort of thing doesn't do at all."

I firmly refused to picture Kriztina in one of Litvinchuk's cells. The Slovstakian slang word for jailer translated as "knucklebreaker." A finger broken and healed at a strange angle was their version of a jailhouse tattoo, a badge of dishonor marking you as a onetime guest of the knucklebreakers—a crook or a dissident, and it didn't matter which.

"Is she hurt?" I hated how small my voice sounded. I wasn't sure I had a compartment big enough to fit all the things I was feeling. It was too much. The booze wasn't helping. The booze never helped.

"It's an internal matter." For a second, I thought she was making a horrible torture joke—like *she was hurt, internally*—but then I realized she simply meant that what happened between Litvinchuk's knucklebreakers and Kriztina was none of Xoth's business and thus none of hers.

I didn't count to ten, because that never helped me. I thought, *This is one of those count-to-seven situations,* which did sometimes help me. "Herthe, I am not in a position to learn more about Kriztina, and while this isn't a Xoth matter, I'd consider it a personal favor if you made inquiries." This was memospeak, the way we wrote to each other when we thought about how our emails would play if they got hacked and dumped, or subpoenaed. I learned it from Carrie Johnstone herself.

Talking in memospeak was a coded communiqué: *I am so angry that if I spoke my mind, I'd say something we'd both regret.* Ilsa was fluent in such grammars, and would, as intended, understand my statement to translate as: *Don't make me chase Litvinchuk with the means at my disposal, because they are not subtle means. You will really hate the things I would have to do to get leverage over our mutual friend. Also, need I remind you that I no longer work for Xoth and you have no ready means of disciplining me should you decide I've stepped out of line?*

"I can certainly make inquiries, Masha. I understand that this situation must be very stressful for you." Translation: *I hear you. I'll ask around. Don't do anything stupid. (Or else.)* "Remember, the press you'll encounter outside of Slovstakia is very hostile to the regime and will go to great lengths to discredit it. Always take care to ask yourself what's outside of the frame." *It's fake news. If you're smart, you'll ignore it.*

Thing was, she was half-right. The US and EU press *did* hate Slovstakia. It was one of those countries whose autocratic dictator was friendly with the other side and bought its arms from them—and didn't have any natural gas, important museums, or other useful assets with which to buy favor with western powers. Its oligarchs bought Chinese and Russian luxury brands, not French and American ones. I wondered if I went back and watched the Car Wars videos, whether I'd see the same attacks from different angles, cut to make them look like two separate attacks. It wouldn't be the first time something like that had happened. Slovstakia was a basket-case dictatorship, but its enemies liked to find ways to make it look even shittier.

"Thank you, Herthe. It is stressful. She's a good friend, and she isn't a criminal." Which wasn't strictly true, but we both knew that I meant "criminal in the eyes of international human rights NGOs" not "criminal in the eyes of the Slovstakian justice system." Technically everyone alive was a criminal under Slovstakian justice, one way or another.

"I will do everything I can." *Don't do anything stupid.*

"Thank you, Herthe." *Message received. That* was more Herthe's style: careful subterranean dealmaking, not threats.

Thing is, I think Ilsa actually liked me in a weird, bent, German spook way. Those commie spooks were long on personal relationships; not like my old American boss, who only liked you if she thought she could get something out of you.

"I saw that you flew out this morning. Your final pay has already been transferred to your account."

"Thank you."

"Masha, you are a very talented, very brilliant, and very stupid young woman."

"I am aware of this, Herthe. Is there something I can help you with?" I choked down rage. I'd been fired, and then something *really* ugly had happened. I'd been spending a lot of time pointedly *not* thinking about this. She was making me think about it, and that was bringing up all the humiliation and shame of having been expendable enough to fire just because I'd been engaged in some harmless-ish fuckery. The fact that it was 100 percent my fault and that it had rendered me incapable of helping my friends just made it 1,000 percent worse.

"I wanted to let you know that just because you are not working for me anymore, it doesn't mean that you cannot talk to me. I want you to be safe, Masha." See? All about the long-term relationships. She'd be every bit as solicitous if she was rendering me to a black site. Even when it was business, it was personal.

"Don't worry, if I go down, I'll leave Xoth out of it."

That cryptographic, absolute silence.

"Hello?"

"Masha, what I am about to say is said with the best of intentions. Have you ever considered psychiatric counseling? I have seen many people in our line of work self-destruct. The combination of secrecy and power, and . . . some of the other aspects of the job—the *human* aspects—can drive smart, thoughtful people over the edge. If you would like, I can recommend some names of discreet people."

"I'll be fine, Herthe. I'm sorry, that just came out wrong." I knew plenty of people who could benefit from counseling or even a heavy course of Thorazine. A certain former boss. Not me.

"Because the people who don't get counseling when the self-destructive be-havior begins? Masha, those people *die*. I have seen it. You may be young enough that you think it can't happen to you. I think very highly of you, Masha, and your wit and strength, but I have seen people *much* stronger and smarter than you get into serious trouble."

I nearly said something again about not having to worry about my taking Xoth down, but I was able to recognize my self-destructive impulse and curtail it. See? Progress. No need for me to see a shrink, especially not one who caters to Ilsa's spook pals.

"Thank you, Herthe. I'll give it some thought."

She tsked, something she was extremely nuanced at, this tsk meaning some-thing between *asshole* and *hopeless,* and that made it clear she understood that I was blowing her off.

She had a point.

I tried to work, but all my brain seemed to want to do was reload my email to see if Kriztina had sent me anything, which she hadn't, and obviously that was just fine because Kriztina lived in a little compartment I had built to last.

Sitting in the lounge, trying so very hard not to dwell on my mistakes, I could tell that I was on the precipice of the dismal, endless canyon. Depression is a fucking liar, but it's a convincing one, and I could hear it whispering to me already, telling me that I'd ruined everything, that I'd never work again, that I'd never be loved by anyone, that I'd end up in exile because someone would sue me in the USA for my complicity in getting their family disappeared; reminding me that I had no idea how many of those disappearances I was complicit in, but that it was nonzero.

I missed the USA, which was something I did rarely, but well. I'd grown up in the Bay Area and had my glory teen years in the trough between the first dot-com bubble (dog food by internet) and the second one (take this gig economy job or we'll make you into dog food), when the rents were merely too high, instead of blistering. Back then, the Castro was still the gay ghetto and not a realtor's dream of painted lady houses ready to be flipped three times in three years at a 100 percent markup every year. Back then, there were under-ground dance clubs, all-ages places or places where they didn't check your ID, and I'd dance my ass off with my girls until two in the morning, then howl through the streets like a dingledodie, drunk or just hopped on youth and hormones and horniness, and get into mischief. I had a LiveJournal. I had a Blogger blog. I wrote a MySpace virus. That was who I was.

In that time, you'd find people doing weird, marginal stuff everywhere: ten kids living in a giant warehouse, calling themselves "artists" and building huge Burning Man art-cars in the living room while teaching XML at San Francisco State as an adjunct, or spinning on Wednesday nights at the DNA Lounge, or gigging with a post–Riot Grrrl band that did anime theme-song covers and original songs about the patriarchy. Half the people I knew were "community moderators" and the other half were haunting the thrifts for underpriced scores to put up on eBay (this was before eBay finished its great project of normalizing the contents of every basement and attic in America).

I played the early ARGs, the ones that required you to have a WAP interpreter on your dumbphone, and my girls and I would *win*, all the time, because we were better than any puzzlemaker you could name. There'd be dudes who'd hide their clues in resources that you could only find on microfiche, things that had never been digitized, and we would ferret that stuff out so fast it might as well have been a first-page Google result.

One day—the fateful day, the day that turned Marcus Yallow into M1k3y (God help us all)—terrorists blew up the Bay Bridge. That was a hell of a day. I knew right away that there was work to do. The thing is, I had loved San Francisco growing up, thought of it as *my* town. I was never afraid there, there was no place I wouldn't go. Crackheads fighting in the Tenderloin would get out of *my* way, and I thought I could freeze catcallers with one blaze from my laser hate-vision. I had thighs like tree trunks from running up its hills, and ill-advised piercings all over the damn place because once you get to know a world-class piercer, it was a pleasure to allow her to practice her artistry.

So I took it personally when those *fuckers* blew up *my* bridge and trashed *my* city. I sent, like, three hundred emails to the DHS volunteering to do whatever it took to help them make my city safe. Of course, every one of those emails disappeared into a black hole, because duh, I was just a kid.

But I was a *smart* kid. I didn't have to be able to wiretap the internet to tell what was going on. There were plenty of clues, if you knew what to look for.

Kids showing up to school with home-burned discs and photocopied instructions for flashing your freebie Xbox Universal to tap into the "Xnet" (imaginative name, "M1k3y") and help fight off the big bad DHS.

It was unbelievably easy to break into the impenetrable, cryptographically secured Xnet: all I had to do was take home one of those homemade discs, copy the installer image to my home PC, and add in a backdoor that caused any machine to open a reverse-shell to a computer I controlled (it was a corporate webserver owned by a dog-grooming company in Brandon, Manitoba, because no language in human history has contained the phrase "As competent as a dog groomer's network security"). From there, I could capture everything: passwords, screengrabs, files. About half of my music collection dates from those days, because I ran a script that looked for anyone who had an MP3 library that contained more than three songs that I'd high-ranked in my own player, and when it found a match, it copied over all of the target's music. It was a plunderphonic idea.

More significantly, I quickly got inside the planning for all the Xnet army's "ops," their RFID switcheroos and their sprinkling of false-positive bomb residue in public places. I didn't turn it over to DHS, not at first. Instead, I built a very careful dossier, tracked who the leaders were. No one had ever told me about information cascades, but I independently reinvented them and built out org charts, calculating the ideal nodes to take out in order to disrupt these fun-lovin' criminals.

I had two problems: First, not all of these kids deserved to be punished. Some were actively questioning whether it was cool to deliberately mess with the DHS's security measures, trying to argue for moderation even as their idiot buddies were demanding that they HACK ALL THE THINGS. Anything I did to call down the wrath of God on these kids would catch 'em all.

Second, no one at the DHS wanted to hear from a teenaged girl, no matter how super-leet she was and no matter how much dope intel she'd amassed on Cal-Qaeda, the bandit army of children who'd made fools of them all.

But I am nothing if not resourceful. Never underestimate the power of a kid who is time-rich and cash-poor, as a foolish boy once said. The DHS leaked a *lot* of signals and HUMINT, all those LinkedIn profiles and old online résumés, all those press conferences and the names at the bottoms of procurement bids on fed websites. Slowly, piece by piece, I compiled a separate dossier on the DHS: specifically the officials overseeing the San Francisco terrorist response team. If Xnet had as much brains as bravado, they would have done something like this, targeted specific people, disrupted the chain of command. That's how, you know, *guerrillas* do it. As opposed to dumbass kids.

Cascade analysis again. When this person gave an order, these people hopped. This person's talking points came out of this person's mouth a week later. My cascade analysis was full of arrows pointing at arrows, back and forth, reflecting the slow journey to bureaucratic consensus, but there was one node with more arrows pointing away from it than all the others, more arrows than all the others put together. Under that node, a name: Carrie Johnstone.

Johnstone was everything I wasn't: super-straight, with a haircut that was so blunt and squared off it looked like it had been specially constructed for her by the Army Corps of Engineers. Second-generation military, navy brat who'd grown up in ports all around the world, poli-sci major, and then washed out of special forces training—broke both her legs, just like Snowden, which was an irony she didn't appreciate at all when that came out. Also, she was hot, you know, ice-queen style, the kind of blue eyes that someone will inevitably call "piercing." She was an old-school country fan, Merle Haggard and Conway Twitty and absolutely no Willie Nelson because she didn't smoke weed and didn't want to know you if you did.

All this I figured out once I'd done the legwork to get her message-board handle, Americhick1776 (barf). I wasn't sure at first whether that was her, because she'd been careful, but there was this open-source library called Anonymouth, which would do "adversarial stylometry" on texts and tell you whether there were matches for idiosyncratic punctuation, vocabulary, sentence structure, and spelling errors. I trained it on the public postings she'd made under her own name, then fed it corpuses I'd scraped from Americhick1776, Thankgodimacountrygirl, USAOKBYME, and Bornintheusa1979, and the Americhick1776 corpus was an 86 percent fit for Johnstone, while the next-best match, Bornintheusa1979, scored a mere 41 percent. From there, it was simple to scrape all the posts she'd ever made, set up alerts for her handle, walk her social graph on the laughably primitive pre-Facebook networks (none of them possessed the mighty anti-scraping mojo that Facebook commands), scrape all her friends' media posts, and build up my detailed picture of where she went, when, and with whom. A prehistoric Usenet post from her early college days revealed her parents' home phone number, and reverse-directory searches got me their addresses. Credit reports revealed their finances as well as the mobile carriers they used. Social engineering to those carriers coughed up their cell-phone numbers, for which they had not changed the default voicemail passwords (neither had anyone else alive at that time). A couple weeks' worth of diligent eavesdropping netted calls from Johnstone, including one where she left her office phone number (her cell phone didn't work in her shielded DHS trailer). I cross-referenced this with her personal online activity during work hours to figure out when she goofed off at work, and then I had motive, means, and opportunity.

I bought my burner phone—while wearing a hoodie and platform shoes— from a 7-Eleven on Market Street and took BART to Oakland, placing my call from the marina, where my sight lines were good and there were no cameras. She didn't answer at first and I got butterflies when I rolled into voicemail, but I hung up, counted to thirty, and called back.

"Carrie Johnstone." I knew her voice intimately already, I still got a thrill. Those other times, she'd been talking to other people. This time, she was talking to me. Those were rehearsals. This was opening night.

"Ms. Johnstone, you don't know me, but I'm a patriot and I have some intelligence on the so-called Xnet, and I would like very much to share it with you."

She didn't miss a beat. "Please hold one moment." Click. "I'm recording this. Please continue."

My mouth went dry. I tried unsuccessfully to swallow and cursed my thundering heart. "I have command structures, logins, passwords, and chat logs. I have planted backdoors on key members' computers and have them under continuous surveillance. I have information on upcoming plans."

"I see." She paused, making me squirm. I had to pee, all of a sudden. "What is it you want in exchange for this?"

"You mean money?" It was a blurt. I hadn't even thought about money. My parents weren't rich, but they weren't poor, and I'd gotten contract web work since I was old enough to have a bank account.

"What else?"

"A job?" Blurt. My mouth had a mind of its own. But I was going to own this. I said it again, without the uptalk. "A job."

"Huh." She had a good "huh," like a teacher who'd just been pleasantly surprised by a student. "Then I guess we should meet up."

I knew a lot of people in the infosec industry, but mostly they didn't trust me, because I am not trustworthy. A few of them knew that I was the person who leaked all that juicy stuff to Marcus, but they all knew I worked for Xoth, and before that, for Xe, and before that, for the DHS. I wasn't a whistleblower; I was, at best, a leaker.

Working for The Man was difficult. There was the bureaucracy, which was only slightly better at places like Xoth and Xe than it was in the government agencies we serviced, because to do business with the DHS, you had to impedence-match them, have parallel bureaucracies. Then add the fact that the people working for DHS often came from Xoth and Xe, and that the people from Xoth and Xe often came from DHS, and pretty soon you could look from the pigs to the farmers and the farmers to the pigs and not be able to see the difference.

But there is this about working for The Man: it paid hella good. My years with DHS had given me a taste of the money you got working for USG in one of the shadowier agencies. Carrie Johnstone had convinced her bosses that she needed to be able to compete with the dot-coms for technical talent, had to be able to offer something that was within spitting distance of the stock-options-and-foosball utopias of Palo Alto and Soma, and they'd come through with her own black budget. I even got a pension—not a big one, because I went private pretty damned quick, but it's indexed to inflation and pays out to my spouse if I happen to have such a thing at the time that I croak.

Then I followed my frenemy and mentor Carrie Johnstone into the private sector, and that's when I got a taste of the *real* money.

I had enough cash in my pockets to last me for weeks; but there was enough salted in tax havens around the world to keep me afloat for years. I had drawn a salary, got bonused at the end of every year, got stock options that vested quarterly, and then there were the commissions on any job that I was the designated "sales engineer" for. Plus they flew me first class and let me keep the air miles.

If it wasn't for the fact that I had to fly to some real basket cases serviced only by their own obscure national carriers, I would have had 33rd Order Mason gold cards for all three of the major airline networks. I stayed in five-star hotels, complete with room service, and had a company card for "entertainment" meals. Xoth billed on a cost-plus basis, meaning that they took all their actual "costs" for any given job (that is, my $8 minibar cashews and $12 miniatures of Lagavulin), added 25 percent, and billed it to the government of Slovstakia, or the DHS, or whomever else they were "servicing" at the time. The more I spent, the more they made.

It's very glam to live in a Berlin squat and fuck idealistic teenyboppers and go on freegan dumpster-diving missions with dropout MIT kids who are experimenting with molecular gastronomy. I do it every now and again, by way of a holiday. But the best thing about that kind of holiday is finishing it in a nice, anonymous international-style hotel with a rooftop pool, a spa massage, and yoga classes taught by Olgas—lady Borises, that is—with Barbie-doll figures and flawless skin.

I didn't need to sofa-surf with my girlhood pal at her place in Oakland. I just *wanted to.*

Carrie Johnstone didn't like any of the restaurants I proposed, not even the Trader Vic's in the East Bay, which I thought was pretty sophisticated given that I was a seventeen-year-old who was stuck ordering off the virgin cocktail list (come for the Soft Banana Cow, stay for the No Tai Mai Tai).

But Johnstone's jam—as I was to come to understand—was the kind of steakhouse with private dining rooms and wine lists thicker than their steaks.

See, once she'd had three or four big glasses of red—mid-'80s Bordeaux, on her government AmEx—she got a little loud and indiscreet, and private rooms meant she didn't have to dispatch snatch squads out later that night to send the people from the neighboring tables to black sites for hearing too much. Private rooms also meant that nobody gave a shit that I was seventeen, which is how I became the kind of seventeen-year-old with definite opinions about whether oaky reds were ever worth the premium (they were not).

The first meeting, I thought she was testing me when she poured me a glass, only later did I figure out that glass two was when things got sloppy and the girl-talk came out. I've talked with Marcus about Johnstone, I know he thinks she's a hundred-foot-tall fembot with laser eyes, but the reality is that she's only so tightly wound because she's got a lot of loose and messy stuff to hold in. Which is to say, she's not all that different from Marcus. Or me. (But she's got surprisingly little in common with Ilsa, She-Wolf of the SS).

She was absolutely riveted by what I had to tell her during glass one. Then glass two came out and by the time it was three-quarters gone, we'd switched to her boasting about all the stuff she had going on, the number of people reporting to her, her sexy new cell-phone trackers, the data analysis she was doing on the toll trackers she'd got from FasTrak, the fights she'd had with Google and Yahoo over getting into their data-centers.

I won't lie, I was impressed. When I was thirteen, I'd figured out how to get into the voicemails of all my school friends. It wasn't hard: I just had to use an internet telephone program that let me spoof my number. Back then, if you called into voicemail from your own number, you didn't need to enter a PIN; I'd dial into T-Mobile or Sprint's voicemail number with my friends' numbers spoofed as my caller ID, and listen to all their saved messages and any new ones.

It was clearly wrong, but man, was it thrilling. There was virtually no chance of getting caught, even if I got sloppy and forgot to mark their messages as un-heard after listening to them—when was the last time you paid any attention to whether your voicemails were correctly flagged as new or old? Everyone hates voicemail, that's its dirty secret, but back then texting wasn't the go-to way to avoid people while still communicating with them, so voicemail was a treasure trove of sensitive information, gossip, and dark secrets. Voicemail, it turns out, is a terrific method for expressing your absolute disgust and rage with your friends, to recriminate with your ex over an ugly breakup, and, in a couple memorable places, to let your hookup from last week know that they'd better get their junk looked at by a doctor before they start pissing flames.

I can feel your disapproval. Go ahead. The reality is, the only reason you never did that shit is because you hadn't thought of it. I 100 percent *guarantee* that if you had started, you wouldn't have been able to stop. Thing is, we're all prisoners in our bodies, we'll never know what anyone else truly thinks or wants or feels. The great mystery of being a human being is trying to figure out WTF all those other human beings are doing. Listening to those private moments, as boring and banal as they were, taught me more about who I was than ten years of psychoanalysis could have.

Then there's the thrill of power, the sense of knowing things about the people around you that they don't even know about themselves. Think of the weird games that people play in middle school, that thing where trios of girls form and then take turns excluding one member, and imagine knowing all the stuff that they're saying when they think no one can hear them. You think in middle school you wouldn't have listened in? You're a liar.

Thing is, when Carrie Johnstone told me about the stuff she was able to do with the data sources she was sucking in, I recognized a kindred spirit. I eventually gave up on voicemails—I got a little group of friends myself, and they were good people, and I couldn't bring myself to spy on them, and then all the other spying just felt wrong. But if there was one thing my finding Johnstone proved, it was that I still had the instincts.

What I didn't have—what Johnstone had—was automation. The toolsuite she described for auto-classifying information cascades, for assembling intercepts into searchable databases, for spotting the single weird grains of sand on the beachful of data she lived on, it gave me a feeling that was unlike anything I'd ever felt before. The closest equivalent is horniness, but this feeling was all above the waist.

As she laid it out for me, I found myself wondering about ways to improve it. Johnstone was getting her code from intelligence contractors, the neolithic ancestors of Xoth, and they were optimized to make code that impressed Johnstone's bosses, the ones who wrote the checks for no-bid procurement contracts. But the people who had to *use* the software were never actually consulted in the purchase cycle, so why bother to make the software any good for those people?

The thing is, Johnstone knew something was wrong with her tools, but she couldn't explain what, exactly. Besides, the defects in those tools gave her something to humblebrag about—as in, *You wouldn't believe what a pain in the ass it is to correlate location data from a couple million cell phones with MySpace friends lists.* Just listening to this, I could tell—I could *feel*—that these tools sucked and that I could make them better.

"Carrie?" I'd gotten through my whole glass of wine and Carrie was on her third. It had been "Carrie" instead of "Miss Johnstone" (never "Ms.") after the second glass.

"Masha." She focused on me with an effort.

"Can I speak frankly?"

She turned her head this way and that, as though she'd only just noticed that I was a freak teenager. "Shoot."

"Have you ever thought of—" It spilled out in a tumble, all the crazy shit I'd dreamed of being able to do whenever I'd contemplated getting the whole world on God Mode, with the ability to see and manipulate all its data. I started out careful, watching her wobbly, boozy poker face for signs of trouble, but then I got on a roll. I poured myself another glass of wine somewhere in there, and by the time I ran down, it was empty. I felt hot and clammy at the same time.

"Huh." She stared up at the ceiling for a long time, then poured out the last sip of wine and drank it. "You know the expression 'Don't teach Granny to suck eggs?'"

As it happened, I didn't, because I was a teenager from San Francisco, not one of the Little Rascals, but I looked it up later and, as I'd suspected from what happened next, it wasn't good.

"Listen, little girl, I've been doing this since you were a larvum. I'm very, very good at it. You, on the other hand, are a child. You've been very helpful tonight, don't get me wrong, but don't go thinking that we're all seat-warming dumbasses waiting for a clever little twat like you to show us the way."

A compartmentalizer like me can do poker faces. I did one. I think I probably managed it, even. But I felt like I'd just been slapped. Johnstone could go from sloppy and friendly to hot and furious in nothing flat. It was a scary trick and I'm sure she knew it. I wanted nothing more than to leave that table and that room and that restaurant, and I couldn't. I had put myself in this situation, had sought it out. I'd *stalked* this woman to get a meeting with her and I had a feeling once Carrie Johnstone had you on her radar, you didn't get off it.

She went on. "I'm telling you this because you need to know it. You're half-bright and you've got potential. I could see working with you. But you technical people have a disease: it's called 'solutionism.' You see every challenge as a problem and every problem as having a solution and every solution as being a piece of technology. You hare off after those solutions without ever stopping to see whether there's another, worse problem that'll burst into life the moment the current one is 'solved.' In fact, those new problems are good news! They're what you solutionists call 'a feature, not a bug,' because when you've got a new problem, you've got another reason to hunt for another solution. You never have to sit back and look at the people, the systems, the politics—just the technology that can be used to distort them to suit your needs."

She looked at me for a long time, a thousand watts of stern disapproval and impatience. I was supposed to say something but I was half-drunk on wine and half-drunk on terror, and my mind was blank.

"Sorry?" Mice have squeaked louder.

"I'm sure you are. I don't want you sorry, though: I want you smart. Think about what I've said. I'll get in touch. You can go now."

I was so stunned that I just . . . did. She was already paging through her PDA, a huge government-issue number with rubber bumpers and a stubby antenna. This was before smartphones were much of a thing, and whatever it was she was holding, it ceased to evolve not long after, became an extinct cousin of everything we see today. Back then, it was the closest thing to a digital armament I'd seen and I wanted one with the white-hot intensity of a thousand suns.

I found myself on the street at the part of the Financial District that is almost the Tenderloin, equidistant between hookers and expensive Scotch. The cool, wet night air sobered me up. I tried to figure out what had just happened. Had I been offered a job? Threatened? Both?

My mom gave me a look when I came through the door and said, in Russian, "You stink of booze."

I gave her a level look back. "Better brush my teeth, then."

I felt her eyes boring into my back the whole way up the stairs.

I'd walked away from a job in the infosec world, but I wasn't stupid enough to think I was going to walk away from the industry itself. I had a very specific skill set, and the only place to use it was in spying on people, or, possibly, helping people avoid being spied upon. When I felt hopeless—which happened on the regular during my Xoth years—I fantasized about moving to Berlin, finding some "social enterprise" investors, and doing a startup that built easy-to-use opsec tools for protesters to use. In those dreams, it was a kind of penance that nevertheless paid well, making me rich while I saved the innocent Kriztinas of the world from the short-fingered Borises itching to zap their tender places with cattle prods.

I knew it was a stupid dream. The world wasn't going to pay for privacy until it was way, way too late. Privacy was like cigarettes. No single puff on a cigarette would give you cancer, but smoke enough of the things and they'd kill you dead, and by the time you understood that in your guts, it was too late. Smoking is all up-front pleasure and long-term pain, like cheesecake or sex with beautiful, fucked-up boys. It's the worst kind of badness, because the consequences arrive so long after—and so far away from—the effects. You can't learn to play baseball by swinging at the ball with your eyes closed, running home, and waiting six months for someone to call you up and let you know whether you connected. You can't learn to sort the harmless privacy decisions from the lethal ones by making a million disclosures, waiting ten years, and having your life ruined by one of them.

Industry was pumping private data into its clouds like the hydrocarbon barons had pumped $CO_2$ into the atmosphere. Like those fossil fuel billionaires, the barons of the surveillance economy had a vested interest in sowing confusion about whether and how all this was going to bite us in the ass. By the time climate change can no longer be denied, it'll be too late: we'll have pumped too much $CO_2$ into the sky to stop the seas from swallowing the world; by the time the datapocalypse is obvious even to people whose paychecks depended on denying it, it would be too late. Any data you collect will probably leak, any data you retain will definitely leak, and we're putting data-collection capability into fucking *lightbulbs* now. It's way too late to decarbonize the surveillance economy.

I needed a confessor. Back when I was at the DHS, I was everyone else's confessor. After going out for work-drinks, someone would quietly ask if I could stick around, then tell me all about their qualms about what we were doing. That was before we knew about Snowden, but he wasn't the only spook who carried around a copy of the Bill of Rights and Executive Order 12333, the secret Reagan-era directive that our bosses used to assure us that everything we were doing was legal. Serving as everyone else's crying shoulder made me feel like I was on the side of the angels. Even if I wasn't doing anything about the things I learned.

Working for Carrie Johnstone's DHS unit was like being in the mafia, but we didn't have to bribe the cops to protect us. We were the cops. I started in a trailer in "Siberia"—the far end of the chain-link compound on Treasure Island where Johnstone had had the ops guys set up her unit—with eight other junior analysts, working after school and weekends on processing "intelligence reports" from the SIGINT units. It was frustrating as hell, because I could tell that the data was being poisoned by Marcus and his Xnet morons, and even if it wasn't obvious from the data, it was obvious from their comms channels, which I was deep into.

So I dutifully filed report after report pointing out that all this intel was bullshit, that the systems that were supposed to be figuring out what was going on were being fed crap, so they were producing crap. Garbage in, garbage out.

After a month of this, I was ready to quit, but for some reason I didn't. I'd run into Johnstone at least once per shift and she'd bore into me with her eyes and ask me how I was enjoying the job and I'd give her my sunniest smile and tell her it was an honor to serve and I just couldn't be happier. I wasn't going to give her the satisfaction of letting her know that I was going quietly insane in that trailer. It didn't help that the other analysts were all gung-ho mother-fuckers from West Point who took the job so seriously they could use the term "homeland" without a hint of irony.

Those guys were the worst. The only thing that made it bearable was that the patriot gang worked totally different hours to me—I'd roll in at 4 p.m. after school and work until 10, while most of them were off the clock at five sharp, giving me a solid five hours in silence without having to worry about some GI Joe wannabe staring at my tits.

The only downside was that I got legitimately lonely sometimes, stir-crazy with that fundamental human need to just shoot the shit. Some of the janitors were nice, though they wouldn't come into my trailer if I was still in it, so I'd have to go for a walk and just happen to bump into them if I wanted to kill some time.

One night I was doing just that and looking up at the moon, a fingernail crescent wreathed in Bay Area mist, when I smelled cigarette smoke. That was a big no-no, the whole compound was plastered in no smoking signs and the MPs would give you a ticket if they caught you at it. I looked around and spotted the ember of the cigarette rising to an invisible set of lips, glowing briefly, descending. I squinted.

"They make an exception for the boss." Carrie Johnstone sounded exhausted.

"You okay?" It was a gamble. She wasn't the sort of person who went in for touchy-feely girl-talk.

She gave me her patented freeze-ray vision. I compartmentalized. She took another drag and blew a plume into the fog.

She sagged. "Politics." Another drag. It stank. "Look, all this—" She waved an arm. "It comes with a cost. Money, all right? And personal capital. Thing is, I'm using up my budget for both." She looked around. "All these people here, they're here because I'm here. Without me, it all goes. There's plenty of people sharpening their knives for me in DC, you better fucking believe it."

By now I'd learned enough to stay quiet.

She stamped out her cigarette. "I probably just need some sleep. It'll all look better in the morning."

I took a chance. "Thank you, Carrie. It's got to be a heavy load."

For a second I was sure she was going to rip my head off. I braced.

Her eyes glinted with tears. She blinked hard. "Thanks." Her voice was husky. She went back to her trailer and I went back to mine.

I spent the rest of the night pulling together a file with everything I knew about the Xnet kids: names, attributable actions, phone numbers, addresses, and information-cascade diagrams. I put it all on a thumb drive—this was before we all freaked out about BadUSB and thumb drives became a vector for network-destroying malware—and went back out to her trailer. I knocked on her door, looking into the camera mounted over the keycard reader, and waited. Despite the bone-deep fog chill, I felt sweat trickle out of my armpits.

She kept me waiting. I wondered whether I should just go, but then the door opened.

"What?"

I handed her the stick.

"What's this?"

"Independent project." I tried to make my voice project confidence, but it still came out in a kitten squeak. Johnstone could turn me into a terrified toddler.

She stared at me, held the thumb drive in her hand like she was weighing it. Then she nodded. "Okay." She smiled, a tight little thing that didn't reach her eyes. "Thanks, kid."

"You're welcome." Better—more confident this time.

"You can go now."

I took the hint. The MPs took me to South Beach and I caught a night bus from there. I'd Amazoned a bunch of manga that I'd been meaning to read, taking advantage of my new paycheck and my new commute to dig into them. My old friends and I were barely on speaking terms anymore, because I hadn't had a free evening in a month, and was half-asleep at lunch these days, but I'd made a point of keeping up with their raves for *One Piece* and *Kuroko's Basketball,* and I was determined to have something halfway intelligent to say about them, even if it meant keeping a Japanese-English dictionary in my backpack.

*One Piece* swept me away into its treasure hunts, and reminded me of my old besties and our days of kicking ass at Harajuku Fun Madness in the streets of San Francisco. After the attack on the Bay Bridge, we'd all been affected in our own ways. I had been a shitty friend, I could own that. But they hadn't been much better. Tanisha and Becky had some kind of monster fight and wouldn't talk to each other anymore, and if any of us brought up the subject of the other, they'd shut down and make an excuse to leave. Lucia became weirdly needy, texting at 3 a.m. and demanding to know what you meant by some offhand remark two days before.

I should have been there for them. I had introduced all of them to each other, and had been the hub around which our friend-group revolved. But I'd been busy chasing idiot children who were making war on the war on terror, and I'd let them slip away from me. I put away the comic and pulled out my phone and stared at the amputated stumps of our texting conversations, all of them waiting for replies from me.

I tapped out replies to each friend, apologizing for my disappearing act and asking what was up more casually than I meant. I had six missed calls from my mother, who I'd put on mute weeks before because otherwise she interrupted me all night when I was working. She was convinced I'd hooked up with some dude and was out all night fucking his brains out, and to be honest, it was easier to let her believe that than to explain where I was really going. For one thing, Mom could get a little nutso ex-Soviet about surveillance, and for another, it was flattering to learn that she thought I was getting *any* action with boys, after years of her telling me my chubby thighs would doom me to eternal spinsterhood.

Mom and I had been on the outs since I was a tween, when I started demanding the right to use my BART pass to go where I pleased, with whom I pleased. She and I got into these epic battles where she'd try to lock me into the house or take away my money. She'd grown up walking the streets of Leningrad at all hours while her own parents worked in some dank government ministry, and teen me was sure she had no business telling me that San Francisco was less safe—or that I was less savvy—than the circumstances of her girlhood. Plus, I'd been expected to help with the cooking and housework since my dad died when I was eight, and if I was old enough to be treated like a little adult, I was old enough to act like one outside the house.

Thinking about my mom made me think about Carrie Johnstone. The symbolism wasn't lost on me. Was Johnstone looking at the data I'd handed her? Was she going to call me before I got home and tell me I was her new BFF? Was she going to drop the USB stick in a desk drawer and forget about it forever? Would I show up for work the next day and have the MPs bar my way, firing me with swiftness and secrecy to match my hiring?

It was my stop. I went home.

The dudebros in my trailer actually dropped their jaws when I put all my shit in a box and carried it into Carrie Johnstone's command trailer. I could tell they were dying to ask me what dark female witchery I'd performed to warrant this promotion (they had a very high opinion of their work on the grounds that they talked about it constantly—and they had a very low opinion of mine because I never did). Had I synchronized my menses with the boss and thus fooled her into thinking I was more competent than I was?

I took enormous pleasure from saying nothing at all.

Johnstone waited two days to talk to me about the thumb drive. I don't know if that's because she had more important things to do than look at my data, or because she wanted to keep me sweating. Maybe the latter, because by the time she finally called me, I was jumpy as a rabbit and pathetically grateful not to be in trouble.

My new job was "special assistant to the director." I had no idea what that meant.

"Do you stand by this chart?" She had my information-cascade analysis on her screen—a twenty-seven-inch tube display that actually buckled the table it sat on. She smelled like cigarettes and her eyes were bloodshot, but her hair was *perfect* and smelled like expensive product, like something you'd smell in a plastics factory.

The dudebros would have snapped to attention and said, "Hell yes! Gung ho!" I wasn't them. I looked hard at the chart. I pointed at one spot. "This line is thicker than it should be. I'm not that confident that this guy is directing those five, it might just be coincidence, or he might just be reading the news more than they do. I think he deserves a dotted line, in any event."

She looked at me hard. "I like careful analysis." Later on, I'd realize that what she meant was, *I like for* other people *to be careful, so I can have the room to be as reckless as I want to be.*

I didn't get a desk next to hers, but I did get my own space at the back of the trailer, and I could hear everyone who came in and reported to her, listen in on her side of phone conversations. She liked to do her dirtiest work on the phone, and if I emailed her about a hard question, she'd shout for me to come over to her desk and discuss it. She never told me that this was all about what got put into writing, but she didn't need to, because I'm no idiot.

M1k3y wasn't Malcolm X or Leon Trotsky, but he knew how to write an inflammatory post that got crazy shares. Watching his new communiqués go viral through the Xnet became my new hobby, and based on who shared and how, I was able to cluster the Xnet supporters into different interest groups: fuck-shit-up nihilists, Latino kids, black kids, weekend warriors, super-nerds, big talkers, super-sharers. I wrote a primitive bot that played Clockwork Plunder by helpfully winding up anyone it bumped into, then tried to chat them into revealing their real names and friends using a variety of ruses. I created viral quiz sites that told you what kind of Xnetter you were after you filled in a long questionnaire, and then gave you a unique address to share your results with your friends, letting me know who was friends with whom. That worked like crazy, and my cascade diagrams got *super* detailed.

Often, but not quite every day, Carrie Johnstone would wander back to my end of the trailer and look over my shoulder. I sent her daily updates—and kept my files on a shared drive—but she liked to watch me work.

Two weeks in, the arrests began.

It wasn't a decapitation strike, not quite. If you'd spreadsheeted the cascade charts and sorted it by each name's sphere of influence, then the people Carrie Johnstone sent the police to get constituted a big chunk of the middle third—people who "commanded" maybe four or five others—and maybe 10 percent of the top influencers. That week, she rarely showed up at the trailer. If she did make it in, it was just for a few minutes of intense conversation with various people around the base. Even with the crazy-long hours, she was always super-fresh, wrinkle-free, perfect makeup, hair even more severe and perfect than ever. A steady rotation of assistants showed up with fresh outfits for her, still bagged from the dry cleaners, and she changed in a porta-potty and did her makeup with her webcam. If there was anything more freaky than her ability to go from friendly girlfriend to ice queen in zero seconds flat, it was her ability to do makeup with all the angles reversed in the webcam software. Also, I couldn't believe that she wasn't taping that thing over, like all the time.

The Xnet kids didn't have a chance. They were chaffing our RFID detectors, sure, and using anonymity and privacy tools, and trading BART cards around to make the Bayesian inference engines go bananas, but all that stuff was about fighting *mass* surveillance. Once we decided to *particularly* spy on those brats, they were toast. We phished them with emails and IMs with malware attachments that took over their Xboxes (hey, kids, here's a tip: when you all run the same version of a "secure" OS that's supported by a handful of crazy part-time volunteers, your enemies will have their pick of vulnerabilities to exploit against any of you). Then we turned their Xboxes into network exfiltration boxes that crawled *all* their devices, from their TiVos to their inkjet printers, and took them over.

Our biggest problem wasn't getting the data, it was making sense of it. These smartypantses were so wide open, we were sucking up their lives faster than we could look at them.

"Hard drives are cheap. Store it all, do keyword searches on it as it comes in, then when we find good stuff go back and search what we already have."

Carrie Johnstone didn't like this plan. She'd come in a few minutes before midnight, just as I was getting ready to head out. One of the perks of my new job was that I rated a ride home from a black-car driver, billed out to the DHS. Mom hadn't caught me getting out of one of those gleaming black rides yet, but when she did, I was going to have to have some kind of story to tell her. Maybe I'd tell her the truth.

"Of course we're going to store it, but we're also going to process it. I don't want to have to explain to my bosses why we missed the early warning signs after the next attack."

I chose my words carefully. She was easy to set off, even (especially) if you were one of her favorite pets. "We're looking for needles in haystacks. Most of what we pull out of the haystack is going to be hay. It's just math: when kidiots outnumber terrorists a thousand to one, our matches are going to flag nine hundred ninety-nine harmless morons for every bad guy. If we store it all, then we can go back in time whenever we want to—if we discover that someone is scarier than he seemed at first, we can unravel his whole social network, everyone he talks to, everyone *they* talk to."

"Being reactive isn't good enough. We are going to be *proactive*. We are not having another attack on my watch." She was so cold, it was all I could do not to shiver.

"Miss Johnstone—" I broke off. "Look, it's math. You can't argue with it. There's thousands of them and dozens of us. We can hear what they say and watch what they do, but there aren't enough hours in the day for us to pay attention to it all. If we auto-flag everyone who *might* be a monster, we'll mostly get idiots, and we don't have the manpower to sort that pile out, either."

"Sounds like you don't trust the tools—"

Damn right I didn't. Ever write software? "Trustworthy" is not a word I'd use. "Computers are good at measuring things. But I don't know how to measure if someone is a threat or not based on the data we collect from them."

She cocked her head. "The vendor who supplied our software built it to catch bad guys. Can it do that, or can't it?"

"It can." I swallowed. "So long as you don't mind catching not-bad guys at the same time." *In other words: arrest everyone and you'll be sure to catch the criminals.*

"I can live with that."

"But—"

She held up a hand and showed me a war face like Rambo on bath salts and I shut up fast. My heart was yammering, thundering. She could do that to me, just slice me open with her body language and her glare. It was a trick that the best in spookdom seemed to master, or maybe it was the one thing that predicted career success in the spooky industries. Ilsa could do it, and she didn't even have to snarl, just ice you with her eyes. I never learned to do it, but I got better at resisting it, which saved my sanity later.

I didn't know what to say. I wanted to promise her anything, whatever it would take to win her approval. But I also knew I'd have to actually do whatever it was I said I could do.

She waited for me to think this through, then she turned her back on me and started out of the trailer. At the door, she turned around. "I'm going to set up some meetings with some of our strategic partners. Companies that can give us the raw power we need to do what the country demands of us. I want you to come to those meetings."

I knew she meant that she wanted me to cut school and come to daytime meetings, which would mean my mom getting phone calls. She was telling me to choose between my mom's rage and hers. Put like that, it was an easy decision.

# CHAPTER 3

**M**ass arrests are messy. The ops people running Gitmo by the Bay had big budgets, but they couldn't make concrete dry faster or make mattresses and kitchen stoves magically appear in San Francisco. What's more, they couldn't just hire people off the streets to do this work: they had to use people with security clearance, and most of those came from companies like Xoth, who understood that when they were being paid by the day to build more cells, there was no reason to rush things.

There were arrestees who needed to become detainees. Carrie Johnstone's orders to snatch people without worrying about false positives meant that we had to double up on cells, then triple up. Johnstone promoted "problem solvers" like the guy who figured out that he could use his personal credit card to order pizzas from all over the city, send flunkies to pick them up, get reimbursed by Uncle Sam, collect tens of thousands of free air miles on his card, and solve our lack-of-kitchen problem all in one go. He wasn't a bad guy—he even ordered half of them without pepperoni so they'd be halal, which probably saved a bunch of dudes from going hungry or rethinking their articles of faith.

But ready or not, the prisoners kept coming. Luckily for us, the security measures after the attack had tanked tourism in San Francisco and another smartypants got the bright idea of searching for hotel bankruptcy auctions. Before you could say insolvency, we had all the mattresses you could ask for.

My job was about three hops back from this, but that didn't mean that I had clean hands. Here's how the system worked: I figured out potential command structures and handed them off to Carrie Johnstone for "further analysis" and "truthing"—reading their email and/or spying on them to figure out if my software was making good guesses. Johnstone then sent snatch squads out for the people who got "truthed." She'd found a federal judge in Arizona who'd sign the warrants, so part of my job was figuring out how each suspect was tied to Arizona—did they phone there once? Did they get junk mail from there? If I couldn't find a connection, I put them in a different file and Johnstone took care of that on her own, in ways I was smart enough not to ask about. They got warrants too—that much came out later in the hearings. But where those warrants came from was put under seal and no one ever bothered to tell me, and again, I was smart enough not to ask.

Once they were in custody, Johnstone and her HUMINT specialists ran the interrogations. I was in no way going to get near that shit, because I knew enough to know that it was the kind of thing that'd give me nightmares for years to come. I took the sanitized transcripts and used them as leads for more computational analysis, which fingered more suspects, which led to more snatches. Lather, rinse, repeat.

Did it work?

No.

Here's the thing: it could have. Sort of. I mean, again, if you don't care about false positives, you can arrest every terrorist by arresting everyone. Terrorists are part of "everyone." But we weren't arresting everyone. Some people didn't look suspicious enough to arrest (meaning they were either innocent or very good at their jobs), some people looked funny but had connections to prosecutors, civil rights lawyers, politicians. Or they were rich. Not that they got off clean: Johnstone kept a file on those semi-untouchables, and I figured out later that some of them got leaned on to help us by letting us into their company's data-centers or having a sneaky look at the company's email servers to see who was doing what. That was all HUMINT and not my department.

I was SIGINT and my job was to write and tune software that was analyzing the data Johnstone got for me, one way or another. Lots of people had that job, one way or another. Even back then, there were armies of code monkeys at Google and Amazon trying to make those sites work better. They'd move a button ten pixels to the left, or change the blue used in link underlines, let a million users see that version of the page, compare their clicking behavior to a million users who saw the present version, then make changes that nudged people toward the desired outcome.

But there was a huge difference between what those legit data scientists were doing and what I was doing: they checked to see whether their predictions came true. If some Amazon code monkey predicted that moving a button would boost sales, she'd measure sales before and after the move to see whether she was right. But I was blithely predicting that some people were terrorists and others weren't, and I never found out if I was right. Take false negatives: almost no one is a terrorist, and almost all terrorists are not doing anything terroristic almost all of the time. So if my code predicted that a real terrorist was a non-terrorist, the chances were I'd never find out I was wrong.

As for false positives, well, the same logic applied: since even actual terrorists were not terroristing most of the time, the fact that we arrested you but couldn't find any evidence of terroristic activity didn't mean you weren't a terrorist—it just meant you weren't a terrorist *right now,* so we couldn't know when we had the wrong guy, and so we held them all.

It was like the difference between witchcraft and science: I was using secret methods to curse people, and no one got to review my methods and point out their flaws (there were many, many flaws: I was a good programmer, but I only had high-school statistics courses to rely on), which meant that I just doubled down on them. The longer I did this, the clearer it became that the goal wasn't to put the right people in jail, just to make sure that there were *some* people in jail. I was acting out an official, security-based syllogism: "ZOMFG, someone blew up the Bay Bridge! Something must be done!"

I was doing something, but it wasn't something I was proud of.

What I truly hated about Marcus Yallow, above all else, was this: he gave people hope when no hope was called for. He told them that they could master their computers and their networks, communicate in private and secret, form networks of mutual aid and use them to bring down the powerful and unjust. But I've been on the other side of the data-center, I've seen how hard it is to cover your tracks, to be perfect in your opsec, to know who and what to trust, to write code that is flawless.

The reality is, there was a kind of blip when a minority of working stiffs—white dudes, mostly—held a little more political power, that lasted for less than a century. Now, humanity was returning to its baseline: all or nothing, with a tiny super-rich minority able to control everyone and everything else. The smarter your device, the harder it would be for you to outsmart it. Technology didn't create the brief democratic blip, and it didn't kill it, but now that it's dead, technology will sure as shit make sure it never comes back. Those days are done.

So you can go and fight in the streets for the world of your dreams where everyone is treated fairly and unearned privilege is replaced by equal opportunity, but you might as well be fighting against gravity. Our modern oligarchs don't even have to put you in jail to render you impotent: they can just turn your phone, car, TV, and thermostat into virtual ankle cuffs that tell them everything you say and everywhere you go, and rat out all of your friends.

The trick isn't to fight the aristocracy, it's to find one who isn't too terrible, who has his hands on the reins of power, and make friends. Make yourself useful. The quid pro quo in feudalism is the protection of the lord from the marauders sent forth by the other lords. They have fearsome power—the power to turn your car into an instrument of execution, for example—and you need protection. Believe me, you really need protection.

Take Xoth. We made a product there that would infect your phone just by sending it a malformed WhatsApp message. The thing was, it didn't content itself with infecting phones. Every time it found itself on a wireless network, it cautiously probed that local net for devices and tried to log in to them, using standard password combos like admin/admin admin/password and my favorite admin/[no password]. A surprising number of devices would accept these logins, from smart lightbulbs to smart thermostats to smart sex toys. Almost all of them ran some flavor of embedded Linux like BusyBox, and so once the malware penetrated them, it used a simple roster of BusyBox commands to lock the devices down—so that other malware couldn't get into them—and then install copies of itself. This stuff was surprisingly common. If you have twenty smart devices, it's a good bet that one or two of them are controlled by someone else, statistically speaking. Mostly, these devices are just enlisted to take part in spamming operations, denial of service floods, or cryptocurrency mining, but there was also a whole universe of stalkerware that used compromised devices to spy on their owners. From CCTVs that streamed a view from your home to a secret server to routers that made a copy of all your traffic for your attackers to look at later and redirected your laptop to sites that served malware that grabbed all your keystrokes, these compromised devices could watch you around the clock, from every angle.

Marcus Yallow got people like Tanisha in trouble—Tanisha knew just enough about computers to be a danger to herself and others. Just enough to believe that she could use them to organize her friends, just enough to believe that she could escape detection.

Tanisha thought she could win. She couldn't. Not while people like me were on the job.

Shit. That's the compartment I never, ever opened. The part that called bullshit on all my girl's-gotta-eat justifications for working for Carrie Johnstone, for Ilsa, She-Wolf of the SS, for Xoth.

I ordered another vodka from the lounge bar. It cost a lot of money. I had made a lot of money.

I wasn't at Gitmo by the Bay when the California Highway Patrol raided it and arrested Carrie Johnstone. I was in Mexico with a lot of cash, a busted hand, and a new phone, because Marcus Yallow had busted my hand, stolen my phone, and left me alone in the back of a southbound truck.

The Baja was full of surf bums and vacationing frat rats drinking Coronas and wearing sombreros. I found it easy enough to fit in—bought a hat and a bikini and sat on the beach by day and went to the bars by night. It was fun for about seventy-two hours. Then I wanted to poison their margaritas and make them eat their board shorts. I bought some mace and used it on the next three guys who tried to grab my ass, before I decided I was headed to self-destruction territory and that it was time to take a detour. I rented a little white house on the top of a mountain and bought a rusty old desert bike to go to and from town, though it was weeks before I managed to ride it all the way to the top.

In the clear rooms in Gitmo by the Bay, where we weren't allowed to have *any* electronics, I got good at thinking of questions without being able to google the answers right away, stacking them up in a little box I'd draw in the corner of my notebook page to refer to when I was back in the infosphere.

I got into the same habit on the hilltop: I'd wonder how many grams were in an ounce (while trying to follow a pancake recipe on the back of a flour bag), or how you said "chain oil" in Spanish, or what was in Executive Order 12333 again, and then I'd have to jot it down and wait until I got to town (and signal on my burner phone) to google it. Living on this information diet meant that I started to think through the kind of nutrition I was putting in my brain. Half the crap I'd intended to google turned out to be irrelevant by the time I got to town and had to choose between looking it up and people-watching or looking for a new hammock chair to hang from the tree outside my little white house. As to the remaining half, well, I got pretty good at writing down the answers, because otherwise I forgot them—which, in turn, made me realize I didn't really care about the answers after all.

Then came the day I forgot to bring my phone with me on a shopping trip and didn't notice until I got back to the top of the hill, pedaling like a champ, barely sweating, thighs like tree trunks, and realized that I hadn't checked it once, and it hadn't made a difference. Instead, I'd spent my time in town haggling over avocados and tamales, watching the hookers watch the frat boys watch the hookers, observing the divemasters' lackeys dragging SCUBA bottles from one dive shop to the other according to some shifting web of allegiances that my information-cascade-attuned brain wanted to unravel.

The six months I spent in the desert—well, on the mountain that I could see the desert from, along with a hundred bars and dive shops—were amazing and weird and made me a better person. I even learned to dive, and I developed a friends-with-benefits arrangement with a Dutch guy who'd started off as a dive bum, graduated to bartender, and emerged from his pupa as a fully formed bar owner with his own place on the beach.

I only found out about the raid on Gitmo by the Bay by accident, when I let Anders take me to Sunday brunch at one of the fancy places and there was a *New York Times* on the rack. It only took a single glance for me to get sucked in by the headlines, and from there I dove into my phone and started googling. That night, I had the worst night's sleep of my life. Not because I was worried about Carrie Johnstone: I idolized her, but I didn't actually like her or anything. Not because I was worried about myself, about being implicated in the raid—I was already an unofficial fugitive from the DHS, an off-the-books "consultant" who'd fled the country under suspicious circumstances. A bench warrant for my arrest might be an advantage—a way to get sent to a nice safe American jail, rather than being rendered to Libya.

No, I spent my night tossing and tortured entirely by the nagging feeling that there were important things happening that mattered to me, but that I didn't know about, and I wanted to know more. I wanted to get out my phone and keep googling, and when I reached the end of Google, I wanted to start over from the top, in case I'd missed something. I was *hungry* for information, but none of the information I consumed did anything to reduce that hunger— it just made me *more* hungry, like some kind of faerie food that could starve you to death.

My phone was plugged in on the bedside, serviceless. Still, I kept picking it up and *almost* getting dressed and riding into town in the dead of the night. Finally, like a drunk who waits until the chime of noon to crack his first beer, I mounted my bike at the first light over the hills, totally wrapped in bright lights and reflectors—Mexican drivers, twisting mountain roads, dawn, and bicycles being a suboptimal combination.

I was the first customer at Rosa's, in before the smell of the breakfast burritos started wafting out the screen door, drinking her awful coffee and tapping away at my phone while Rosa's daughters bustled around the kitchen. Ten minutes later, I'd taken my laptop out of my bag and I was on the café's wifi, because I needed (!) to use browser tabs for the kind of deep googling I was doing.

I left Mexico a week later.

With Carrie Johnstone in California detention and the feds and California legislature brawling with one another—it got so bad that California threatened to withhold its tax transfers and to ban the IRS from operating in the state!—I decided that all the people angry with me had more pressing matters to attend to, and that in the good ol' USA I might find myself one of those lawyers that Marcus Yallow had such confidence in.

(Also: I was thinking of looking up Marcus, because I still owed him for my busted hand.)

(Also: maybe the stress of all that had happened had busted things up for him and his girlie.)

My trip to Cabo had been a thirty-hour bus ride down tight-twisting roads— look down from the hairpins and you could spot the rusting remains of buses that hadn't made it—with puking babies and even (not making this up) a caged chicken for a brief part of the ride.

My trip back was in a Southwest Air 737, where they didn't even card me as I pounded Jack after Jack, using drink coupons I'd downloaded from the internet and printed on convincing paper stock (the same site told me where in Cabo to go to find the paper). The immigration lady at SFO didn't bat an eye at me, just bobbed her head between my passport and my bloodshot eyes and then turned her face away from my booze breath.

My mom cried when I came through the door. I let her hug me. It wasn't a terrible feeling. She scolded me in Russian for being drunk, which is practically what Russian was invented for. I was back in my own room, in my own bed, when I realized I hadn't said goodbye to Anders.

Carrie Johnstone didn't go to jail. Eventually, she went to Iraq, with Zyz, who made her a vice president. Before that, she came to recruit me.

My mom didn't know what to make of this woman standing on her doorstep with her precise haircut in disarray, wearing tracksuit bottoms and a sweatshirt instead of her customary suit. Mom recognized her from the TV coverage, which she'd watched obsessively while I was in Mexico, correctly guessing that the nightly news had something to do with my disappearance.

"May I speak with Masha?"

I heard her voice from the kitchen, where I'd been nuking a frozen bagel that I'd covered with a triple-thickness of Kraft slices. Carbs and edible oil products: the ultimate comfort food.

"I've got it, Ma." I could tell my mom was caught between offering her coffee or throwing her out on her ass. I took advantage of the pause of her indecision to jam my feet into a pair of crushed tennis shoes and shrug on a hoodie from the pile on the stair post. "Let's get a coffee." I didn't meet my mom's eyes as I closed the door behind us.

Once we were well out of earshot of the house, Johnstone said, "The park up there is better, where the dog walkers go. It was pretty empty when I walked past." She pulled a beanie hat out of the pocket of her sweatshirt and pulled it down over her hair and now I got why it had been so messed up before. Carrie Johnstone didn't wear hats. But that Carrie Johnstone also didn't have to worry about being recognized in public.

"You hanging in okay?" That was more surprising than the hair. Since when did she care?

"I'm surviving." I wished I'd taken the bagel with. "You?"

"Me? I'm *amazing*." The way she said it, I couldn't tell if she was kidding or crazy or what, it was that fervent. She was staring at me with burning eyes. "I'm about to deploy. Iraq."

"You joined the army?"

She scoffed. "Me? A govie? Never again. I'm working for the private sector now. Remember those useless contractors who built that analytical app you nursed along for me? Ass-clowns like those guys can get billions from Uncle Sugar for underdelivering and overpromising. So imagine what happens when someone *competent* gets into the market, someone who understands the mission and cares about delivering it?"

"Sounds great." I didn't quite hit the neutrality I'd hoped for, but it was close.

"It is. It is really, really *great*." She took my shoulders and spun me to face her, stared into my eyes. At first I thought her eyeliner had smeared, then I realized it was the remains of yesterday's makeup, ground in and unwashed. "Masha, did you ever wish you could just slice through all the bullshit and go straight to the heart of the matter? Ever really *know* how to get your job done but not how to get around the people on your own team who got in the way?"

She looked like she was inches away from a psychotic break. This close, I could smell her, a stale smell that I associated more with the prisoners I had helped question than Carrie Johnstone and her shiny hair. It wasn't a bad smell, but it was an ominous one, coming from her.

"Well, *did you*?"

"Sure, sometimes."

"Sometimes. Because *I* shielded you from the worst of it. I bet you thought *I* was getting in your way. What you never understood—what I could never explain—was that I was protecting you. If I ever gave you an unreasonable no, it was because I'd fought off a thousand *no*s that were a thousand times worse. But you know who never had to go through all that bullshit? The private contractors who were supplying us with all that useless shit you were wrestling with in the first place. They were outside of the chain of command, living in blissful, rarefied, consequence-free heights, laughing at us mortals. I'm going to those heights, Masha." She took my hands and squeezed them, stared harder into my eyes. "I want to bring you with me."

"Thank you, Miss Johnstone—"

"Masha, don't answer right away. I'm deploying in a week. I can give you that long. Starting salary for a senior intelligence technologist is $250,000 plus bonuses, and you get room, board, transport, and an allowance for desert and combat gear."

There wasn't enough money in all the world to convince me to move to Iraq, no allowance large enough to buy me the combat gear I'd need to feel safe in that quagmire. And the idea of locking myself in some remote walled fortress with a disgraced, unhinged Carrie Johnstone? Shit.

"Miss Johnstone, that sounds incredible—"

"Don't answer right away, I said. Think this through. We could do something that no one else ever managed. We could serve as the crucial vector between the pressing national security priorities of this country's governments and the poor bastards who have to try to make it into a reality. If we don't take this job, someone else will, the kind of bozos who fucked us eleven ways to Uranus while we were trying to clean up around here. The kind of profiteer that gets people killed and then walks away having made serious bank.

"The people behind me run a serious concern, they get the job done, and they provide full stack services, from transport to food to security—with the guards and armor we'll have between us and the world, we'll be safer than anyone in the region, including the vice president when he deigns to visit. It's six months in the field, one month in a forward logistics site—basically private resorts in places like Dubai and Singapore, five-stars with spas and massages and boat drinks. Cabana boys. One month paid vacation a year. Private on-site medical. Top chefs and real food." Money isn't the only thing, but it's something. "Pension, too. Stock options. It's a startup, just like the fuckers around here, but with contracts into the next decade and investor runway for the decade after that. They're in revenue, they're in profit, and they're only two years in. It's a growth industry, and they're going to be gobbling up a lot of competitors. More than one of the big old fish have tried to gobble *them* up since, but they're not interested. They're the swallow*er* type, not the swallow*ee* type."

She broke off and gave me a long, intense stare. Now she didn't look disoriented and desperate. Now she looked like she was *on fire*. "They're called Zyz. Look them up. Like I said, I leave in a week, and I get to bring a team. I want you on it. If not . . ." She shrugged. "No hard feelings." But her disapproval radiated.

My mom wasn't happy with any of this shit, not all the time I'd spent out on Treasure Island, not my disappearing to Mexico, not my showing back up unannounced and emotionally wrecked and smelling of tequila and ocean salt. Ma could always explain, in two languages, exactly how bad she had had it and the sacrifices she'd made to get me the advantages she'd lacked, growing up through the collapse of the USSR, leaving Russia as a single parent with a baby in her arms (that would be me), coming to a country where she didn't speak the language and working two jobs just to keep me in the materialistic, spoiled manner to which I'd become accustomed.

And so on.

Long before the attack on the Bay Bridge and all that followed, I had learned to tune her out completely, simply stopped rising to any of her bait. Before that, though, we'd had plenty of screaming matches. I don't know which she preferred, but for me, the clear winner was détente, the silence of my refusal to fight back, the very Russian tactic of saying nothing and doing exactly what you were planning to do after being told unequivocally that you were forbidden to do it.

I perfected this tactic over my months working under Carrie Johnstone, refusing to answer questions about my long hours and my school's increasingly urgent messages about my truancy, while dropping just enough hints that my mother figured out that I was doing secret government work related to national security. If there's one thing Russians understand, it's secretive government work. The thought of me working as a spook probably scared the shit out of her, but I *know* it made her respect me and stop asking me a lot of questions that she didn't really want to know the answers to. For the first fifteen minutes after I got back from Mexico, it had been all hugs and sweet burbling in Russian baby talk, reminding me that whatever else we were, she was my mom and I was her grown-up baby. Fifteen minutes later, we were back to détente, me in my room with my door closed, emptying my suitcase and digging through the drawers of clothes I'd forgotten I owned. Me sneaking down to the fridge while she watched TV and pretended she didn't notice.

When I got back from my meeting with Carrie Johnstone, she followed me up the stairs and into my room.

"Masha."

"Yes?"

"What did that woman want?"

So much for not asking questions you don't want to know the answer to.

"Nothing, Ma."

She bit her lip and looked out my window. "Masha." Her voice sounded pressurized, like the word was a cork stuffed down the throat of something that could blow at any second.

"It's nothing, Ma, really. She wanted to know if I had any suggestions for a job opening at her new startup." If I was going to take the job, I wouldn't have told her that. Mom should be able to figure out from the fact that I'd dropped the hint that the hint didn't matter.

She switched her gaze from my window to my face. "Don't leave like that again, Masha. Promise me."

I felt like slapping her. We had a deal. She didn't ask me about where I went, I didn't tell her. She didn't make me feel guilty about making her worry, and I never asked her to worry about me. The anger was so intense that the room tunneled down with black crawly edges. A compartment breach. I swallowed and made my shoulders relax and wiped the grimace off my face; stuffed the emotions back into their compartment and told them to stay there.

"I won't leave like that, Ma." Not saying how I *would* leave, but she didn't seem to notice, either, because I'd said it in English and she missed nuance in English, or because she decided not to notice.

"I love you, Maria." No one called me Maria, least of all my mother. It was a reminder of my Russian Orthodox father, who only stayed around long enough to make sure I didn't get a Jewish name. It was another reminder that I was once her baby.

"I love you, Ma." Because saying anything else would be taking notice and then having a further discussion, and I wasn't going to do that.

When the door closed I sat on my bed for about thirty seconds before making up my mind: I was going to Iraq.

# CHAPTER 4

I flew to Iraq on a passenger jet, in business class, with free liquor, warm nuts, and a fully reclining bed. On the layover to Dubai, I got a mani-pedi and a massage. In Baghdad, a rep from Zyz met me *before* I cleared customs. He looked like a jarhead, but his gear was a thousand times better than anything the Marine Corps gave out, and he was wearing a class ring from the Citadel, the private military academy you go to if you can't get into West Point or the Air Force Academy and you have a lot of money to burn.

"Ms. Maximow," he said, before I even had a chance to register that he was holding a sign with my name on it.

"Yes?"

"Highbury." He held out the hand, the ring. I shook it. "Welcome to the Green Zone. Let's get you cleared." He smoothly took my laptop bag while I was still gaping, and set off across the polished concrete floors, the soles of his combat boots silent as my sneakers. The air-conditioning was weirdly intermittent, alternating columns of icy, blasting air and humid, sticky sections that smelled of sweat and lemon cleaning products. I followed Highbury like a baby duck down a long, high corridor to a customs and immigration concourse thronged with miserable-looking people: Middle Easterners, Africans, South Asians, fanning themselves with their customs paperwork—almost all men, almost all staring at us as we approached.

Swiftly, Highbury veered off to one side, tracking down a narrow, human-free corridor along a wall, like the out-of-bounds sidelines of a sports field, and

I followed along behind him, conscious of all those stares. Ahead of us stood a guard with an automatic rifle slung casually across his chest, sporting a thick, bushy mustache beneath his beret. He watched us closely as we came toward him, and Highbury held up a laminated ID on a lanyard across his chest like a talisman. The man took it and studied it at close range, and then nodded. Highbury shook his hand, and I saw some American money pass between them, in full view of all those poor bastards sweating in the all-day line, and then we were clear of the line, headed to the baggage hall. The carousel was stationary and there was dust on its chrome, large signs in Arabic and English posted above warning about the penalties for smuggling. As we stood by it, the security door on the wall opened, letting in a blast of superheated, dusty air and another mustachioed man, this one in sweaty overalls, wheeling my suitcase behind him. Highbury flagged him down and asked me for my bag claim-check. He handed it to the guy, who compared it to the tag, then handed it back with a nod. I saw another greenback pass between them as Highbury shook his hand.

The customs "inspection" was another golden handshake, and then we were in the arrivals area, with crowds of people and armed men all around us. Four younger, less-well-equipped clones of Highbury pushed their way to us and fell in around us, two in front and two behind. Highbury acted like this was expected, so I played it cool too. Later on, I figured out that some of this was to impress me as a new recruit, and some of it was Highbury being a big swinging dick because Highbury was a dick and never passed on a chance to show us all how big and swinging he was.

Our phalanx made its way outside—more of that hot, dry, dusty air, a thousand smells, the sounds of horns and sirens and commercial and military jet traffic screaming overhead—and hup-hupped into a car waiting at the curb, a huge Hummer with armor plating that—I later learned—was the envy of the US military, who had to weld their own hillbilly armor on their Humvees. The driver, another GI Joe doll, didn't say a word as he popped the locks, let us in, and put it in gear. The air-conditioning was on so high I got instant goosebumps, and all the time zones I'd just crossed got together and kicked my ass in unison, leaving me with swimming vision and a ringing in my ears. I watched the traffic move around us, watched our guards watching it, making unobtrusive hand signs to one another when they saw something interesting, which I came to realize was, basically, young men of Arabic extraction. There were a *lot* of those. Our guys were busy.

"Welcome to the Green Zone." Highbury looked supremely relaxed. He busted out some Hubba Bubba and offered it to me, but not the jarheads. I shook my head. He pocketed it. "First time?"

I nodded. "First time anywhere except the USA and a trip to Vancouver, plus Russia, when I was little."

He smiled and chewed. "You'll love it here. We got all the home comforts. Can't beat the weather, either. Gets a little hairy once you're out of the Green Zone, but then you get to the forward operations bases and you're back in the lap of luxury. Pizza Hut, Starbucks, and wifi. I hear you're especially interested in the wifi."

He was monologuing like a tour guide trying to pretend he didn't have a coke problem. I didn't see any reason to piss him off, but I didn't want to be this guy's friend, either, not least because his vibe was more than a little rapey. I nodded, nodded, and tried to understand the scenes through the windows: a shining mall fronted with metal detectors and guards with rifles attached to their belts with heavy chains; bomb sites; a row of shining Mercedes; fortified installations that could have been hospitals or government buildings; apartment buildings ringed with walls and sandbags; low-rise compounds with low-rise walls topped with barbed wire; sparse trees with homeless beggars beneath them; guard towers with machine guns; taxis and tour buses; Hummers and MRAPs; palm trees and families pushing strollers.

"Checkpoint." It was the first word the driver said, pulling over to the side of the road. Highbury clambered over the jarhead next to him to the window, rolled it down, and squinted into the sunlight as a teenager with an automatic rifle peered in at us. I assumed he was local—mustache, olive skin—but the accent was Texas to a tee.

"IDs, sirs?" Now I realized the teenager was wearing US military insignia.

Highbury popped his gum and grinned, dug out the lanyard with his laminated ID, let the kid hold it through the window. "Hot day for it."

The kid wiped his zitty forehead. "Every day, sir."

I was wondering when the rest of us would have to show ID, but the kid studied Highbury's card for a moment longer and then handed it back. "All right, sirs, ma'am, you have a good day and be safe, all right?"

"All right." Highbury made it sound like everything was, indeed, all right.

The kid disappeared behind darkened glass.

"That was, uh, *cursory.*" I wondered what the kid's threat model was and whether he even knew what a threat model was.

The driver had just put his hand on the gearshift when there was a tap. Our boy was back at the window. Highbury lowered it.

"Sir?"

"Yes?" He peered at the kid's name tag. "Ramirez?"

"Yes, sir. I was wondering—" He blushed, making his zits glow. "Look, sir, I speak pretty good Arabic, and half the time people think I'm a local. I went tops in my class in Santa Fe. From what I hear, you guys sometimes have contract work for us to do, during R&R, off-shift? What I hear, it can turn into a job offer when my hitch is up?"

Highbury smiled and smacked his knee. "That is *initiative,* son. Hell yes, we do. Someone give me a pen?" He held out his hand and a second later one of the others had slapped a Sharpie into it. He uncapped it and seized the kid's hand and wrote something on it. "That's my email. You send me a note reminding me where I met you, and we'll see what we can sort out. Sound good?"

"Yes, sir!" Ramirez was *delighted.* Like, scarily so.

Highbury shook the kid's hand awkwardly and enthusiastically through the open window, then gave a little wave as he raised the glass again. The air conditioner began to cool the interior again as we pulled away.

"Kid's got initiative." Highbury stared out at the road, which was lined with bomb-proof bollards and more sandbags, Jersey barriers, and wire-coils. "'Course, he's also a scrawny little govie fuck the color of a two-day-old turd."

The goons laughed dutifully. Working at Gitmo by the Bay had made me into a fully paid-up member of the White Privilege Club, good at pretending not to hear racist bullshit when it was just us whiteys yukking it up. I wasn't about to start my life in Iraq as the Social Justice Warrior from San Francisco who can't take a fucking joke, so I poker-faced and stared out the window too.

We were heading onto the open road, cleared of any kind of hiding place all to the outer range of an RPG on both sides. Scrub, sand, blowing trash. A convoy blew past us, MRAPs in the front and rear, a couple big rigs between them. The drivers were all army, American boys far, far from home, like me.

"I'm going to get some sleep." Highbury produced a padded sleep mask from a bag by his feet. "Want one?"

"I think I want to get a look around," I said.

He laughed. "It's pretty much like this for the next sixteen hours. We'll stop a couple times for piss-call; apart from that there's not going to be much to see, unless something goes truly shit-shaped."

"That's okay."

"Take one for later. Trust me, you'll get all you want of this view in the next couple months. Never pass up a chance to get some sleep, that's my motto. Learned it from my dad. Marine Corps. Could sleep standing up with his eyes open. Life skills."

The goons laughed. I smiled and took the mask and put it in my pocket.

He got out another and slid it over his eyes. I didn't make eye contact with the goons. The view out the window crawled by like one of those backgrounds from the Flintstones, an endless loop recycled to give Fred and Barney something to walk past.

After an hour—maybe it was more?—I put on the sleep mask and tried not to think about the goons staring at me while I slept.

The first piss-call was pure terror, sniper's crosshairs ghosting on the back of my neck as we filed out at a dusty ex–truck stop, now deserted except for a few guys that Highbury claimed were moonlighting off-duty Iraqi military. They smelled of stale sweat and smoked like crazy. The women's bathroom didn't have any paper or soap and the plastic hinges crackled in disused complaint when I lowered the toilet seat.

Inside the dim, cavernous building, Highbury's men broke out rations: power bars and ramen noodles that they heated in a filthy microwave. I choked down a mush of overcooked noodles swimming in clumpy salt-broth and reminded myself that I was jetlagged and culture-shocked and the tears pricking at the backs of my eyes were not to be trusted. Compartmentalize, girl.

We had Gatorade to flush it down. "Don't forget to drink up." Highbury finished his in one long chug, belched, and pitched the empty bottle into an overflowing trash can. "Just because going to the can is a pain, it's no reason to let yourself dehydrate. Getting IV fluids is worse than a dirty toilet."

The men nodded as though this was the wisest thing they'd ever heard, and not the kind of anodyne wisdom you got from Burners, and I silently chugged my Gatorade. It was Yellow-flavored. Yum.

Lather, rinse, repeat: the miles disappeared under the Hummer's wheels, the landscape rolled past in Flintstonian redundancy, the men farted and ate MREs, and we stopped for fuel and toilet breaks in places that were all minor variations on the first. I learned that two of the goons smoked, which was something that no one I knew in San Francisco did. You could buy cigarettes in some of the truck stops, apparently; one of the guys went off and dickered with one of their guys and came back with three cartons of Marlboro Reds whose health warnings were in Chinese. It was a real cosmopolitan, crossroads-of-the-world experience.

I was asleep when we pulled into the forward operating base at dawn, waking to a prod in the shoulder by Highbury. I made myself not jolt, and opened my eyes to see a US soldier, this one a lot dustier, older, and scarier looking than little Ramirez, peering in at me.

"Your ID, please, ma'am?" His armband read MP, and he had a coplike inflection, like this was a traffic stop in the Mission and not—I blinked, looked around a little—a guardhouse in the dawn light surrounded by chain link defending a no-man's-land around a tall, walled compound surrounded by sandbags and bollards and spikes. I handed him my California driver's license, which he fed into a scanner in the gatehouse. He prodded uncertainly at a chunky keyboard for a while, then handed it back to me. "Welcome to FOB Grizzly."

The gates swung open and we pulled through. We drove past a large, open field that was apparently a kind of boneyard for armored vehicles, everything from Hummers to sixteen-wheelers and tankers, then turned down a street of wide, warehouse-style buildings, toward a denser, more built-up "downtown" that looked like a US Army base: a mess hall, a PX, barracks, officer housing, some nondescript office buildings. Soldiers walked around in desert camo, some of them holding legit Starbucks Frappuccinos or Pizza Hut takeaway boxes (both responsible for the twenty pounds I would later put on).

We pulled into a parking spot near the front entrance to a set of interconnected prefab trailers. One of Highbury's guys opened the car door, another grabbed my bags, and a third badged us into the trailer, touching an ID to a wireless reader zip-tied to an eyelet on the doorframe. I stepped from the air-conditioned Hummer into the already warming day, then into the air-conditioned trailer, like an astronaut drifting from a shuttle to the space station. The door closed behind me with a heavy clunk, and after my eyes adjusted to the tube-lit gloom, I saw a reception desk, low cubicles, a row of doors leading to offices and conference rooms. Could have been back on Treasure Island, except for a dusty smell that came in on our clothes, and a musty, mildewy smell from the upholstery kept in airtight, ever-moistened darkness.

"Welcome home." Highbury patted the empty reception desk. "You're gonna love it here. I saw you eyeballing those Pizza Hut boxes. Wait'll we get a Jamba Juice next year—all the wheatgrass shots you can drink!"

I barely heard him. A door had just opened, and out of it—Carrie Johnstone. Every hair perfectly in place. Business-casual. Not an army uniform, but a uniform nevertheless. She crossed to us like she was gliding on roller skates. Perfectly in her element. This was her show.

"So glad you could make it." She shook my hand—dry fingers, loose grip. Some Californian instinct in me wanted to hug her, but I tamped it down. This wasn't hugging territory. We were two women in a place that was grotesquely male; any sign of feminine softness in front of these Glock-packing dudebros would definitely be fodder for lesbian "jokes" later on, either among themselves in private, or on sticky notes gloatingly left on my keyboard for me to discover.

"Come into my office." She closed the door in Highbury's face, showed me to a chair. "Coffee? I can send someone to Starbucks." I could tell she was trying to impress me, casually name-dropping: *yeah, we got a whole strip mall here in FOB Grizzly.*

"Don't think so—my sleep's weird enough after napping on the ride, and the jetlag. Just want to let it all normalize."

"Good thinking. But don't get too synced up. I still haven't decided if I'm going to run you on DC or Iraq time, depends on how much you're going to be liaising with the DoD and how much you'll be behind the scenes." She caught the tamped-down flare of surprise on my face. "Don't get a swelled head. You're the best analyst I've ever worked with, but that brilliance is counterbalanced by . . . *personality complications* that put me in an awkward position when it comes to putting you in client-facing roles." All the while, she was clicking at her mouse and tapping her keyboard, talking to herself more than me.

The realization that I was thousands of miles from home, in a war zone, with this woman in charge of every detail of my life slammed into me, a hammer blow to the ribs. I tried not to show it. She wasn't paying attention to me anymore anyway.

Then she was, fiercely eyeballing me. "Don't worry, that's for me to do. No one's perfect and there's lots of opportunities for growth out here. I think I'll start you as an analyst all the same. Get you on local time, you'll get to know your team." She flashed me a grin. "Welcome home, Masha! You're going to love it here."

When they called boarding for my flight, I got that going-back-to-the-USA feeling. I always went back, no matter how fucked up it was, because America, fuck yeah: milkshakes and giant movie theaters and highways and barbecue and simple politics with only two parties that mostly agreed on mostly everything that mattered, like bombing the shit out of everywhere else. I was going to go back because Tanisha was there and not in jail, while Kriztina was in Europe and in a cell. I could be at the Slovstakian jailhouse door in three hours from a standing start, and there would be not one fucking thing I could do once I got there. Kriztina was a mistake, as was the whole Slovstakian affair. I'd kidded myself that I could make things better to make up for all the ways I was making them worse, and the reality was that I was just making them worse from both ends at once, and they'd met in the middle. Kriztina didn't need a mentor, and I didn't need a protégé.

All my life, there'd been women who'd showed me the ropes, shaped me, made me someone more than I was. They hadn't been good women. Ilsa, Carrie Johnstone—even my mother. Every one of them was deficient as a human being. *I* was deficient as a human being. Why had they taken me on? Why had I let myself be taken?

Being a skilled compartmentalizer didn't mean that I hadn't ever thought of these questions before. These questions were how I got so good at compartmentalizing. Unlike certain grandstanding assholes I could name—ahem Marcus Yallow—I was self-aware enough to know what shit I was deliberately not being self-aware of.

Let's open one of those compartments, shall we? Realistically speaking, every teenaged girl spends a lot of time convinced that something is deeply, profoundly wrong with her, and I was no exception. All the world hates a girl, in special and vicious ways that goes way beyond even the mountain of shit we shovel onto young dudes. They get toxic masculinity and we get "you throw like a girl" and "scream like a girl" and "you're such a pretty girl." Mansplaining and creepers on BART and whistling out of car windows. I internalized the full measure of girl-hating, hating the sound of my recorded voice, the sight of my photographed face, my own body in the mirror. I hated my handwriting, the loopy letters I'd taught myself to draw when we first moved to America and I'd had to unlearn Russian and figure out the strange English glyphs all the perfect girls could write perfectly.

I hated my hair and the way I walked. I hated my tits and I hated my bras. I hated my mother and I hated all the girls in the world, more than anything. Even more than boys.

I don't believe I was special in this regard. There's a lot of self-hating girls out there in the world. We're the secret, seething, silent majority. Some starve. Some cut. Some try to screw their way to happiness.

Me, I idolized strong, powerful women who seemed to have risen above it all. Never mind that they were drunks or sadists or war criminals. They were leaning in, doin' it for themselves, and that was what counted. Compared to being trapped in girlhood, alcoholism and war crimes were small potatoes.

It doesn't take a genius to figure this out. I knew this about myself after that first dinner with Carrie Johnstone, lying in bed awake and trembling, replaying the conversation and the extremes of terror and confusion and, yes, awe. Women like Johnstone were the brightest stars in my sky. They had been girls and now they were their own women. I could be my own woman too.

Kriztina, back in Bltz, all dimples and brave chin, fighting her fight while I went to America to help my friend defeat the massed armies of the DHS and the NSA and the Oakland PD and the local dogcatcher. Not to mention all those people working for Xoth and its competitors—smarter, hungrier, and better paid than any of their public-sector customers.

I got out just in time. Squint at me and you could see the larval form of Carrie Johnstone. Brightest star in the sky, for the right kind of young woman.

In the words of Ice-T, "Do I look like a motherfuckin' role model?"

People had problems. Anyone who chose *me* as their guiding star had *two* problems.

Truth was, it felt good to have someone like Kriztina—brimming with potential and energy—look at me like I hung the moon in the sky. Truth was, I was nervous about seeing Tanisha and my old friends, people who'd done things with their lives they weren't ashamed to talk about.

Zyz provided quite a variety of services to the US Army. We sold them smart-cards and data-centers, encrypted phones and "battlefield intelligence" appliances that were supposed to integrate data from insanely heavy, balky sensor packages that we also provided to the infantrymen. These failed even more than could be explained by the incompetence with which they had been designed, and it was an open secret that the GIs were sabotaging them so they didn't have to carry them around.

But more than anything, we provided SIGINT. Jihadis and insurgents had bad opsec, used stock shortwave radios or worse, SMS messages carried by the national telco. They made up half-assed codes, including—hilariously—a book code based on the Koran, because no one would ever guess that someone who'd given his life over to fighting for Islam might have memorized an *ayah* or two.

Zyz worked with other contractors, mostly Halliburton subsidiaries, to funnel all this stuff to analysts like me. I had a team of translators at my disposal, Arab-English bilingual for some values of bilingual. The American contractors stateside were the worst, the English-speaking Iraqis were worth their weight in gold. Between them, I was able to get a pretty good slice of all the comms flowing through their networks, such as they were.

My favorite trick was to build up my cascade analysis by watching the propagation of useless opsec tricks. Some bright boy would get the idea to paste a whole ton of garbage text into the end of every email, and I could use that dumb trick to track who thought that guy was worth listening to. Even better, I could identify the jihadi thought leaders by watching how a "trick" like this would spread slowly, from person to person, meandering around the social graph, until it reached a magic node that used it in a message, and then, bam, suddenly everyone was doing it and I'd be like: that guy, that guy right there, that's the guy.

I'd pass his details onto the infowar types and pretty soon I'd see clever fakes in the streams, and even better, things that look like fat-fingered acciden-tal forwards of shady messages to people who got dissed in them. These guys were not the most even-keeled types to begin with, so a little bit of psyops was often enough to spark irrational bun-fights—a very useful term I learned from one of my British-born translators—that were as dysfunctional as any internet flamewar, except that they were being fought by unstable, underslept armed boys who could settle their fights by busting in on one another's tents with guns blazing. It was a beautiful thing to watch, in a terrible way.

The psyops was seriously my favorite part of the job. From my perspective, mapping and remapping the information cascades, it was devastatingly effec-tive. Our adversary was an insurgent force held together by radical ideology that they found so compelling they'd give up everything, pass the death sen-tence on themselves, and go out to commit murder. Many of them came from distant countries and—I could see from their messaging—were on the receiv-ing end of a continuous stream of messages from their heartbroken families begging them to come home.

Fighting these guys in the desert was for losers. They had suicide vests, we had jarheads in Humvees. The jarheads tried to find the suicide vests by knock-ing down peoples' doors and throwing everyone to the ground and screaming at them while they tossed their homes. This just put more sorry-ass teenagers into suicide vests. But the stuff we were doing—finding and exploiting the fracture lines in their own organizations, trolling the shit out of them—took bad guys off the field by pointing them at each other. It made them stop trust-ing each other, made them point fingers at each other, accusing one another of being secret double agents and provocateurs.

If there were any double agents in that mess, they weren't ours. But it's not hard to make someone erratic look like they're working both sides, especially if the person you're trying to convince is even more erratic. These guys were barely stable as it was. All it took to throw them into a glorious state of higgledy-piggledy were some well-thrown (metaphorical) bombs. I was in charge of range-finding, and after I called the range, another group of specialists—sometimes they were in UAE, sometimes it was a team in Bulgaria—fired the munitions. I reported back on the strikes, and they were pretty glorious to watch.

Carrie Johnstone was indecently happy with our work. No one at Zyz had ever done work like this. They were more about providing scorchingly expensive substandard battlefield laundry services and hiring dishonorably discharged sadists to guard army convoys. She'd convinced the top dog—an infamous millionaire playboy and war criminal named Dick King—to let her create a new "product" for their government clients, and this was the proof-of-concept that they'd use to sell it to other clients around the world.

I kept the same hours as the jihadis, and my overseas translators kept the same hours as me. I didn't get too friendly with them, but the details of their personal lives leaked through—*Sorry, baby's crying, BRB*; *Bloody kettle's packed in can't think without my tea*—and gave them personalities that I tried to ignore.

I didn't want to be anyone's friend. The soldiers on the base kept up a formality with us civilians that radiated more contempt than any amount of overt hostility could have managed. "Yes, ma'am" and "no, ma'am" can be angrier than "fuck you," given the right kind of spin. The Zyz contractors were either the aforementioned dishonorably discharged types, or brogrammers whose insufferable high-fiving and sadistic glee felt only slightly ickier than the fact that I was secretly high-fiving myself, inside my head, every time one of my predictions played out. The other civilian contractors—the kids behind the counter at the Pizza Hut and the Starbucks—were insular, the Filipinos sticking with one another, likewise the Bulgarians.

That left Carrie Johnstone.

She'd stop by my desk a couple of times a day, sometimes bringing me a Frappuccino or a muffin, quietly telling me how much Dick King appreciated the excellent work I was doing, hinting about the giant bonuses we could both expect at the end of the year, bitching about her Pentagon liaisons in a way that made sure I knew how many stars those generals had, how big their budgets were, and how eagerly they were eating up my fine work.

Johnstone was the closest thing I had to a friend at FOB Grizzly, which is exactly as pathetic as it sounds. I am, by nature, a curmudgeonly hermit, but even I start to miss human contact after sustained deprivation. So when Carrie Johnstone asked me to join her for dinner after my shift (to "celebrate our mutual success"—yes, she really talked that way), I was embarrassingly happy about it.

Johnstone's quarters were in their own trailer, provided by Zyz and outfitted with a full suite of Ikea furniture that was so new it was still off-gassing that new-furniture smell from the glue in its composites. She had a kitchenette in one corner along with a mini-fridge full of frozen comfort food from a Trader Joe's somewhere in the world. She transferred the fried mac n cheese balls and steak-and-ale pies to big plates, throwing in some carrot sticks in a contemptuous nod to the vegetable kingdom, then busted out these monster Bordeaux glasses with goblets the size of toy beach pails. She filled them from a bottle of something red and sharp-smelling.

"Your health." She managed to lift her glass with only one hand, which was an impressive feat. I clinked my glass to hers and politely pretended not to notice that the beef in the middle of the pie was still frozen. Even frozen, it was better than yet another Pizza Hut from the Grizzly food court. It was clearly not bothering Carrie Johnstone.

"Have I mentioned how great your work is, Masha?"

*Only about a million times.* "You have. Thank you. It's been fun." The words came out of my mouth and I realized that it was true. Being in Grizzly wasn't fun at *all*, it was lonely and weird and sometimes scary, when the guys came back from patrol with casualties or the bombers overflew low and heavy. But the work? That had been amazing, like a text-adventure game combined with a logic puzzle.

"Is there anything you need? Anything you want that could make it better? Zyz has the resources to help you out here, just say the word."

I shrugged. "I feel like maybe I'm running up against the limits of my computer science chops? I'm pulling out these really big data sets, bigger than any I work with, and I'm writing these little Perl and Python scripts to analyze them, but they take forever to run. I could maybe just keep throwing computers at it—if you had a couple of big tower PCs with a lot of RAM lying around, I'd love to have them—but I could really benefit from having some computer science PhDs to take my spaghetti code and turn it into something a little more efficient. Or a lot more efficient, to be honest."

She gave me a long, considering stare. "You know, I've been hiring people to do jobs like yours for years and you're the first one who's ever admitted that she didn't know enough about programming to solve her problems."

That stare was supposed to intimidate me. I didn't let it. "Were they all dudes?"

"Men? Yes."

"There you are, then. Statistically, only ten percent of programmers are really in the killer leagues, but dudes all like to think that they're defying the odds and sitting up there among that elite decile. I have good ideas, but I'm not about to kid myself that I'm the greatest programmer that ever lived." I swigged wine. "However, I would be an *excellent* boss for that programmer. Give me the tool, I'll get 'er done."

She laughed long and loud and guzzled her wine, and when she set her glass down, there was a gleam in her eye. "I knew there was a reason I liked you." She raised her glass and I clinked it with mine.

"It's mutual." It was. There, alone in the desert surrounded by all those strangers, Carrie Johnstone was literally my best friend for five thousand miles. That wasn't a very nice thought, but it was much better than no friends for five thousand miles.

"I'll talk to HR tomorrow and we'll start getting some résumés to you. You want to interview them?"

"Sure." I wondered what kind of programmers they'd send my way, who would be able to pass the security clearances. Shiny-faced grads from the Citadel? It'd be fun to have some of them to boss around.

The best part of first class is debarking priority. Whether you'd managed to sleep—as I finally had—or stayed up all night watching videos and drinking free smoothies and eating free ice cream—as most of my male, suit-wearing co-passengers in first class had—fourteen hours in the sky is a long time, and there's nothing worse than rounding it off by standing in the aisle while three hundred people blearily wrestle down their carry-ons and shuffle off the plane. I sprinted down the jetway and into the immigration and customs hall and went straight to the front, a perk of being on the day's first flight.

I hadn't checked a bag—another advantage of first is that no one gives you shit if you push the limits on carry-on—so I motored out past the customs guys and into the arrivals hall. It was pretty much the perfect zipless fuck of long-haul flying and there was no way I was ever going to be able to go back to cattle class; even with my savings from Zyz and Xoth I couldn't afford to do this all that often. It's hard to pay your own way when you're used to someone else picking up the tab.

It was 6 a.m. and the airport was just starting to get busy. I thought about taking BART but what the hell, after dropping more than $5K on a plane ticket, what was $75 more for a taxi?

"Oakland," I said. "I'll get you an address as we get closer."

The driver nodded and put it in gear. I had swapped a US SIM into my phone in flight; I had a monthly calendar reminder to top up my burner SIMs to keep them from expiring, using a long list of rotating prepaid credit card numbers. I never knew when Xoth would send me somewhere my phone wouldn't work. I texted Tanisha.

> Morning girl

There was a long pause. We crawled through traffic.

> What time is it where you are?

There she was!

> Same as you. I'm stuck on the 280, just leaving SFO in a cab

> Fuck yeah, Masha's in town!

> Still OK to use your guest room?

> This is Oakland, Masha. My place is so small the mice got hunchbacks. You're on the sofa

> That'll do. You are the best, Neesh. Send me your address? We're coming up on the Bay Bridge

> You'll be another hour then, this time of day. I'll get breakfast stuff from the market. What you want to eat?

> I'll take you out somewhere. My treat

> Damn. Big spender

> Just send me the address

I leaned over and gave it to the driver and tried not to flinch as he veered all over the road while pecking it into the ancient smartphone magneted to his dashboard. We came up on the Bay Bridge traffic and the sea of red brake lights. We started to travel by inches. The drivers' faces around us were blank and resigned, dead-eyed through the windshields. Inch, inch, inch. Bad even by Bay Bridge standards.

"Is there an accident ahead?"

The driver shook his head. "Checkpoint." He pointed ahead. I followed his finger and saw, in the distance, flashing blue police lights. We got closer and I saw better: a cherry-picker with a cop high in the sky, pointing a directional antenna at cars, and below, a section of lane blocked off with traffic cones and water-filled bollards, cars being waved into it. We passed it, and saw the cops, full body armor and visors, automatic rifles and heads-up displays, tearing apart the possessions of the drivers they'd pulled over. The miserable commuters who'd rung the jackpot—brown-skinned, resigned—watched miserably from the sidelines, answering questions from more cops.

We watched it in silence. I tried to imagine what kind of sensors the guy up in the cherry-picker was using. Some kind of IMSI catcher for sure, a license-plate reader, and maybe something that's trying to fingerprint cars based on the unique identifiers of the radio-emitting tire-pressure sensors in each wheel.

Focusing on logistics helped me distract myself from the deeper significance of what they're in service of—how the hell did something like this pass Fourth Amendment muster? Were they somehow classing every one of those stops as "voluntary," as in, "you're free to go at any time, but if you do that's probable cause for arrest, search, detainment?" Slovstakia had a great constitution (on paper), but this gag was so familiar there that everybody knew it was a joke. Despite all the evidence over the years, I'd assumed that America would be a little subtler than this.

"Well, that happened," I said, to break the spell.

The few times I'd been back to SF since my first overseas posting, I'd been involuntarily impressed by the new Bay Bridge, its bold design and incredible lights at night. It was ten million times more impressive than the new World Trade Center, proud and beautiful without being a monument to forever wars, a symbol of resilience, not revenge.

Now it was all checkpoints. There was another one at the other end of the bridge, and when I craned my neck to see the toll plaza for the city-bound deck, I saw a third.

We saw multiple Oakland PD officers in full battle gear, the kind of thing I'd seen a lot of at FOB Grizzly, and twice we saw MRAPs—big tanks, minus the gun turret—parked by the roadside.

Around them streamed Oaklanders. Lots of smart professionals—white, sprinkled with brown—taking a break from their gentrification duties to put in ten hours at some tech salt mines. Lots of homeless, listlessly panhandling them, carrying signs with printed-out memes and witty slogans I'd had so-cialed at me by virality bots and well-meaning old people. This was a highly connected homeless population, and of course I'd expect nothing less from the second, subordinate head of Silicon Valley.

They were locked in a classic tech arms race to locate and seize attention, the same fight that every disinformation bot, con artist, political party, marketing campaign, advertiser, religious figure, jihad fighter, meme warrior, self-publisher, and malware phisher was fighting. Every one of them on this crowded battlefield, fighting for your eyeballs and earballs and your sweet, sweet insecurities and desires and shame.

Oakland had more homeless people than I'd ever seen in a country not actually at war, and the local scene had moved past the pathos arms race, that medieval game of performing misery and enfeeblement to convince the passersby that you were among the Deserving Poor and not a mere "moocher."

These homeless people had straight backs and jocular signs that were ha-ha-only-serious, pulled from the same imageboards and social media that the people scuttling past them used every day. They were asserting their member-ship in the same human club as everyone else: *Give me money because it could be you next.* It was far more disturbing and harder to look away from than the usual alms-for-the-poor routine.

I checked my phone. We were getting close to Tanisha's place. The traffic cleared for a block or two and then we were at her door. I peeled five twenties off my roll and passed them to the driver who raised his eyebrows at the cash, then asked if I wanted a receipt. Out of habit I said yes, because I'd been able to expense my taxis for a decade, and watched his face contort. For reasons I will never understand, Bay Area taxi drivers act as though filling in a receipt was harder than taking their GED. I almost took mercy on him when I remembered that I'd just throw it out, but then something sadistic took over and I reminded him of the day's date and told him that I also needed him to write his car number on the receipt. When he was done, I carefully folded the little slip of paper and made a show of putting it in my wallet. I don't know why I did it—maybe I was trying to perform my adulthood and prove that I was still a grown-up despite being unemployed.

When I looked up, Tanisha was standing on the sidewalk staring at me, arms folded, eyebrows cocked sarcastically, with lethal quantities of sass.

I smiled sheepishly and shrugged, then clambered out of the cab and got my bag. "Hi, Neesh."

"You going to give me a hug, or am I gonna have to come and *take* it?" A second later, she was squeezing the air out of my lungs. Her smell brought me back years, a dizzying moment in which the person I'd been was superimposed on the person I was. Not pleasant. That me that was in Tanisha's arms now was a *lot* less morally defensible than the me she'd held the last time we'd seen each other.

I felt a tremble inside, one that threatened to make me start shaking on the *outside,* and that was so unthinkably ghastly that it snapped me back under control. I disentangled myself. "Let's get inside before someone mugs us."

Tanisha gave me a friendly shove and picked up my bag. "Come on, then."

She led us up four flights of worn wooden stairs with chipped navy blue handrails that ended in elaborate brass finials to her door, which I was pleased to note had good locks. She used three separate keys, including a complicated one that controlled top-and-bottom bolts set into the tempered steel doorframe. She unlocked it all and gave me her eyebrow again: *See, I know what I'm doing.*

I knocked on the wall next to the door. "Lath and plaster. Doesn't matter how good your door is if you can go through the wall in five seconds with a wrecking bar."

"Come on," she said, and led me inside. It wasn't big, but it was cozy and clean and it smelled even more like her than she did, like her bedroom on a hundred sleepovers a hundred years ago. I recognized a quilt on the sofa as coming from her parents' house, a framed print of *Guernica*, a giant Oxford English Dictionary with a little magnifying glass in a drawer that I'd always coveted, her bass on its stand in a corner next to a little pig-nose amp. The feeling of being superimposed was so strong I wobbled and had to brace myself on a wall. Tanisha was suddenly in my face, looking concerned.

"You okay?"

"All fine. Just jetlagged. Long trip."

She wasn't buying it. She put her arm around my shoulder and steered me to her sofa. "Sit. I'll get you a drink. Plenty of things wrong in the world, but you keeling over isn't going to help."

She disappeared into her tiny kitchen, taking a water glass out of the dish drainer and filling it from a filter jug on the counter. She pressed it into my hand. Being looked after this way felt amazing, but also humiliating. I let go of my pride, especially when Tanisha tucked that quilt around me. I'd been under that quilt so many times, binge-watching DVD sets with Neesh and sneaking drinks out of her parents' liquor cabinet.

Tanisha handed me a Tupperware of cut strawberries and I bit into them, getting more of my past into my mouth as California produce burst between my teeth and washed my taste buds with sweet juice. I closed my eyes to savor them and literally dozed off immediately, just for a second, jolting awake to see her grinning at me.

Fuck this. I unwrapped the quilt and stood with dignity. "Breakfast now."

Tanisha opened her mouth to tell me to sit down and take it easy and I spoke before she could. "Breakfast. Now."

Back in Bltz, I'd sometimes take Kriztina to the hilariously weird "American Diner" for breakfast. Now, I was eating breakfast in a Californian diner in America: the kind of place with three kinds of milk (none of them animal-based), paleo smoked duck bacon and sweet-potato pancakes, and chia pudding with mango and pistachios. It was all better than I wanted to admit, and the coffee was exactly the kind of fussy bullshit that Marcus Yallow would have nerdgasmed over. It wasn't bad.

The server brought two plates of pancakes while Tanisha and I grimaced at each other from our perches on the crest of middle-aged spread.

Tanisha reached out with one finger and touched my shoulder. "You fucking came."

"Well, you did call me."

She poked me again. "I *called* you, fool. I didn't ask you to fly halfway around the world."

I changed the subject. "How's Becky?"

"Haven't talked to her in a long time, but as far as I know, she's still in everybody's business, like a one-woman intelligence service. Like always."

"Why don't you talk to her anymore?"

Tanisha side-eyed me. "Becky is a pain in the ass to be friends with. Lots of people lost touch with her. Like you, right?"

"It's an occupational hazard. I lose more friends that way."

"Not me, though."

"No."

She pushed aside her pancakes, only half-eaten, and I wished I had her self-control.

"But you had someone in mind, right? Masha, tell me what's going on. I'm your friend, I can help."

I shook my head. "I left behind some people in Slovstakia. Friends. One of them was a pretty good friend."

She shook her head. "God, not a boy."

"No, a girl."

"Whatever. Heartbreak is boring."

"It's not like that, Neesh. She's more like—" I fished for the word. Not *protégé*. "A little sister."

"Yeah, they can be a pain in the ass. Well, if you're worried about her, just give her a call."

"I can't."

"Come on. Just wake her up. Or wait a couple hours for the sun to go up there."

"It's not that, Neesh. She's in trouble."

"Trouble?"

"The kind of trouble you're worried about getting in." I looked hard at her: *Don't ask more.*

She looked back at me, nodded. Sighed. Again.

I had their numbers, literally. Every jihadi in the field. They'd switch SIMs but not phones, and I'd correlate the IMSI of their handsets with the new SIM. They'd switch phones but not SIMs and I'd do the same, but in reverse. They'd switch both—these were the elite elites, the paranoid paranoids—and I'd watch their calling patterns, and within a day, I'd have IDed them.

I had their numbers, so I had their locations. Their social graphs. Their information cascades. I had their porn-watching habits. I had their SMSes. I itched to get their Google searches, but that was hard because Google had better security than every other service they visited—strong SSL certificates that hid everything after the slash, so all I could see from my vantage point was https://google.com/—and then . . . nothing.

"I wish I could get past the slash," I griped to Carrie Johnstone over giant goblets of wine one night.

"For all of them?"

"No, just a few, just to validate my theories."

"Theories?"

"Yeah. Most of the time, these knuckleheads are talking about the same half-dozen subjects: griping about the food, boasting about their prowess in battle, fantasizing about the chicks they'll score, or sending emails back home to their families to let them know that they're doing the right thing and it'll all be over by Ramadan.

"But sometimes, they get these wild hairs up their asses, you know, rumors that they're being infected with bioweapons created in secret CIA labs, or that Mossad is booby-trapping their rations, or whatever. I see spikes in search activity by some of these guys when the rumors start to spread, and then those same subjects get all over their messages, squelching them and insisting that it's all BS.

"So my theory is that these are the guys who are smart enough to search for debunking information when they see rumors, you know, the ones who got As in their media literacy classes or whatever before they became full-time terrorists, or whatever the local equivalent is—"

Carrie Johnstone swallowed her wine and held up her hand. "The local equivalent is growing up in Saddam's Iraq."

"Okay, that. What I know is that when *I* google these rumors, I get some of the same debunking info these guys are pasting into their chats, but not always. Anyway, my thinking is that if I could see how those guys search for that info, we could change the info they get when they try—feed them disinfo, point them at each other by showing them different results."

She looked at me appraisingly. "I like the way you think. Let me snoop around, see what I can do."

Three days later, she loomed over my desk, dropped a pad of Post-its.

"What are these?"

She grinned wolfishly. "I can get you past the slash. You give me a phone number, an email address, or a max address—"

"MAC address," I corrected her before I could check myself. She grimaced.

"Whatever. Any of those. Turns out there's some people we're working with who've been hoping to do some live-testing of a few advanced tools."

"And I write it down? On paper?"

"We don't want a digital trail." She made a face. "Funny, isn't it. Used to be when you wanted something secret you didn't write it down on paper. Now you don't write it down on a computer."

When she was gone, I turned over our conversation in my head. Someone— the NSA? A competitor?—was inside our systems. Carrie Johnstone had an- other channel to reach someone—the NSA? A competitor?—who could do stuff to computers and phones with a MAC address, email address, or phone number. That meant that they were inside one of three or four ISPs, either through infiltration, bribery, hacking, or taking over a base station or satellite uplink. That made sense—we owned the Iraqi ISPs six ways to midnight, and I had seen stuff come across my desk that had to be fed by the satellite ground stations.

But how, exactly, were they going to get past the slash? It was possible that they'd hired a bunch of math geniuses who'd figured out how to break modern, "unbreakable" cryptography. It wouldn't be the first time a widely held mathematical certainty turned out to be a mere conjecture with pretensions. But I worked for Zyz, and I was considered a Big Brain in it, and *I* wasn't that smart.

You didn't need to break the math to break the crypto, of course. The crypto was implemented in code, software written by huge teams of programmers, no smarter than me, in big companies with sociopathic managers and tight deadlines. That software would have mistakes, and those mistakes would produce bugs. Send a device a specific bad instruction and it would open up like a Hoberman sphere, allowing the attacker full access to its mysterious interior.

Companies found and fixed their bugs, but they were slow, and not everyone updated everything. For example, if you were a badly educated, paranoid jihadi living in a cave, you might just not want to squander your precious internet access downloading large security updates that might actually be poisoned fakes that opened you up to hackers.

Even better than betting that your targets wouldn't update your software was to target bugs that no one else knew about—bugs for which no updates existed. These had a name, "oh-days" (only noobs called them "zero-days" so I made a point of calling them that, just to put hackerboys' teeth on edge), as in, "It's been zero days since the existence of this bug was known to the manufacturer and the public, therefore, no patch for them exists and every system is vulnerable to attacks that use them."

Some companies had bug-bounty programs where they'd pay you to tell them about the bugs in their code, but in those markets, the high bidder was usually not Microsoft, Apple, or Adobe, it was a company like Zyz who'd give you top dollar. Of course companies tried to counter this by appealing to researchers' sense of civic duty, as in, "You must tell us about our bugs so we can protect the public from evil hackers. Remember, you and the people you love use this software too." Which would be a lot more credible if those same companies didn't often end up just sitting on bugs after they'd been told about them. Imagine that you found some killer, showstopper bug in Windows or iOS and decided to Do the Right Thing and deliver it to the vendor instead of selling it to Zyz or one of our competitors. Then weeks tick by, then months.

Then you go back to the company and demand to know when they plan on doing something about the bug you turned in and they tell you that they've decided it's not urgent enough to warrant an out-of-cycle patch, and they're going to fix it in the next version of the product, which is a year away at least. By the way, the bug-bounty agreement you signed? It has a gag clause, so any attempt to tell the world that the company is sitting on a dangerous bug would result in you being stripped of your livelihood, your house, and everything you've ever saved.

All of a sudden, "civic duty" starts to feel like a synonym for "gullibility." Zyz might make you sign an NDA when you sold it one of your 0-days, but we'd pay you a lot more and wouldn't insult you by pretending that we had any intention of doing anything to fix it.

It turns out that companies aren't great custodians of bad news about their products, especially around their quarterly earnings calls. Who'd a thunk it?

I knew about all of this in the abstract, but I assumed that any 0-days Zyz was sitting on were used sparingly, to catch the baddest of the bad guys, Saddam's top generals and spies. But here was Carrie Johnstone, offering me a full arsenal, one for any operating system or platform. How much of this stuff did we have?

(A lot, it turned out. Writing bug-free code is hard, and the fact that the big tech companies had all but declared war on security researchers and bad news about their products meant that every bug that got discovered ended up being weaponized, rather than fixed. There was a glut on the market.)

A week later, I boiled down my list of potential targets to a top four, and I carefully wrote down everything I had on them—all their numbers and identifiers—on a slip of paper that I walked over to Carrie Johnstone's desk and put directly into her hand. Then I went back and took the sheet of paper below that one on the pad—a blank sheet, with the impressions of the pen I'd used on the sheet above it just visible when I turned on my desk lamp and held the pad at a forty-five-degree angle—into the shredder under my desk.

I was meant to be choosing targets based on their ability to provide intel. Instead, I chose them based on the different systems they used. I wanted to know what kinds of tools Zyz had in its toolbox. I had almost no interactions with Zyz. We were "compartmentalized," and the only direct Zyz contacts I had from day to day were with Carrie Johnstone. The other people in the Zyz building at FOB Grizzly were mostly shadows, glimpsed in the dim air-conditioned cubicles. Sometimes I'd see them at the food court and exchange a few words, but they weren't the same tribe as me. Most of them were ex-military—not necessarily US military, though—and all of them were at least a decade older than me. The older women gave me those suspicious looks that older conservative women reserve for young women with suspicious piercing scars in their ears and nostrils, and the older men gave me the looks that old dudes give *all* younger women. Gross.

So I knew almost nothing about Zyz, except that they paid really well, and they seemed to have a lot of confidence in Carrie Johnstone. This didn't really speak well of them, but since I also had a lot of confidence in her, I was in no position to talk. They certainly had some lucrative contracts from the Pentagon, but I wasn't going to assume that meant anything—least of all that they were even marginally competent. So my purpose was, in part, to figure out who I was working for: mere looters who could talk a good line in sales meetings, or ninja black-ops off-the-books Delta Forcers who got all the dirty work?

(It was possible they were ninja looters who could both talk a good line and also do military magic, but I was betting you either got one or the other.)

I was going to find out which one soon.

# CHAPTER 5

"So tell me about this Black-Brown Alliance," I said, leaning back on the diner's bench seat, slowly digesting my pancakes as coffee and jetlag warred for control of my eyelids.

"We grew out of Black Lives Matter. They threw everything at BLM: spies, provocateurs, terrorism charges, RICO charges, disinformation campaigns. BLM kept growing. States passed laws that let them charge million-dollar fines to activist groups that called demonstrations where there was property damage—*any* property damage, even a kicked-over trash can. BLM crowd-funded the fines and got stronger every time, and so other people picked up on it, and then you had Brown Lives Matter, which came out of the Council on American Islamic Relations, who'd been fighting similar shit that was still different enough that they wanted to get at it their own way. Then there was Latinx Lives Matter, organizing around immigration raids.

"Yadda, yadda: after a while we figured that since we were all on the same side, we should coordinate together and it turned out there were some people whose favorite thing was to be that bridge between the different groups. It was like the old SNCC, the Student Nonviolent Coordinating Committee, the people who loved to be facilitators, and that's how the Black-Brown Alliance was born."

"Sounds like progress."

Tanisha made a face. "Yeah, it's great, all right. We're the scariest monster of the mass white supremacist psyche: black folks and Muslims and Arabs and

Persians and Mexicans and Salvadorans and Hondurans and Colombians, a sea of brown and black faces stretching as far as the eye can see, having one another's back, refusing to be divided. You name a cause, we're on it: Fight for Fifteen, debt strikes, immigration amnesty, Planned Parenthood, prison reform, voter suppression, the war on the War on Drugs, and locking up every single dirty banker and CEO in America—" She was counting them off on her fingers. She made a fist. "The whole fuckin' enchilada, as my white, liberal burrito-eating friends would say."

I looked at Tanisha, really looked at her, trying to see her as a stranger would see her. Tanisha'd always had inner strength that was hidden behind her easygoing peacemaker role in our friend group. Now that strength shone through. Without trying, Tanisha looked *tough,* like someone who'd take any shade you threw at her, weaponize it, and use it to cut you open from throat to belly. Someone who knew everything going on around her, ready to react to it like a judo champ turning your punch into a throw and lobbing you over her shoulder without even seeming to move.

She was Woke Wonder Woman.

Tanisha took a sip of coffee and poked at her abandoned half stack. "Then we started putting names on the ballot. We wrote a ticket, fifteen campaign pledges hitting all our major goals, and we fundraised to put up five hundred candidates at the state and local levels who'd back them, then spent even more money on voter registration drives and challenges to dirty vote-suppression tactics in every one of those races. Our good friends in the Democratic Party said we were being too idealistic—especially the corporate Dems whose asses we were primarying. Three hundred seventy-two of our candidates got into office in the first cycle, and that's when the hammer came down.

"All of a sudden, every one of our rallies turned violent when masked Black Blocers started throwing rocks and punches. No one knew who these people were—that's the point of the Black Bloc—but we heard stories of these people being allowed to slip through the police lines and disappear. Then videos showed up, and yup, it sure as hell looked like these dudes were smashing bank windows and setting fire to cop cars and then walking away whistling while the cops arrested everyone *else.*

"At the same time, our internal mailing lists went super toxic. Mean arguments broke out and just as soon as they seemed like we'd put 'em behind us, they'd flare up again, twice as bad as before. Our ugliest moments leaked onto social media, ended up in the press, got used to shit on our candidates when they were pushing for better labor laws or housing laws or voter laws, like, 'You gonna listen to this idiot? Look at how fucked-up her friends are—what makes her competent to make laws?'"

I started to get a sick feeling in my stomach. I knew this playbook. I'd *written* this playbook.

"We knew we were infiltrated. We knew we were hacked. We weren't stupid. So we took countermeasures. New devices, new messaging platforms, new opsec. We followed the recipes we found online from the Committee to Protect Journalists, from Cryptoparty, the EFF's Surveillance Self-Defense Kit.

"But a lot of that stuff? It's about letting you know when you're hacked— not about making you hack-proof. Stuff like binary transparency. We all update the second a new version drops because we all want to be patched against whatever is latest and worst, so we started paying attention to the binary transparency alerts, even though they're almost always false alarms."

"Until they aren't."

She looked at me and sighed. I waited for that second sigh.

"Yeah, until they aren't." She got a Faraday pouch out of her bag, handed it to me. "That's the old phone. I haven't turned it on since I got the alert. Been using this one." She pulled out another phone, cracked screen, scuffed case. "It's old but I was able to patch it up. Got a burner SIM. But—" She sighed. Then again. "Well, it's only a matter of time. What do I do? Stop updating? Stop using a phone? Might as well give up on Black-Brown Alliance altogether."

"You don't need to do that. But you *will* need to up your opsec to the next level. That means downloading open operating systems for your phone, compiling them yourself, checking the checksums manually, installing them. It's a huge pain in the ass, and you and all your friends are going to have to do it perfectly, every time, or you're going to be cracked wide open. Security is a team sport, and your data is only as secure as the sloppiest person in your group." It felt good to say this. It felt dirty to say this. When I'd been at FOB Grizzly, I'd targeted the highest-value adversaries, but also the sloppiest. Couple times there, I'd had guys who had the *tightest* opsec game, no way into them, but they were sending messages to some dumdum who didn't bother to patch, didn't bother to encrypt, recycled their passwords . . . I may not ever get entry to my target's devices, but everything that opsec ninja sent to his clown of a lieutenant was mine anyway. That was both an obvious matter of common sense and a trade secret of Zyz, Xoth, the NSA, Mossad, GRU, and the Eagle Scouts' intelligence arm. Everybody knew this stuff and no one was supposed to talk about it. *Don't mention the war.*

Tanisha narrowed her eyes. "That sounds impossible, Masha. 'Just don't make any mistakes' is a wish, not a plan. I think you even told me that."

"That's why you need a full-time security operations person."

"Only that, huh? Why didn't I think of—"

"I'm serious, Neesh. You can't do this with individual training and personal vigilance. You need someone whose only job is making sure that you're all dotting your tees and crossing your eyes, and that someone can't be a rando you send to some training sessions."

Tanisha shook her head. I knew that headshake well: it was the shake of someone trying to convince themselves that things really weren't that bad. "Masha, all my life you've been telling me that security wasn't a pro sport, that anyone could do it with a little effort. Now you're saying we need a full-time opsec czar."

"Security *is* easy, if you're not worried about untargeted, opportunistic attacks from dumdums and petty crooks. You don't need to run faster than the bear, you just need to run faster than the other guy. Even if your adversary is the cop who traffic-stops you and tries to crack open your phone, the opsec moves are pretty straightforward, so long as you prep them in advance: minimize data on your phone, minimize passwords on your phone, encrypt everything, know your rights, scream for a lawyer, shut up, and sit tight.

"But when you're actively targeted by a *government*? By the *US government*? That's a different story, Neesh. You're not playing in the amateur leagues anymore. This is the majors. All-star. We call those guys 'advanced persistent threats.' 'Advanced' because they're really good at it. 'Persistent' because they're going to staff their desks 24/7 with good people who will watch you *all the time* waiting for a single fuck-up to exploit. You need advanced, persistent defense."

Again with the headshake. "We don't have that person, and even if we did, we're not an army. I can't order people to change their lives to do nothing but react to what our worst enemies are doing to us. The point here is to set a positive agenda, not let white supremacy dictate our lives to us."

I didn't say the snarky thing that was on the tip of my tongue about wishful thinking and tell me again about not letting white supremacy boss you around when you and all your friends are wearing hoods 24/7 in Gitmo.

Because she was right.

"You're right."

She checked to see if I was snarking, saw I wasn't.

"Go on."

I shook my head. "What can I say, you're right. They want you to act in certain ways. Top priority would be to get you all to stay home and shut up. Failing that, they want you to fall apart after they get inside your loop and make you all distrust each other. If that doesn't work, they'll settle for you putting all your time and energy into stopping them from attaining their other objectives.

"Problem is, if you just go on as you are now, you're going to end up shattered, busted, and neutralized. You need better security and you need to be able to attain it without changing who you are."

She crossed her eyes and stuck her tongue out. "Obviously. But how do we do it?"

I'd tried to teach Kriztina and her friends, train them. It hadn't gotten them very far. Doing the same thing over and over but expecting a different outcome wasn't the formal definition of insanity (see *The Diagnostic and Statistical Manual of Mental Disorders, 5th Edition* for more), but it wasn't good tactics.

"What if I do it?"

She blinked. "What?"

"What if I come on board, full-time, as your security professional. You all give me your devices and I'll set them up. I'll take over your servers and harden them. I'll be available, 24/7, to keep your systems up and answer your questions. My job will be to figure out how you can do the things you want to do, not to convince you that you don't really want to do them. I'll do it for the duration, until you're sick of me or the world has been remade to your satisfaction."

The words rang in my own ears. I couldn't believe I'd said them, but I had. It was a formal declaration of allegiance, taking sides in a fight where

I'd always balanced on a beam right down the middle of things. Having said them, I felt *amazing,* my heart thundering in my chest, my blood singing in my ears. I was going to *do it,* pledge myself to a sacred cause and change the world.

This must be how Marcus Yallow felt all the time.

It was a hell of a drug.

Then Tanisha sighed, and sighed again. "No."

I held my breath.

"I'm sorry, but no. We don't need a white savior, Masha."

I sat with my feelings for a moment before saying anything. Was that fair? Tanisha was an old friend, one of my oldest, but we hadn't spent much time together since I was seventeen. People change. Had she become an asshole? Had I? One of us was being an asshole, I was pretty sure of that.

"Fair enough." There was only a little wobble in my voice.

I was pretty sure my poker face was holding.

"All right, then." Tanisha sighed. She drank some coffee. Second sigh.

She looked out the window. The Oakland commuter crowds had thinned, now it was boys on the corner, moms pushing strollers, homeless people, cops.

"You let me know if you think I can help," I said. Inside, I was planning my escape. I could ditch Tanisha, head back to Mexico. I could learn to surf. I mean, why the fuck not? Good a place as any to be when the end came, whatever that was.

"I'm sorry." Tanisha was still staring out the window. "I know you probably feel this is unfair. I guess it is unfair. But it's unfair all over. It's unfair that we have to form the Black-Brown Alliance. It's unfair that the government and the cops want to destroy us. It's unfair that our phones and networks don't keep us safe. It's unfair that you came all this way and that we don't want you to be our tech-support security ninja. But the thing I've devoted my life to is making the world more fair, and that means that sometimes I have to do hard things. I didn't promise you a job with the Black-Brown Alliance. I'm sorry your plan for us isn't a plan we can work with. Maybe we—you and me and my comrades—can come up with something better. But maybe we can't. Sometimes hard problems don't have easy solutions."

*Sometimes hard problems don't have easy solutions.* It came out of her mouth all polished and perfect and I knew it was a thing she'd said before, to other people, and I wanted to pounce on it, all teeth and claws. But I was trying hard to be the person that Kriztina had wanted me to be, to be as good as Tanisha, to adult so hard that I wouldn't let my hurt feelings eat my good sense.

"I hear you." Which seemed like a safe, adult thing to say. Poker face. "I hope we can come up with something too."

I picked up breakfast, reminding Tanisha that it had been my invitation. Neither of us said anything about me already spending five grand on a plane ticket to offer her the on-site help she'd never requested and that, it turned out, she didn't really want. Oh well, easy come, easy go. The breakfast was just a drop in the bucket, after all the money I'd raked in being such a spectacular sellout.

*Compartments, Masha. Remember your compartments, girl.*

The sunlight and the cops and the people and the smells of Oakland triggered my jetlag, sending it crashing over me. I was going to need a shit-ton more coffee or a long sleep. My stomach was already bubbling with excess acid and I just wanted to pull the covers over my head for other perfectly good reasons.

"I think I need a nap."

Tanisha put a warm arm around my shoulders. "Good idea. You have to be wiped as hell. I've got to get to work anyway."

"Where do you work?" My question reminded me that I didn't know the answer, and that reminded me that I was kind of a shitty friend. No wonder Tanisha didn't want my help. *Shut up, self-pitying Masha. Compartments. Sleep.*

"Customer service for a software company. I sit at home with a headset and help corporate drones unstick their enterprise chat software. It's a job."

She ticked her head at my scrunch of surprise. "You're wondering how I could possibly know enough about technology to help someone else? First of all, I'm not that dumb, but second and most important, I'm not the kind of person anyone designs technology for. No one in the history of the world ever raised VC by talking about the major bank they'd earn by tempting radical African American women to use their tools. Since the first time I turned on a computer, I've had to fight the code to make it work my way, for me. Unlike those bros"—she gestured out the window—"I've never used an app that wanted to make *me* happy. These office drones who call me, they're using software bought by some dude who looked like one of those guys, designed by someone who looked like one of those guys, and which treats them as cost-centers and tech-support problems, not people.

"I'm *good* at tech support for that kind of person. Better than those guys could ever be."

We watched the tech bros stream down the sidewalk toward BART and their rideshare pickups. I was so tired, and Tanisha's words made me more tired. Just thinking about whether I was an honorary tech bro made me want to crawl under a blanket.

"I believe you," I said. "And now I need to sleep."

She carefully sized up my face, didn't like what she saw. "You do, girl. Let's get you home."

One thing I learned in all my years as a tech person: tech is more about sales than it is about code. There are companies out there that make "products" that barely run, but they've got the right kind of sale-dudes, bros who can convince other bros to give them lots of money for stuff that no bro will ever have to actually use—that's the job of monkeys further down the evolutionary ladder: customer-service reps, grunts, fast-food clerks, tellers, check-in staff. Those people earn so little money that the business can afford to have them stuck in endless glitch loops, waiting while progress bars crawl across their screens (those progress bars aren't going to watch themselves, after all).

The first time I logged in to Zyz's spyware back-ends, I knew I was using code that one bro had sold to another. The menus made no sense, the UI liked to crash, the error messages had clearly been written by someone who didn't speak English as a first language. Someone had built this for Zyz and sold it to them, and now Zyz was billing the US government at crazy markups for me to dick around with it and try to get it to run.

Once I'd worked out which combinations of commands would cause it to crash, which ones would merely make it hang for hours at a time, and which ones would seem to work, but actually give back deceptive or incomplete output, I got to grips with it, stealing photos and texts and browser histories from my targets' devices.

Things got even faster when I figured out the lame-ass encryption used for the app's database and sucked it into MySQL—an open-source database used by everyone in the world except greedy contractors who wanted to mark up Oracle licenses—and started probing it with real database queries. Then I started to get a sense of just how much data we could suck out of these guys' devices: all of it. That's what I called the program: AOI, for "All Of It."

We were totally inside those gadgets, and I could suck up so much data and poll the devices' locations and status so frequently that it was clear whoever had built this had given exactly zero thought to how suspicious their malware would be as it sucked up bandwidth and chewed through the battery. I made a note to myself to give some thought to figuring out how I'd fix that so that I could stay inside my targets' gadgets without tipping them off.

Meanwhile I was exploring everything past the slash: validating my guesses about where these guys were getting their info, which posters and which messages would set off cascades of communication and action. I started to match their activity levels to their locations, building up a picture of the rhythm of their days: how often they stopped to check their phones, what their charge levels said about their access to power, when they moved at a walking pace and when they covered ground at driving pace.

Then I started in on the photos. These guys weren't using image-sharing sites, but we knew that they posted their trophy shots to private message boards, some of which we'd been able to get access to because these bozos recycled their passwords.

But the shots they kept on their phones were a lot darker than the stuff they shared with other jihadis and the jihobbyists they hoped to lure to Iraq. The first one I hit on showed a grinning soldier—a kid—with his gun to the head of a weeping older man with short, iron-gray hair, the man on his knees, the kid's smile huge and luminous. The next shot: the man on the ground, a pool of blood around his head, the kid's gun and hand and forearm dripping blood, the smile still there, flecks of blood on the kid's face.

That was the first execution shot, but not the last. These guys weren't just fighting us, they were murdering people, lots of people, but only a few at a time, families left dead in their living rooms or buried in shallow graves behind their homes, captured in stills by lo-rez phone cameras whose lenses were dusty and smudged.

I clicked through them at a deliberate pace, taking in their features, unconsciously thinking through how I'd classify and file them, checking the EXIF metadata on the photos and making notes of which targets were dumb enough to leave the location-tagging turned on so I could auto-extract the GPS coordinates later and plot this stuff on a map. Click, click, click. The death images usually included at least one older man, all with soldierly bearing, and click, click, click, it clicked for me, these were Ba'athists, the old military, being executed by the militias we were chasing. I couldn't remember if Ba'athists were Sunni or Shia, but our targets were Shia, and the guys they were killing were Saddam's old loyalists, so they were Sunni? Maybe?

Click, click. I was breathing heavily and sweating in the dim, air-conditioned Zyz trailer. Time had fallen away in the room. I was so far from a window, and they were all so heavily tinted anyway, it could have been the middle of the night or the middle of the day. Sometimes I worked straight through, not having any friends to distract me or parents to make demands on me.

Click. Then I saw the first rape photo. It had taken a long time to get there, and I let out a long breath. Some part of me had been braced for this picture, knowing it had to be in there. She was young. Younger than me.

I don't want to write about her.

She was dead in the next frame.

She wasn't the last one.

Click. Click. Click.

I was so tired when we got back to Tanisha's place that I couldn't even be bothered to find my toothbrush or my tights. I skinned off my yoga pants and tee and slid into the silk sleep-sack I traveled with everywhere, then toppled onto her sofa, using a sofa cushion as a pillow. I was nearly asleep when I remembered with a jolt that I hadn't charged my phone or laptop and dragged myself up to snag my backpack, connect my power cable, find the US adapter, unplug Tanisha's cute side-table lamp (a ceramic Hummel shepherdess with a lamp sticking out of her head, painstakingly repainted in neon colors) and plugged in my laptop, then plugged my phone into it and put it under my pillow. I dropped off to sleep with my hand curled around it.

When I woke up, my heart was thundering and I didn't know why. Something had scared me out of a deep, deep sleep and for a second the feeling was so intense I couldn't even think clearly enough to remember where I was. Tanisha's blinds were drawn and the room was in half light, and I could hear Tanisha's muffled music through her bedroom door. I took a couple of breaths and oriented myself: full bladder, dark room, sore muscles, crusty eyes, shitty taste in my mouth and . . .

My phone in my hand.

It made a noise, not a loud one, but not a good one. One I'd chosen myself, as a very specific alarm tone to sound in a very specific set of circumstances. It was a phased loop of European ambulance sound, distinctly computer-generated, with some menacing clipping to give it the ear-feel of being played super loud, even at low volumes. My phone had only made that noise three times before, and all three times it had been because I'd gotten too close to gear that *I'd* set up, for Xoth.

Technically, the alarm wasn't coming from my phone. It was coming from my phone's *case*: a battery case that gave me an extra day's battery life, but which also had its own onboard processor, and which had a small, wired SIM-shaped tentacle that it inserted into my phone's SIM cage; the actual SIM lived in a slot on the case, and that slot was powered by a little programmable controller that monitored all the signals going in and out of the phone.

If my phone was supposed to be off but was covertly sending data, I'd hear that alarm. But that wasn't the only trigger: the case also let me know when the phone tried to connect to a fake cellular tower, an IMSI catcher. Stock phones could spoof their IMSIs when they thought they were talking to a fake tower, but with the case, I could just log and ignore any attempts by a fake tower to handshake with my phone. Finally, my case would let me know if the tower it was connected to tried to poison my baseband radio, the tiny, low-powered computer that handled all the communications between the phone's cellular radio and its operating system. Baseband radio security sucked, and anyone who took over the baseband radio would be in a permanent blind spot that the operating system and its apps could never see into.

The phone case had a cheap OLED screen on its back, scratched from all the times I'd dropped my phone, but still readable. I stepped over to the window, cracking the blinds to let the daylight fall on the display, then used the volume buttons on the case's edge to scroll through the attack log.

Right up to the moment I saw the log, I had been thinking, *Well, this is a weird false alarm, I wonder what's going on,* part of my project to get my heart to stop thundering and the blood to stop roaring in my ears. But as I read and reread the error console's output, my pulse spiked again and I had to consciously regulate my breathing.

Someone had tricked my phone into associating with a fake cell-phone tower. They hadn't actually got my phone, of course, just my cell-phone case, which had carefully spoofed its output to the fake tower to see what would happen next. What happened next was pretty goddamned scary: someone had targeted my phone for a malware attack on my baseband radio, trying to poison my phone. The case had trapped the attack in a honeypot—a simulation of a phone baseband radio—that watched and logged as the fake tower delivered its attack and then followed it with a rush of neatly packaged malicious software, apps that would run in my phone's background, letting the attacker take over the whole sensor package—cameras, mics, GPS, accelerometers, the fingerprint sensor—raid my filesystem, the usual spy-in-your-pocket routine.

The thing is, my phone's case impersonated a different make and model of phone every time it talked to an IMSI catcher as part of its spoofing, and the attack that it had received was a strain of malware that was tuned to a specific fake model and firmware level. That meant that an adversary had gone looking for this phone, found it, probed it, prepared a weapon to attack this specific phone, and taken it over. In other words, this wasn't a bunch of dumdums with some toy they downloaded off the internet, it wasn't local deputy-dog law enforcement using some off-the-shelf stuff they'd paid too much for in a secret deal with a surveillance supplier—this was an advanced persistent threat, a government or someone working for a government, using the kinds of serious firepower whose caveman ancestors I'd tested out at FOB Grizzly.

I grabbed my laptop, then fished around under the lamp for the switch. I put in my earbuds and cranked up some music, then cabled my phone case to my laptop and dumped its logs. I had an idea.

The attack had been tailored to a specific phone, so I could run the logs through a simple analysis and figure out when my phone had been noticed by the bad guys. If the attack was tailored to the model it impersonated at 10:28 a.m., then that was when I'd been targeted. There it was: I was targeted at 9:18 a.m., and a quick scroll through my phone told me that this was just as we were coming through Tanisha's door.

Shit.

I tucked my laptop under my arm, and quietly turned the doorknob for Tanisha's bedroom. She was sitting at a laptop with wireless earbuds in, talking in a calm voice to someone, somewhere in the world, about finding an error log and reading her the top entry. She saw me and held up a finger. I shook my head. This was urgent. She shook her head back, never losing her sweet-as-pie tone with her client. It was weird to hear her being so pliable and patient, like the poster child for Emotional Labor Awareness Week. I made an impatient wind-it-up gesture, aware that I was being a dick but also understanding that this was important.

When she finally hung up, she was coldly furious. "What. Is. It?"

"Gimme your phone?"

That made her angrier.

"Come on, Neesh. Seriously."

She shook her head, sighed. Sighed again. Gave it over. I slid the paperclip out of its slot on the side of my phone case and ejected her SIM. Then I unplugged the router that was behind her computer. With no wifi to connect to and no cellular network connection, it couldn't talk to the rest of the world. I found its wired port—still covered by the manufacturer's seal—and pried it up with my fingernail, then went back to my bag for a cable and a USG.

Like the baseband radio in your phone, the USB port in your laptop is actually a separate computer, and not a very good one. The system-on-a-chip that controls the USB port has a whole, shittily made, ancient, insecure operating system, and moving a USB device from one system to another is all it takes to transfer a virus, one that your operating system will never detect, one that can totally compromise everything you do on that infected system.

Enter the USG, an open-source hardware gadget that some Kiwi hackers whomped up in New Zealand and turned into a serious business as paranoid people like me got increasingly worried about what happened when we attached "innocent" devices to our laptops. It was a little dongle that had a "female" USB port on one side and a "male" USB plug on the other, and two more little systems-on-a-chip inside it, except these ones were a lot better than the USB controller in our laptops, with open, auditable operating systems. One handled input, the other handled output, and they filtered all the instructions between USB devices and computers, throwing out anything that looked sketchy, like a hardware firewall for your otherwise unguarded USB ports.

If you were only a little paranoid, you could buy a USG from these Kiwis, stick it in your laptop, and go to work. If you were a little more paranoid, you could compile the firmware for the gadget from source code, and check to make sure it had the same fingerprint as the firmware that was running on it when it arrived. Even more paranoid: flash the firmware with source code you compiled yourself. Most paranoid: buy the components, get a soldering iron, build your own USG, compile the firmware from source and flash the gadget, so that someone targeting you would have to somehow know which commodity electronic components you were buying and compromise them.

Guess which one I did.

I plugged her phone into my cable and plugged my cable into the USG, then plugged the USG into the phone. I used my phone to quickly google instructions for rebooting her phone into developer's mode, so I could directly access its firmware from my laptop, and after holding down all the right buttons in the right way and getting the timing right (which took four tries), I was able to safely manipulate the software on her phone with my laptop.

First, I took fingerprints for the OS and her apps and started feeding them into Google. Predictably, most of them matched known apps and modules, and the rest were unknown. But then one of them hit: it was a known Android rootkit, one that totally compromised your phone and all its operations. Another query—comparing it to the attack my phone's case had rebuffed—and I confirmed that it was the same attack, tailored to her phone.

"I think whoever is taking over phones is doing it by proximity to you, or possibly your phone, though I'd bet on the former. I bet everyone in the restaurant's been pwned, not to mention all your neighbors."

Tanisha blinked a couple times. "What does that actually *mean*?"

"Someone—probably Oakland PD, or maybe state cops, or possibly feds, and/or some contractors for any of the above—controls enough cellular towers, real or fake, to identify which phones are close to yours, and when it finds them, it sends them tailored attacks that seize control of their phones."

"What do you mean 'seize control'?" I could tell from Tanisha's dawning look of horror that she already knew the answer, though.

"You know: cameras, mics, fingerprint readers, location, and network traffic. Any photos or other files on the device, plus access to all your cloud data: messages, calendars, shared docs. Access to your encrypted chats, because they're grabbing the decrypted cleartext from your phone. Some or all of that is already exfiltrated to their databases, and the rest is available on tap from your phone whenever it's on and connected to any kind of network."

She had paled, and I watched her clutch at her thighs to keep her hands from shaking. I was scaring her on purpose, I admit it.

"What do we do?"

"We?"

She shook her head. "Don't be an asshole. I know you're butthurt because I won't let you be the Black-Brown Alliance's in-house opsec ninja, but Masha, we're both in this."

"Yeah." I thought for a moment. "Neesh, I totally get your objections, really. But I'm at a loss here. The people who infected you and tried to infect me are going to figure out that I'm *not* infected pretty soon. I'm really close to your node on our little social graph here, because we've called each other and such. Plus, it's not hard to figure out who I am and what I know, especially if you're a cop. So they're going to come after me again and again, and they just have to find one mistake I've made, while I'm going to have to make *no* mistakes."

"Are you sure they'll come after you?"

I shrugged again. "I don't know, but it seems like a useful assumption at this point. They hate you enough to slap a bug on everyone you meet, after all."

She looked like she might cry. I knew that look. I'd seen it on Kriztina's face when I explained the facts of life to her.

I didn't like thinking about Kriztina.

"Come on, Neesh, what's long odds to someone like you? You're already fighting an uber-resourced, uber-organized adversary—I mean, you're willing to declare war on patriarchy, white supremacy, and late-stage capitalism, but not malware?"

She laughed grudgingly. "Okay, I get your point. But I *understand* all those other things and I don't actually *need* them. Shit like these little distraction rectangles"—she hefted her phone, looking for a sec like she might toss it against the wall, which was not a terrible idea, all things considered—"I need them but I don't understand them. Not like you. Not like *them*."

I thought for a second. "Well, I have some good news for you, then. Practically *no one* understands these things. Certainly not the cops and their bosses. They barely understand how to fill out a purchase order for the cyber-weapons they hit you with. They certainly don't understand how they *work*."

I didn't schedule a meeting with Carrie Johnstone. Some instinct told me that I shouldn't leave any documentary trail. I used my phone camera to take pictures of the stuff I could see on my screen, then printed those pictures on a little inkjet I bought from the PX for cash. I wiped my phone down to factory reset and reinstalled it afterward. I thought about snapping the printer's mainboard in two and throwing the whole thing out, but if your threat model includes bad guys putting malware in your printer's firmware to see if you're defeating the audit logs on your work computer, you're already screwed, because those same bad guys would have first taken steps that included surrounding that computer with hidden cameras and so on.

I knew that Carrie was working the DC shift, hitting her desk at 2:30 in the afternoon—7 a.m. at the Pentagon—and going back to her quarters at midnight to drink wine and eat low-carb sweet potato MREs from the PX while she watched pirated episodes of *The Sopranos*. I arrived at her quarters ten minutes after she did, giving her time to take a piss and change into her sloppies: track pants and an oversized tee. Wine-drinkin' clothes.

She answered the door with a large glass of red and a hostile expression, looking me up and down before grunting, "Little late."

"I know." I didn't explain why. Carrie Johnstone had good radar for when it was smart to talk about why you were meeting and when it was smart to keep your mouth shut until the door was closed.

She stepped to one side and gestured me in with the wineglass. I kicked off my shoes and calmed my breathing.

"Wine?"

"Yes, please." Not because I wanted it. I didn't. I wanted a clear head. But drinking wine was Carriejohnstone-ish for "Just us girls." We sat down with our glasses on either end of her right-angle Ikea sofa and she switched on a couple floor lamps so that she could better watch my expressions.

"I've learned something important."

She made an unconvincing smile. "We like important learnings. It's why we pay you so well. Tell me about your important learning, Masha." She was a little drunk already.

I swallowed. "You know how, back in the Balkans, there was this thing, 'ethnic cleansing'?"

"The Balkans didn't invent that, dear." She was more than a little drunk maybe.

"Oh. Yeah. Well." I swallowed again. "I'm inside our guys' phones now, getting much finer-grained intel on their movements and activities, and . . . Look, we focus on them attacking us, attacking our guys and the guys we backed, Chalabi and his crew?"

"Is there a question in there?" She wasn't going to make this easy.

I looked her in the eye. "That's what we're focused on."

"Yes."

"But that's not what *they're* focused on. Those jihadi belligerents, they're not out there with their IEDs and RPGs because they just want us out. They hate Saddam's old guard, his Sunni loyalists, just as much as they hate us."

"Yes, they certainly do."

"Thing is, those old Saddamists, they don't have FOBs and air support and Humvees. They're all back on their old homesteads, hiding out, trying to blend in, and these jihadis, they know where to find them."

"I imagine that's rather unpleasant for them." Her smile was broader than ever.

"They're going from house to house, executing these old Ba'athists. Their families, too. Women. Kids. The women—" I swallowed a third time. My mouth was bone-dry. I took a big mouthful of wine.

When she spoke her voice was all syrup. "Sounds like you need some counseling, Masha. There are parts of this job that are difficult to cope with, and that's something Zyz understands. We've got excellent psych counselors, and there's no shame in talking to them. You'd have to be crazy *not* to need to talk to someone, the kind of things you see on the job here."

"Talking with a counselor, yeah, that'd be great." *That'd be great if I didn't have my well-developed system of expert, impregnable compartments.* "But that's not what I'm here for."

The words hung out there. She drank her wine. Her poker face was pretty good. Maybe she just wasn't feeling anything.

"What I'm here for." My mouth was pasty-dry and sour from the last gulp of wine. I wished I had water. "I'm here because there's a *lot* of killing going on, and I think we have a duty to do something about it."

"Why does Zyz have a duty to do anything the US Army isn't paying it to do?" Not like she was being a hardass, just like she was wondering it aloud, like *Why is the sky blue?*

"Zyz may not, but the army does. We broke this place, so we bought it. Those killings are being carried out on our watch."

"Masha, I have to be frank with you. I don't think the US government has any appetite for risking American lives and spending American treasure to save Saddam's men from vengeful militias. I mean, good riddance, right?"

"They're not militias. They're the terrorists, the same guys we're fighting. What's more, they're not just killing Saddam's men. They're killing civilians. Lots of them. Women. Children. Girls. And before they kill them—" My mouth was so, so dry.

We held each other's gaze. I was saying, *There are women and girls who are being raped and then killed and then butchered out there, and it's happening on our watch.* She was saying, *This is above your pay grade. I have decided it's not our problem. Stop making a big deal out of it.* Or maybe, *If you shut up about this now, we can pretend this didn't happen. Keep talking, and we'll have to do something about it, and you might not like it.*

"Masha."

"Miss Johnstone."

"Masha, the capabilities that you have used to discover this intelligence are not widely available to US adversaries, and their existence is not widely known. Any action we take on this would jeopardize that secrecy, and the viability of those capabilities. The possible tactical uses of the ability to compromise our adversaries' personal systems take priority over revenge killings."

*Did you think that careful sidestep up just now, or had you drafted it in advance?* I put that thought in a compartment and sealed it.

She put down her wineglass. "Which is not to say that this isn't useful, if disturbing, intelligence. I would like a full report, please, so that the right people can factor it into their decision-making process. I will see to it that this is shared at the highest levels. I want to be clear that there will likely be no overt action based on your discoveries, but that doesn't mean that nothing will happen."

*Translation: it means that nothing will happen.* Get in your compartment. *Murdered kids and raped girls don't generate procurements or help us claim oil fields.* Back in your compartment. *No one is paying us to save the Sunni women of northern Iraq from brutal rape.* In your compartment.

The way this was supposed to go down was, I'd nod and let her know that I understood the lay of the land, I'd go back to my quarters and have a stiff drink. I might even get a raise.

There was another way this could go down: the Marcus Yallow way. Stick a thumb drive into my computer, copy the incriminating data, send it to someone, one of those hacktivist types who'd publish it in a trice—or risk sending it to a journalist, risk that they'd ignore it, risk that they'd turn me in, risk that they'd have such terrible opsec that they'd lose control of the data, handing it and me over to the US government or some random band of masked "hacktivist" griefers.

Then there was a third way this could go down: I could find the number for the whistleblower hotline, call it, and watch as my career and reputation were trashed.

I didn't like any of these options. Objectively, being a party to genocide was the best of a bad bunch, which was, you know, a sad commentary on our civilization, but I knew the job was dirty when I took it, right?

I made myself drink some of the sour, warm wine. It was thick and didn't want to go down my throat. I swallowed until it was gone. "Okay," I said.

Carrie Johnstone seemed to remember that she was a human being for a moment and hastily said, "Masha, I mean it about the counseling. Seeing that stuff, knowing that you're connected to it, even in a very roundabout way, it can eat at you. Talking with a pro, it's not weakness. You'll feel better."

Old-school punk rock lyrics: "You'll probably feel better if you talk about it, so why don't you talk about it?" Why was I thinking about old-school punk lyrics? My compartments were rupturing, that's why. I'd learned those lyrics from Ada, who was Trudy Doo's little sister. Trudy Doo was a punk legend in San Francisco, frontwoman for the Speedwhores, zero-fucks-given punk musician turned cypherpunk, who ran an indie internet service provider called Pigspleen that would host anything, keep no logs or records, and fight every law-enforcement request to the max. Marcus Yallow worshipped her. Marcus Yallow would leak all of this information with a righteous, self-destructive entitlement that you had to be a white dude to really even approximate, that confidence that you wouldn't end up in jail, that you wouldn't get rendered to Syria.

My compartments were leaking: "Why don't you talk to someone?" Carrie Johnstone meant talking to someone who was on the company payroll. In the US, what you said to a counselor was privileged. They couldn't tell your employer what you told them. Chaplains in the army had the same deal. But military contractors in forward operations bases, incorporated in a tax haven like St. Maarten or Guernsey, what were the rules they had to live by? Iraqi law? If I spilled my guts to some Skyped-in Zyz contract "counselor," would I have to go to a court in Baghdad to enforce the rules? The reality was that I was absolutely in the power of Carrie Johnstone and her bosses. They could shoot me in the head and dump me over the FOB Grizzly wire and there would be no repercussions.

Would Marcus Yallow be stupid enough to leak Zyz's secrets under these circumstances?

There was a distinct possibility he would.

What an asshole that guy was.

I realized I was just staring at Carrie Johnstone, watch-cursoring as I tried to compute all this stuff, put it in its compartments. If I were her, I'd be thinking, *She's about to blow!* and planning that bullet through the head. I was fucking this up.

I blinked deliberately. "Thanks, Carrie. I appreciate that. It's, uh, good to know that there's someone I can talk to if I need it. For now I think I'm okay. I mean, I want to give you the space to talk to your bosses and see what they think should be done with this. We're the good guys, right? They won't let this stuff go on forever." She was nodding now, and I had the feeling that we were steering to an end point where we'd both be able to claim that everything had been done right. "I mean, there are lots of conflicting priorities here, a whole national and regional theater. I can't know everything."

She nodded. "Masha, you're a smart girl." She finished her wine and set down her glass, visibly relieved that I wasn't going to be a party pooper. "You've done incredible things. I mean, just with this tool, you're getting more out of it than anyone ever thought—shit, you're getting it to do all the things the sales guys said it would do, and no one believed them.

"If there's one thing we can learn from this work you've done, it's that we're entering a new era in warfighting, one where the kind of SIGINT you're able to generate and analyze will make more of a difference than all the boots the US Army can put on the ground.

"The Pentagon can't develop those capabilities on its own. It doesn't have the internal structures to support that kind of research, and there are too many big shots with stars on their shoulders whose personal empires are based on the status quo. They would kill something like this before it could ever get off the ground. Believe me. I *know*. That's where Zyz and our competition come in. The US military can't be its own change agent for the same reason you can't lift yourself up in the air. Some outside force needs to act on it. That's Zyz, that's what we *do*. You can be a part of that—a key part of it, Masha. You have the technical capabilities, the insight, and the drive. I've seen it in you."

I was supposed to feel good when she said this. It was a kind of booby prize for my willingness to go along to get along. I did feel good, but the feeling was weirdly distant. Or I was distant, a hundred feet above the situation, watching it in shift-tilt miniature, knowing the good feeling was there, but not *feeling* it. Perhaps I was standing atop a ziggurat constructed of carefully stacked compartments.

"Thank you, Carrie." The distant me, all that way away, sounded convincing.

"Thank *you*, Masha. You're a force for good in this war and in the world. Never forget it."

I gave her back my still-mostly-full wineglass on my way out of her quarters, and I saw her sip from it out of the corner of my eye, just before the door clicked and I was standing out in the deserted base in the cold desert night, under the yellow glow of the outdoor lights.

I walked back to my quarters. They were filthy. How did I even amass enough stuff to make a mess that large? I'd been going back and forth to the PX on autopilot, buying whatever took my fancy. I was making so much goddamned money, every penny of it tax-free, that I hadn't even had to keep track.

Now, looking around my hoarder's nest, I realized that I hadn't ever used most of it. I hadn't even opened the boxes, sometimes. Cosmetics, a little fold-up DVD player, a sewing kit, packages of underwear, an Iraq war snow globe, a neck pillow with a built-in speaker . . .

Where would one even start cleaning it up? I'd just pile some portion of this detritus into a bag when it was time for me to move on or go home, whatever home meant, leave the rest behind. Someone else would deal with it. I was tired. So tired.

I turned off the lights and lay down without bothering to brush my teeth or wash my face. I closed my eyes. I saw things on the back of my eyelids. They weren't good things.

I got up, turned on the lights.

Half an hour later, my place was spotless. I'd even vacuumed. Two huge trash bags stood outside my door. I'd take them to the FOB dump in the morning. I was exhausted.

Still, sleep wouldn't come.

I remembered that the photos I'd brought to show Carrie Johnstone were still folded up in my jeans pocket. I'd never even shown them to her. She hadn't asked to see them. I had a burn bag next to my desk in the office, but none in my quarters. The kind of thing you'd put in a burn bag, it wasn't ever supposed to come home with me. I took my jeans out of my laundry bag, took the photos out of the jeans. The printouts were folded into quarters, with the images on the inside so I wouldn't have to look at them when I handled the papers. I put the printouts on my side table, still folded, and got back into bed. It was like they were a light, shining on the backs of my eyelids when I closed my eyes.

Fifteen minutes later, I was in the tiny bathroom, and the photos were in the sink. I set them on fire. They curled as they burned, and exposed flashes of the pictures inside. A face. An arm. A torso. I couldn't look away.

They were practically all ash when the smoke alarm went off. Even by FOB standards, the sound was loud, in a way that, say, passing overhead jets couldn't be. I hastily turned on the taps and swept the soggy ashes down the drain, seeing that the fire had scarred the hard-wearing plastic of the sink. I tried to reset the smoke alarm and nearly broke my leg falling off my rolling office chair, and then it stopped on its own.

I waited for someone to come and investigate the alarm, but no one did. Fire suppression was handled by another contractor, of course, so I could probably burn to death and all it would mean is that the contractor would get another $40 million to upgrade the sprinklers.

I clearly wasn't going to sleep. I got dressed, showered, and went to my desk, where I did my job with robotic perfection all day, and then I did it again, and again. Three days later, I got a promotion.

Carrie Johnstone showed up at my cubicle as I was packing up for the day, putting my notes in my desk safe and shutting down my computer. She watched me finish up.

"Got a second, Masha?"

I followed her woodenly into her office and waited while she closed her door and settled herself behind her desk, sitting down on her little sofa when she told me to.

"Masha, you've done excellent work here, met and exceeded every expectation." I was about to get fired. "I think you know that, but it bears repeating. Excellent. Really, really, just . . . *excellent*." She was so uncomfortable. Probably trying to figure out how much she'd have to offer me in hush money.

"That's why I'm going to miss you so much." Oof. I'd been expecting it, but . . . oof. I felt like my head was a balloon, detached from my body, bobbing against the ceiling, watching the scene. She grinned. It was a very uncomfortable grin. "But I can't argue with the logic of it. You see, my boss's boss—the

founder of Zyz, Dick King, has been reading about your refinements to the All
Of It program, and Masha, he's *impressed*."

I began to understand that I wasn't being fired.

"It's clear to everyone in the business—in the whole industry—that this is
our future. All that shit where the CIA was dressing up agents in Lawrence of
Arabia drag and putty noses and sending them into the field to try to figure out
what was going on, that's dead. It's fun kicks for the agents, but all it produced
were *anecdotes,* not *facts.* The plural of anecdote isn't fact." Her grin got more
genuine, like she knew she'd told a real funny there. "The data don't lie. So
we're going into the data business. It's the new oil. It's the new *gold,* Masha.
Bigger than gold. And you're very, very good at data, girl."

I wasn't being fired, I was being promoted.

"The new business unit is being set up in Mexico City. It's a great location, better than this shithole—real culture, real food, a short plane trip back
stateside if you need healthcare. Plus the region is *begging* for these kinds of
services. We're getting the best and brightest there, Masha, and you're going
to be a star."

My face smiled at her. "That's amazing."

"You get a week in the Green Zone before you go, it's a little thank-you and
good-bye present from Zyz Iraq. You can spend it in your hotel room binge-
watching Netflix if you want, but I strongly recommend seeing the sights. The
Green Zone is like Mardi Gras crossed with Vegas. You can get anything, do
anything. Go to a pool party and find yourself drinking boat drinks between
a senator and a billionaire. There's never been anywhere like it, anywhere on
Earth. And you've earned it, Masha."

I said some things, and they were probably the right things, because Carrie
Johnstone offered to take me out for a drink when I said them, to celebrate,
and so we did, and we must have talked about something, but I can't tell you
what it was. I remember stumbling into my quarters, now neat as a pin from
my obsessive organizing, and realizing that there wasn't a single thing there I
wanted to take with me when I left. I picked out a couple changes of clothes
and some basic toiletries and stuck them in a shoulder bag, looked at the rest
of it, and shrugged.

Two days later, I was on my way to the Green Zone in an up-armored

Hummer, sandwiched between four goons, watching the desert unfurl through the smoked windows.

A gainst my better judgment, I took a hack at deworming Tanisha's phone. I knew I'd seen something about being able to reset baseband radios to factory defaults by shorting a couple contacts, so I patiently melted the glue that held its case together, working with a blow-dryer and bunch of Tanisha's bass guitar picks to gently work the case apart. Neesh loved the show and I certainly felt like a total ninja, peeling open the phone on Tanisha's little breakfast bar, laying the pieces down on a clean T-shirt weighted at the corners with heavy lowball glasses from Tanisha's cupboard.

But once I had the phone laid bare and had looked up the right pins to short and then did so, carefully, with a pair of Tanisha's tweezers, it remained infected—I cabled it up, booted it into diagnostic mode, and had a look at the ROMs and confirmed it, then did it again, just to be sure. Either the instructions for reinstalling to factory default were wrong, or this malware had squirmed so deep into the baseband that it was in the factory defaults. Which was a neat trick.

"Sorry, this thing is toast."

Tanisha made a face. "I need my phone."

"We'll get you a phone."

Now she looked upset. "You can't just buy us phones."

I looked around the apartment. "Call it rent?"

"My lease doesn't let me sublet." But she was grinning a little and I knew I had her.

"I know a place in San Francisco where we can get cases like mine, we'll take the BART over and—"

"Did you just call it 'the BART'?" Tanisha looked horrified, and only half-joking.

"BART. Shit, Neesh, I've been an expatriate for more than a decade. What do you want from me?"

"Just try not to embarrass me in front of my friends."

I didn't bother to close up the phone, just put it in a baggie with its assorted parts, films, screws, and connectors and handed it back to its owner. If Tanisha

was going to cave in to the temptation to make calls before I could replace her phone, she'd have to figure out how to reassemble her phone first—like when my mom froze a credit card in a block of ice so she'd have it for emergencies but couldn't impulse-buy with it.

The guy behind the counter at the place that sold the high-security cases was clad head to toe in rigid, deep blue Japanese designer denim that was so stiff he creaked when he walked. They only took cash and cryptocurrency, which was cute, but I gave them cash. Neither of us wanted to create a paper trail of who owned a case that could detect government malware—I could think of a hundred ways to exploit such a list.

Then we walked into a T-Mobile store and I paid cash for a pay-as-you-go phone that would fit the case, and we went to a crappy café where the staff made espresso by putting a pod in a machine and pressing a button and drank crappy coffee while I vetted the apps that the new phone tried to reinstall when we connected to Neesh's accounts. A couple of them were unsalvageable: games that just refused to work unless you gave them way more access than they needed, like your phone number and your full storage. I straight up banned those, then went through the rest of the apps and changed their permissions to the absolute minimum, throwing away anything that insisted on more access than it needed.

By the time we were done, Tanisha was a mixture of bored, frustrated, and curious. I always stopped what I was doing to explain it when she had questions, which she appreciated, but it also made the whole process take longer. Plus, she was going through mobile-device withdrawal. I thought we'd hit the bricks again when I was done, but of course she needed to go through her apps and answer all the alerts that came in while I was working. So then it was my turn to be bored.

I had been avoiding checking in, wanting/not wanting to know if there was news about Kriztina. I had done everything I could not to worry about her, because it was her idea to stay in Slovstakia, and she was a big girl who had to be responsible for her own decisions.

(Even when those decisions landed her in a torture chamber.)

But it was only the usual background noise of spam and recruiters offering me jobs with companies even more morally challenged than Xoth (business

was good for that sector) and news alerts about news I didn't care about. Neesh was in her own world, so I put my phone down and did the unthinkable, actually observing the other flesh-and-blood humans around me to distract myself.

I didn't recognize him at first. I recognized his girl instead, that searing asshole-to-earlobes jolt of jealousy that made me embarrassed to be me even before I'd consciously registered what I was feeling. Then, next to her, noticeably taller than her even when sitting down, him.

He'd grown a stupid scruffy beard and let his hair get longer and he had a honeymoon tan, but it was unquestionably Marcus Yallow. Unquestionably Marcus Yallow was of course *not* drinking one of the crappy coffees from a pod, because Marcus Yallow would sooner die. Instead, he had a dented, stickered metal water bottle with a carabiner that he slurped from while he ate an oatmeal raisin cookie.

I hate raisins. Sweetened rabbit turds.

I had stared at him for too long—inevitably, he noticed me and looked back. His eyes narrowed, then widened, then he smiled like he was recognizing an old friend, then he looked trapped as he realized *which* old friend he'd just recognized and who he was sitting next to. There was a quarter of a second in which we could have both looked away and plausibly pretended not to have seen each other and then it was past and the world spun on its axis.

He waved, and so his girlie looked over and *she* recognized me and waved too, because of course she did, she married him and I went off to the other side of the International Deodorant Line to spy on dissidents with bad opsec. She was safe.

Then Tanisha recognized him, of course.

So, all of us now trapped in this dance together, they got up and walked over. I hugged her first and then him, a mannered kabuki in which I acknowledged her claim and then affirmed that I was big enough not to have a grudge. Introductions followed and they sat down with us, inevitably.

He cocked his head at me. "You're back in the USA?"

"Yeah. You too, huh? How was the honeymoon?"

They made noises, told us about Ange's grad school graduation ceremony, but didn't subject us to slideshows on their phones which meant that they knew which way was up. She was a little sunburned from their beach time, and it looked incredibly cute on her, a contrast with all the pale nerds around us, bleached gray by the light of their laptop screens. "Why'd you come back?"

I was about to say something meaningless and then Neesh busted in with, "I was hacked by the Oakland cops."

Was she a little bit proud? Yes, she was. Badge of honor, right? Also: she knew Marcus. It was like dangling a steak in front of a hungry dog. Like releasing a crippled mouse in front of a frisky tomcat. He grew two inches, widened his eyes, and leaned forward like he wanted to leap across the table.

"What happened?"

"We don't know for sure." It wasn't nice of me to cut Neesh off, but I also didn't want her to mangle the explanation. I sketched it out for him: the binary transparency warning, the baseband attacks, the attacks on known-proximate devices. He lapped it up. I watched his girlie's face. She wasn't as technical as he was—though he wasn't as technical as he *thought* he was—and I wondered if she would follow it. But she was clearly keeping up, interrupting a couple times to ask for clarification. I was sure that there were a few things Marcus himself didn't understand but wouldn't admit to, lest he seem ignorant in front of the ladies.

"Now I have this." Tanisha held up her phone in its chunky case, turned it over and pressed the recessed button to light up the display on its back. White type marched down the black screen, logging all the chatter between the baseband radio and the tower. This far from Oakland and the Super Fusion Center, everything was normal, though once both of our phones had chirped in unison as a cell-site simulator in a van drove past us down Market Street, briefly capturing the identifiers from everyone in the café, sidewalk, and nearby offices.

Marcus lit up and made a *May I?* and she nodded.

He whistled as he scrolled through the logfile on the back screen. "This is the best one I've ever seen. Slick. All the ones I've seen were 3-D printed and kind of plasticky."

I couldn't help myself. "There's a co-op, ex-Palantir kids who vested out and started a maker space. They mill the aluminum and print their own circuit boards. Friends of friends. There used to be a waiting list but now that they've ramped up production there's no problems."

He nearly dropped the phone when I said the P-word. I didn't let myself smile.

"You trust it?"

As in, *Do you trust that people who made their fortunes spying on people wouldn't screw you over?* I rolled my eyes. *Oh, baby, if you only knew.*

His girlie—his wife—his Ange—picked up the phone. "What are you going to do about it?"

I launched into a little canned opsec monologue about what I wanted everyone in Neesh's cell to do, which apps they'd use, which proxies, which gadgets. She waited me out and nodded.

"But what are you going to *do* about it?"

I didn't know what the hell she meant, but I also didn't want to look stupid in front of her. I turned to Neesh instead, like, *Hey, I'm just an ally here, what do you think we should do?*

Tanisha didn't care about looking stupid. "What do you mean, Ange?"

Ange looked at Marcus, like, *All you people and your dumbass ideas.* "I mean, like, are you going to ask your lawyers to sue the Oakland PD or the feds or whoever? Are you going to publish a technical analysis of the malware? Are you going to fight back?"

Oh, *that.*

Neesh smiled. "I get you. That would be a good battle to get into, but you know, in the BBA, we're fighting the war. White supremacy. Late-stage capitalism." Ironic inflections that were pure Neesh, ha-ha-only-serious. "I don't think we'll get justice out of the OPD this time, no matter how egregious the shit we catch them doing is."

And girlie-Ange actually thought about that for a good long while, hadn't been just figuring out what she'd say when Neesh was finished. We all watched her. "That's a good point about OPD. I was there when they hit that guy with the tear-gas canister, shot him in the face with it, killed him. He was a veteran, too. No charges. So yeah.

"But what about all the people they're spying on with this stuff? The people who have the bad luck to walk past your apartment or sit in the same café as you. You said they were targeting anyone who got too close to your SIM, right?"

I nodded.

"So all those people, some of them are possibly not crazy radicals, no of-fense. Some of them are probably rich white people who won't like knowing that they've had their phone bugged because they happened to buy a latte while you were in the room. Maybe if you get *those* people angry about this, they'll be able to make life harder for OPD and all who sail on her."

I realized that Marcus and I were giving her the same look, which was something like, *Oh, man, that sounds like a lot of work and I wouldn't even know where to begin.* I mean, I know how to make a phone harder to wiretap, but aiming angry rich people at powerful police forces? That was sorcery.

She recognized the look, but she didn't care what we thought, anyway. It was Tanisha's show, after all.

Neesh looked thoughtful. "I don't like the idea of getting justice only be-cause rich white people don't like getting caught by cops who're looking for us. I mean, that's not exactly fighting white supremacy, is it?"

Ange didn't get defensive, which was super-admirable, and kind of irritat-ing. "That's an excellent point."

Tanisha clearly hadn't expected her to give up on her cool idea so easily ei-ther. Neesh continued to process, and both Marcus and I strained not to jump into the silence. Marcus because, well, Marcus, and me because silence made me think about my own shit, and my own shit included Kriztina and her own attempt to make Slovstakia and all its Borises be fair and free and all the things we were supposed to be in America. But I held my tongue.

"But you're right that this is some grade-A bad, indiscriminate spying shit," Tanisha said at last. "What if we could find some lawyers to get an injunction forcing them to cut it out? And then what if some of those rich powerful people they've been spying on filed a fat lawsuit? We keep trying to force Oakland PD to get public comments before they buy new spy-gear, maybe if they lost their shirts for not doing that . . ."

Marcus beamed at Ange. "I love it when you point out how dumb I am."

I didn't roll my eyes.

Tanisha started tapping out notes on her phone. "I'm going to talk to some lawyers about this. Masha, do you think you could write up a forensic report on my old phone?"

I didn't sigh. "Yes, I can do that."

Marcus was bouncing up and down in his seat. "You'll need to be able to replicate the attack. Tanisha, can you change phone numbers to a burner account and give me your SIM? We can get a bunch of cheapie phones and prepaid SIMs and work up a demo. I could write it up and send it to Black Hat—it'd be killer. Unless you want to present it, Masha?"

J. F. C. "You can have the glory." Like I'd want my name out there as someone who you could call if the cops were spying on you. Might as well paint a giant target on my ass too.

He didn't notice the sarcasm. Ange did, but she ignored it. Now she and Tanisha were deep into it, figuring out what their legal strategy would be. That left me and Marcus in our own little conversational bubble.

"That was an epic wedding present."

"I'm glad you liked it."

He smiled. "It was all anyone could talk about at the reception. I'm sorry you couldn't make it."

"I was overseas."

He nodded and carefully didn't ask where I'd been and what I'd been doing.

"I'm really glad you're back in town and working with these folks." He tilted his head toward Tanisha. "We need it. It's dark times right now. I can't believe how bad it got and how fast. Like, I'd spent years telling people that the internet could be the world's most powerful surveillance tool, but even I was surprised by how quickly it all changed."

I took a deep breath and made sure my voice was level. "It didn't all change, Marcus. It was always like that. You're always talking about internet history, but you ever hear of CALEA?"

He frowned and then had to admit that there was something he didn't know.

"It's a wiretapping bill, passed in 1994. It says that any switch that handles voice has to have a backdoor so the cops can tap into it remotely, without getting help from the phone company. It was sold as a way of tapping *phone* conversations and not as an internet-tapping law, but of course, it was only a couple years later that we started sending voice over the internet and the FBI started insisting that all switches come with this backdoor. Literally since the earliest days, there've been cops and crooks figuring out how to use the net to spy on people."

He opened his mouth to say something and I held up my hand.

"That's the problem, Marcus. There isn't a pure, surveillance-free internet to go back to. The spying on the internet today is *exactly the same* but more so. You'd have seen that if you hadn't been so drunk on your little hacking adventures, tinkering around with your homemade laptops and playing woke James Bond."

He rocked back and then rallied quickly. "I prefer 'Cyber Che Guevara,' actually."

The other two were now watching us like tennis spectators. "I'm not surprised." It was a lame volley, and even though I'd scored some big points on the serve, I could tell that I was losing. "My point, Marcus, is that if you want to protect people from spying, you might just have to protect them from computers, not with computers."

He grimaced. "How does that work? You want people to stop using computers?"

I started to say *no* and then *yes* and then I shrugged my shoulders. I hated this. How had I ended up with the duty to protect the meek and powerless from the strong and powerful? That was exactly what I signed up *not* to do. The spectators were spectating, and the clock was ticking for me to surrender to Marcus Yallow. So I did what I had to do.

"What's the best way to secure a home camera in your bedroom that's connected to the internet?"

He snorted. "Are you kidding?" He opened his laptop and showed me the EFF sticker he'd put over the camera's eye.

"There's an old martial arts story, Marcus. A student asks her teacher, 'O, Sensei, what should I do if I find myself walking down a lonely alley at 2 a.m., and there's no one around and no streetlights and there are three armed men all bigger than me who attack me?' And the teacher says, 'Don't go down an alley at 2 a.m., and if you do, choose one that's well lit, with people around you.'"

Ange smiled. Marcus looked thoughtful. When did he get thoughtful? Marriage was working out for him, apparently. It had to work for someone, I guess, or we wouldn't keep doing it.

"Okay," he said. "But abstinence-based education doesn't work. Telling people not to use computers will just make them write you off."

"I'm not talking about abstinence. I'm talking about mindfulness. The opposite of abstinence isn't promiscuity, it's fucking who you choose, under circumstances you give some thought to." Talking about fucking made him visibly uncomfortable. Good. "At a certain point, when the question is 'Why does it hurt when I do this?' the answer is 'Don't do that.'"

Tanisha leapt in. "But if you tell people not to use Facebook at all, that just means that they'll use it behind your back. Not using Facebook isn't an option."

"So we use Facebook to teach people about alternatives to Facebook. Get them so they move their default communications off the platform, one inch at a time, until Facebook withers behind them. Because ultimately, if they're planning to change the world on Facebook, they need to expect that the world will take an interest in them and dig into their Facebook accounts."

Tanisha thought about it. Marcus looked like he wanted to jump in and then reconsidered it. He was getting smarter. No wonder it was so hard to hate him.

Tanisha spoke deliberately. "So let's try it. Maybe if we sue the Oakland PD over hacking our phones, it'll be easier to convince people that it's worth becoming technology vegans."

I gave her a thumbs-up. "I like that analogy. Even if we can convince them to be technology vegetarians, we'll be making progress."

So that's where we got to, in the crappy coffee place on Market Street: a group of semi-friends with two phones in cyber-armor, getting ready to sue the Oakland PD and teach the Black-Brown Alliance about mindful technology use. We were scrappy underdogs, but we had a plan and we were going to run with it.

I should have remembered that the first casualty of any battle is the plan of attack.

They hit us on the way back across on BART. The train had pulled out of Embarcadero station and into the tunnel—the new one, all shiny and well lit as befitted a defiant gesture against the terrorists who'd blown up the original—when it came to a stop and the conductor came on the intercom and crackled out an announcement about a brief delay.

The belts of the Oakland PD officers who entered our car were hung with less-lethals and networking gear, and each wore what looked a little like marksman's glasses with black rectangles of electronics on each temple: they were recording everything.

They moved down the car, slowly panning their glasses across each person's face. I could hear something in their gear buzzing every time they got a lock and a successful recognition and then they'd move on. People reacted with careful, controlled neutrality. All conversation ceased.

We looked at one another, Tanisha and Marcus and Ange and I. They were getting closer. We were underground, underwater, in a train, in a tunnel. There was nowhere to go. If they were looking for us, then they were going to get us.

They locked on Marcus. A brief pause. Those shooter's glasses had a little display in them too, I saw. These guys were glassholes, wearing dysfunctional tactical versions of the even more dysfunctional and long-abandoned Google Glass glasses (try saying that three times fast). Then they alighted on Tanisha. The cop stiffened up like he'd been shocked. We all saw it. He was white, young, brown-haired, a little chubby—a babyface. His partner was older, South Asian, white sidewall haircut and skinny. The two of them closed in on us.

"Ma'am," White Cop said to Tanisha. "Can we see some ID?"

Tanisha looked around the car. Everyone was watching us and trying not to let it show. A couple people—both black guys, both young—had their phones out and were recording. That was gutsy, and maybe stupid. I could see Marcus wanted to get his phone out. He kept it in his pants.

"Am I under arrest?" Like a bust-card come to life.

Marcus was pale now. I knew his story. My guess was that he was reliving a specific bad moment out of his past. I had an idea of which one.

"Not yet." Whitey was a comedian. His partner didn't like that.

"Am I being detained?" That was the next bust-card question. The one after that was *Am I free to go?* which would be hilarious given where we were.

"We'd like to check your ID, ma'am. You are legally required to identify yourself." The older guy was trying to keep everything cool. He could feel those cell-phone cameras drilling into his back.

"I think you are supposed to show him ID," Ange said. The older cop gave her a tight smile.

Tanisha slowly reached inside her jacket—they both tensed up and so we tensed up and so everyone who was watching tensed up too—and drew out her wallet with two fingers, opened it and brought out a California non-driver ID. We used to tease her about being the only one of us who never wanted to learn to drive.

The younger cop took it, examined both sides, then tapped it to a reader on his belt. Seconds crawled. We heard the buzz in both cops' systems.

"We would like you to come with us, please." The old guy said it calmly and in a voice tone pitched to carry, talking for the camera phones as much as for Tanisha.

"Am I under arrest?" She was so calm. Calmer than I'd be. I wondered if it was the first time she'd been arrested. I hadn't thought to ask.

"You are being detained."

"I invoke my right to counsel. I invoke my right to silence. I do not consent to a search of my person or belongings." She said them like a mantra, loudly, crisply, like a manifesto. One of the black guys recording her whooped. Someone clapped a little. It was a hell of a performance: an underwater civics lesson, delivered in a crowded tin can.

The cops just nodded like they'd heard it before. I'm sure they had. We all looked at each other like, *Are we going to let them lead her off?*

"I'd like to accompany her," Marcus said.

"Can I see your ID?"

Marcus swallowed. This was clearly going to go around and around in circles. Marcus could grandstand for days.

I held out my hand at him and took out my own ID, not nearly as slowly as Tanisha had, but still avoided getting gunned down where I sat. The young guy took it, nearly fumbled it, scanned it. Whatever data came up, it was more than would fit on his stupid little heads-up display, because he took out his phone and scrolled for a while, conferring with his partner.

Everyone stared at me. Everyone. I was someone the cops had to whisper about before deciding their next move.

"You're staying," the young one said. People stared harder. I was a snitch. An undercover. A diplomat. A VIP. The president's niece.

"I'm going." My mouth was dry. "I'm going and I'll either follow you until you cuff me or I'll come along quietly and not get in the way."

The young one rolled his eyes. "You are under arrest for obstruction." He began to recite my rights. Numbly, I held out my hands for the cuffs. The old one made a twirling motion and I turned around and put my wrists together behind my back. The cuffs were plastic, tight, but not painful. Maybe one of my little group said something. I couldn't hear over the roaring of the blood in my ears. What the actual fuck was I doing. The old one led me, the young one took Neesh. She wasn't in cuffs. We walked through the car and the cops said something to the conductor, who quietly asked the passengers, one on one, to clear out. They retreated to the other end of the car. The train jolted to a start. Its motion made me remember to say, "I am invoking my right to silence. I am invoking my right to an attorney. I do not consent to a search." Tanisha gave me an unreadable look, and the young cop rolled his eyes so hard they fell out and onto the dirty carpet of the BART car.

Our friends stood at the front of the crowd at the other end of the car.

"We're getting you a lawyer," Ange called after us. Marcus was tapping furiously on his phone. "We have their badge numbers!" Ange's voice carried remarkably well over the sound of the wheels starting to move again.

The cops turned us around. The train pulled into the station and the conductor's voice came over the platform PA to ask everyone to stay where they were during some important police business. That was us. The cops led us over to the elevator and touched in to its emergency call button with a cop-phone and the elevator dinged a moment later. They brought us up and up to the surface, where there was a police van and a whole cadre of cops. It was only as they put us into the van that I looked around me and realized that something was amiss. There was a silence in the street, an absence. Not so many people as there should be, though it had been a long time since I'd spent any time in Fruitvale, but something was . . . wrong. A cop—I didn't see which—put his hand on the back of my head and guided me into the back of the van. A pair of benches ran down the sides and no one else was in there, but there was graffiti, scuff marks, a smell that was close and hot and sour.

Tanisha was right behind me. We sat together. Two prominent CCTV bubbles were set in the back of the lockup, ringed by IR LEDs to keep the scene lit even in low light. We'd be showing up as hot bright ghosts on the video, false-colored with neon tones. Software waited patiently to record and text-to-speech transcribe our words. Maybe there was something doing sentiment analysis, hunting for incipient violence or self-harm.

"Well, that happened." Tanisha's smile was tight and brave.

I shook my head. "I'm sorry."

Side-eye from Tanisha. Two sighs. "You're pretty crazy for someone who's supposed to be all wise and calm and shit."

"Gotta stick up for my friends."

That tight smile. "You are a crazy person. What do you think they were looking for?"

"With you? You know. That thing we did today. Same thing. They'd been watching you and then you did something that suggested that you'd figured out what they were doing. Before you did that, they thought you might be dangerous. Once you did it, they decided you *had* to be dangerous." I shrugged. "My bad."

She actually laughed, and even though it was a small and brittle laugh, it was very welcome. "Masha, I *am* dangerous. Haven't you figured that out yet?"

Ha, ha. Only serious. I looked at her. We'd known each other since we were little, really little—we'd met in the third grade. She'd been quiet and serious, with straightened hair that she wore with barrettes. She studied like crazy and beat herself up when she didn't ace her tests, and hung out equally with the black kids and the white kids and the Hispanic kids, never being anyone's bestie.

Until we went on a field trip to the Chabot Space and Science Center and there weren't enough tables at lunch, so we ate together on the floor around the corner from everyone else, and I convinced her to sneak off with me to the earthquake house. We'd surfed that house like crazy until we got busted by a security guard and had to sit in the lobby for the rest of the day, ears ringing from our teacher's scorching denunciations. After that we were tight, calling each other late at night. (We learned to synchronize our watches and turn off all the ringers on all the phones before bed, and then one of us would call at a specified time and the other one would pick up. I invented that trick. Even then, I was the opsec specialist.)

By high school, we had fought and broken up and made up a dozen times and we were tighter than ever. Neesh continued to ace every test and do every extra-credit assignment, while I was the kind of nightmare student who calculated the minimum work necessary for a C-minus and did exactly, precisely that, with such polish and perfection that the teachers knew exactly what I was doing. I don't know how I developed my contempt for academia, but I eventually turned it into a little canned rant challenging people to explain how someone could be 74 percent competent at math or literature, and what the difference was between 74 percent and 75 percent. I think the reality is that I just didn't like being cooped up in school.

Eventually I started skipping to play alternate reality games. I fit the profile. But it was Tanisha who got us permission to form a school team and get excused from classes to play. It came with my promise that I'd bring my grades up to a B-minus (which I did with my patented C-minus laser-like, fuck-you precision). Before long, we were racking up incredible victories, beating every other team in the city thanks to our special truancy dispensation, combined with Neesh's devious puzzle-solving mind.

That was when I started to realize what an amazing set of superpowers my innocuous friend possessed. And that she'd had to develop these superpowers because no one takes little black girls seriously, not even in liberal-ass San Francisco. She'd had to be ten times better than me to get 10 percent of the slack I'd gotten. When I disappeared into Carrie Johnstone's demesne, I'd seriously considered recruiting her. Johnstone would have paid me a hell of a bonus for recruiting someone as smart as Tanisha, and I could have easily taught her to code, and much better than I could. But I knew that Tanisha would never work for the DHS.

She would never stoop that low.

# CHAPTER 6

The Green Zone *was* like Mardi Gras crossed with Vegas, lit with IEDs. Good-bye, FOB Grizzly's Frappuccinos; hello, Manhattans in prechilled coupe glasses served by buff guys with eastern European accents and cheekbones for days. Zyz kept a floor in a Hilton by the airport, with a couple of our guys by the elevators 24/7, and a nonstop party in the hallways that they smiled beneficently at and kept gently contained to our floor. I'd hardly put my bags down in my room before there was a knock at my door and I found myself facing a welcoming committee of three of my Zyz co-workers, tank top–wearing Californians with great bodies and white, white smiles. Frida and Denver worked in "logistics support" and Marco was a "procurements liaisons specialist" and it took me all of five minutes to figure out that their actual job was to get drunk and party with people from the US government and their preferred contractors.

I told them that I was between assignments and that I'd done confidential work at a FOB and they didn't bat an eye and quickly moved the subject on to my favorite cocktail and whether they had the right mixers for it.

The rest of the week passed in a literal drunken blur. Taking Carrie John-stone's advice, I went to three pool parties and drank boat drinks between a general and an admiral; a billionaire and a senate majority leader's chief of staff. Close enough for government work. Every. Single. One. of them tried to fuck me. The chief of staff needed a literal knee in the balls to be dissuaded. I missed the first time, getting his thigh, but I thought fast and tripped him and then kicked him while he was down, because that is how it is done (thank you, self-defense class). His expression went from lust-crazed to rage-crazed to insensate with pain in three flashbulb moments I can still recall clearly to this day.

By the time the week was over, I was so ready to go. The first time I treated my hangover with a Bloody Mary, it was cute. The third time, it was like I was poisoning myself. Then Frida hooked me up with some Provigil and my morning routine became two of those, each washed down by their own Bloody, followed by that weirdly intense wakefulness while I cruised the malls with my new besties or party-hopped, followed by a huge lunch at some five-star place in the lobby of a hotel brand that you could find within two blocks of Union Square in San Francisco.

I had two flings, neither of them memorable enough to discuss in detail, and one awkward case of puppy love from one of the Zyz goons by the elevator door who stumbled through an awkward declaration of his crush on my last day there. He was adorable and so, so stupid, and I didn't laugh in his face or anything, but I did tell him in no uncertain terms that I wasn't interested, that he shouldn't get in touch with me when he rotated back to the USA, and that he should keep himself safe and enjoy his life without me in it. I did my best, honestly, but I could tell he wasn't happy about it. Not my problem. I wasn't getting paid to use my big brains nursemaiding the fragile male ego.

Besides, I was off to Mexico City.

I had two hours in the Dubai airport, where I got a massage and a dubious herbal "hangover remedy" from a juice bar, then fourteen hours to JFK in first class, where I quickly succumbed to the free booze and started a dead soldier collection that a less jaded me might have found embarrassing. I was the only woman in first on either flight.

The US immigration officer—Latina, Brooklyn accent, middle-aged, tired—could see that I was half in the bag and when I told her I'd been a military contractor in a FOB in Iraq, she'd thanked me for my service and waved me through. I rechecked my bag to San Francisco and ate a stale pretzel, then did six more hours in a significantly shittier first class than I'd gotten on Etihad, sobering up and developing a pounding, jetlagged hangover that stayed with me at SFO as I got into a cab and told the driver to take me to the Nikko. My deal with Zyz meant I didn't have to stay with my mother.

The check-in clerk at the Nikko did that Japanese thing with my credit card, taking it with both hands and then giving it back the same way with a little bow. She wasn't any more Japanese than I was, and it reminded me of my stupid youth as a Japan-worshipping gamer and anime freak, though of course I'd been into pretending to be Japanese as a hobby, whereas the white girl behind the counter would probably get fired if she didn't get those little details right.

I was afraid that I wouldn't be able to sleep, but by the time I'd carded into my room I could barely keep my eyelids open. I thought about setting an alarm and didn't.

I ate the Japanese buffet the next morning, haunted by the ghosts of my friends Tanisha and Becky, and the times we'd saved up to visit the Nikko's fancy in-house restaurant for seaweed, salted salmon, and even natto, God help us.

I didn't call them, though. Instead, I texted my mother and let her know I was in town, and was she free that night? She called an instant later and the connection was crappy enough that I barely understood her, but, in laborious Russian, I set a time to meet her after work at a Russian place in the Richmond that she and I had eaten at for birthdays and special occasions when I was little. I got off the phone before she started crying but I still felt like a shitty, shitty person.

The thing was, I wasn't the Masha that my mom had known (I hadn't been that Masha since well before the Bay Bridge bombing, to be honest). I wasn't the Masha that Tanisha or Becky knew, either—and Marcus Yallow had never really known any Masha, but he especially didn't know that one and wouldn't have liked her very much, I'm sure, and it was thoroughly mutual.

*I* liked that Masha, though, unfortunately for me. My week in the Green Zone had been weirdly meditative, despite all the noise and partying and booze. None of the people I'd been with there were anything like friends. It was more like we were all temps hired by a really weird, wasteful company to enact a kind of performative debauchery, and while I had plenty of drunken conversations and a little sloppy, instantly regrettable sex, there wasn't anyone I connected with beyond the skin-to-skin contact. Even that poor crushing floor-guard and I had only glanced off each other, him falling for a performance of me, me deeply disinterested in anyone who'd fall for such a performance.

But with all that time in my own head, I'd been able to do some long-overdue thinking. My time at FOB Grizzly had been lonely, but busy. Too busy for any kind of introspection. Deliberately, if I'm being honest. Some part of me knew that if I spent too much time thinking too hard about why I was doing what I was doing (rather than how to do it better), I'd regret it. That part of me was right, of course, and that's how I'd ended up back stateside, on my way to Mexico City.

With the time I'd had to think in the Green Zone, I'd decided:

*a) That the world had some seriously shitty humans in it; and*

*b) That I had the power to stop at least some of them; and*

*c) That computers were going to be used to do that kind of thing no matter what I did; and*

*d) That there were plenty of shitty humans who would happily work on either side of the issue; and*

*e) If I wasn't working on catching bad guys with computers, it would up the overall shittiness of the whole project, and that wouldn't help anyone.*

I didn't add f), that I would make shit-tons of money by lending my ethically centered mad skills to the project of turning every computer in the world into a surveillance device (that went without saying).

The Masha that emerged from the Green Zone was a pragmatist on a mission: to catch bad guys, and to not let the other bad guys use computers to figure out who to disappear, torture, and dismember.

In that order (because pragmatist).

That Masha didn't want to have to hassle with all the dreary emotional labor of being a daughter and a friend to people who had all kinds of crazy, badly informed ideas about how the world should work. That Masha had the disposable income to put emotional labor behind her, to pull off the guy trick of paying people to do the work that women and poor people secured through favor-trading. New Masha didn't need a mother to nurse her when she was sick, didn't need besties to loan her money until payday, didn't need a dude to make her feel pretty on bad hair days or scratch the occasional itch. New Masha was an island fortress: FOB Masha, self-sufficient and impregnable. FOB

Masha had an AmEx Black card and could simply buy whatever she needed, and then pay the people responsible to leave when her needs were met.

But there was still some squishy remnant of Old Masha stuck to FOB Masha's shoe, the part that couldn't land in the same city as her dear old, dreary old mom without taking her out for blini.

My mom didn't cry until after the waiter brought the drinks. She wasn't really a crier and we didn't have the kind of relationship where she cried on my shoulder (or vice-versa, at least not for many years), but the room was full of disapproving Slavs glowering at my subpar daughtering so I let her cry on me, though it got snot on the amazing ninja-style hoodie I'd paid $500 for at a boutique in the Mission that sold clothes that looked like the stuff from *Assassin's Creed.*

When she was done, she blew her nose on a napkin and went into the bathroom to fix her makeup. The waiter had brought champagne (French, not Russian, because I was paying and I wanted the good stuff) and dark rye with salted butter. I ate carbs and fat and drank cold bubbles until she got back.

"Masha, I'm sorry. I was so worried for you over there, in that place. Every day I wondered if you were dead."

"You could have emailed."

Mom smiled. She'd shown up that night smelling like the perfume she wore on rare dates, and for her office Christmas party, and makeup that she'd repaired in the bathroom. She'd had me when she was eighteen, and despite several yo-yo flirtations with babushka-grade hips, she'd filled our fridge with diet food and nutrition shakes, and beaten back our Ashkenazi genes and their insistence on moving bagels from our mouths to our butts with perfect efficiency.

Young, slender, made-up, and smelling like a duty-free, my mother could have passed for a grad student on a big night out. In reality, she was an executive secretary who had wiped the nose and held the hands of an unending parade of mediocre white men who had been promoted through the ranks of Bank of America and never cared to bring along the personal assistant who'd been shopping for their wives and answering their emails. She had a killer game face, a smile that promised to be nonjudgmental and helpful no matter how fumbling your efforts to off-load your work onto her. She collected a small bonus every year and if any of her bosses had ever gotten handsy she hadn't bothered to tell me about it. As far as I knew, she was happy.

"I didn't want to disturb you, Masha. I knew you were doing important work. Government work." She looked down, picked up her champagne glass, touched it to her lips, set it down. "I didn't want to send an email and get an answer from your boss telling me you were dead." Ah, that much-vaunted Russian subtlety.

"Jesus, Mom."

"You asked." She had almost no accent left, but it came out when she was stressed. That "sk" in "asked" had an edge on it like the tip of a Cossack's horse-whip.

"I didn't die, Mom."

She rolled her eyes. "I know that. You also didn't call me."

"I called you today."

Mom's great Russian sorrows could become towering Russian rages in an eyeblink. This one was getting close. I was picking a fight with her, I dimly realized, because then she'd say terrible things that would justify my continuing to not call her while I was in Mexico City. Baiting her into letting me off the bad daughter hook.

"I'm sorry." Adults apologize. FOB Masha was an adult. "You're right, I should have. I knew that you'd be worried about me and things were stressful over there so I chickened out on having those hard talks with you. It was selfish and bad of me."

If I'd slapped her across the face, it might have startled her more. Maybe. But her jaw was practically scraping the table by this point. It felt good. FOB Masha didn't front. If I had an apology to own up to, I owned up to it. It wasn't like I cared about losing face. I had zero fucks to give about face. I knew who I was.

"Thank you." I'd never heard her use a voice quite like that. She looked at me, reached up with a tentative hand, and, when I didn't pull away, stroked my hair. "You're so grown up. Strong. Smart." She looked me up and down. "Beautiful. I'm very proud of you."

She'd said all those things to me before, but never in that order, never while locking eyes with me, never once I'd remade myself as a fortress of solitude and strength. It was weird; my utter severing of my need for her approval was the one thing that finally granted it to me.

"I'm sorry," I said again, because it had worked so well before. "It was shitty of me not to stay in touch. I'm going to Mexico City on Friday, that's where work is transferring me. I'll be almost in the same time zone. I'll call you, okay?"

She smiled like she was humoring me. "I'd love that." She didn't know I meant it.

"You can call me too."

"I will."

By the time dinner was over, I'd told her G-rated versions of the highlights of my Iraq tour, the dusty roads and the goons and the Green Zone. I didn't tell her about the work itself, except that I was "catching bad guys" but that I never left the FOB. As I told the stories, I heard them as from a long distance, heard how I made myself more of an active hero than I'd been, not a prisoner of fate going with the flow. Who was I trying to impress? Mom? Me? FOB Masha had some holes in its defenses. They needed shoring up. I would work on that in Mexico City.

By the time I paid the bill, I was more than half-crocked and I swear my mom was too. I'd never seen her drunk, not even when coming in from a rare late date. She was rubber-legged and huggy, with a huge smile that stirred memories of a long-ago childhood with a long-ago mom.

I took her home in a cab and told the driver to wait while I walked her to the door. She was drunk enough that she didn't realize that I still had a cab waiting and was surprised when I hugged her on the doorstep. I pointed at the car. "Got a hotel room."

That started the waterworks. She held on to me like a shipwreck survivor and switched to Russian, the language of maudlin motherly sentiments, telling me how beautiful I was, how much she loved me, how proud she was. I was conscious of the driver watching us through the windshield while the meter ticked up. I unwound myself from her bear hug, kissed her cheek, and got back in the cab.

I didn't see my mom again on that trip. Instead, I went to the Kabuki baths and had a massage, got my nails done, went to the movies alone at the

Metreon, and spent hours in the hotel gym, watching CNN while I ran on the treadmill.

Mexico City couldn't come too soon. I was itching to get back to work.

The cops separated us after they processed us. I was in a cell with a homeless woman who sat silently, whole body shaking, moving her lips without making a sound. The cop who put me in the cell told me not to worry, there was nothing wrong with her. I tried smiling at her when the cop left, but she stared right through me.

Time passed. The cellblock was quiet, people speaking in church whispers. Cops walked past with prisoners or without, on mysterious errands. I hadn't gotten my phone call yet, but I was sure that Marcus Yallow was out there calling every lawyer he knew, which wasn't the worst possible outcome.

Time passed. They'd taken my phone. I'd have to drop it in a shredder when I got it back. Who knew what mischief they were getting up to. There's a class of security problems called the "evil maid" attack, in which you have to figure out how to defend yourself against a hotel chambermaid who's been co-opted to work for your adversary and attacks your hardware while you're out of your room—say, having a swim, which I badly needed at that point.

Once your adversary has unrestricted, unsupervised access to your hardware, you lose. The number of undetectable ways to poison hardware was effectively limitless. A phone or a computer is actually several complete systems, with cheap, fully programmable systems-on-a-chip serving as controllers for your USB, networking, and other components. Plug the right device into the system and you can completely compromise it. My fancy network-sniffing case might tip me off if the device started to betray me, but there are subtler ways available to a sophisticated adversary pulling off an evil maid attack. I had my glitter nail polish on my laptop screws, but now that the bad guys had my phone, how could I trust the pictures I'd taken recording the pattern dispersal of the glitter?

This was the thing that Marcus Yallow and his co-worshippers failed to understand. Crypto and gadgets might be securable against enemy spies and criminals—maybe, depending on how targeted you were—but when it came to the government whose police force had jurisdiction over you, could arrest you and take your stuff away, it was game over. The government didn't even have to be very good at it: companies like Xoth would supply them with everything they needed.

Time passed.

I discovered the hard way that the toilet was plugged. The ensuing mess flooded the floor, and as it spread toward my cellmate, she gave me a withering look and pulled her feet up onto the bench.

Time passed.

The cop who finally came to get me stepped right over the mess on the floor like it wasn't there and led me out of the cell. I wondered if this was my phone call, or whether they'd feed me, or whether I'd get to see Tanisha.

Instead, they brought me to Carrie Johnstone.

She had taken over one of their interview rooms and was three-quarters of the way through a Frappuccino. Not one hair was out of place, and not one of them was gray. Her makeup was impeccable, and if she hadn't had Botox, then she was at her lifetime peak of visible serenity. She wore a structured, concrete-gray sleeveless top that showed off her toned arms and her collarbones, and her perfect manicure set off a diamond big enough to choke a housecat next to a slim wedding band with a single glittering rock.

She nodded at me as I was shown in, then nodded at the cop to let her know that she could leave. Once the door clicked, she gestured at the interviewee chair with a single finger, flashing that rock again.

"Congrats," I said, pointing at it as I sat, ignoring the growling from my stomach and the thudding of my heart. If Carrie Johnstone was here—

"Yeah. We had a destination wedding. Scrub, in the British Virgin Islands, no commercial aviation, only charters. We got a good crowd." Her way of telling me that since I'd left Mexico City, she had started hanging out with a better class of person than me. Even at my lofty pay grade, I wasn't in any position to charter a jet to her exotic island destination. "We got Paula Abdul to play. It was epic."

"Congrats," I said again. I wanted to lean across the table and drain that Frappuccino, mainline the sugar and caffeine and fat right into my starved bloodstream. She took a long slurp and set it down. Carrie Johnstone had logged a *lot* of hours in interrogation rooms on at least three continents. She knew what she was doing.

"You're lucky I was in town," she said.

"Hell of a coincidence."

That just hung out there. I had a guess already. She was waiting to see if I'd whip it out and lay it on the table where anyone could see it. Stupid poker-playing. I hate poker.

"When did Zyz get the Oakland PD contract? Is it just the Super Fusion Center or are you handling all their ops?" Meaning: *I know that Zyz is behind the malware I flushed out of Tanisha's phone—the same malware that bounced off my phone like a tennis ball because my opsec is better than your offense.*

She smiled. "All of it. SFPD next, I think, because integration just makes sense. That's why I'm out here, closing that deal. It's a big one. *The* big one, for me. My bonus—" She mimed dropping a boulder on the table. "BOOM. Private jet money, no more chartering." *See what you missed by quitting Zyz?*

"Congrats."

She shrugged modestly. "Hard work pays off. What can I say, we're the best."

"Uh-huh." I would have killed for that Frapp.

She took a final long slurp, making milkshake noises with the straw for longer than was necessary. I prayed for a timely brain freeze, but she was seemingly impervious. "So, Masha, what the fuck are we going to do."

"Is there a 'we'?"

She hitched up the corners of her mouth into an eyeblink of a smile for a grim nanosecond. "That depends on you. Do I need to spell this out?"

I shook my head. "You've sold Oakland PD on some kind of zero-day base-band radio exploit and they're being *really* indiscreet in their deployment of it. If word gets out, they'll have a serious lawsuit on their hands and probably a state investigation, if not a federal one. As far as the SFPD will see it, you guys sold Oakland PD a tool that got it into a horrific PR mess, and that'll be the end of your bonus." I mimed dropping a boulder. "BOOM."

"So you need me to be quiet about this, and also to convince Tanisha to do the same. Or you could bring the DHS in, send me to a supermax while my lawyers argue pretrial delays for a year or two, long enough to close the deal and ride out the vesting schedule. Do I have it right?"

"We wouldn't send you to a supermax. Those places are *nasty*." She made a showy shudder and then grinned at me. "You're pretty smart, Masha. But I knew that."

*Smart* was what Carrie Johnstone had called me in Mexico City, right before I took my little vacation.

Everyone in Mexico City was smart. Zyz's headquarters were in a gated office park by the airport, a little like a FOB, down to the Starbucks and the Pizza Hut, but I didn't live there—I had an apartment in another compound, just as heavily guarded, about five miles from the office, which could be a ten-minute drive (if I worked until midnight) or an hour (if I tried for a rush-hour commute). But most of the people I worked with were in the same building, and we all used the same black-car service to get back and forth, or to go into the middle of the city to party in the kinds of bars that were at the tops of tall towers whose basement elevator banks were behind hard security checkpoints. It was a hermetically sealed life, shuttling from airport to office, office to home, home to clubs, clubs to office—like we were living in a giant habitrail and the black cars were how we navigated the tubes between the common spaces and the living quarters.

Zyz was a giving and generous hamster owner, and it tipped new hamsters into the structure for us to socialize with: military personnel—mostly US, then UK, then Canadian, then a grab bag that included at least one person from the military of a country that Zyz was *definitely* not supposed to be selling stuff to (spoiler: it rhymes with "Shmarain"). These newcomers would drop in to deliver technical assistance or (more often) technical requirements: difficult integration challenges involving legacy systems, language localization problems, weird custom software written by the smartest programmer in the local technical college or by the president's daughter's boyfriend at a heavy markup.

They had *ambition,* these visitors. A typical question: "What if we could access every text stored on every phone in the borders and within one hundred kilometers of the border in neighboring countries?" A lot of these guys (they were almost always guys, and a depressing number of them hit on me in despicable, perfunctory ways) were early adopters, and after a couple drinks at the club after work they'd be gleefully spitballing ideas about what we'd be able to do when *everyone* had smartphones—these always-on cameras with GPSes that might even be used to start cars or as a substitute wallet.

I usually kept my mouth shut during these bullshit sessions; first, because I got tired of being interrupted all the time, and second, because I knew if I started talking I'd eventually get around to pointing out that they were of course already carrying one of these magical spy devices. Everything they could think of doing to millions of people just minding their own business was probably already being done to them. After all, these guys weren't randos who had forgotten to patch their phones—they were spooks and contractors to spooks. Exactly the kind of people who'd attract active threats deliberately targeting them, specifically. When they bothered to mention this kind of thing, it was with a lot of bravado about how great their opsec was. They clearly thought that the kind of spying they were so hard for was going to be exclusively directed at *other people*.

Two months in, sitting at the club in a crowded VIP booth with a guy from the NSA's Tailored Access Operations group, I noticed that he was being as silent as I was, amid all the Zyz boasting. He was young, no older than me, and had a kind of spectrum-y vibe that I'd gotten pretty good at spotting outside my own occasional glimpses in the mirror. He'd been drinking Cokes all night, and I was drying out from a couple weeks of overindulging so that was where I was at too. So we had that in common as well.

When the party broke up at about eleven—when the DJ changed over and the oontz music started throbbing—he stuck close as we left and contrived to share a black car with me back to the apartments. Zyz put up its guests in the same compound as us long-termers.

Once we were in and the divider was up, he looked soulfully at me and I thought, *Oh shit, not another creeper,* but then he said, "I'm not hitting on you." Nice thing about people on the spectrum, they weren't afraid to speak their minds.

"Okay."

"But I want to talk to you about something private."

"Okay." I waited. The silence stretched. Mexico City's lights whipped past the tinted windows as we cruised the largely empty night streets.

"Private," he said again. "Maybe on your balcony." He added hastily, "Or mine? Seriously, I am *not* hitting on you."

I believed him. I was also starting to get an idea of maybe what this was about. "My balcony. I probably want a drink and my liquor cabinet is very, very good."

All the Americans at Zyz Mexico City were fiends for Cuban rum, and I'd been skeptical at first because surely it was just the forbidden fruit effect. But after my first taste of Havana Club Selección de Maestros—the master distillers at each of Havana Club's plants picked their favorite fifteen-year-old barrel and then they were all blended—I'd bought a case of the stuff.

He was visibly nervous for the rest of the ride. Oh, he made adequate enough small talk about the work we were doing around the office—he'd been training me on XKeyscore, a new tool for searching massive troves of NSA intercepts— but he kept trailing off and looking at his fingers in the dark car.

He took off his shoes when we got to my apartment door, which was adorable. I sometimes forgot to take mine off until bedtime. The cleaners who came in twice a week took care of scuffs on the white tile.

I poured myself two fingers of spectacular rum and offered him some, but he shook his head, visibly tenser by the minute. But he did follow me into the kitchen when I went for ice and before I closed the freezer door, he caught it and held it open while he took his phone out of his pocket and put it in the freezer compartment. He nodded meaningfully at me. I rolled my eyes for show, but he was Tailored Access Operations, so if there was a way to spy on someone through a phone that seemed to be switched off, he'd know about it.

I powered down my phone and put it in the freezer, wondering if he was hoping to capitalize on the freezer's shielding, or the hum of the compressor, or both, or something else.

I didn't say a word as I unchained the balcony door, removed the charley-bar, and slid the door open (among its many charms, Mexico City still had romantic cat-burglar types, or so I'd been told). We both stepped out. The white noise from the street was distant but audible. It was late enough that almost none of the lights were on, and I stepped back inside and killed mine. Because opsec.

Once the door was closed, he slumped. He took a set of deep breaths, straightened, opened his mouth, shut it. I sipped my rum. He held his hand out and I passed him the glass and he took a slug, passed it back.

"I happen to know a thing or two about you. That's a thing that happens when you work where I work. I know your work history. I know what happened to your hand—and how."

What he meant was, *I know you helped Marcus Yallow bust the DHS and blow the whistle on the secret detention center on Treasure Island.* They'd called it Gitmo by the Bay, because that's what passes for humor among spooks and the people they spook on. I'd helped load Marcus into the back of a moving truck to get him and me out of the country and he'd slammed my hand in the truck's gate and stolen my phone, with its cache of damning photos. He'd never actually apologized for that.

I was starting to get a bad feeling. Carrie Johnstone knew where I'd come down on the whole Gitmo by the Bay thing in the end, knew what I'd gotten up to with Marcus Yallow. We'd discussed it once or twice and she'd dismissed it as youthful exuberance, a lack of appreciation for the big picture. It only came up when she'd had a couple large glasses of wine and was in the mood for some ambiguous teasing that might or might not be pure sadism.

I didn't think that Carrie Johnstone had put that in my personnel file, because that would be the kind of thing that would make it very hard for me to work for her. But she'd clearly put it somewhere, and this guy had found it.

I wished I could remember his name. I'd learned it (assuming it was his real name), and immediately forgotten it. We got a lot of visitors and I couldn't be bothered to learn their names. Their emails were all that counted, and those had sigfiles to jog my memory about who they were and who they worked for.

"You know about my hand." I flexed it. It didn't hurt anymore, except after long typing sessions, and that could just be the baseline technology ache.

He nodded.

"What's your name again?"

He looked startled, then he smiled, which I hadn't seen much of so far. "Raymond. Ray, usually."

"Hi, Ray." I let him shake my hand, just to prove that it didn't hurt anymore.

"I know about your hand, and I know what kind of person you are, and that's why—" He stopped and looked out at the city, at the other balconies, at the ground below us. He dropped his voice. "I brought you this." He held out his hand again, like he wanted to shake with me, but this time he passed something small and squarish and plastic into my hand, warm from his body. "Only eight gigs, but that's all I could scrape without being obvious. The passphrase is the body of the first email that Marcus Yallow sent you after his trial, with all the spaces removed."

I slipped it into my pocket and thought hard. "Do I want to know what it is?"

He looked out again. "I want to tell you."

"Yeah, I figured you would. Do I want to know?"

"It's torture. Stuff we intercepted from the CIA, or, you know, maybe you could say they shared it with us. Bad stuff. Not all of it done by contractors, though there's some of that. Some of it was done by govies, too. But all of it is stuff we know about, stuff we're funding or aiding or turning a blind eye to. Bad." He looked out again. "Bad."

"What do you think I'm going to do with this? I'm not the Senate Intelligence Oversight Committee and I'm not the *New York Times*."

"Yeah, I noticed. I don't know, to tell you the truth. The thing is, I didn't sign up for this shit. I believe in the mission. My parents are both in the service. I went to West Point. I believe in the mission."

"You said that."

"But I do. Look, you know what it's like out there. There's bad stuff, stuff that needs to be dealt with. I'm proud of what we do, at least when we're taking care of all *that*. But I didn't sign up to be complicit in the kind of stuff I was finding out about. I tried to talk to my bosses about it, but they weren't hearing it. I thought about pushing it, or even going public, but then I looked at what they'd done to other people from the agency who spoke up. Guys like Thomas Drake and Bill Binney—they ruined them, trashed their reputations, called them traitors, sued them, prosecuted them."

"And they didn't make a difference, either."

He shook his head. "Not totally true. But they didn't make as much of a difference as you'd hope. They didn't fix things, even if they made things a little better. And no offense, it's getting worse because of people like you, contractors. We're moving all the really bad stuff into your in-baskets, writing you fat checks, then your bosses lobby my bosses to do more of it. Then, when my boss is ready to quit, your boss gives him a job at five times his government pay, and he goes back to the agency as private sector to lobby his old reports to keep throwing money at their old boss's new company."

"It's the Circle of Life."

That made him smile a little. "The Human Centipede. A positive feedback loop, where Process A accelerates Process B, which accelerates Process A, until the whole thing is going so fast it explodes."

"You think I can keep it from blowing up?" The little drive felt oddly heavy and warm in my pocket.

He shrugged. "I just wanted someone else to have the same data I had. In case—" I saw that he was trembling. "I see the people I work with, these old guys. They went in with the same ideas I had, and now, after decades inside, they're willing to burn down all their ideals rather than making a stink. I don't know exactly how that process works, but I can already feel it working on me." He looked away. "I thought that if someone else knew what I knew, someone whose moral compass was still fixed, that it would keep me honest. Like I wouldn't just let myself slip away. I don't know."

I was starting to get an idea. "Ray, can I try to translate all this for you? Like read it back and you can tell me if I've got it right?"

He nodded miserably.

"You're complicit in some really evil shit, but it pays the bills. You don't want to quit, because you like playing secret squirrel and knowing all the 'I could tell you but I'd have to kill you' bullshit that those jerks who sell their companies to Facebook at twenty-five and retire will *never* know. You found me in your creepy stalker searches and did a little background research on me and decided that I could be your Jiminy Cricket; now you're dumping all these radioactively hot leaks on me, so that I can somehow 'keep you honest,' like we're diet buddies or something, like if you don't blow the whistle on this stuff, I'll dump the docs for you. Do I have things more or less right?"

"When you put it that way . . ."

"Yeah. When I put it that way, it makes you sound like a coward who picked a stranger to do your dirty work because you don't have the courage of your convictions."

He held out his hand. "Okay, give it back."

I hadn't expected that. It made me like him more. "That's *better*. Good one, Ray. But I'm not going to give it back. I'm going to hold on to it and keep you honest. Because to tell you the truth, you were right about me. I believe in the mission, but I don't believe in the kind of moral flexibility that your bosses are so good at, not that my bosses are any better. And so long as we're telling the truth, I could fill up my own thumb drive with the stuff I've been asked not to think too hard about. I think maybe it's easier to do the right thing about someone else's dirty secrets than your own."

He smiled just a little. "Have you ever heard of credit-default swaps?"

"Finance thing. Company A holds a million dollars' worth of mortgage bonds from New York and Company B holds a million in mortgage bonds from London, and they swap the risk of them defaulting. New York tanks, Company B pays up—if it's London, Company A pays."

"Basically. I assume some of your risk and you assume some of mine, so if something really bad happens to me, you'll pick up some of the tab, and vice versa. We probably wouldn't swap London and New York because they're both big finance towns on the Atlantic exposed to a lot of the same climate and economic risks. But maybe New York and New Delhi—or Coca-Cola bonds and Tata bonds."

He was starting to remind me of Marcus Yallow. I heard the term "mansplaining" later that year and I remembered this conversation.

"Yeah, I get it."

"Well, this is like a swap, I guess. I'm giving you some of my moral risk, the risk to my conscience that I will chicken out and talk myself into sitting on this stuff forever like those zombies I work with."

"So I get to give you some of my risk too?"

He looked puzzled, then got it and shook his head. "No, it's just a metaphor." Then he realized what he'd just said. "Though, uh, I guess if there was stuff you wanted me to hold on to, for insurance—"

I waved him off. "I can take care of my stuff. Just wanted to know where I stood. This isn't a swap, it's just me assuming some of your debts."

"Risk."

"I think we can agree that the stuff on that stick is both risky and that your knowledge of it was a kind of debt to your conscience. So it's risk and it's debt."

"I guess the analogy is imperfect."

"Depends on whether its purpose was to clarify the subject or just make you feel better about dumping this shit on me." I didn't have any urge at all to make him feel better about his brave decision to put me in a position where I had to make a brave decision. He looked pained. Good.

"I can take it back—"

I took a step backward. "No, you can't, not really. We're now both into deep-shit territory, potentially, and this is the only leverage I have if things start to go bad. You're not getting it back."

He shook his head. "I think I was right about you, Masha. When I read your file and did some digging, I started to get an idea of what kind of person you are. The thing I saw, right away, was that you didn't kid yourself about what you were doing and why. I knew that if I brought this to you, you'd get it."

"Ray," I said slowly. "You are laboring under the misapprehension that you and I are in some kind of consensual relationship in which we share a set of common goals. The reality is that you've just hijacked me into something that's very, very dangerous, because you didn't have the guts to handle it yourself." I let that sink in. He opened his mouth a couple times to say something, closed it. "I can understand why you did it. You found yourself in a hard place. You know yourself well enough to be suspicious of your own integrity. That's admirable and even ethical. But let's not pretend that conscripting me into being your conscience was an ethical act. It was dirty as fuck."

"I'm sorry." He clearly was, too. The guy might be a spy but he was definitely SIGINT, not HUMINT. I wouldn't trust him in a kindergarten poker game. "Yeah, I get that."

"I see you do. Maybe it's time for you to leave."

He did, without fuss. A couple times I almost told him that it was all right, but I never did, because it wasn't. Part of me was furious with him for doing this. Part of me was just furious that I hadn't thought of doing it first. I transferred the files to my computer before bed, putting them in a plausible deniability partition that I spent a lot of time thinking of a passphrase for. Once I had the files stored there, I queued up a job to write zeroes over every sector on the thumb drive, over and over again, until I got up in the morning. I'd fill it with encrypted porn afterward, and use a weak passphrase. That completed the plausible deniability picture, all right.

I stared at the ceiling for a long time before falling asleep. The questions raced around my mind: Delete the files? Look at them? Report them?

Not that, I knew. Never that. Ray had that right, anyway.

I saw Ray a couple times more around the office that week and it was as awkward as if we'd hooked up. More awkward. A mere exchange of fluids would have been less consequential. We hadn't been practicing safe hex.

I ran into him with his roller-bag in the elevator lobby on his way down to catch his car to the airport. We were alone, except for the cameras.

"Safe flight."

"Thanks. It was, uh, really great to work with you, Masha. I mean it. You're doing amazing work here, and you're personally, well, you're good at your job. If you're ever in Fort Meade, look me up. I'll get you a tour. Maybe we'll hire you away from these private-sector types." He smiled. He looked sweaty.

"I don't think Uncle Sam can afford me. There's a certain manner to which I've grown accustomed to living."

"I hear ya. Maybe I'll hit you up for a job, then."

"Above my pay grade, Ray, but I'd write you a reference."

His elevator came, sparing us one more instant of excruciating banter. He shook my hand—sweaty palm—and left.

I didn't hear from him again until someone from the National Reconnaissance Office visited to work with us on merging satellite data with cellular location data and quietly slipped me a thumb drive, telling me that "Ray said you'd take care of it." My stomach did a slow roll when he said those words, half-convinced that Ray had been caught and this was a sting, half-convinced that it *wasn't* a sting, but that Ray was getting drunk in seedy Falls Church bars and telling anyone who'd listen that there was a chick in Mexico City who'd take their leaks off their hands no questions asked and see that they found a good home. It was hard to tell which would be worse, honestly.

I spent the rest of the day trying to find a way to sneak off with the NRO guy—American-born Chinese, Caltech comp-sci guy, anime hair—but he dodged me. When I saw him with his roller-bag, I took the service elevator to the ground floor and beat him to his airport car.

"I need to fill in some damaged baggage paperwork," I said. "You don't mind if I ride with you, right?"

He knew he was licked and threw his bag in the trunk without a word. He rated a town car with a privacy screen between the passenger compartment and the driver. It wasn't secure, not even by the standards of Ray and his phone-in-the-freezer balcony routine, but I made a point of putting my phone in my bag and then putting that in the trunk where the NRO guy could see it. He sighed and put his phone in the front compartment of his roller-bag.

Once we were under way, he turned on the radio—a Control Machete marathon that a local station had been heavily promoting—and cranked the bass all the way up, which either meant that he was into jeep beats or he believed that audio bugs had a hard time contending with bass interference. Then he leaned his head close to mine and said in the quietest voice that would carry over the music, "You can erase the damned thing if you want. But Ray said—" He broke off. Some secrecy instinct told him not even to whisper certain things.

"I bet he did. What is it?"

He gave me a long, considering look. In the dim light of the tinted windows, his eyes were dead and spooky: *You really want to know?*

"I'll erase it if you don't tell me. Drop it into the shredder." We had a big shredder at the office, kind of thing you could put a whole laptop into. When we did client assignments in some countries—Russia, China, Saudi—we would take burner laptops and work on remote servers, then drop the laptop into the shredder when we got back. Our internal ops team didn't work cheap; it cost less to replace a commodity laptop than it did to pay one of them to strip a machine down and look for physical bugs, dump the firmware on all the systems-on-a-chip controllers and make sure they hadn't been poisoned. That shredder could chew through a laptop in under a minute, titanium frame and all—a USB stick wouldn't last two seconds.

More of that dead-eye. Maybe it was the light. "Targeted assassination. Drones. In undeclared theaters of war."

*You had me at targeted assassinations.* I nodded. Did I want this stuff? I did, to my surprise. The US government and its contractors had a *lot* of dirty laundry, so much that no one knew how much. These guys, they'd all signed up to help their countries, and pretended there wouldn't be any dirty laundry on the way. The lucky ones learned to ignore the dirty laundry. The unlucky ones, it gnawed at them. They were going to Do Something, had to, to protect their images of themselves as being good guys, on the side of the right. They'd talk to each other, gather evidence, and . . . What? Leak it to the press? Take it home and hide it under the bed?

They might as well give it to me. I wasn't any better than they were, of course, but at least I could tell when I was kidding myself about which side I was on and what its shortcomings were. Whether its shortcomings were the sort of thing the International Criminal Court cared about.

"Okay," I said.

He raised his eyebrows. That wasn't what he'd been expecting. I wondered what Ray had told him about me.

"Okay," he said.

In its own way, Mexico City was as much of a hermitage as FOB Grizzly had been. Nominally, I was less isolated. On a good day at Grizzly, I'd speak to a Filipina Starbucks barista, a Bangladeshi Pizza Hut clerk, and Carrie Johnstone. My Mexico City crew "socialized" at least once a week, getting loaded at the club, and then there were the "bonus" nights when we were entertaining visiting clients and got to drink top-shelf booze on an expense account.

But I can't say I liked or even got to know any of my teammates. Sometimes, I couldn't remember their names—it was easier for me to tell who was who when I was in our source-code repository than when I was actually talking to people. They all blended into a kind of homogeneous median miltech-bro, West Point or Air Force Academy or Big 10, neat hair and sexist jokes, casual racism about Mexico and Mexicans, and bad spelling in their check-in messages.

So when Carrie Johnstone dropped by for a visit, I discovered to my surprise that I was glad to see her. I didn't like people, but I didn't like being lonely, either.

Her visit was a big deal. She was now VP of the branch of the company that our office was a kind of R&D department for. There were rumors that she was going to spin it out as its own thing and that we'd all convert our minuscule stock grants in Zyz into hefty equity stakes in the new company, which the miltech-bros were convinced would set them up for life. We were definitely "industry leaders in a growth field."

She set up in a corner conference room and drew the blinds, rotating in a steady stream of managers and managers' managers. They'd emerge looking wrung-out and retreat to their desks to deliver whatever it was they'd promised to "action ASAP," as our internal memos liked to say.

Us coder grunts pretended to work as the parade went by, straining our ears to eavesdrop on the whispered conversations between our bosses, trading rumors on the unofficial chat channels we used when we wanted to talk without letting the company in on our conversations.

Then I got an IM pop-up on my desktop, which made me jump and I had to suppress a squeak. I had alerts turned off for everything under almost every circumstance, because I didn't like being interrupted. Everyone in the office knew that I tabbed over to my email every twenty minutes or so, and if they wanted to talk to me, they should send an email and wait. If the office was on fire, they could come over to my desk and tell me so.

But I did have a small white list of people whose IMs would punch an alert on my screen, and one of those was the office manager, Iliana, who let me know when there was something at the front desk that needed my signature and when there was a driver waiting for me. I wasn't expecting either.

> Ms Johnstone would like a word with you

I looked up at the closed conference-room door and experienced the weirdest mix of relief (she *did* want to talk to me after all), pride (she didn't want to talk to any of these other assholes in the coder pens), and trepidation (am I in trouble?).

I walked to the conference-room door with all eyes on me, thought about knocking, but then grabbed the handle and let myself in, thinking of all those eyes on me, seeing me just barging in like me and the boss lady went way back, which we did.

At FOB Grizzly she'd been a little disheveled: haircut grown out, makeup sometimes smeary, often a little sweaty. That day, she looked as put-together as she ever had in our old days in San Francisco. That day, her bob and bangs were so blunt you could have used them to level a shelf, her makeup was so perfect it could have been laser-printed right onto her face.

She smiled at me and I decided she'd had more Botox as well, and made a guess that she was stationed in L.A., especially given the Beverly Hills look of her tailored lady-suit. She made me feel like I was wearing old sweats and rocking bedhead.

"Hello, Masha. It's such a pleasure to see you again." She held out her hand, half rising from her chair. I shook it: perfect nails, cuticles to die for.

"Hi, Carrie. Good to see you too." I slid into a chair across from her. She poured me a glass of water from an iced pitcher and slid it to me on a coaster.

"I have to say that we're all very pleased with the work you've done here." She took a sip from the glass beside her. "I didn't tell you this before I sent you out, but this division had been on thin ice before. The mobile implants they'd built were so unreliable and their progress was so slow that we were ready to give up on them. But after the work you did at Grizzly, I knew you'd be the perfect person to kick their asses into gear. You met and surpassed that expectation. You should be very, very proud of what you're doing here."

I was, at least in that moment. Unadulterated praise from Carrie Johnstone was so rare and she was usually so mean that it felt like I'd just taken home the gold in the spying Olympics. I tried not to let it show, because I knew that any sign of neediness would be filed away in Carrie Johnstone's memory for indefinite retention and eventual exploitation. But man, it felt *good*.

"Thank you, Carrie. It's been fun. Challenging. I like working with smart people."

"Then you must hate working here." She gave me a half smile and I gave her a half smile back.

"It's not bad," I said. "They just don't have a lot of field experience, so they tend to think of answers that solve their problems, not the problems the users will have in the real world. Maybe if we rotated them in and out of client sites . . ."

She nodded vigorously. "That is an excellent suggestion. I can't believe I never thought of it. It's so good to see you again, Masha. It's been too long."

*You said that already.* "Thanks, Carrie."

"Do you pay any attention to smart appliances?"

I rolled my eyes. "Stupidest idea ever. No one needs a toaster or a fridge on the internet."

"So you don't pay attention to it?"

"To be honest, no. I mean, I always figure that any sentence that contains the phrases 'brand identity,' 'action item,' or 'internet of things' is automatically bullshit."

"You don't think people will buy smart gadgets?"

"Oh, they'll buy 'em. People are dumb. But you shouldn't—and I won't."

"But someday, you can imagine targeting an appliance in an adversary's home?"

Oh. "Yeah, I can imagine that." I'd given it more than a little thought, to be honest. Smart cars, connected to the internet, smart thermostats, smart insulin pumps. Hearing aids turned into remote listening devices. Lethal shocks delivered to wireless pacemakers. Yeah, I'd thought about it. On reflection I wasn't surprised to learn that Carrie Johnstone had been thinking about it too.

"Well, there's been some talk about developing some internal capabilities on those lines. Talk at a very high level. We have some external customers who are *very* interested in that."

The documents I'd been given: torture, mass surveillance, rendering and murder, drone strikes. Add to that the ability to kill people in their boots by dumping a whole reservoir of insulin into their blood at once, or to listen in through their ears, to freeze them where they lived or run their cars off the road.

"I can see why they would be."

"Masha, the business that gets to this first is going to have it made. The people in that business who run that program—well, they're going to be able to write their own ticket. Zyz did five hundred million in billings two years ago. This year, it was three billion. With a program like this, it could be thirty billion. More."

There were opals in her earlobes, a string of pearls around her neck. That suit was hand-tailored. Carrie Johnstone wasn't hurting for money.

"You come up with some good ideas for this, we can set you up as an independent contractor: You'll go in as a cost-plus line-item expense, so the more you charge, the better our markup is—just make sure your number passes the giggle-test. We can still bonus you with options and you'd still have access to admin and travel services. You'd triple your take-home, and you could domicile yourself in Luxembourg or Panama and Uncle Sam wouldn't see a dime. It's the kind of thing we do for our smartest people, the ones we really want to take care of and keep happy.

"And you are smart, Masha. Very, very smart."

Carrie Johnstone buzzed in a cop and sent him out for burgers, like he was her PA or something. "What are you having? Cheese? Bacon? Please don't tell me you've gone vegan, Masha, I couldn't stand it."

I was still jetlagged and my appetite was all over the place. "Bacon double cheeseburger, fries, chocolate milkshake."

"That's my girl." She nodded at the cop. "Same for me. Get extra ketchup for the fries, okay?"

The cop's face was wooden as he turned on his heel and left the room. Carrie Johnstone gave his departing back a sarcastic, sprinkled fingertip wave and then let out an exaggerated satisfied sigh when the door clicked shut.

"Let's talk about Tanisha," she said, palms on the table, head cocked a little to one side.

I poker-faced it. "All right."

"She's not running with a good crowd, your friend Tanisha. Black identity extremists. Kind of organization where you scratch the surface and it's all Russian infowar stuff, targeted ads getting people riled up and in the streets." She shook her head slowly. "It's a pity. I can tell her heart's in the right place. It's right there in her file. But you can't deny that there's a legitimate interest in keeping an eye on that sort of thing."

I didn't roll my eyes. "The Black-Brown Alliance is a Russian front?"

"I didn't say that. Just that it's some muddy waters. The rank and file believe in the cause, but they don't have good information. They've been nudged and shoved around, pushed into a very ugly, confrontational politics that is designed to create civil unrest. Pushed to think of the police as enemy soldiers. Manipulated with weaponized, half-true stories about criminals being shot by law enforcement that make them look like victims instead of perps."

Now I did roll my eyes. I couldn't help it.

"Masha, you know this playbook. You *used* this playbook. Why is it hard to believe that someone would use it on your friends? Do you think those assholes in Iraq were stupid?"

That was actually a pretty good question. I realized I had, at some level, believed that they were simply stupid.

For as long as I could remember, the worst sin in my world was to bullshit yourself. If you had to do something evil because it was convenient or because it was inevitable or because it was well paid, then sure, be as evil as you need to be, but don't pretend that you were acting virtuously.

But I hadn't ever consciously thought through the possibility that you could be smart, self-critical, and just plain *wrong*. Misled. Tricked. Conned. Those kids whose loops I'd been inside of, with their trophy photos of rapes and murders: I'd always put them in the "stupid" box, partly because of the terrible, unforgivable things they'd done, but mostly because it had been so easy to pwn them.

And yet. Kriztina and her friends weren't stupid and the stuff I'd installed had totally compromised them. I knew the people who'd developed that stuff, the people who'd bought it, the people who'd sold it. They weren't supergeniuses. They were as flawed and self-deluding as anyone, and maybe more than most. They were able to comprehensively dominate a large slice of the world with tools that were so obviously flawed and badly thought through they wouldn't have lasted ten minutes as commercial software in the open market.

I'd been kidding myself. In some corner of my psyche, I'd convinced myself that the spy tech I worked on worked on people who were just too dumb to defend themselves, and in some way deserved to get spied on. But the reality was that the deck was stacked in my favor. The companies supplying their tech, their apps, didn't know or didn't care about people like me, and nothing my targets did would keep me out, not in the long run.

They were defenders: they had to make no mistakes, ever. I was an attacker: I had to find one place where they'd made one mistake and use that to slip past their defenses and destroy them. They never stood a chance.

"It's the Russians, huh?"

Carrie Johnstone nodded. "Who else? The Chinese hold too much US debt to bother with this kind of tactic, and the EU is too busy tearing itself to pieces to pay attention to us. No one else has the attention span or budget to try it except the Israelis, and they're on notice not to mess with things over here."

Did I believe her? Carrie Johnstone had lied to me plenty of times. Nothing personal. It came with the job. She probably didn't want me to go to jail, both because she felt some kind of demented affection for me and because she wanted me to owe her a favor, not a grudge. Convincing me that Tanisha was a Russian stooge could be a way to get me to abandon Neesh and her friends.

But yeah, I had used those tactics. You didn't have to be stupid to fall for them, either.

I had never paid much attention to Tanisha's actual politics. I'd always thought of her stuff—and Kriztina's, for that matter—as a side in a strategy exercise. They wanted to do X; they were fighting people who wanted to stop them, and keep Y in place. X and Y were just placeholders, and the only thing that mattered about them was that one side was the insurgents and had to use insurgent tactics, and the other side was the authority and got to use authority tactics. What did the insurgents and authority want? Did it matter?

It mattered a lot to Tanisha. Did it matter to me? I was white and rich and knew how to make the system work for me. Tanisha could make the system work too, but chose to work against it. Chose to fight for people she didn't even know. I knew Tanisha well enough to know that doing that work probably made her feel very good about herself, but I also knew her well enough to know that *not* doing the work would destroy her. She couldn't sit by and watch bad things happen. Never had been able to. Better to look yourself in the mirror knowing you tried your best.

Or, as Marcus Yallow liked to say, *When in trouble, or in doubt, run in circles, scream and shout.*

"Smart Russians."

"Don't be funny, Masha. Your friend is in a lot of trouble and there's still worse that can happen to her. I know you want to help her. You always want to help your friends. It's an admirable quality. I can give you a way to help her."

"What's that?"

"A get-out-of-jail-free card. You and her, you just drop this business. She quits her little protest group, just cuts it out completely, and I'll see to it that whatever happens next, it doesn't happen to her. That is a *very* fair offer, Masha."

*Yeah, that's mighty white of you.* "And you get your SFPD contract, and your bonus, and—"

"Yes, that's what we get out of it. Masha, once that deal is done, Zyz is going to need to staff up quick. There's not much talent out there with the kind of skill set—"

I couldn't help snorting. "Zyz isn't going to hire me."

She shook her head. "Even after everything, you still don't understand how Zyz operates. Masha, we are a *results-first* organization. Money talks, bullshit walks. We hire the right person for the job, because we're a team, not a family. The fact that you have had disagreements with us in the past"—she pretended not to notice my snort—"doesn't disqualify you from working for us in the future. We don't bear grudges. We're a meritocracy. We care about what you can do, not what you've done or who you are."

"Well, that would explain the goons working your security."

"I know you're joking, but that's actually a really good example. There's plenty of guys working for Zyz who've been in one kind of trouble or another for aggressive use of force in the field. Thing is, you *want* aggressive guys working in those roles, and you can't ask a man to aggressively do his job and then get pissy when he gets too aggressive. When that happens, you've got to give him feedback, maybe some training. But if you fire everyone who's ever squeezed off a couple more rounds than necessary, you'll end up with no one at all, or a bunch of pacifists guarding your back. We're realists, in the real world. No one is perfect, but we can build systems that compensate for our imperfections and get the job done."

I didn't point out that Carrie Johnstone herself was quite the beneficiary of this flexibility, given her own history with "overly aggressive" surveillance, detainment, and interrogation. She knew. Hell, it proved her point. Carrie Johnstone Got Shit Done. If you're a Get Shit Done type of person, sometimes you'll make a mistake or two. The DHS hadn't been able to tolerate Carrie Johnstone's occasional errors in judgment and they lost her; Zyz was smarter and so they got to keep her. That was Carrie Johnstone logic. It was very tempting. If I had never met Herthe, I might have believed in it.

"I need to talk to Tanisha before I commit to anything."

"Yes, I imagine you do."

"Can you make that happen?"

"I'll do what I can. I'm just a civilian contractor, after all." Her smile told another story. They took me to a new cell, much nicer, and all my own.

Carrie Johnstone called me smart but if I were really smart, I would have deleted every incriminating file and told every one of those spook-boys who visited me from Langley or Fort Meade with a USB stick to jam it up their tight, white asses. But I didn't and I didn't and then there came a day when I got a USB stick from a guy who was more squirrelly than most, a guy who wouldn't say a word about what was on it. I'd developed a rule, I would only take new files from people if they'd tell me why they were handing it over. Partly because I wanted to know what I had (though I'd verify that later), and partly because I wanted to make them own up to their own situation: participating in something they found so terrible that they were leaking it to me, but not so terrible that they were willing to quit doing it, or go public, or sabotage it.

This guy, tighter and whiter than most, had only been at the Mexico City office for thirty-six hours, a flying visit on behalf of his superiors at the Air Force Air Mobility Command. He maintained their "persona management" tool, which let their overworked, thin-stretched Arabic-speaking operatives each impersonate up to twenty people online, keeping the biographical and other details for each identity separate. He was finding ways to use the chatbots to trick their targets into installing our mobile malware, which wasn't really my department, so I didn't have much contact with him beyond the obligatory booze-up the night he arrived.

When he slipped me his USB on the way out of the office, I did my usual and followed him downstairs and refused to get out of his airport car until he talked. "No," he said, and put in earbuds, leaned back, and closed his eyes.

I followed him into the terminal, to the check-in counter and then to the security checkpoint. Before he showed his boarding card to the guard and slipped through, I grabbed his arm and pulled him aside.

"Tell me or I'll flush it down the toilet."

He gave me a stony look. "Do what you have to." He shrugged his arm out of my grip and walked off through security. I watched him go with a sinking, awful feeling.

I checked my cash—about a hundred bucks, mostly in pesos, my usual walking-around money, and I stepped out onto the curb and got in a cab, trying to keep my breathing even. In my halting Spanish, I asked the driver to take me to La Condesa, where there was a strip of all-night internet cafés. I used the front-facing camera in my phone to look over my shoulder a couple times and didn't see anyone following me.

I stepped out on an empty corner and walked around the block once, stopping to look behind me in shop-window reflections, then I went into a café, laid down cash, and signed a fake name in the register. I sat down at a grubby ancient PC covered in a single-molecule-thick biofilm of stale Burger King and the DNA of teenaged boys, whose spoor was thick in the air around me.

Turning the monitor to angle away from other people, I started torrenting porn, mostly gay stuff, while I secure-erased the USB the spook had given me. Once I'd filled it with zeroes five times, I dumped all my torrents onto it and closed the session, then sped out and found another cab, which I took to my place.

I hid the USB in my cutlery drawer with the other ones—I'd given them all the same treatment, every time I'd finished dumping them to my plausible deniability partition—and took a shower. I stank. Fear sweat.

I was getting ready for bed when the knock came. I'd put on my most all-American pajamas, a pair of Juicy sweats and an oversized USMC tee, because optics. I made myself take three deep breaths before I called out, "One sec" and ostentatiously flushed the toilet.

I put the chain and the two slider bars on the door before cracking it. My boss was there, a bland Irishman named Callum who had done something for MI5 in another life and who was more administrator than anything, could have been managing a froyo stand or a construction site just as easily. He was accompanied by two guys with the characteristic look of Zyz security, 'roidy and twitchy, Crossfitters who listened to talk radio podcasts on their corkscrew earpieces and shopped exclusively from the tactical section of the Cabela's catalog.

"Callum?"

"Masha, can we come in?"

I closed the door and undid all the locks and opened it again.

"What's going on?" That felt like what I'd say if I didn't know what was going on.

"Your employment contract allows us to conduct random spot checks of your premises and personal effects as part of our ongoing security. We're instituting a new anti-breach protocol. Your contract also prohibits you from discussing this with your co-workers." His eyes were looking all around my place, hunting out the hiding spots. "We'll be taking disc-images from all your systems and mobile devices. Do you have any personal devices or mass-storage media that have not been issued to you by the company?"

"Several," I said, this being true. I mean, start with the four games consoles under the TV and the pile of old phones in my desk drawer, right?

"Please produce them."

As I could have predicted, the goons followed me on both flanks as I moved around my apartment, unplugging things and handing them to him. I was weirdly calm, and so were they, and I knew that we both knew that this was a performance for one another. They knew I was up to something, but not exactly what (or the whole situation would have gone down differently, either with a no-knock entry or a covert job while I was at the office). I knew that they knew, but not how much or what.

So I produced. Once that was done, I asked to get dressed.

"We need to search your bedroom before we can leave you alone in it," he said, sounding apologetic. "Procedure."

"What if you search my bathroom and I take some clothes in there?"

"That's reasonable."

I waited with him for forty-five minutes as they searched. When I was finally able to use the bathroom, the medicine cabinet, toilet paper, and towel bars had all been removed and leaned against the wall and the light fixture was dangling, still live, from the ceiling. I got dressed.

They found the thumb drives in the cutlery drawer around 3 a.m., as I was drowsing on the sofa and waking periodically whenever the goons crashed or banged a drawer or cupboard.

"Masha?" Callum's voice was gentle, like a father waking a child who's fallen asleep in the back seat on the drive home.

I opened my eyes and focused them. He was holding a handful of USB sticks. I knew they'd been found.

"Oh."

"You didn't surrender these mass-storage devices."

"They have personal material on them."

"You were required to surrender all mass-storage devices. It's in your employment contract."

"What if I terminate that contract?" I had rehearsed some of this, in the half-sleeping hours while they turned my apartment upside down.

"We still get to keep these."

I shrugged.

"If they are encrypted and you fail to turn over the keys, we will swear out a criminal corporate espionage complaint. We already have counsel standing by with our contacts in Mexican law enforcement to arrange for custody in the event that such a course of action is necessary. We'd prefer that it wasn't."

I closed my eyes and opened them. I was so tired. This moment had been a long time coming and I'd rehearsed it so many times. Living through it in that half-awake state felt like another rehearsal, fogged in unreality. "I would like a lawyer."

"The only way that's going to happen is if you are arrested by Mexican police, at which point you will be able to contact your counsel of choice. For the record, it's not what Zyz would prefer. Is it your preference?"

"No."

"In that case." He let it hang out there.

"Pen and paper?"

"Of course." He withdrew a small spiral notebook from his breast pocket, then a shiny chrome "zero-gravity" pen, and passed them over.

I wrote the passphrase for my porn drives, held the notebook and pen back out to him. He didn't reach for them.

"Masha, I want you to think very carefully about what you're doing here. If there are any other passphrases, any hidden partitions, on those drives, and we find out about them, it will be very hard for you to argue that we should trust you any further. This situation will proceed most easily for you if we establish a basis for mutual trust and respect." Three a.m., and he looked as tired as I felt, but he was still able to remember the cues for his little speeches, the branching narrative in the text-adventure game he was playing with himself. I wondered how often an MI5 agent from Antrim Town had cause to discuss trustworthiness and mutual respect. I wondered if I should have offered him a shot of the Black Bush I'd bought at the duty-free the last time I'd flown in.

I met his bloodshot eyes. "Callum, just take the notebook."

He did.

"Coffee or whiskey?" I asked.

He looked quizzical.

"Are we done, or staying up?"

He stepped into the kitchen for a moment to confer with his goons, staying in the doorway where he could keep an eye on me. "Whiskey," he said.

I went to my liquor shelf and got down the Black Bush and poured a stiff three inches into one of the water glasses that the goons had pulled out of my cupboard and put on the counter. I didn't offer one to Callum. Let him get his own duty-free.

I sipped it as they left with my laptop and phone and thumb drives and games consoles and DVD player. Once the goons had boxed everything and carried it out, Callum gave me a long, considering look from behind his dark-ringed eyes.

I met his gaze. "There's nothing on those thumb drives," I said, finally.

"That's good to hear." He kept looking at me.

"Good night, Callum."

He nodded like I'd made an interesting point and stepped out into the hallway and let the door close behind him. The whiskey burned down my throat. I guzzled it. Callum hadn't said whether I was expected (or even allowed) at work the next day, but as far as I was concerned, I'd just put in a shit-ton of overtime. When I found myself nodding off on the sofa, I didn't bother to haul myself into bed, just let it happen.

I slept until noon, and decided the company-supplied cleaners could put everything back together.

Without a phone or a device, I couldn't call a company car, so I walked off the compound, and then, because I couldn't think of a single solitary reason to go into the office, I wandered around the neighborhood.

I'd seen plenty of these streets from the windows of company cars, and I'd ducked out to the OXXO store on the odd Saturday afternoon when I'd woken hungover and wanted a pint of ice cream and a fistful of jerky. But walking around, on a weekday, by myself? It was a new experience.

The people around me belonged where they were. As far as I knew, they hadn't lived in four countries, they didn't spend most of their time in armored compounds or in big cars driven by big guys with suspicious bulges under their jacket armpits. They actually lived lives, these women with strollers, these old men talking in cafés, these beggars looking at me with frank stares. They carried phones, they talked on those phones, messaged and hopped from tower to tower. They were each data-streams, converted from analog humans doing things to data that could be quantified and analyzed, by people like me, who didn't belong anywhere.

I missed my phone.

I wondered what Callum would do with my trove of hot guy-on-guy porn. It was, in fact, reasonably hot, for the excellent reasons that a) it lent verisimilitude to my claim that the drives were my secret wank-bank; and b) if I was going to spend a bunch of time assembling a plausible deniability trove of porn, I might as well enjoy myself.

I walked the sidewalks until I forgot that I was doing something weird, until I was just putting foot in front of foot as I'd done as a teen, walking the streets of San Francisco after the Muni buses stopped running, that autohypnotic long march walk that left the mind free to go where it would and mine went where it would, back to the thought I'd refused to let myself think since the start of all this.

While I was downloading porn through my proxies or in internet cafés, I had also been logging into a virtual machine I had bought with a prepaid credit card, on which I ran a little media server loaded up with pirated movies that I could stream from hotel rooms, which was convenient. Even more convenient: the giant whack of storage I had in the cloud let me run a plausible deniability partition that mirrored the one on my laptop, indistinguishable from random noise unless you knew the passphrase, containing every file that had ever been leaked to me.

If I never got my laptop back, I could still get all that data back, providing

I could find a safe place to do so, an unmonitored internet connection where I would be unobserved.

It was time to make a decision: I had been collecting this data for more than a year, storing it without looking at it, without doing anything with it. Now I was in serious danger of losing the ability to choose to do something with it in the future. Now I was at the crossroads where I either did something with it or pretended I'd never received it. If I were Marcus Yallow, I'd be telling myself that I owed it to those brave lads who risked everything to get me these docs, but of course they had risked nothing and put me in tremendous danger, so fuck them, each and every one.

The only duty I owed was to myself and the whole world. These docs were a mixed bag of sins minor and major, voluminous in the way that only files scraped from a nation's computerized nervous system could be, impossibly vast and yet small enough that I could download them all in a few minutes and stash them on a thumb drive that came six to a pack in the checkout aisle at Walgreens.

But what would or could I actually do with them?

I didn't get home until dinnertime, unexpectedly hungry from a day's worth of pretending I didn't have a body. The Zyz co-workers I passed in the lobby pretended they couldn't see me. Word gets around.

I'd had the foresight to buy a phone and a laptop from the local Best Buy, which was just like the American version except the signs were all in Spanish. I fired them up, installed ParanoidLinux on the laptop and a bunch of extensions on the phone that would damp its emissions, and then sent an email to Callum requesting a leave of absence to go to Burning Man.

I was pretty sure he would be glad to have me gone. I was also sure I'd be watched the whole time, which was why I wanted to go to the Burn—it had no network access, no CCTVs, and was what Marcus Yallow would call "a glorious higgledy-piggledy" of a place. Plus, Marcus was going to be there, and I'd finally found a use for him.

They brought Tanisha to my new cell before the half burger I'd saved for her got cold. I passed it to her along with the fries I'd set aside. She surrounded them with her digestive system like a ravenous amoeba before pinning me on her gaze. "You must have sold out big time to get this, huh?"

"I didn't make any promises. But they offered me a deal, yeah. For both of us. You're going to hate it." I told her about it.

"And you get a job out of it?"

"I guess. If I want it. But more importantly, we both get out. Otherwise, there's going to be a lot of procedural stuff that keeps us locked away for a long, long time. Zyz has got a lot of money on the line, and their objectives are aligned with the local cops and prosecutors. That's not going to be an easy victory to score."

"Fuck victory." Her eyes were glittering.

"Yeah, well."

"No, seriously. Masha, I'm sorry, girl, but you don't understand this thing. Fights like this aren't fights you win, they're fights you *fight*. If we curb the Oakland PD and out Zyz, they're not all going to take up Buddhism and move to a damn ashram. They're going to hang around like a bad smell, like Voldemort reassembling his power from the back of some poor asshole's head, until they can come back for more. This isn't a thing you do, it's a thing you commit yourself to. It's a thing *I* commit myself to."

"Your commitment level isn't going to matter if you're in jail."

She folded her arms. "Plenty of people have gone to jail for what I do. I wouldn't be the last. Not like I didn't know it was a possibility. Fact is, the law isn't on their side, just the power of the law. Right lawyers, right judge, I could kick their ass, force them to swear off all that bad stuff you're thinking of helping to install for them."

"That's a hell of a risk for you to take."

"It's mine to take. Meanwhile, that's a hell of a compromise you're willing to make."

"Neesh—"

She held her hand up. "Just shut up, okay? I can run your whole side of this dialogue for you. 'Better to live to fight another day.' 'Prison's a scary place, especially the kind of prison they got for people like you.' 'Pick your battles.' It's the Serenity Prayer, coward's edition. I've heard it."

I opened my mouth to say, *So what do we do,* but she shook her hand at me:

*Shut up.* I shut up. Maybe this was the last time we'd ever talk. I didn't want it to end in a shouting match. Especially if she was about to disappear into the prison system for an indefinite stretch.

"Masha, I know you think that the 'struggle for justice' is a corny fantasy, but you live in a world where people have weekends, don't get maimed on the job, and have constitutional rights, at least some of the time. You live in a world where I'm not someone's *property*, where I can *vote*, where I can marry a woman or a man. That's because sometimes, the struggle for justice gets *somewhere*. Do you know how that happens? Do you have a theory of change?"

I shrugged. "The arc of history is long, but it bends toward justice?"

She made a fart noise. "You know what makes it bend, Masha? People hauling on that mother, with all their strength, with all their lives. We pull and pull and pull, and then, bit by bit, it bends. People hear Dr. King's quote and they think, oh, well, if the arc of history is going to bend toward justice then all we have to do is sit back and wait for it. But the truth is, it bends because we make it bend, and the instant we let up, even a little, it snaps back."

I got hammered by a wave of déjà vu, remembering an argument I'd had with Marcus, when he was telling me about meeting John Gilmore, one of the guys who founded the Electronic Frontier Foundation, all excited because he'd met the guy who said, "The internet interprets censorship as damage and routes around it." Marcus had been all wound up by the revelation he'd had after talking to this Internet Graybeard: the internet doesn't automagically stop censorship because of its mystical censorship-busting properties. It was because people who used the internet learned that censorship was Very, Very Bad and so they signal-boosted, mirrored, and rerouted stuff that was blocked, and nerds like Marcus built tools to automate this.

Marcus had been head-explodingly excited about this idea, the sense of holy mission it gave him. Every time I saw someone getting harassed by white nationalists or doxxing trolls or bot armies and asking why no one could do anything about these technologically supercharged shitheads, I thought about Marcus in that moment.

But here was Tanisha, saying the arc of history is long, but we can bend it toward justice. The internet interprets censorship as damage and we route around it. Why did all the idealists in my life have to be so committed to personally making a difference rather than finding a comfortable place from which to watch the great forces of historic inevitability play out?

Goddammit.

"So you want me to go to jail on the off chance that I might be able to help you bend the arc of history from behind bars?"

She looked at me for a long time. "Masha, sometimes I can't tell if you're obtuse or lazy or what. I don't want you to go to jail, girl, I want you to *fight to get me out.*"

Well, of course she did. The Masha way was to take the payoff, move along, live to fight another day. The Marcus way, the Kriztina way, the Tanisha way, was to burn every bridge, piss in the ashes, and then run directly into the machine-gun nest.

I like directness. "Tanisha, can I ask you a serious question that I mean with absolute sincerity and zero emotional valence, like just straight-up ask you?"

She actually laughed at that. "Masha, no one will ever say no to a question posed that way. Go."

"What if I say no? What if I take the deal and don't auto-destruct in a bid to get you out without you having to take the deal?"

Her face was expressionless. "What about it."

"What happens with us?"

"You mean, will we still be friends while I rot in prison for a long stretch, maybe until I die?"

I didn't say anything.

"I think you know the answer." She sighed. Sighed again. "Thanks for the burger, Masha."

I called for the guard.

# CHAPTER 7

hit the bricks twenty-five minutes later. I was going to have to buy a new phone (this one could obviously never, ever be trusted again), but in the meantime, I couldn't help firing it up to get my messages. The cops had probably already retrieved them, so why should I be the only one who hadn't read them?

Marcus, of course. A steady stream of updates about his energetic attempts to get me free, both ineffectual (because he sucked at that kind of thing) and useless (because they take your phone away when they arrest you) and then even *worse* than useless (because he was feeding the cops his strategy notes and narrative, giving them a chance to head him off before he got started).

He wanted to speak to me, naturally.

I had no idea where I was. The building I'd just left—a towering monster with narrow slit windows that looked like the kind of thing you'd shoot arrows out of—bore a sign reading GLENN E. DYER DETENTION FACILITY, which rang some bells, a hunger strike or something when I'd been a kid.

I had to use my phone again, to check maps. For an untrustable device, I was certainly making a lot of use of it. But the cops and Zyz had just shown me the door, so they knew where I was standing in any event. Turns out I could walk to BART in a matter of minutes. That van ride had seemed a lot longer than it turned out to be.

Now, of course, I was going to use my phone again. To phone Marcus Yallow. Perfect opsec requires perfect people. I was tired, heartsick, and miserable. I was not perfect.

"Assume we're being recorded," I said, instead of *Hello*.

"Oh. Uh, yeah. All right. Are you okay? Where are you?"

"Meet me at Fruitvale BART." I hung up. I wasn't okay, and I didn't want to talk about it. I half put my phone in my jacket pocket, then stopped. So long as it was working, it was going to tempt me to use it. I thought about Ulysses and smashed it as hard as I could into the corner of a standpipe sticking out of an office building. It took two whacks until I could see the mainboard showing through the smashed screen, and three more before the mainboard was visibly cracked, with multiple severed traces.

I thought about Ulysses and brushed the fragments of glass off before putting it in my back pocket. I never put anything else in there, and sitting on my phone at this point would only improve the situation I was trying to create.

Ulysses was an early hacker. Normal Greek heroes who had to sail through siren-infested waters had an opsec protocol to keep themselves from being lured to their watery graves by the sirens' irresistible songs: they would fill their ears with wax to create a firewall that was impenetrable by the sirens' freespace acoustic network infiltration attempts.

But Ulysses wanted to be able to hear the sirens and live to tell the tale. So he came up with a hack: he had his sailors tie him to the mast so that no matter how tempted he was, he couldn't choose to jump into the sea.

Economists call this a "Ulysses pact"—the bargain your strong, present-day self makes with your weak, future self. You can make a Ulysses pact by throwing away all your Oreos the night you go on a diet, or only taking enough cash to buy three beers when you go to the bar, or, if you happen to be at Burning Man attempting something very scary and risky, by leaving all the acid at camp after ingesting your hit, so that when you start to peak, you literally can't give way to the otherwise irresistible temptation to eat all the rest of it and see just how high you can make that peak go.

Ulysses pacts aren't an admission of weakness, they're a show of strength: a way to use your strong self against your weak self. Could I resist using my compromised phone? Fucking right I could: I could resist using it by smashing it to smithereens.

With no phone, I had to stand at the top of the Fruitvale BART escalators, trying to blend in without staring at a distraction rectangle like all the other

LTE zombies around me. I settled for sitting on a bench and stretching out my legs, then staring at my toes, a decidedly uninteresting pose of someone who had the familiarity with long bouts of sitting that comes from being unemployed and, quite possibly, panhandling. No one wants to have to talk to a panhandler. Staring at my toes let me subtly lift my eyes a little periodically to scope out the top of the escalator and see if Marcus and his girl were debarking. They'd probably try to phone me when they arrived, and might wait for me by the turnstiles. I was hoping they had the native wit to check upstairs if they didn't see me down there.

Hope died that day. I found them by the turnstiles and they said they'd been waiting for me *forever,* which seemed like a stretch and also suggested they might have given the matter some thought and concluded that I might wait for them where standing around wouldn't be as suspicious.

Marcus and Ange were flustered and sweaty, having spent several hours calling the lawyers they knew and the activists they knew and trying to spring me, which was nice of them, even if I'd sprung myself.

"Let's go for a walk," I said. "Are your phones backed up?"

"To my laptop," Marcus said. "I don't trust the cloud."

"Very smart. How about you, Ange?" I couldn't say the last time I'd spoken her name before.

"Yeah, to my computer."

"You don't have anything on there you wouldn't be able to replace? Like, if you lost them?"

They looked hard at me.

"And those phones, they're not fancy or sentimental or anything?"

Ange was getting the picture. "You want us to throw our phones away?"

"Something like that." I pulled out mine.

Marcus looked terrified and exhilarated. Ange smiled at him. "This is just like the night we met, remember? The keysigning party in North Beach where you smashed the laptop afterward and soaked it in seawater?"

Great. What did it say about me that Marcus was smashing hardware years before I took up the hobby? Not that his keysigning party didn't sound like a hell of a first date.

I'd scoped out a standpipe in a niche between two buildings and I led them to it, forming us into a semicircle so that we'd look like we were smoking weed instead of smashing phones. Marcus went first, three good whacks that went right through the mainboard. Ange did it in two and made a joke about her boxercise classes paying off.

They'd been using an Oakland hackspace as their base of operations (of course) while they tried to get me and Tanisha sprung. I tried not to roll my eyes when Marcus suggested we all go back there. We were about to plan something stupid and dangerous; I didn't want to do it in a place full of nosy strangers who might want to "help." But even if I had a key to Tanisha's place, we obviously couldn't go *there*.

So we went to a hotel. The Extended Stay America on the way to the Oakland airport was cheap and the check-in clerk didn't bat an eyelid when I told him our flight had been delayed and we'd been rebooked for the next day and were going to use the half-sized toy apartment they rented us as a base of operations for killing time. Like all the best lies, this one contained one significant truth: we *did* need a base.

"We should assume that Carrie Johnstone knows that we're all together, but she doesn't know what we're doing."

Marcus and Ange exchanged a look. I knew Marcus had a kind of conditioned terror reflex where Carrie was concerned, from the "stress questioning" she subjected him to when he was an impressionable young fellow.

Ange spoke up while Marcus was busy trying to get his shit together: "Why would you assume that?"

"Zyz is the technological infrastructure of Oakland PD. OPD has cameras and Zyz has facial recognition. We didn't take any countermeasures to stop them from recognizing us, so the chances are we were imaged on the way here and at least one of our faces was flagged, brought to a human, escalated to Carrie Johnstone, and matched. But I made sure we didn't go past any city cameras after we left Coliseum BART, and I bet that OPD can only access store cameras and other private sources with a warrant, and not in real time. So they know we got off BART at the station closest to the airport and they don't know anything else."

"They know we're not at the airport, though?" Ange said.

"How would they know that?"

"So many cameras there—if we were there, they'd see us, and they didn't, so we're not."

"Can't argue with that. But there's a third possibility: we went through the Oakland airport and we didn't get recognized by the cameras."

She cocked her head at me, but Marcus got it (of course).

"Adversarial perturbation," he said knowingly (of course) (and of course, he was only half-smart: sure, he'd heard of my infrared-reflecting makeup, but my only supplier for it was on the other side of the Atlantic Ocean).

"CV dazzle is very big this season."

"I know you two are showing off," Ange said. "But I half understand, so let me try and we'll see if I get it right. I'm sure you'll correct me if I don't." She rolled her eyes at us. "Machine learning is just a kind of statistics. You feed a bunch of faces to a computer and give it labels for them, then ask it to do the math to figure out the relationship between them. That's called the 'model.' You check a model by feeding it some new faces and ask it to make inferences, like 'this profile photo belongs to the same person who's in this front-view pic,' or 'this is a picture of Ange Carvelli, who I already know about from my training data.'"

Marcus was looking at her with pride, which was a little condescending.

"If the model can make accurate guesses, we call it reliable and turn it into a product. But we've only tested the model on faces that no one tried to disguise. It's a security system that's never been tested on its enemies. Maybe it works on the enemies, maybe it doesn't. Probably it doesn't, though, right? Because a lock that no one ever tries to pick stays unpicked, whether or not it works.

"The thing is that these systems use statistical inferences to figure stuff out—a face is at such-and-such an angle when I see the following ratio of things that I think are eyes in relationship to a thing that I think is a nose. Here's how I correct the face when it's at an angle to discover the ratio of those things and all the other things I think I can recognize on a face. That kind of thing.

"Well, those things are brittle, right? Because the computer isn't picking hard-to-confuse markers to understand faces from different angles—it's picking *easy-to-spot* ones. Those easy-to-spot markers might be really easy to confuse.

"And they *are*. You can wear eyeglasses or even the right kind of makeup and it confuses those facial recognition systems, because they've only been trained to recognize people who aren't trying to trick them—who aren't 'adversaries' and who aren't tweaking their look with 'perturbations' to fool it. Right?"

Marcus and I nodded at the same time, which, you know, ugh.

"Play this right, and the bad lady might think that we've gone to the airport but disguised ourselves from the cameras.

"No one can review *all* the images from *all* the cameras that they have at the airport, or hell, even in a BART car. It only works if you can rely on software to do all the watching, and it can only do that watching if it can't be easily fooled. Can it?"

Marcus shrugged. "I don't know. They're always changing the models, trying to make them harder to fool, but they have to anticipate all the ways that we would try to fool them and we only have to think of one way they didn't anticipate."

I decided to inject some realism: "Of course, we have *zero* idea which model they're using, and which countermeasure might work against it."

Marcus shot back. "But Carrie Johnstone doesn't know that. And we have *some* idea, because we know who Zyz hired, because they all update their LinkedIn profiles; from there we can just read the papers they published before they disappeared into spookland, and make some informed guesses."

"And if you guess wrong, we all get arrested."

Ange ostentatiously rolled her eyes. "Folks, Tanisha is in jail. From what we understand, Carrie Johnstone plans on keeping her there until her deal closes. The only reason Masha is free is that Johnstone thinks she'll play along for money. But Masha says she wants to help us get Tanisha out, even though it'll burn her with Carrie Johnstone, who is a torturing criminal piece of shit. Carrie Johnstone is almost certainly watching Masha, and if she figures out that Masha *isn't* going to do what she promised, she can have the Oakland PD arrest all of us faster than you can say 'red team.' Is it *really* important to figure out which one of you two is the bull-moose nerd in our little clan?"

Marcus gave her a drippy look. "Sorry, babe, you're right."

"You forgot to mention that Carrie Johnstone is about to close in on all of Tanisha's friends and make their lives a living hell as some kind of sales demonstration for the SFPD, just to show them how effective her stuff is."

"Yeah, I forgot that part."

"I'm pretty sure that Tanisha would hate us if we managed to get her free but didn't do anything about them. So anything we do has to do something for them, too."

Ange shook her head. "You don't get to do anything *for* people with a just cause. If you're competent, and if they give you permission, you can do something *with* them."

"Sure, yeah. But the reality is that we can't do anything *with* Tanisha's friends until she's out and can help us get in touch with them and figure out what they'd like from us."

"Uh, I know them," Marcus said. Ange nodded. "I've been going to a bunch of their demonstrations. They have their own cryptoparty and I've been learning how to run my own by watching their trainers."

Even though it was horribly predictable that Marcus was playing wide-eyed tagalong on the Alliance's movement, this was actually good news. If they already knew they should be doing something to protect their communications, that was half the battle. Indifference is a lot harder to correct than simple ignorance. Still, cryptoparty training materials were pretty good, but they were a generation behind the kind of stuff Zyz was marketing to Oakland PD.

"What about the lawyers you'd been talking to about getting me and Tanisha out?"

Marcus shook his head. "I hadn't heard back from any of them. Someone at the Electronic Frontier Foundation is canvassing their lawyers for a recommendation for a criminal defense attorney and I've texted this guy at the ACLU about six times, but he's not picking up."

"Why not just call the best criminal defense lawyer in town and hire them?"

That took him aback a little. "We could do that, assuming we had a lot of money, and knew who that lawyer was."

"I have a lot of money," I said. "Why don't you figure out who that lawyer is?"

Ange followed Marcus's advice and started pulling up all the LinkedIn profiles for current Zyz employees and checking on any research papers they'd published about machine learning. It turned out that there were two major

groups: one trio from a small facial recognition company that Zyz had acquired and another larger group of machine-learning generalists who'd started
a company backed by In-Q-Tel, the CIA's investment arm. Zyz had been a
co-investor, and from their CVs, it looked like their company was effectively a
division of Zyz in all but name.

As she refined her search and collected their papers, it became clear that
both groups had deep benches in facial recognition, spun out of a lab at Stanford where all of them had studied under the same prof. And yeah, there *were*
a bunch of adversarial perturbations that the models they'd created were theoretically vulnerable to. There was even a template site where you could upload
a picture of your glasses and it would produce a pattern you could print and
stick to the frames that would (again, theoretically) blind the algorithm to
your face. As in, it wouldn't even recognize it as a face. You could choose what
it recognized it as: an avocado, a helicopter, a machine gun, or a porg.

"You should go as an avocado," Ange said. She wasn't kidding. "If a CCTV
spots a helicopter or a machine gun in the street, it might flag it for human
attention."

Of course Marcus had a couple of paranoid USB sticks that encrypted their
data to a key you unlocked with a passcode keyed into a tiny numeric keypad
on the stick's body, and a couple of deluxe USB condoms that used a pair of
Raspberry Pi mini-processors to monitor all the USB traffic in and out of the
device, blocking anything that looked like BadUSB. And of course he'd built
it himself at a hackspace, all blobby solder and firmware he'd compiled himself. Yes, it was good opsec. Yes, it was the kind of thing you needed to have
thought of *before* things went wrong. But it was *such* boy-spy-adventure-novel
stuff.

Ange downloaded a PDF of a custom perturbation pattern for me and put
it on a stick and I took the whole unwieldy gadget down to the hotel's business
center and plugged it into one of their virus-riddled public computers. It was
like drinking out of a communal tin cup chained to a pump in a town suffering an Ebola outbreak, but we'd taken every major precaution. I printed out
my template and hit the reception up for a sewing kit that came with a pair of
cheap folding scissors, then paid cash for a pack of sugar-free gum.

Ten minutes later, I'd outfitted my sunglasses with the paper skin, decorated with abstract computer-vision dazzle and stuck down with denture-destroying blobs of chewing gum. I had the hotel call me a cab and slid into the back seat with my face turned away and my chin tucked down low in my chest for the short ride to Best Buy. I bought six phones for cash, choosing a newly released Nokia model that the phone counter had stacked up in an endcap display. Because the phones were out in the open, I could observe the chain of custody as they were taken from the stack to the cash register and then into my possession. I'd noticed another generic airport hotel on the drive to the Best Buy, and from there I was able to get a cab to the airport itself. Making sure my dazzle-equipped shades were on firmly, I went into the terminal and put a prepaid credit card I kept around in a vending machine and bought six prepaid SIMs. Then it was back into another cab and back to the Extended Stay.

All told, the errand had taken maybe thirty minutes, but when I reentered our "base," it was totally transformed. The bed was pushed into a corner, they'd found extra chairs, and someone had had the bright idea to use the mirror as a whiteboard; it was now covered in dry-erase marker checklists and plans, with categories like LAWYERS and COMMS.

The LAWYERS column had four names with checkmarks and stars next to them. Ange saw me staring at it. "Checkmarks are lawyers we've gotten references for; stars are lawyers we've confirmed availability with."

"I've got comms," I said, and shook out the bag of phones. "Marcus, can you unbox these and get them all plugged in and charging? Here's some SIMs."

I kicked off my shoes and folded my sunglasses away. "They good lawyers?"

Ange nodded. "This guy has been getting white-collar criminals off for twenty years. You remember that billionaire's kid who drunk-drove 280 and killed six millionaires' kids? That was this guy's lawyering."

"He sounds like a wizard."

"Wizard-ninja. And he's willing to talk to us, assuming we have the money."

The work I'd been doing paid very well. *Very,* very well. But I wasn't doing it anymore, and while I'd been a pretty good saver, I wasn't a member of the order of frugal nuns, living in sackcloth and squirreling away every penny. I had stupid money in banks around the world, but not crazy stupid money. A guy like that could eat up my savings and not even notice, and there wasn't enough GoFundMe dollars in the world to pay him in full.

Was I willing to throw away everything, potentially, to get Tanisha out?

"Can't hurt to talk to him. What's his deal?"

"I've got his scheduler's number and they're holding a slot in"—Ange checked her phone—"forty-five minutes."

"Okay. Plan B?"

"This woman. Ten years litigating for ACLU and now she's in private practice. She mentioned pro bono. I didn't tell her that maybe we had some money."

"That was smart." I looked around the room. Marcus was busily setting up the phones. I wanted to get on a computer.

"Can I use your laptop?"

Ange made a sour face. I liked her for that. Sharing a laptop was like sharing underwear. "I'll boot it from a stick if you can make me a bootable Tails image?"

"I've got one here," she said, and rummaged in her backpack, coming out with a little stick that she fitted into Marcus's USB condom and then stuck into her laptop, powering it down and passing it over. I admired her paranoia briefly: it was her own laptop and her own USB stick, and she still took anti-BadUSB precautions? She had more potential than I'd imagined.

I booted up and got the machine on the hotel's network. Every bit it transmitted was routed through Tor and the machine itself wouldn't keep a record of the keystrokes I entered or the bits I sent or received.

Unless.

Unless Ange was actually working for the other side and had given me a sabotaged laptop with a crooked version of Tails. Unless Ange had been compromised by someone who physically accessed her machine and installed a keylogger or other malware on it. Unless there was a bug in Tails that the bad guys knew about and the Tails project team didn't.

It was a lot of unlesses. I took a deep breath and logged in to my email. Carrie Johnstone would be communicating with me over that channel, and I needed to be able to keep track of where she was at in order to stay safe. It was also how I'd reset my passwords for things like my banking so that I could log in to them without having access to my own laptop and all its encrypted data. It was how I'd boot up the dormant virtual machine I kept running on

Amazon's cloud, the one that would serve my backup back to whatever new laptop I bought next.

And, it turned out, it was how I'd hear from Kriztina again.

> Dear Masha,

it began. It was not encrypted, which meant that she was either getting sloppy or she'd lost control of her laptop, phone, and keys. I was betting on the latter. I was feeling very aware of how often you had to stick your laptop in a shredder and start over, and Kriztina was many things, but not sloppy.

> How are you? I think of you often, and what your intentions were when you told me to give up and go into hiding.

> I was picked up not long after I last saw you. Two days, going from friend's house to friend's house. I couldn't sleep, couldn't eat. We'd been hearing about the Finecab attacks, so many rumors, watching the videos, not sure what to believe. I was so nervous and scared it was almost a relief when they knocked at the door.

> They took me to Uslon prison, stripped and put in a solitary cell. It was very cold. The window glass was broken out and I wasn't given any clothes. I did exercises to try to keep warm, push-ups on my mattress so that I didn't have to let my hands touch the frozen cement floor. I would get so tired, but whenever I stopped, I would start to freeze up, feeling my bones start to lock in their sockets, and I had to keep going. I tried to tear the mattress off the bed to wrap myself up in it but I was too weak and it was too slippery.

> I was half-frozen and couldn't see or think straight when they let me out and put me in a heated cell with regular prisoners. They heaved me in without any word. Someone covered me with a thin blanket. It stank, and so did the floor and the people even. I was mixed in with criminals and beggars and addicts and politicals like me. We formed cliques in the big cell, but no one fought or bickered. I knew a few of the politicals, though they were from different factions, and they loaned me a few pieces of clothing and helped me get some water down my throat.

> We talked, of course, like politicals do. Just this and that, trading tips and theories of how it would all end, but then they brought in someone else, Sasha, from our group, and he was bleeding and talking about the cars, which he'd

seen firsthand. I've read the news reports since, of course, but that afterwards stuff doesn't really capture how frightening it was in that moment, when no one knew what was going on. Even now, days later, I jump every time I see a small car, the same model as the Finecabs, I find myself marking bollards that I could duck behind, stairways I could jump onto. The government has only used that little trick once, but it was a very good investment for them; everyone in the country is too busy worried that death could come at any moment to think about how to overthrow the state jk (not kidding).

> They held me for two days and then they just let me go. All the politicals, in fact. Let us go and told us our charges were pending and we should be ready to present ourselves to the police. We all stood in the cold, blinking at each other, wondering what was going on.

> That's when I saw your old boss, the German one. She was standing off to one side across from the jail, all dressed in a fur and thick gloves like a movie spy. She saw me see her and she closed one eye and then looked away. So I guess she is to thank?

> I told the other politicals to throw away any electronics that had been confiscated while they were in jail. A few of them wouldn't do it, or said they'd do it later, and I could tell they were talking themselves into thinking that their phones and laptops could be trusted because they couldn't afford to replace them. I smashed my laptop and phone in front of them and then some of the others did it and finally most of the rest followed on. I suppose peer pressure is good for something.

> When I got back in touch with everyone, I learned the terrible news. Pawel had been killed by the cars. That's what we call it now. The cars. Not even a capital letter.

> The capital letter isn't important, of course. Pawel being dead is important. I can't help but think that it could have been me run down in the street, that while I was hiding and fantasizing about freedom, everyone I love was being chased down like dogs in the streets outside.

> And then when I imagine what kind of trouble you might be in, I see you with Gabor, running from the cars.

> I don't mean to be dramatic. Maybe I just need some sleep.

> We're not going to give up. Pawel's death was supposed to scare us into

submission, but if he is dead, we owe his memory something. I know that this is how the long grudges of history start. Everyone in Slovstakia understands that fights like this go on and on, for generations, so that eventually everyone is killing everyone over something their great-great-grandpa did. I know that when I take up Pawel's cause, I'm creating another one of those grudges, another immortal monster that my grandchildren will fight over. But what else could I do?

> A grudge it will be.

> Masha, I'm full of stupid emotions today. Love and hate, grudges and sentimental longing. I'm sorry you're not here and I'm sorry I'm not there and more than anything else I'm just sorry.

> So I guess that's the point of this email. I'm alive (for now) and I'm sorry (forever). Be as safe as you can be and choose the right side.

> Solidarity.

> Kriztina

I think I just stared at the screen for a very long time, because then Ange touched my shoulder lightly and I closed my lid.

"Okay?" she said.

I blinked hard at my stupid tears. "Let's get Tanisha sprung."

Long story short: I got to Burning Man. I rendezvoused with Tanisha and Becky, and it was *glorious,* me and my girls together again, catching up on everything that was worth getting caught up on, dancing our brains out at the huge dance camps, drinking some of the genuinely outstanding tequila I'd bought at the Mexico City duty-free.

And of course, I found Marcus Yallow and his girlie and gave them my insurance file, slipping them a thumb drive so cleanly that there was no way we could have been watched, then escaping into the night with a shitload of style and mystery, which pleased all three of us endlessly. We toasted each other with the last of the tequila as I packed my bag and got ready to split.

And then . . .

I was most of the way to my rental when I ran into Carrie Johnstone and her friends from Zyz's security team, which meant I got my own little private helicopter ride from which we watched the fire and explosions below, which are the kind of things that Burning Man is supposed to have, but not *that* kind of fire and explosion, not the sort that is accompanied by panic and screaming. Carrie Johnstone's satisfaction with the carnage was *obscene*.

The next three weeks? Not glorious.

Carrie Johnstone wanted to be sure I understood where she was coming from: that this was just business, but that it was *serious* business. Zyz's role as a US military intelligence contractor depended on its discretion. If there were to be a leak that could be traced to Zyz, that would bring repercussions that were bigger than either of us. And of course, Zyz's ability to do business with other countries' intelligence services depended on its relationship with the USA. So this is *important,* Masha. You need to *understand,* Masha.

I had a dilemma. I had my insurance file out there in Marcus Yallow's twitchy, overactive hands. I could tell her this, use it as leverage, try to bargain my way free. But once I admitted that the insurance file existed, I'd be admitting my role in its production, and there would be consequences, of that I was sure.

Worse consequences. Worse than the consequences I was already facing: just enough food to keep me from passing out, just enough water to revive me when I stopped being able to speak intelligibly. Every now and then, my guards used me as a punching bag, or put me in with prisoners who knew that they'd get an extra ration for every bruise they gave me. I lost a tooth. Then two.

It was hard to think straight. I told them stuff. Then more stuff.

Then, one day, I was transferred. They'd recovered the data from Marcus Yallow, and I'd convinced them that there weren't any other copies floating around. Everyone suddenly got a lot more chill. I was moved from the kind of oubliette where you go to be forgotten forever to the kind of facility that you grow old in. The Costa Rican authorities told me I was being held on drug charges, which were the Costa Rican version of murder charges, thanks to generations of politicians who used the bogeymen of Colombian narco-trafficante to carry them to election victory upon zero-tolerance policies.

The new facility was comparatively luxurious, but not exactly homey. Once I had a few decent meals and got back in my head, I started to probe the system for weaknesses. I considered breaking out, but that wasn't my idea of a good time, since it would leave me a fugitive in Costa Rica, a country that prides itself on "not having a military" but gets a little prickly when you mention its massive, militarized "police force" who use military ranks, sleep in military barracks, and wear army fatigues.

Every jail has jailhouse lawyers, and my jailhouse lawyer was an actual lawyer, which was refreshing. She had a racket in there, money and special favors from everyone for helping them with their appeals and divorce papers and asylum claims and custody battles. When she got wind of what had happened to me, she laughed and said it would be a piece of cake: my idiot employers had gotten me locked up on such flimsy charges that getting me bailed out would only take a couple targeted pieces of legal karate. The only snag was convincing her that I would actually transfer real money to her when I got out, because there wasn't anyone out there I could hit up to front it. I wasn't going to call my mother. Obviously. And Tanisha and the rest of the old gang had negative net worths.

But I convinced her, in part by convincing her that the sums she was asking for didn't actually make much of a dent in my savings so it'd be petty as well as stupid to rip her off. In part I convinced her by doing a bunch of menial, demeaning jailhouse chores for her like delivering packages and gossip, cleaning her cell, and reading to her from the English-language tourist newspaper that the prison was willing to bring in since it had exactly zero pieces of real, substantive news about Costa Rican politics and affairs.

When the day came for my parole hearing, she coached me on what to say about my solemn intention to remain in the country until my hearing, where I was anxious for the opportunity to comprehensively clear my name, return to the USA, and cease to be a burden upon the Costa Rican people. She also assured me that if I skipped town without delay and then hired a good white-shoe lawyer to represent me, I could probably make the case go away without any ugly Interpol business in my future. She was a hell of a jailhouse lawyer, and I made sure I paid her every cent I'd promised and a sizable bonus besides.

The ex-ACLU criminal defense lawyer we ended up hiring to free Tanisha didn't like doing business on the phone, which I certainly couldn't fault her for. To her mind, planting actual physical bugs in her office was unlikely, only because of the enormous consequences for anyone caught doing it, so she deemed that the safest place to meet was face to face.

We discussed all this on a weird, vanishing message system I'd never heard of, one that showed thick gray lines that toggled to text when you scrubbed them with your finger, in order to foil people who tried to take screenshots of the messages before they disappeared. It was closed source and probably had lots of chewy defects that someone was already figuring out how to exploit, but I only needed it to be secure for a couple of hours, and I was willing to take that risk.

But I didn't want to move my little group all the way across the Bay Bridge to the Financial District. We were vulnerable in ways the criminal defense lawyer wasn't—if they picked *her* up, she could make life pretty unpleasant for them, all on her own. If they picked *us* up, we'd have to hire her to ruin their days. Once I explained it that way she immediately stopped bargaining and messaged that she'd called a cab. Give her credit, she understood logic when it was laid out for her.

It was rush hour and the drive would take at least an hour. I changed twenties for fives at the front desk, then cleaned out the lobby vending machine, filling a plastic laundry sack with energy bars, salted nuts, rolls of candies, crackers, chips, jerky, and, this being Northern California, vegan jerky-alike.

We fell on the snacks like wild animals, then, as the hunger abated, a silence fell over the room.

"You okay?" Ange put her hand on my forearm.

"Yeah. Just . . ."

"Tanisha."

"Yeah." I blinked hard. Kriztina's note had gotten under my skin. Why had they taken her? She wasn't the threat. I was.

Or was I? I had no idea *who* was a threat. Were those jihadis in Iraq threats? Maybe to the people in the villages they were terrorizing, but they weren't any threat to me and they sure as shit were no threat to Zyz. In fact, those fuckers were Zyz's gravy train. Without them, Zyz would be millions (billions?) of dollars poorer. Threat? Those guys were a feature, not a bug.

Same went for Tanisha and her Black-Brown Alliance. I had paid zero attention to what they were doing, except to note that it was attracting Zyz's attention. Again, activity worth tens of millions to Zyz. Were they a threat, or an opportunity?

Now that I thought of it, I couldn't name a single thing that Tanisha and her friends had done. She'd told me plenty about them, but none of it had made a mark.

I spread out my hands. "Honestly, I have no idea if anything we do matters one single, solitary damn. I don't know if anything that Tanisha and her Black-Brown Alliance does matters."

Marcus looked affronted. "Of course what they do matters."

"How?" I said. It came out quieter than usual.

Ange put her hand on his arm. "It's not easy to explain, because they keep winning these partial victories, like they got bodycams for the cops, but then they couldn't get the rules right, so the cops get to see their bodycam footage before they write up their reports—meaning they get to see how much they can lie about without being contradicted by the video evidence. They sued the Cities of Oakland and San Francisco to force them to disclose what kind of surveillance gear they were buying, but only got to see the totals and the companies they went to, and not what was purchased or how it was deployed.

"Back in 2017, the City of Oakland passed a law requiring the cops to publicly consult when they wanted to buy new gear; it basically killed the idea of the Fusion Center. But then, within a couple years, they got the rule killed: 'no more red tape,' and that's when Oakland Privacy joined forces with the Black-Brown Alliance. But they've been fighting a rear-guard action ever since."

I shook my head. "So, useless, in other words."

Marcus said, "No!" but before he could go on, Ange cut him off, more calmly. It was hard not to like her, but I was giving it the old college try.

"It's not useless. It's just incomplete. The reason they can get away with this stuff is that most people don't even spend that much time thinking about it. They think of other people being shaken down and spied on, not themselves. They think of other people having their data leaked, not themselves. They think of other people being shot by the cops, not themselves."

"Because they're racists," Marcus said.

"Yeah, there's plenty of that. If your skin is the right shade, you probably *won't* get shot by the cops if you get stopped, and you also probably won't get stopped. But when it comes to having all your stuff recorded and then abused or leaked, your skin color doesn't matter. The problem isn't just racism, it's hyperbolic discounting."

Marcus nodded sagely, which meant that I was sure as shit *not* going to ask what that meant. I didn't have to. Ange could tell I didn't know what she was talking about.

"It's an economics idea. If someone wanted to buy the rights to publish all your texts and passwords, you'd probably ask for, you know, like ten billion dollars. And if you were told that securing yourself against that disclosure was, say, ten bucks, it would be obviously rational for you to spend that ten dollars. Even if the publication of all that personal information was ten years away, it would make sense to spend ten dollars today to save yourself from a bad outcome that you've already valued at more than ten billion.

"But the human brain really sucks at pricing those long-away risks. It makes some sense to lower the value of things that are far away—like, if I tell you that I'll give you ten dollars' worth of hamburger meat in forty years if you give me one dollar now, it's a ten-ex return on your investment, but you can probably do better work with that dollar in the intervening decades, so it's not that great a deal, even at a thousand-percent return.

"That's called 'time discounting' and there are lots of ways to add up how much of a discount you should apply to events that are far in the future, so there's no one right answer about how big the discount should be, but there are definitely *wrong* ones. Not buying fire insurance is a form of time discounting, because your house fire is some unknown time in the future, but the insurance policy is so cheap, and the cost of an uninsured fire is so crazy high, you'd be nuts not to just buy a policy.

"'Hyperbolic discounting' is when you discount something too much, just because it's some time in the future. White, happy San Franciscans and Oaklanders would give almost anything not to get stopped in the street, forced to turn out their pockets, pulled over for no reason, shot when they reach for their driver's license, or just get the shit beaten out of them for 'failure to comply.' But though avoiding that future is worth everything to them tomorrow, it's worth basically *nothing* to them *today*. They're discounting the discomfort of living in a police state a couple years down the line by nearly one hundred percent."

Marcus jumped in. "The point is just that people usually only figure out that things are turning bad when they turn bad for *them,* and by then it's too late. The time to act is when you still *have* privilege and power, not when you've had it stripped from you."

Ange smiled at him like he was a clever pupil who'd gotten a lesson right. "So the Black-Brown Alliance are pretty much fighting on their own. I mean, they've gotten together in a coalition that includes Arabs and Asian Muslims, Latinx people, and black people, but white people not so much, especially rich white techbros who are rock-solid certain this is never going to affect them personally, so they don't have to participate."

Marcus said, "Yeah but no. I mean, even if this never affects them, they should care, because other human beings are being treated like shit in their country—in their city! That's what gets me, the empathy gap."

Ange tilted her head. "I'd rather count on self-interest than empathy, but sure, okay. Get one and you'll get the other—like, I bet someone who's been strip-searched on their own doorstep for no reason probably has more empathy for other people who are getting the same treatment."

Despite myself, I couldn't help but think that she was a good influence on him. Marcus's phone alerted. He looked at it. "Is this them?"

It took a moment to figure out what we were seeing on the phone's tiny screen: drone footage of a huge street protest in front of a nondescript bunker of a building, four or five stories tall, with no windows and many visible CCTV bubbles. The protesters were overwhelmingly brown-skinned, carrying signs that were impossible to read from the drone's overhead angle. But that angle *did* reveal the cops massed around them, and, beyond the cops, the MRAP armored cars and ranks of police buses and vans. The cops were assembling a kettle around the protesters, a cordon that would lock them in so they could be dragged away in ones and twos, searched, cuffed, or let go. The protesters, meanwhile, were doing some kind of weird flocking thing where they moved in seemingly coordinated waves, slipping through the cordon like schooling fish, leaving the cops to try to reform their kettle.

"It's Sukey!" Marcus beamed. He drummed his hands on the hotel desk. "Some of them are wearing anklets with buzzers on them that vibrate to tell them which direction to go to beat the kettle and the rest of them follow.

People are home watching the drone footage and identifying routes to freedom."

"Marcus helped invent it," Ange said.

I was pretty sure I could think of a bunch of ways of defeating it: shut down the internet, or use machine-vision and information-cascade analysis to identify the people wearing the anklets and divert cops to take them out, cutting off the system's leadership. I'd dismissed Marcus's little gimmick as a toy back when it first came on the scene, but watching it in action now, it was actually pretty damned impressive, like watching a marching band do precision maneuvers, or like watching quicksilver squirt through some reckless YouTuber's fingers as they did the Mercury Challenge.

"What are they protesting?" Marcus and Ange looked at me like it was a stupid question. I didn't let them woke-shame me.

"It's the Black-Brown Alliance," Marcus said at last. "They march for an end to stop-and-frisk, profiling, evictions, and police killings. It's a weekly thing."

I shook my head. "Weekly? Sounds exhausting." I thought of Kriztina and her friends and their regular rallies in the central square. "Don't people just stop showing up, until only the nutjobs and hard-core are out? Sounds self-marginalizing."

Marcus held up his phone again. It was another demonstration, this one in Civic Center, at San Francisco City Hall. It was visibly larger than the Oakland one. The drone was steady and it had sound, chanting, but I couldn't make out the words.

I smacked my forehead: "They're dividing up their forces in *two* protests? Goddammit—"

"Three," Marcus said, tapping his phone. "San Jose," he said. This protest was even bigger. "Black-Brown Alliance has rolled up a lot of different single-issue groups around here, and in San Jose they merged with the housing justice folks and the Unhomed people, who were already really plugged into the East Palo Alto anti-eviction groups, and—"

I stopped listening. I was trying to make sense of the images I'd seen. These were some of the biggest demonstrations I'd seen in the USA, and they weren't special-purpose protests, timed for an election or a declaration of war or an inauguration—they were *weekly*. Jesus. I mean, I didn't really pay attention to politics much, but I felt ashamed for having missed something this big, something Tanisha was involved in. Some part of me had assumed that if the state had taken a fine-grained interest in Tanisha and her friends, it was because someone like Xoth had sold them on the need to do so, without considering the possibility that they were actually doing things that had the potential to really, genuinely change everything.

I have some pretty huge blind spots.

I smiled, and I could tell it looked fake and weak. I felt fake and weak too.

Getting out of Costa Rica wasn't easy, but I did it. The thing is, Zyz had paid me extremely well to develop the very technologies they would use to try to stop me, which meant that I knew how to beat them and I could afford to do so.

Once I was back in the USA, I had my final contact with Carrie Johnstone. I called her from a safe house in Miami, a place where a guy who'd once been a doctor treated people with no questions asked. He'd been certified as a veterinarian, which meant that he could still write and fill prescriptions, which helped, because the injuries I'd sustained on my way to Managua—the city I flew to Miami from—were not pleasant. A doc there had fixed me up with some tablets that I knew better than to bring over the US border; I'd eaten as many as I dared to get through the flight and across the border and flushed the rest down the airplane toilet.

The doc was willing to hand over Rxes for stuff that was way better than my Nicaraguan MD had provided, so I skated through the next week in a pleasant haze of pills, periodically overshadowed by half-sober moments of realization that I was going to have to talk with Carrie soon.

After a week of this, I had run out of excuses not to call her. Of course I still had her number, stashed away in one of my encrypted cloud backups that I'd mirrored to a burner laptop in moments between pills. Turns out progress bars are a lot more watchable with the right opioids.

She didn't pick up on unfamiliar numbers, of course, so I left her a message: "It's me." I waited an hour and called back.

"Hello."

"Let's deal."

There was a long silence while she thought about it. Or maybe while she messaged someone in telcoms to see if they could trace the call. Zyz did a lot of integration deals with carriers, helping them sell into spy agencies and telcoms ministries, then worked with them to install surveillance gear without breaking the national phone system and provide training and support to the spies, cops, and petty, grudge-chasing government employees who would be using the gear once it was in place.

"I don't think so." Carrie Johnstone could do cold voices.

"I think you will." Unspoken: *Because I can hurt you worse.*

"Go ahead."

"That data wasn't supposed to get out. It was my *insurance file.* It got published because of what *you* did. I didn't leak that data. Other people leaked it to me, and I didn't want to go down for it. This was your doing, lady."

Dead air. I waited until I heard her breathe to make sure she was still on the line. I was warming up to my subject but I didn't want to lose control, either.

"What's more, what went live wasn't everything." This was a lie. But she couldn't know that. "I'm not dumb enough to put all my eggs in one basket. Especially not *that* basket." She *hated* Marcus Yallow. Any shit I could talk about him would only endear her to me.

"And?" Still ice-cold, but there was a tremor in there.

"And that's where we stand. You keep going after him, I will have to stop you, because if he goes down, I go down. Nothing you do now will get his leaks taken down anyway. That food coloring is all up in the swimming pool, lady, and you can't ever get it out again. You should be focusing on how to rebuild, not how to exact vengeance from Marcus fucking Yallow." *Or me.*

"Or you."

Yeah. "You can get rich or you can get revenge, but not both."

Silence. She breathed very softly, but it sounded like a sigh. "Yeah."

"Yeah?"

"Yeah." Still icy, but already moving on to the next thing. I didn't kid myself that she was forgiving and forgetting, but she was definitely compartmentalizing. That's something I can spot a long way away.

"We're good, then."

"We're good."

"Take care of yourself."

"You too, child." She hung up on the last syllable. We'd meet again, I was sure of it. In the meantime, it was time for me to go find Marcus fucking Yallow and tell him I'd bailed out his stupid ass again.

# CHAPTER 8

The lawyer was late arriving at our hotel room/lair. She knocked at the door. "It's Aino McCulloch."

Ange let her in, made her instant coffee, got her seated. She was middle-aged, thin as a bird, with tilted eyes and skin so fair and well maintained that it looked like bone china. Her hair was fine and ash-blond shot with gray. She wore a smart little suit and expensive tennis shoes. After she'd seated herself, she switched off her phone and put it in a Faraday pouch, then asked if we needed to borrow pouches for our phones.

I liked her already.

"Traffic was insane," she said, squaring up a yellow pad and a pen on the hotel desk. "The protests."

"We saw," I said. "So, there's a lot to tell here, and some of it is very sensitive. You're not our lawyer, right?"

"You mean, is what you tell me privileged? That's a prudent question. I'm not your lawyer, and so what you tell me isn't privileged, though I am discreet, as you are aware and as my professional code of ethics requires. As I understand it, you would like me to represent a friend of yours, but I'm not her lawyer yet, so even what she tells me won't necessarily be privileged. You should talk to me like you would talk to a reporter on background—someone trustworthy and honorable who'll try to keep your secrets, but whose legal protections and duties are a complex stew of imprecise and ambiguous rules of thumb."

Marcus and Ange just nodded like this was old hat. I'd spoken to a lot of lawyers in my professional life, but they usually worked for my employers or (more rarely) for me. I did a quick mental rundown of what I'd have to tell her for everything to make enough sense for her to decide whether to take on Tanisha's case, and decided it was doable.

"All right. Can I just brain-dump some stuff for you? The basic who, what, where, why, and how?" She nodded and clicked her pen, then wrote the date at the top of the top sheet of her yellow pad, with TANISHA SAMS and P.1 next to it.

By the time I was done, she was at P.25 and was shaking her hand out and rubbing at her wrist. She dropped her pen, sipped at her ice-cold coffee, and made a face.

"From what I can see, there are several interlocking issues here: you want to blow the whistle on these military-industrial complex types you used to work for and out them and OPD for using surveillance gear that's illegal or at minimum warrantless and improper.

"You want to keep their pals on the police force from coming back after you and locking you up on some bullshitty pretext, just to keep you out of the way.

"You want to get your friend out of jail, where she is being held on a bullshitty pretext.

"Is that a good summary?"

I thought about it. "You've got the shape of things."

"Does Ms. Sams want me to be her lawyer?"

"The last thing she said to me was 'Get me sprung,'" I said, "So yeah, I think that's a good guess."

"Then I suppose I'd better go and see my client."

"What about money?"

She looked me up and down. "Got any cash?"

"A little."

"Cards?"

I swallowed. "They leave a trail."

She nodded. "That they do. But a trail that points to me is going to scare the shit out of the kinds of people you want to scare the shit out of." She grinned. I shrugged. She dug her phone out of its pouch and fitted a reader to its port, and I passed her my AmEx Black. A swipe later and I was three grand poorer, and she was messaging some paralegals in her office (with Signal, I noted—for a lawyer, she was practically a US Cyber Command Delta Force ninja) while waiting on a Lyft, the rumpled yellow pad stuffed back inside her bag.

"She seemed nice," Marcus said, once the door had clicked shut. Ange gave him a kick under the table.

I personally had lots of practice sitting around in hotel rooms, but the rest of them were antsy and hungry for something that wasn't vending-machine food.

I thought that the safest thing to do would be to sit tight, wait for our nice lawyer lady to get in front of a judge and make some noise about Tanisha's corpus failing to have habeased, but I was outvoted.

We went for vegan soul food, because this was Oakland, so of course we did. We ate seitan and collards and Ange did her hot-sauce thing. For a moment there, it felt weirdly utopic, like I'd successfully adulted, using money and technical knowledge to solve a problem that a bunch of people had been headless-chickening over, saving the day. Now I got to go out for craft beers and trendy food with reasonably nice and interesting people. Maybe this was the start of a new life for me.

Marcus's phone buzzed. He glanced at the screen, and the blood drained out of his face. "Shit."

"Yes?" I kept my voice calm.

"When you two were both in jail, I called everyone, not just lawyers and stuff—activists, journalists, hackers. I . . . made a video."

I didn't say anything because I couldn't be counted on to keep my voice calm.

He passed me his phone, tapped some.

> This is Marcus Yallow. A few minutes ago, Oakland PD took my friends Masha Maximow and Tanisha Sams off a BART train in handcuffs. Tanisha is a co-founder of the Black-Brown Alliance and Masha is a hacker who specializes in surveillance and operational security, and she'd discovered that OPD was illegally hacking phones of anyone in the vicinity of Tanisha and other Alliance organizers. I believe that she was arrested to prevent this news from getting out.

I pinched my own thigh under the table to make myself focus on the rest, which was basically more of the same. Marcus's big, dumb, sincere, urgent face, well known to the sort of person who knows about people like him, confident and earnest. He made me sound like a whistleblower and Tanisha sound like a martyr. He made it sound like we'd been dragged off the train with bags over our heads and sent to Gitmo by the Bay.

"You didn't mention this, Marcus," I said, finally.

"To be honest, I kind of forgot about it. There was so much else going on. You know, I just tried *everything,* because you never know what will work, and I figured that the longer we waited to sound the alarm, the more we'd be playing catchup while you were being rendered to Bahrain or something."

"When in trouble, or in doubt—" I said.

He shrugged. "Yeah, or throw it all at the wall and see what sticks. Thing is, the video stuck. It, uh, went viral." He tapped his phone again. "Eight hundred thousand views, give or take. Ten thousand retweets. Fifteen thousand likes." He showed me the analytics screen. The totals were rolling up as I watched.

"We need to let the lawyer know," I managed.

"I think she's probably going to find out, one way or the other." He turned the screen back toward me. I recognized the building that they were protesting in front of: it was the jail I'd just been released from, and the thousand-plus people in front of it were holding up FREE TANISHA signs with her picture. A few of them had FREE MASHA signs, too.

I had a momentary panic—thundering heart, wet palms, the feeling of blood draining to my gut—and I made myself stay calm. Then I had a flash of Carrie Johnstone's face, what she'd be doing right now as she sat on the phone with her boss or the SFPD's procurement point person, watching the protests in front of the jail. She'd doubtless have seen the video, would know that Marcus was involved, and would be in a white-hot fury.

I started thinking aloud. "They're going to be raging. Zyz and the SFPD. They'll start lashing out, and Zyz is going to be panicking. Oakland PD is going to be shitting bricks, because they're the ones who bought and used this stuff without a warrant and then arrested Tanisha to shut her up about it after infecting her with it."

Marcus stuck his chin out. "But now that thousands of people know what they've done, there's no way they'll be able to keep the news from getting out, and so there's no point in keeping Tanisha."

I shook my head. "Marcus, that game theory only works if you're sure that the other side isn't controlled by enraged, vindictive assholes. Here's another framing: up until a few minutes ago, we had something they wanted—confidentiality—and we could bargain with them for it. Now we've thrown away our only bargaining chip, and we got nothing from our adversary from it. We have nothing they want, and they have something *we* want: Tanisha."

He was getting defensive and pissed. "Come on, we were never going to offer confidentiality to them—Tanisha already told them that she wouldn't do that."

"But that was before we sent an expensive criminal lawyer out to bargain with them. That was something she could have dangled in front of them to get them to the table, or offered and then taken away. She's got nothing now."

He was about to say something else, something stupid for sure, and Ange shut him up. "You're right, Masha, as far as that goes. But we didn't know we'd get a fancy lawyer to take your case. We didn't even know that you'd get out and that Tanisha would be stuck inside. So we did what seemed best at the time and now we can't take it back. The wrong question is 'who's to blame,' the right question is 'what do we do with these facts,' so let's ask it."

"Yes," I said. "Yes. You're right. Someone does need to talk to the lawyer, get her a copy of this. She'll be rattling cages, waking up judges, calling state senators—that kind of thing. We can't afford to have her surprised by this situation. We need to tell her *everything* you did, everyone you talked to." I had a sudden realization. "You talked to reporters, too, didn't you?"

"I've got about six of them trying to reach me right now," Marcus said, looking defiant.

"I'm sure you do. Don't call them back. Call the lawyer, get her on the phone, tell her *all* of it." I thought a second, remembered shoulder-surfing her phone. "Wait, she's on Signal—message her instead."

Marcus nodded and got a little roll-up keyboard out of his bag and tethered it to his phone's USB port and started typing.

Ange was right. The way out of a crisis was to deal with it as it was, not as

you wished it were. The people down on the streets were a huge wild card and nothing we did was going to change that, so it had to be a part of our plan.

Marcus's fingers were a blur on the chiclet keyboard. He looked up from his phone. "She's not happy about it. Quote, 'this makes my job much harder,' unquote."

*Boo-hoo.* I was already past being pissed and had moved into getting shit done. She was getting paid enough to deal with this. "Ask her whether we can help."

Clatter. "She says we should sit tight."

I'd figured. This was where I was supposed to shine, knowing when to act and when to lie back and wait. Marcus was supposed to rush out and take action. But I knew that they'd be maneuvering Stingrays into range around each of those protests, if they hadn't already, and they'd be hacking the baseband radios of every cell phone that each one of those people were carrying. They'd be turning them into covert mics, running automated cascade analysis to spot the leaders, looking for old arguments to start up again to sow discord so that when they started making arrests, they could fool half of them into ratting out the other half.

It was like my mind had split into two: on the one hand, I was thinking like the Oakland PD—or more precisely, like someone from Zyz running operations for the OPD—and on the other, I was feeling like I was responsible for these protesters, like they were a band of Slovstakian dissidents I'd adopted and was now in charge of ensuring didn't get scooped up and tortured or hounded to the ends of the Earth. There was no way I was going to be able to secure that crowd's devices, though, not even with an army of skilled technicians.

Sometimes, the best thing to do really is to sit on your hands and wait for someone with specialized knowledge and skills to fix stuff.

"Back to the hotel," I said. They groaned.

We walked. It was a nice evening, and the fog was pretty, rather than oppressive, and it left less of a data trail than an Uber or a Muni bus.

By the time we passed Coliseum and were headed to our hotel, it was full night and I was feeling my jetlag. We passed a 7-Eleven and I proposed a snack

run (yeah, I paid again, from my dwindling supply of cash—I'd need an ATM soon); we were just apportioning the bags when we heard the crash outside.

I'd heard car wrecks before, and this one was wrong, even by crash standards. It took me a second to figure it out: it was all smash, no brakes. Usually, there was a brake squeal before the smash, the panicked prelude to the crush and groan of tortured metal, the tinkle of glass. This was just: *wham,* no runup, no brakes.

It was very, very wrong.

I looked around the 7-Eleven. It had a huge picture window, like every 7-Eleven, lined with shelves and racks, each more useless than the last when it came to absorbing a hypothetical car crash. Maybe if we crouched all the way back at the far side of the store, between the last row of shelves and the cooler—

Another crash, a scream, glass tinkling.

—or maybe successive rammings would trap us between crumpled rows of display racks and razor-sharp shards of reinforced cooler glass.

I heard whimpering, realized it was coming from me; Marcus and Ange had gone pale and were eyeballing the shelves nearest to us, clearly doing the same kind of mental mathematics as me.

"I think we have to get out of here," I said. "We need to find something solid to hide inside of."

The clerk—a young Latinx guy who'd barely said two words to us—was confused-giving-way-to-fright, his eyes wide. "What's going on?"

"Did you see the news from Slovstakia?" I said. "The cars that started running people down?"

He cocked his head. The world comes at you fast, and most Americans had never heard of Slovstakia. "Maybe?"

I shook my head. "Someone hacked all the self-driving cars and sent them to run down protesters. There's protests all over Oakland today—"

Another crash, followed by two more, these ones with squealing brakes as human drivers tried to avoid the collision, a different kind of information cascade, a cascading *failure* where noncombatants served as force-multipliers, suicidal robo-cars startling nearby human drivers into their own crashes.

"—and I don't know for certain, but I think that the same thing is happening here."

There were sirens now, and screaming, and the screech of tires. I watched as a car mounted the curb in front of the 7-Eleven's parking lot and smashed into a pole. Across the street, another car had crashed into the window of a Subway store, and its engine was revving as it tried to keep going, nosing aside the tables and burrowing its way in like a fox down a rabbit hole.

"Fuck, let's go," I said.

Ange was the first out the door. "Keep heavy things between you and the road," she called. "Fire hydrants, poles, parked cars." That sounded like good advice. I followed behind her.

Where could we go? The majority of autonomous-capable and fully autonomous vehicles in Oakland were commercial, mostly trucks and other heavy equipment. I wouldn't want to be in a three-story house after one of those plowed into the ground floor at full speed—not even if the building had a full suite of California building-code seismic bracing.

Marcus and Ange were by my side, sprinting with me from car to pole to car. The four-lane road was lined with plazas, motels, strip malls. Nothing that I'd want to try to shelter in. It was dark, and it felt like every car was on a murderous trajectory, though most of them were just panicked drivers sprinting for somewhere safe, just like us, except they were behind the wheel. Two fender benders later, we were on a long street of low-rise apartment blocks with wide lawns that offered zero shelter from an onrushing car. Rows of parked cars down the curb lanes bristled with menace.

"I don't like this." I was panting. Too much time spent behind a desk, too little spent on a treadmill. Marcus and Ange hadn't even broken a sweat.

"I think we should go to the jail," Ange said.

We both stared.

She started to tick off reasons on her fingers: "One, it's fortified. Two, Mc-Culloch said she'd send a legal assistant there to help with Tanisha, so we'll have someone who knows the law available to us. Three, that's where the protesters are and they may need help, or maybe they can help us."

"I hate this idea and those are very good reasons."

Marcus and Ange exchanged a complicated look that reminded us all that they had a whole married-couple-style nonverbal communications system worked out. "Yes," Marcus said.

I sighed. "Anyone know the way, or are we going to have to turn on a phone?"

Marcus knew the way. He'd been to other protests there, and he led us there by way of side streets. When we crossed major roads, we did so while swiveling our heads back and forth, looking for rushing cars. Each road we crossed was emptier than the last one. Word was getting around. There were cars pulled over, double- and triple-parked. Once, we saw a self-driving car smashing itself apart, trying to batter its way free of the cars that other drivers had parked around it to immobilize it. The other cars' drivers and onlookers stood a cautious distance away, recording with their phones and startling every time the captive car managed to budge one of the vehicles hemming it in.

As we drew up on the jail, the night fog took on the blue-red glow of the bubble lights of the police vans parked on the approach. Cops in riot gear stood in shadow around their vehicles, maneuvering large pieces of equipment on motorized dollies: a portable guard tower on an accordioning cherry-picker base, rolls of fencing, large lights. Some of the vans bristled with antennas, and I could hear and smell the laboring generators.

Over that hum: protesters. Sporadic chanting—LET THEM GO LET THEM GO, BLACK LIVES MATTER, WHOSE STREETS OUR STREETS—tight voices, giggles on the edge of hysteria. I realized it had been a long time since we'd heard any car crashes or tire squeals. Had we outrun the Night of the Living Cars?

We needed communications here. We took out our phones. They already knew who we were. I had Signaled a bunch of texts to Aino McCulloch in between sprints, asking her to warn her paralegal that we were on our way. But she hadn't answered. Who knew what kind of techno-apocalypse was unfolding where she was?

The police hadn't kettled the protesters, not yet. After watching the videos of protesters evading their kettles with ease, I understood why. Oakland PD was brutal af, but they weren't terminally stupid. If something didn't work, they'd stop doing it (eventually). I wondered if they were going to try to create a fenced-in outer perimeter before trying the kettle again, to limit the protesters' maneuverability. It would only work if no one noticed that they were putting up the fencing, of course. The sky was alive with the red lights of zipping drones, and some of them probably belonged to the protesters livestreaming to the web and people playing the protest home game, watching the police formations and marking clear routes through them.

If it were up to me, I'd enumerate the SIMs on all those drones and stop them from getting internet access, either by tricking them into connecting to a fake cell tower simulated by some of the gear in those antenna vans, or by ordering the phone company to refuse service to them. Of course, if I had all of Zyz's toys, I could also use their baseband radios to try to take the drones over and do anything from landing them to crashing them to just turning off their cameras.

I realized that Marcus and Ange had plunged past me, heading straight for the protesters, while I was watching their retreating backs. I considered letting them run off—their problems didn't have to be my problems, after all—and taking off to look for a safe place to go to ground, maybe even getting myself arrested after making contact with Aino's paralegal so that we couldn't be disappeared.

But I didn't. I raced to catch up with them.

The protest was weirdly boring, especially after our nighttime race through the city. Every few minutes, someone would come up with a chant and shout it out, WHOSE STREETS? OUR STREETS! and if they were persistent or had friends who wanted to support their bid, the chant would go for a while until it petered out.

Someone was trying to give a speech, a young woman in a hijab who was talking into her phone; around the crowd, supporters held up their phones, which were apparently retransmitting the livestream of her audio, acting like a distributed array of speakers for an ad-hoc PA system. I guessed there was some software magic that was working to synch up the phones' varying network latency, because the audio was mostly in phase—but out of sync with her lips, which was weirdly disorienting.

"—told that the Oakland police needed their Super Fusion Center for public safety, and that they couldn't tell us what they'd be doing in there for public
safety, and now we learn that they were abusing their power and using all their
toys to retaliate against activists for saying that they'd abuse their power!" That
got a wry laugh that rippled around the crowd. The drones whined overhead
and there was a distant crash that might have been some powerful control
machine maneuvering into place, or a self-driving car committing suicide, or a
crane gone amok in the port.

Even though I'd lived through disasters before and had seen how people
just blocks away from a catastrophe could be relatively calm, and even though
this crowd was focused on its own mission, I was still reeling from the contrast
between the scenes on the streets of Oakland and the obliviousness of these
people. I mean, I was theoretically all in favor of springing Tanisha, but not
until the killer autonomous vehicles were all immobilized.

I saw someone holding up a FREE MASHA sign with a not-very-good
picture of me on it. I didn't recognize him. Someone who had gotten the word
from Marcus Yallow, no doubt, and had decided that a total stranger whose
crimes and misdemeanors were completely unknown to him should walk free.
Marcus Yallow and the Yallow-ites, a botnet and its loudmouthed botmaster.

Marcus was beaming at the guy and looking from him to me. Ange and I
shared a knowing look.

And now the speaker was holding up her phone. "Now we learn that if you
find out what they've been doing, they'll arrest you to keep you from talking!"
Shit.

"We live our daily lives on these things, talk to our loved ones and bank
and go to school and do our jobs, and the Oakland Police Department looks at
them and you know what they see? A listening device! An ankle cuff! A way to
attack us! They buy military surveillance cyberweapons from companies that
supply torturers and dictators and bring them home to shut down anyone who
dares to question whether they can be trusted with spying tools! Am I the only
one who sees the irony here?" Chuckles, calls, *Hell no!*

"No police force in America has been more consistent in demonstrating its
corruption, its burning need for adult supervision, its fundamental untrust-
worthiness."

She was a good speaker, lots of pure magnetism and great voice control, but I could tell she was fishing for an out, some kind of closer that would leave the crowd charged up and ready for action. But of course, that was the problem: What action? Charge the jail? Charge the cops? Sing "We Shall Not Be Moved?"

This was the thing I always hounded Kriztina and her friends about: What do you hope to accomplish today? What is your actual theory of actual change that starts with your bodies in harm's way and ends with a better nation for you and your descendants?

I bet I knew what this woman would say if I asked her: "We need to put the cops *on* notice that if something happens to Tanisha and this Masha rando (whoever she is), it will *be* noticed." I got that. But if the Oakland PD was already convinced that "being noticed" was a largely consequence-free phenomenon, what good would that do? Was it enough to make up for the possibility that these nice people were going to get their heads busted open and their own asses slung into jail if they kept this shit up?

I was sure I'd heard another distant crash. The woman in the hijab had found her closer: "This isn't the first time we've come out for something like this, and it won't be the last. Oakland PD is buying weapons of cyberwar because they are scared as hell of us and our movement. Your strong, brown bodies terrify them. Your attention and scrutiny, it terrifies them. Your resilience, it terrifies them. Your unwavering commitment to justice, no matter what the price, no matter how long it takes—"

"It terrifies them!" The crowd had figured it out and went along with it. I looked around at the helmets and visors that obscured the faces of these "terrified" cops.

They didn't look all that scared, to be honest.

But she'd found her closer, all right. The crowd was straightening up, looking alert. Their morale had visibly lifted.

I heard another, distant crash. Jesus Christ, when the fuck were they going to pay attention to something that *really* mattered?

"She's amazing," Marcus said, reverently.

Ange nodded. "She really is. Yaren Kassab. I remember when she was a high-schooler leading solidarity walkouts during the Arab Spring. Now look at her."

I looked more closely. She couldn't have been out of high school for very long. There were actual kids around me, of course, the high-schoolers and even middle-schoolers who were the mainstay of any Bay Area protest since the kids' climate strikes, but they weren't alone—like in the central square in Slovstakia, there were plenty of older people there, and even families with really small kids, which was batshit parenting. There was a real chance of some broken skulls that night—who brings a toddler along for something like that?

Someone else was stepping up to the mic, an older guy, black, gray-bearded, bald, going a little fat, but tall and straight-standing like a general reviewing the troops.

"Thank you, sister." He was rocking some real gravitas, a James Earl Jones voice with Morgan Freeman cool. "You all know me," he said, and stared out at us, seeming to meet all our eyes at once. He was good at this. "I've been out here for a hell of a long time. I was there with Bobby Seale in sixty-seven, I was out here with Occupy and Black Lives Matter. I've been beaten, jailed, slandered, and spat on. I've been blacklisted and dirty-tricked and psyopsed. I've been Cointelproed. I've been done dirty and done ugly, and I'm *still here*."

It was an obvious applause line, and the audience loudly obliged.

"I've been standing my ground in Oakland with you, with your mommas and daddies, and for some of you, with your grandparents. I've been standing right here, waiting for the arc of history to bend toward justice. That arc doesn't seem to want to bend. It wiggles and it shakes, but hard as I pull on it, hard as we all pull on it, it just hasn't flexed.

"My name is Bayard Wilkins. I'm just one man and I am not going to stop hauling on that arc until it starts to move. Because there's no alternative. You either bend the arc, or it bends you: you stand up, or you surrender. There's no middle ground, friends."

Another applause line. Marcus's and Ange's eyes were shining. Clearly this guy knew just how to preach to his choir. Sounded like he'd had a long time to refine his pitch, anyway.

I'm not going to pretend that his words didn't stir me. Hearing him speak, I had visions of Kriztina and her friends, putting their bodies on the line for a better future, refusing to let some kleptocrat Boris loot their country with impunity. I had flashbacks to Black History Month at Sutro Elementary and watching *Eyes on the Prize* on that dusty VCR every year. I heard echoes of my mother's story of the tanks in Moscow in 1991, the women who convinced the soldiers to go home rather than rolling on their countrymen. All that narrative of the Davids standing up to the Goliaths.

But those had been slow, clumsy Goliaths. Today's Goliaths might not be any smarter, but they had armies of people like me who could make them a searchlight bright enough to pierce the darkest shadows and smart enough to choose which shadows needed piercing.

Somewhere, a car was crashing.

I moved in close to Marcus and Ange. We made a huddle. "Something bad is about to happen here," I said. "Everyone who's not standing *right here* is glued to news about the cars going bugfuck. That means that these cops can do practically *anything* and get away with it. What's more, Zyz is going to be flipping *out* about the fact that all these people know about the illegal surveillance gear they vended to Oakland, and the millions on the line with their SF contract. Their only hope is to change the narrative, to make sure that everyone is thinking about security, not corruption or surveillance or the Black-Brown Alliance."

"You make it sound like they're going to kill us all," Ange said.

"No, just enough of us to make an impression," I said. Another crash, much closer. Wilkins stopped talking and looked around. People were checking their phones, whispering updates to one another.

Electric cars don't make much noise, not even when they're accelerating flat out, but the one that was heading down 7th Street made sure we knew it was coming, blaring its horn and flicking its lights. Just before it crashed into the back of an empty paddy wagon, I saw that it had a passenger in the driver's seat, all terrified whites-of-his-eyes, beating the horn for all he was worth. I lost sight of him in the impact, though after the crash I watched a couple of deputies pull him out of the car, semiconscious, and draw down on him, screaming at him to lace his hands behind his head.

Half the crowd drew away from the crash, the other half drew toward it. Some of the cops had their guns out, and all of them had their visors down and were looking around nervously: "When in trouble, or in doubt . . ."

The police started to shove at the protesters who were trying to get a look at the crash, pushing harder than was necessary, and one of the protesters did the predictable thing: fell backward into someone, who shoved him forward, so he fell into the cop who'd just shoved him, prompting that cop to (predictably) go upside his head with a baton.

The crack of stick on skull was surprisingly loud, even given the general chaos, and the protester dropped like a sack of potatoes, all at once, in a heap on the ground, in a spreading pool of blood.

And then it was *on*. Someone screamed—a sound of fear—and then someone shouted—a sound of rage. I heard someone say, "Fuck this," with real feeling. Now there were people in bike and motorcycle helmets around me, their faces covered with scarves or balaclavas. Suddenly the crowd was boiling forward, trampling the cops, forcing them back toward their vehicles, as the police formed a line of overlapping shields and dug in. The protesters on the front line were caught between the crowds pushing behind them and the cops in front of them, and some of them were getting hit by batons. I saw a few slide down under the press of the crowd, to be trampled underfoot.

But the protesters on the front line knew what they were doing. Amid the shoving bodies, there were protesters whose job it was to pull the fallen people to their feet and drag/carry them behind the front, and I realized most of the pushers were working in pairs with someone who diligently watched for batons being swung over the shields, trying to catch arms or give a well-timed shove in the legs if a cop was unwise enough to bring his shield up.

Not their first rodeo, then.

Normally in a situation like this—and yes, I've been in enough situations like this that there's a "normally"—I would be cool and distant as a star. But my stupid compartments were rupturing. Watching these people, I was once again seeing Kriztina and her people. The bodies, the blood.

Knowing I'd had a part in it.

Knowing that the job I'd set myself to balance some kind of ledger by doing good deeds for the right-hand column to balance out all the evil shit I did in my day job that went on the left was bullshit. No one whose father had been kidnapped in the night and thrown in some Boris's dungeon cared if I was teaching opsec to the rebels in the square fighting for his release.

All those times those baby spooks had slipped me their thumb drives full of their dirty laundry, I'd thought they were weak, too ethical to do their jobs, not ethical enough to stop, half-assing it by bringing their dirty laundry to me.

But what had *I* been doing? I could have told them to cram their drives up their asses, do their own dirty work, and instead, I had hoarded all that data like some kind of obsessive MP3 collector, an ever-growing stash of docs I kept just because I could—

But really, what *had* I been doing with those files? It had been a crazy risk to take. I could have turned them in, every one of them, starting with Raymond, and collected a nice cash bonus for each of them. I could have *not* turned them in, but deleted all the data as soon as they gave it to me. I could have done so many things, but instead, I'd carefully tended those hoards of conscience-files.

I'd made them my own. I'd known what I was doing, the world I was using my skills and hard work to create, and I had been able to look myself in the mirror because I knew I had those files, and as long as I had them, I was doing something to balance out the great ledger. I was working from the inside for change, not selling out.

But I hadn't done a single thing to actually change anything, not until I'd been caught, and then I'd only taken the necessary action to cover my cowardly ass. It was Marcus fucking Yallow who'd dumped my docs, jumping to the conclusion that he was helping me by doing so. Just like he'd dumped my research on the baseband radio malware that Zyz was using to infect Tanisha and her friends. I'd told myself that these secrets were bargaining chips, but Marcus had treated them like bullets, firing them indiscriminately in the direction of Zyz, the Oakland PD, the DHS, the San Francisco PD—anyone who wanted to stop people like Tanisha and Wilkins and the chick in the hijab from standing up and speaking their minds. Marcus didn't care whether his bullets hit anything: he just kept firing toward Big Brother and hoped that eventually he'd hit something critical.

I'd kidded myself that I was a sniper, patiently waiting for the killing shot to present itself in my crosshairs. But a close look inside that compartment revealed that I'd been hunkering down behind a barricade, telling myself that eventually I'd stick my head up, when the moment was ripe—and that ripening had never come.

So who was actually more effective? Me and my clever plans, waiting for a perfect time that never came, or Marcus, who would charge at the enemy lines whatever his chances, relying on blind luck and being a nice middle-class white dude for extra lives if he got shot down?

Marcus was staring at his phone. "They're moving in a kettle," he said. "We need to go that way, *now*." He pointed and started pushing us. Around us, other protesters using the anti-kettling app were also starting to move. As we streamed forward, I saw that the cops had been unrolling the fencing ahead of us, setting it into heavy, water-filled bollards, and the gap was narrowing. I lowered my head and charged. We squeaked through along with the main body of protesters. The ones who were stuck behind the fence moved away quickly, presumably headed for a more distant gap, while we milled around, looking at our phones for more clues about impending kettles we'd have to avoid. I discovered that I was grinning like a crazy person, unaccountably pleased at our daring escape, squirting like watermelon seeds out of the grasp of the Oakland PD. It was a dangerously excellent feeling, playing nimble mouse to the lumbering cats of authority. I could see how it could get to me. I could see how it *had* gotten to Marcus.

But damn, it felt *good*.

Everyone was still tapping around on their phones, watching instant replays of our dash to freedom or caucusing with the people playing the home game, analyzing the drone footage from overhead to spot signs of the OPD moving another kettle in.

So I looked at my phone too. I checked my email, pulling down the refresh like an old lady pulling the arm on a slot machine, and watched as the messages filtered in.

From: Kriztina Kolisnychenko

To: Masha

Subject: Oakland?

Enigmail UNTRUSTED good signature from Kriztina <kriztinak@riseup.net>

Did I just see you running past a police line in Oakland? And are those people holding up signs with your picture on them?

From: Masha

To: Kriztina

Subject: Re: Oakland?

Unfortunately, yes.

Are you OK?


From: Kriztina

To: Masha

Subject: AW: Re: Oakland?

We are not OK, but that is OK. No more lethal car nonsense at least. Did you
hear about Litvinchuk?


I didn't follow the link, because that would be bad opsec, but I did google
Litvinchuk quickly and then I had to do a loop through an online translation
because no one who spoke English had a single fuck to give about the internal
politics of Slovstakia.

After some puzzling over the stilted translations of terse state news agency
reports and profane message-board traffic, I was able to piece it together: Litvinchuk had been purged.

He'd been ousted specifically for taking kickbacks from Xoth, who were
alleged to have built backdoors into their gear for US intelligence to monitor
Slovstakian state communications on top of conducting population-scale surveillance on Slovstakians. Litvinchuk had been denounced by someone from
the far-right ethno-nationalist opposition who had managed to really rile up
the base with accusations of selling out Slovstakia's patrimony and national
sovereignty to the US military.

There was a lot of hay being made out of Xoth's seed capital coming from
In-Q-Tel. I could see where they were coming from—having the CIA in your
roster of shareholders looks shady as hell from the outside—but *everyone* was
funded by In-Q-Tel, even direct competitors of existing In-Q-Tel portfolio
companies. Sometimes these competitors merged and In-Q-Tel trumpeted its
ability to find "synergies" between former rivals, and sometimes they just ran
on, stealing customers from each other; the CIA got an upside no matter who

came out on top, and they ensured that there was always an open spigot of cash for anyone who had a better idea for spying on people. I'd been invited to "join our management team" a couple of times by folks taking on big investments from In-Q-Tel, which was a hilarious indictment of the whole process. If In-Q-Tel was happy to fund companies where people like me were made someone else's boss, they were funding some serious basket cases.

But of course, Slovstakia didn't know that. Xoth *had* been funded by the CIA, and the CIA was, well, the CIA. Assassins, stagers-of-coups, hackers-of-elections. The long, bloody arm of American imperialism. You didn't have to be a former Soviet republic to have a serious dread of the agency, but it sure helped.

But that was a thousand miles away. There was a lot going on right now, all around me. Marcus and Ange were furiously tapping their phones, conferring with other protesters. It seemed like there were more than there had been just a few minutes before. I heard another distant crash.

Then we were rushing again, running past another attempt at a kettle, slipping through another police line. I nearly fell and had a vision of being trampled before I was swept up by someone who yanked my arm hard enough to hurt, but strong enough to keep me from falling. I turned and saw it was an Arabic-looking guy in his twenties in a Stanford sweatshirt and a bicycle helmet. Before I could thank him, he disappeared into the crowd. Soon we were back where we had started, in front of the police station, panting and ragged, triumphant and scared.

A passing kid grabbed at me. "We should get out of here." She looked terrible: whites of her eyes showing, sweat sheening her face.

Kid? She was older than I'd been when I'd shipped out. Is this what Carrie Johnstone had felt when she looked at me?

My phone rang.

That was almost certainly bad news. The caller ID was blocked. Maybe it was a spammer. I almost sent it to voicemail, then I didn't.

"Yes?"

"Masha, how do you imagine this will possibly go well for any of us? I thought you were smarter than this." Carrie Johnstone in ice-queen mode, the rage just perceptible beneath the surface. I suppressed a shiver, but my face must have shown something because Marcus was staring hard at me and Ange followed his gaze.

"Things got out of control. It wasn't my idea."

"I've seen Mr. Yallow's traffic while you and I were chatting and I can see that he was doing his customary headless-chicken impression. But I also see that you are with him—" I looked up at the drones overhead. How many were fielded by protesters documenting the action and helping to slip the kettles, and how many were OPD's, supplied by Zyz? (And how many protester drones were feeding OPD, thanks to some kind of hack supplied by Zyz?)

I resisted the urge to give the sky the finger.

"Glad to hear you're still looking out for me."

"I know you don't believe this, but I am, in fact, looking out for you. You are involved in something big and potentially lethal. Your involvement has been noted by parties other than me. You are going through a door that you can't go back through."

"Lady, I'm just here as an observer. I'm not the one who had me snatched off of BART or locked up a beloved movement leader to protect a procurement bid."

Marcus's eyes were as big as saucers. He'd figured out who I was talking to. Great.

"I wanted to give you a chance. Go into the jail. I'll have someone meet you and put you somewhere you won't get hurt during what's about to happen."

"I'm not an idiot."

"I rather think you are. But this isn't a trick. I want to keep you safe. What you're doing right now is decidedly unsafe."

"I'll take my chances."

"This isn't an offer you'll get again, Masha. Think carefully."

"I have given this offer more consideration than it is due already. Now, fuck off. Then keep fucking off. Fuck off until you come up to a gate with a sign saying 'You Can't Fuck Off Past Here.' Climb over the gate, dream the impossible dream, and keep fucking off forever."

I hung up.

Yallow looked like he wanted to pick me up on his shoulders and parade me around. I felt sick.

"What are we doing here?" The OPD hadn't given up. There was lots of energetic action taking place around their rolling stock. Equipment being maneuvered into place. Then, another crash, this one *very* close.

Ange looked up from her phone. "Three buses full of cops are about to pull in around that corner." She pointed. "Looks like the car crashes are getting closer too."

"What are we doing here?" I said again.

"It was supposed to be safer than the streets. McCulloch's paralegal is supposed to be inside, right?"

"Has anyone heard back from her?" I checked to make sure that the Signal messages had gone through. Who the fuck knew what kind of mess she was stuck in, though. Maybe she was strawberry jam in the tread of a killdozing self-driving car.

"I'll call her," I said. But she didn't answer. I left her another message. Someone was giving a speech again, I couldn't see them, but the protesters around me had their phones out and tuned to repeat the speech, and even so, I couldn't make out the words. My heart was thundering in my ears and my mouth was dry as cotton. I was breathing fast and getting dizzy.

"I think I'm having a panic attack," I managed, before I sat down heavily, breathing hard. A thousand miles away, locked in her own compartment, some part of me was screaming at me to get up, get myself together, be *Masha*, who never panicked, let alone had panic attacks. Every compartment seemed to be bursting open except that one, and their contents were rushing out, blending together, a series of snapshots: the photos of the killings and rapes from those phones I'd tapped; the people in the square in Slovstakia; Kriztina's face that last night in Slovstakia; the beatings I'd endured in jail in Costa Rica; Marcus Yallow's expression as he slammed the truck tailgate on my fingers; his expression when I kissed him and walked away after getting him straight with Carrie Johnstone; Tanisha's face as I left her behind in jail—

"Masha!" Ange had been saying my name for some time, I realized. I looked up into her worried face, and behind it the worried stupid face of Marcus Yallow.

"I'm sorry," I managed, before Ange started dragging me by my wrist to my feet. That's when I realized that people around us were running hard, and that there were big, industrial noises coming from nearby. I squinted into the spot-lights and saw a roll of fence unrolling, fenceposts being fit into water-filled bases and twist-locked into place.

I let her pull me up and tried to run. My feet weren't cooperating. I stum-bled and went down hard on one knee, my skull echoing with the sound of my jaws slamming together, just missing the tip of my tongue. Ange pulled me back to my feet and pain shot down my leg; I limped behind her, hissing every time my right foot came down, dragged, stumbling, shoved by people on all sides as they ran.

The cops killed the floodlights, and now we were *really* running into each other. Ange dragged me a few more steps then stopped and grabbed me, hold-ing me around the waist from behind and we braced our feet to keep upright. I got my phone out and lit it up, then put it in my shirt pocket so it wouldn't be knocked out of my hand. Other phone lights went on, and now I was being dazzled by LED flashlights being shone right into my eyes.

The lights came back on. The OPD had unrolled fencing all the way around us, and now they were maneuvering in heavy equipment: trucks with suspi-cious antennas, prisoner transport buses, water cannons, cherry-pickers that were studded with cameras. The message was clear: Prepare to be pacified, identified, and detained. Resistance is futile.

My leg was killing me. Marcus and Ange were nowhere to be seen. I rubbed my swelling knee. I was trapped, might as well be comfortable.

By the time I met Kriztina, I already knew that she was a key figure in the Slovstakian resistance. I'd only been in-country for two weeks, but it had only taken two days to get the entire country's phone records and email meta-data ingested into the cloud where my analysis software lived and only one day more to run the analysis. Kriztina jumped right out of the visualization; she received a *ton* of email, and when *she* sent out emails, they triggered a waterfall of more emails, calls, and messages that percolated through the population. These were correlated with major protests, and I could see that she was operating multiple identities with their own email addresses because all of these addresses corresponded with the same people. She was already using two-factor authenti-cation on her email account, which also made her stand out in the data.

So I used some off-the-shelf malware to infect a bunch of the people she corresponded with. She used Gmail, but many of her correspondents used local hosting providers that didn't encrypt email in transit; I could see these emails and read them as they went by. I waited for one of them to email her, then emailed them back with a spoofed reply that asked them to open an attachment and a few minutes later, I was inside their computers. From there, I could read all the emails she was sending out. I ran my own translator service in my own cloud—Google might eventually figure out that there was something weird about that one account that kept running other peoples' emails through Google Translate—and while it wasn't as slick at translating as the algorithms at Google, I could still verify that the discussions Kriztina was taking part in were nominally a bunch of equals debating tactics, but when she weighed in, it tended to settle things and then plans propagated out from there.

I did my thing. I built dossiers on Kriztina, her immediate circle, their wider circles who would pick up the messages they created and run with them. I got to know them all, Oksana, Nedeljko, Jasmina. In another era, I'd have used headshots and thumbtacks and bits of colored string. Instead, I just tossed them all into a database visualizer I'd built that did it for me, allowing me to model different gaps in my knowledge to see how stable my predictions about this power structure were.

When I first met Kriztina, I was momentarily unsure I had the right girl. She was so . . . average. She was a kind of Slavic kewpie doll, short, with the tilted eyes and the cheekbones, an inch or two shorter than me, hair in an undercut, clad in layers of knitwear and loose cotton yoga stuff. She was eating pizza and drinking pilsner with a group of her freaky friends, all more subculturally cool than she was, even with the little gold studs in her right nostril.

But then I saw her speak and watched how all the lines of attention in the room shifted to her, how she seemed to be talking to everyone at once, moving naturally to shift the searchlight beam of her attention around in a slow sweep that let everyone feel like they were part of the scene.

I'd known she'd be there—I'd been reading her email for weeks. I'd checked out the little pizza place a few times on my own, and already figured out which tables would give me the best view of the whole dining room.

Kriztina's attention lit on me from time to time as she spoke. I didn't speak enough Boris to really understand what she was saying, but I could make an educated guess: there was a big march coming up that weekend and they were trying to figure out how to get the word out, what to do when the bonehead ethno-nationalists joined in, how to livestream it, what to do if there were arrests.

But also, what they were fighting for, because that was a favorite subject of Kriztina's, talking about how Slovstakia was a rich country with enough for everyone, talking about the looters who'd sucked all the money out of the country and pocketed it, how they had a common enemy in the Big Borises and not the refugees or the Borises next door. It was stuff you could hear anywhere in the world these days, but when Kriztina said it, people seemed to believe it.

Watching her do her thing, I was reminded of Marcus fucking Yallow, though Kriztina was a million times better at what she did than Marcus ever was. I'd met career politicians, people who'd risen to the highest levels of office in their countries, and they all had that same thing, the work-the-room thing. I didn't work rooms: I watched them and understood them and attacked them sometimes, but I never worked them. It was weird to watch someone be so good at something I wasn't even slightly competent at.

She sat there for hours, long enough that I couldn't really keep up the pretense that I was just eating a pizza. People cycled in and out of her table and the adjacent ones and moved on, with a visible spring in their step. Cascade analysis was a scarily good way of figuring out who the lynchpins of a movement were, all right.

When it was just the two of us, Kriztina favored me with a dimple-chinned, solemn look—Borises didn't smile unless they were bullshitting you—and nodded at me. She said something in Boris and I shook my head.

"English." Then I added *sorry* in Boris, which was pretty much my whole vocabulary, along with the usual Ps and Qs and a dash of genuinely filthy profanity.

"Was that interesting for you?"

"It was," I said.

"You work for?"

I shook my head again. I did her the courtesy of not lying. "Not something

I'm at liberty to discuss." I'd meant it to come out as cool and Teutonic as Ilsa the She-Wolf, but I spoiled it by involuntarily grinning—in Boris, only idiots smile easily.

She smiled back. One on one, she'd dimmed the lighthouse sweep of her attention, and without its glare, I could finally notice that zit on her cheek, the place where she hadn't blended her concealer, the unibrow hairs that straggled over her nose.

I picked up my stuff and moved to her table. The waitress looked over and rolled her eyes. Presumably I wasn't the first stranger she'd seen invite herself to Kriztina's table. I didn't mind: star-struck revolutionary was good camo.

"American?"

"Canadian," I said.

"Sorry, sorry! I don't mean to offend."

"American, actually, just fucking with you."

She gave me an up-and-down kind of look and then a little nod with just a bit of a smile, which was practically a Boris knee-slap. I was in.

"Tourist?"

"Not at liberty to say."

"Staying long?

"See previous answer."

She heaved a sigh. "Working for the state security apparatus, then." She looked disgusted. "You've come a long way to help destroy my country."

"It was no trouble—they flew me business class." I meant it to sound quippy and a little mean, but it came out self-conscious.

She ordered us two beers and I poured mine into a tall, frosted glass. She drank from the bottle. "Are we going to have a serious discussion, or just make jokes?"

"We can have a serious discussion, if that's what you'd like."

"I would."

"What would you like to discuss?"

She gave me a long look. "Honestly?"

"Why not?"

"I want to know how not to be spied on."

I nodded slowly. "What have you got to hide?"

Now she *did* smile, only a little. "I thought we were having a serious discussion. I have to hide *everything*. The government here destroys its critics. They pay their trolls to spread lies about you, the police raid your house, you lose your job, mysterious men show up at your mother's work, your father's bar, tell them you're addicted to heroin, that you're being duped by foreign powers, that you're stealing or screwing little children. I have so much to hide."

"They don't do that to everyone, though—just the people who stand against them. If you didn't make a fuss, they'd just ignore you."

"I said a serious discussion."

"I'm being serious."

"Then you're not so smart as you seem. A government that would do this to its enemies isn't going to be careful about who it decides is an enemy. Keeping quiet isn't any guarantee that you'll be safe."

I shrugged. "Hard to argue that making a lot of noise improves your safety, though."

"That is short-term thinking. Long-term the only way to be safe is to change to a better government."

"Pretty speculative bet."

"Yeah. Long odds. But I want to make them better." She smiled at me and her charm flicked back on, dazzling me momentarily. "Now, how do I stop myself from being spied on?"

The protesters in the OPD kettle were all ages, but they skewed young, Kriztina's age, with snappy-funny signs designed to be photographed and socialed. I watched them organize themselves with admirable efficiency. The ones with batteries were setting up charging stations; the ones with drone feeds were holding up their screens for others to see; others were doing first aid or recording each other doing direct-to-camera mini-speeches. I overheard a law student interviewing a protester pointing out which cop had hit her friend.

Over it all, I kept hearing people shouting out words I couldn't quite make out.

I cornered a woman, young, cornrowed hair that turned into ponytails with blue tips, wearing a bulky old leather jacket and leggings over runners' legs. "Are you shouting out 'Hufflepuff'?"

As she nodded, I heard an answering call, "Hufflepuff," and another girl, Latina, sparkly Chuck Taylors and a Ramones/Bernie Sanders mashup tee, emerged out of the crowd and gave the first girl a hug. I realized I could hear others calling "Slytherin" and "Gryffindor" and "Ravenclaw," and other answering calls, groups self-assembling, hugging, showing their phones to each other, ignoring me.

"Excuse me? What is this Harry Potter thing?"

The girl grinned at me. "Dumbledore's Army! It's how we organize our affinity groups. That way you can always find people to get your back—the houses let us find the kind of people who share our tactics and style." She tapped an enamel pin on her lapel, yellow and black diagonal stripes. "Don't worry, we're trans-inclusive. JKR won't have a thing to do with us—we keep waiting for her to sue. You want to join?"

I absorbed this ridiculous idea.

The girl produced a strip of yellow-and-black-striped ribbon and a safety pin. "Do you want in? I'm Lanae, by the way."

"No thanks. No offense, but I never really felt like a Hufflepuff."

"There's other houses. What's your name?"

"Masha."

"What house are you, Masha?"

I decided to play along. "Slytherin."

"I think I heard them over there," Lanae said, pointing. She tapped her phone quickly. "The Hufflepuffs on the other side of the fence are getting everyone's details to give to the legal team. Maybe you should check in with them before you go looking for the Slytherins. Just in case, you know."

"No thanks. I'd like to keep my name from ending up on any kind of list."

Lanae side-eyed me. "Would it be better if you ended up in jail *without* your name written down by someone on the outside?"

"Of course not. I'll just have to make sure I don't end up in jail. Besides, I have my own lawyer."

Lanae looked more closely at me. "Wait, *Masha*? As in Free Masha?" She looked around and spotted a sign, then found a sign with a not-great picture of me on it and pointed. "*That* Masha?"

I nodded. "Yeah. The signs weren't my idea."

"But you were locked up?"

"I was."

"And . . . ?"

"Now I'm not."

"Shit, girl. Is Tanisha with you?"

"No." I didn't see any positive outcome from volunteering any more than that.

"No?"

"No."

"Why not?"

She wasn't going to like the answer. "They offered us a deal. I took it. She didn't."

"What *kind* of a *deal*?"

I guess I was about to go to war against Dumbledore's Army. I'd faced down scarier armies.

"They didn't want me to talk about how they came to arrest us, and in exchange they agreed to drop it. That sounded like a good deal to me. I talked it over with Tanisha and she said she didn't agree, and told me that if I was going to take it, she hoped that I would help her get out."

I watched her digest this. From what I remembered of my Rowling canon, Hufflepuffs liked simple stories with good and evil, ironclad principles that you followed to be virtuous or broke to be wicked. I was *definitely* a Slytherin.

She squinted at me. "Why did they arrest you?"

"Like I said, I agreed not to talk about that."

She didn't like that at all. "So what are you doing to get her free?"

"I hired a lawyer. A good one. An expensive, good lawyer." Why did I feel the need to justify myself to this random (literal) fangirl?

"Where's that lawyer now?"

I gestured to the jailhouse, beyond the fence. "Inside. Or at least, her paralegal is. She was going back to her office to file paperwork and terrorize people by phone. It's a team sport."

"And your position is what, 'person out front, shouting'?"

I listened for a second, waited until we heard another crash. They were coming pretty regular now. "No. I'm here because of *that*. Someone's using half the cars in Oakland as murdermobiles. We came here because we figured we'd be safer with a big building to shelter in."

The side-eye I got for this was epic. "You came to go to jail?"

I shrugged. "Beats going to meet my maker as a smear on the road."

She scowled. "I heard that the stories about the cars were totally exaggerated—a couple cars got into fender benders and it got clickbaited into a major panic. Now you've got assholes driving around like maniacs." She gestured toward the place where the car had run into the fence.

"Nope." No point in arguing.

Lanae's frown deepened.

"Well, it was nice to meet you, Lanae. I'm going to find a quiet place and try to get that lawyer on the phone."

Lanae scowled at me. I wandered off. The floodlights were on from all directions, shining down from cherry-pickers, and the people who'd escaped the kettle were massed on the outsides of the temporary fencing all around. The enclosed area was about the size of the playing field out back of my old junior high, and crowded. The cops had managed to capture a sizable fraction of the demonstrators—at least a thousand of us, and there were more inside than outside.

For now, they seemed content to let us stew. If I were them, I'd be using those drones buzzing over us to triangulate on known figures, making a ranked list of who to take in and who to let go after a quick search and some light questioning.

I had to try calling Marcus and Ange. I turned my phone's networking back on, feeling naked and exposed as I did. So much surveillance gear around but I needed to find them. I was going to be dropping this phone in the shredder when this was all over.

He answered on the third ring. "Are you okay?"

"Yeah. On the west side. You two got out?"

"Yes. We're both all right." I hadn't asked, but whatever. "Have you heard from the paralegal or the lawyer? I've left them both messages and gave them all our numbers." On an unencrypted line in the middle of a police lockdown. Smooth, M1k3y, very smooth.

"Not yet, but my phone was off. I'll check in."

"Things are weird out here, Masha. There's all kinds of news media showing up, way more than I've ever seen for a protest. They're practically crackling, they're so excited. Did you see the chopper?"

I had noticed it circling, higher up than the drones. "Yeah. Military?"

"News. That's a news helicopter for a protest with a thousand people at it. Normally, I'd be so goddamned psyched to see this much press at a protest, because it would mean that anything the cops did would end up on a million screens ten seconds later. But the cops are looking pretty happy about this situation, and there are some slick guys here I recognize from SFPD and Oakland police brass, the cable sound bites and press-conferences guys. They're in dress uniforms and one of them even had a makeup crew going over him with powder. It's *weird*."

"Shit. This can't be good."

I heard muffled speech as he conferred with Ange on something, then I heard both of them shouting, and then their shouts were drowned out by the screams from outside the fence, and booms, and then a series of crashes that seemed to go on forever.

"Marcus?" I couldn't hear him over the din. "Marcus!" I hung up and texted him instead.

> What happened?

No answer. People were streaming past me again, and again half were running toward the crashes and half were running away, getting in one another's way, tripping over each other.

I stopped. I was running in circles, screaming and shouting, and that never got anything done. I stood on tiptoes, dodging the crowd, keeping the weight off my bad leg, trying to get a look at what was going on. The bright spotlights and deep shadows made confusion of everything, though. It seemed like maybe slightly more people were moving away from the place where that huge crash had come from than toward it, and so I decided I'd buck the trend, and began to push my way through the crowd to whatever it was they were streaming away from.

As I got closer, the crowd got thinner, and quieter, and grimmer.

A stretch of the portable fence had been destroyed by a Jeep, its paintwork scratched, its grille battered, its windshield starred. Its front end was tilted on a ramp made from fallen fencing. Behind it were at least three more cars that had rear-ended it, driving it forward and dragging the fencing forward with it, the huge water-filled bases the poles had been set in tilted and dragged across the parking lot. Cops were cautiously circling the wrecks from behind, but on our side of the fence, protesters were formed in urgent little circles around half a dozen injured, some of whom were screaming or crying, some of whom were ominously silent.

I got my wilderness first aid certification in high school, and then recertified at FOB Grizzly, and one thing I'd learned is that any time someone is injured, the most important thing was to step up instead of waiting for someone else to do it. The "bystander effect" means that any time someone is hurt, everyone who's in a position to help is convinced that someone else in the crowd is better trained and better equipped, and will hold back. People can die waiting for someone—anyone—to take the initiative and help.

I limped down the line, taking note of how bad off the wounded seemed to be and whether anyone was actively helping them. There were seven people in varying degrees of pain, and all but two had someone doing *something* for them, so I cruised around the remaining two for a second pass, triaging them. One was a young black guy who was clutching his arm and groaning and thrashing. The other was an older Latino guy who was absolutely motionless within a semicircle of people who stood looking helplessly around at each other and him.

I pushed past them and knelt beside him, running two fingers into his mouth to make sure he wasn't choking on his tongue, then lowering my ear to hear his breath—ragged, slow—then putting two fingers on his throat to feel for his thready, weak pulse. At least he was breathing, at least he had a pulse. What came next? Physical examination. I turned my phone's flashlight back on and pointed at a random girl in the crowd, young, afro-puffs, yoga pants and a bomber jacket and big shoes and one of those Harry Potter badges, and I brandished my phone at her: "Take this, shine it where my hands are."

She stepped forward and leaned down close enough that I could see that her badge read SLYTHERIN and then she took my phone and did as I asked, while I examined the man, probing him from the crown of his head to his feet, looking for abrasions, feeling for bumps. He had a fist-sized goose egg on the back of his head and his pants were shredded at the knees, ugly scrapes running all the way down his shins.

I reconstructed what had happened: the wrecks had plowed into the fence, the fence had tipped forward and whacked this poor guy on the head, driving him to his knees and knocking him out. I finished my check and rechecked his breathing and pulse.

"Is he okay?" the young Slytherin asked. I couldn't look at her without blinding myself on the light from my phone, and waved at her to aim it away.

"He's not dead, he's breathing, his heart is beating. I don't know if he's okay. I think we should turn him on his side so that he doesn't asphyxiate if he pukes. We'll need to use something for a pillow and then I'll need your help keeping his head still when we roll him so we don't strain his neck in case he has a spinal injury. Got a sweater or anything?"

She took off the small backpack she was wearing and rummaged through it, but didn't turn up anything; a guy with short dreads and goggles on his forehead passed me a rolled-up towel that smelled of chlorine. "I came here from swim team practice," he said, and I carefully got it seated under the old guy's head. I got the two of them to take hold of the man and we counted one-two-three and gently rolled him into the recovery position. He groaned and thrashed weakly with his free arm, which I took as a good sign, and I checked his pulse and breathing again.

"You, Slytherin," I said. The girl pointed at herself. "You busy?"

She looked puzzled. "What?"

"You got somewhere you need to be? Someone should sit here with this guy and talk to him and keep him calm, stop people from tripping over him, check and make sure he's breathing and his heart's still beating."

"What do I do if he stops breathing?"

"You know mouth-to-mouth?"

Her eyes got wide. "No."

"Then you shout, 'Who the fuck here knows CPR?' until someone comes over."

I could see that she was about to back off, so I said, "Come on, this guy needs you."

"What about you?"

"I'm going to see who else needs help, because I *do* know CPR. Good enough for you?"

She wasn't happy about it, but she knelt by the guy.

"What's your name?"

"Lisette."

"Lisette, you're doing something important and good here, okay? Shouting at cops is fun and all, but ultimately, if you don't stop to help some poor asshole who's been mowed down by a car, can you really claim to be committed to any kind of social justice?" I wanted to be sure she stayed put.

"Okay," she said, voice small.

"Okay," I said. I shook her hand and looked her solemnly in the eye, sending her a deep don't-fuck-this-up crossed with a you-got-this. Once I was semi-sure she'd gotten the message, I limped away, my knee throbbing.

Three steps away, as I was digging out my phone to try to reach Marcus again, someone tapped me on the shoulder. I turned around and someone else grabbed my phone out of my hand.

"Hey—" is all I got out before I felt the pressure in my side.

"Don't make me use this," said a voice on that side. I turned slowly, saw a guy there—tall, white, mid-twenties, faded OCCUPY tee under a worn denim jacket, black jeans, and combat boots. He was looking at me with pure cop glare.

"Okay." It was clearly his show. He had enough of a high-strung vibe that I didn't want to tempt him.

"This way." He steered me with a hand on my bicep. I limped alongside him, looking around unobtrusively, trying to spot Marcus and Ange on the other side of the fence.

We headed to a place where a small knot of other young men about his age were milling by a dark stretch of fence, and then the men parted and let us slip through. A guy on the other side of the fence separated a stretch of fence from its support pole and let us pass through, and a moment later we were stepping into an armored police bus.

I breathed slowly and tried to ignore the thudding of my heart in my ears.

There were lawyers looking for me, and friends around me, and important people would notice if I disappeared. Not to mention noisy fucks like Marcus Yallow.

The bus was brightly lit inside, but had blacked-out windows. It was definitely a command center of some kind, and long work surfaces stretched down its length, bolted-down monitors and keyboards mounted on fold-out arms. There were at least ten of these workstations, but only three of them were staffed. Once the door had closed behind me, the guy who'd had me by the arm spun me around so that I was facing the wall of the bus and pushed me roughly forward, making me catch myself with my arms out, then he kicked my legs apart and frisked me almost before I realized what was happening. He was good at his job and wanted to be sure I knew it.

When he was done with me, he stepped back and I turned around cautiously. The three people at their keyboards kept their heads down; they had polarizing privacy sheets that made their screens look black from my angle. One of them—an older woman with iron-gray hair in a kind of Midwestern-mom cut—looked up from her screen and considered me. The guy who'd dragged me onto the bus kind of faded toward the back, leaving the two of us to stare each other down.

"Well, hello there." Her voice was warm, matronly. She smiled and it even reached her eyes. "I've heard an awful lot about you. Herthe Netzke sends her best."

I kept my face wooden. "That's nice. Tell her I hope her rash clears up soon and doesn't leave any scars."

The smile vanished. "Have a seat."

I settled painfully onto one of the work stools bolted to the bus floor in front of an unoccupied workstation.

I thought about keeping up the smartass routine—*nice place you've got here, love what you've done with it*—but decided there was no upside there. Iron Mom showed no sign of manifesting her kindly Midwesterner persona again, so we stared at each other for a while. I didn't really have any incentive to give in, so I just waited.

"Herthe wanted me to talk to you about your role with Xoth."

"I don't have a role with Xoth."

"Masha, you don't *currently* have a defined role, but that doesn't exclude the possibility that you could have a role in the future. We have a history together."

"We? As in, you work for Xoth?"

"I'm the regional team lead for Northern California."

"That's a pretty plum job."

"It could be, if."

"If?"

She looked at me. "Our lawyers reviewed your NDA prior to this meeting and confirmed that your confidentiality burden extends beyond your termination. The penalties are severe."

"You could just ask me to keep it under wraps."

She stared at me a while longer, until I carefully recited, "I understand that I can't repeat anything you say here without severe legal ramifications to me and everyone I love."

"I know you think you're joking, but for the record, this conversation is being recorded and will be preserved as evidence in the event that we need to prove that you willingly violated your confidentiality obligations in relation to Xoth or any part of this conversation we're having now."

"Well, now I'm intrigued."

She rolled her eyes. I got the sense that the tough lady act wasn't necessarily supposed to scare me so much as to indicate that this was serious business and no time for fucking around. The fact that I was smart-assing my way through it was putting her on tilt, at least a little, and I decided that made it all tactically sound. But also: it felt good to get to her.

"Masha, I know this may surprise you, but we at Xoth are as horrified as you were to discover that Zyz was attacking Americans with indiscriminately targeted and illegal cyberweapons. We are committed to comporting ourselves in a strictly lawful manner, and we make sure that the terms of every one of our engagements reflect those values."

I didn't roll my eyes, but she guessed what I was thinking about.

"As you understand, we operate in international theaters, with clients who operate under a variety of legal frameworks. In each territory, we adhere to those frameworks."

"So, you're saying that if the Slovstakian constitution says the government is allowed to kill anyone it doesn't like, you make sure you don't do anything that would violate those very strict laws?"

"I'm saying that we follow the local laws, wherever we operate. It's not our job to export American laws to every other country in the world; where countries permit, say, recreational drugs, or prostitution, we don't work to stop them; in the UK we help shut down libel, in Thailand we protect the king from lèse-majesté, and in America we uphold the Bill of Rights."

"And in Slovstakia . . . ?"

"In Slovstakia, we do as the Slovstakians do." She made a little face, like I was being stupid. "Of course."

This wasn't going to go anywhere. Pivot: "You mentioned Zyz?"

"Zyz does not have the same commitment to following the law that we do. We believe that it is in America's interest for law enforcement to be working with companies like Xoth, not entities like Zyz."

"Xoth, Zyz. What is it with you guys and consonants, anyway?"

She gave me the tiniest of smiles. "We used the same branding agency and they didn't disclose the conflict of interest until after we'd had the business cards printed and the signs made. We don't use that agency anymore."

"Good call."

"Masha, there isn't a lot of time. Our understanding is that things are about to get very bad." She tilted her head toward the blacked-out bus windows. "Out there." Beat. "Where your friends are."

Shit. "Okay, give me your pitch."

"As you know, Zyz is bidding on a much larger contract, to provide security services, data gathering, and predictive analytics to the city of San Francisco. But they've been caught by one of Xoth's alumna"—she nodded at me— "doing dirty things in Oakland, the kind of thing that could kill their deal. They're panicking, because they're having trouble rolling over their debts, and In-Q-Tel isn't willing to give them another cash infusion—which hadn't been such a big deal when they were confident they were about to land a plum contract with the SFPD. Creditors would have lined up to lend to them once that deal was inked.

"But *you* pose a threat to all that. They thought they could buy you off and lock your friend up. But that didn't happen and now they're in panic mode. This is a life-or-death moment for them—if they lose the SFPD contract, they lose everything."

I was getting the gist. "If they lose the SFPD contract, they go broke, and then Oakland and San Francisco are both up for grabs."

She stared coolly at me. How had I ever mistaken her for maternal? She was Carrie Johnstone with better facial control. This woman, Carrie, Ilsa: Was it just a coincidence that the only women who rose through the ranks in this industry acted like poster children for toxic masculinity? Was that my future, if I stayed in the business?

"Masha, let me be direct. Your actions in Slovstakia were reckless and Herthe did you an enormous favor when she let you part ways on the terms you enjoyed. Within Xoth, you are considered a loose cannon. But Xoth has ways of working with loose cannons: we like to bring them in as contractors, for specific jobs. It's a very lucrative, arm's-length arrangement that would let you choose your engagements. Frankly, we think it's a good deal for us, for you, and for America."

My snort was very quiet, but I made sure she could hear it.

She shook her head. "Someone is going to provide predictive analytics to American police departments. It could be a company like Zyz. The way they do it is to just have a black box ascribe guilt to various brown and black people on the basis that poor neighborhoods have more crime, so they must have more criminals. And since no one cares when black and brown people complain about overpolicing, no one can tell if they're targeting the right black and brown people, and so they can just claim it's working. After all, 'You got the wrong guy' is exactly what a criminal would say.

"Xoth is better than that. Our *technology* is better than that, as you know. You helped develop it, you helped support it. When our analytics make a prediction, we follow up on that prediction to see if we got it right, and if we didn't, we modify our models. That's the difference between Xoth and Zyz: we care if we're right; they just want to land the next contract."

"So I should help you somehow"—I was getting a sense of *how,* actually—"because you're the snoops that America deserves, not like the scum you run into in the lobby of your branding agency."

"Yes." She looked at me steadily.

"And you want what from me?"

She looked at her screen for a moment. "In nine minutes, there's going to be a terrible accident, just over there." She gestured outside the bus window.

"What kind of accident?"

"You remember what happened in Slovstakia? The night of the cars?"

"I don't have to remember it, lady. I'm living through it."

"No, you're not. Not yet. Everything that's happened so far has been a warmup, dialing in the controls. Now that they have attained their desired degree of precision, they're ready to execute. They learned their lesson in Bltz about going crazy with the self-driving car gambit, so now they're going to go *surgical*."

Translation: Zyz provided the tools that allowed the Slovstakian government to attack its citizens, and they're the ones driving Oakland's murder-cars tonight. And they're about to do something really, really bad.

"I don't know your name," I said.

"No, you don't."

"I don't know if you're here on behalf of Xoth, or just some rando with a bus. You wouldn't be the first social engineer with a props budget."

She nodded. "No, I wouldn't be, and the stakes here are high. We're down to eight minutes, so perhaps it would be good to ask a friend to join us." She turned her laptop to me and I saw a video feed of Ilsa, a hotel-room bed behind her, daylight streaming through the blinds of some distant city.

"Hello, Masha." She stared evenly into the camera.

"No offense, but I'd like to see you do something that would be computationally intensive to fake."

She grimaced. "What did you have in mind?"

"Something involving a lot of frenetic motion."

"You want me to dance." It wasn't a question.

"That would do."

She stood up, opened her wallet, flipped through it, withdrew a German driver's license, and held it up to the camera.

"That could be a macro."

She rolled her eyes. "Masha, your friend Kriztina lives at 301 Nedbalova

Street. Your 401(k) is entirely invested in Vanguard Target Retirement 2060 Funds. Your Slovstakian phone number is 13–256–278–887. You billed Xoth for more than $400 a week's worth of Bulleit Rye from your minibar fridge."

I rolled my eyes back. "What can I do for you, Herthe?"

"Masha, in six minutes, some very bad things will happen; these will be directed by Zyz, and Zyz's senior management intends to use these events as the basis for insisting that the City of San Francisco would be very foolish not to contract for Zyz's security service, and that the City of Oakland has more pressing business than finding blame for a little overzealous baseband radio malware insertion."

I swallowed. Somewhere, in a compartment that I'd locked down and buried deep, there was a rattle and crash. There were people out there that I knew. Strangers, too. People I liked, and just people.

"Again: What can I do for you?"

"I believe you have already discussed the kind of collaboration we envision. If you were to discuss the details of your findings during sales calls on behalf of Xoth with the SFPD, and possibly in discussions with the city attorneys for Oakland and San Francisco, we believe that our position that they should switch contractors will be especially convincing. There is a very large sum of money involved; the company that supplies predictive analytics and related security services to San Francisco and Oakland will have an enormous advantage in other cities in the US and abroad. By the way, we have five minutes to act."

I stuffed my panic-surge into another compartment. "Five minutes. But if I help, you can stop it?"

She glared at the camera for a moment. "Masha, the tools they are deploying to direct the autonomous vehicles were developed by a Xoth contractor who later left to work for Zyz. We have extensive countermeasures that we have never used in the field, but we have a high degree of confidence in their efficacy."

"But you won't use them unless I agree to help you?"

"Without you, we will not be able to easily attribute the attacks to Zyz. So perhaps we will have to let things get worse, before we make them better. If you do not agree to help us, we will need to establish some other angle in making our case regarding Zyz's unsuitability for the job."

"Why not just deploy the countermeasures and then tell everyone you pre-vented mass slaughter?"

Her eyes flicked to another part of her screen. "We may have less time than we thought."

*Or you may be trying to pressure me into caving.* My hands were sweaty; a dribble ran down my back and infiltrated the crack of my ass. I didn't let my-self squirm.

*What was the harm?* The harm was that Marcus and Tanisha would think I was a sellout. Big deal. They already thought I was a sellout, and I thought they were dumbass hippies. None of that would change no matter what I did. And it was true: Ilsa was no Carrie Johnstone and Xoth wasn't Zyz—but of course, there were dead people in Bltz who'd been mowed down by cars compromised by Xoth's malware—malware that Zyz had stolen and set loose in Oakland.

Did I care which secretive cyber-arms dealer supplied mass surveillance and compliance tools in my hometown? Tanisha would tell me that they were all rotten to the core. Marcus would call them all the enemy. I'd worked for both of them, and I knew them better than any of my friends. They weren't lairs of supervillains: they were open-plan offices full of awkward nerds maintaining buggy code that their marketing departments had overpromised on. They were Dilberts, not Dr. Evils.

Plus, Marcus wouldn't be able to disapprove of me if I let him get killed.

"I'm in."

Ilsa cut her feed and the lady with the gray hair clicked her mouse once. "We'll be in touch," she said, and pointed to the door. I let myself off the bus; the dickhead who'd taken my phone was waiting outside, and he handed it back without a word. He was going to be a fun co-worker.

I was outside the fence. On the other side: Tanisha, and, possibly, a paralegal who'd been paid a very large amount of my money to represent us. On this side, cops in great number, my new boss—same as the old boss—and Marcus and Ange.

I had a sudden, overwhelming urge to go home: call a cab, give it my mother's address, get the spare key out of the magnetic box around the side of the house, and sneak into my old room and just ghost all these complicated pains-in-the-ass

I'd found myself tied to. I could block their numbers, blackhole their emails, buy an off-the-shelf Delaware LLC, and start billing Xoth for high-priced consulting fees.

I was jetlagged and bruised, buffeted by shocks and horrors, my knee hurt, and I was done.

I walked away from the bus and the police lines. The protesters who'd escaped the kettle were a hundred yards away, milling about anxiously, some brightly illuminated by the lights the police had hoisted up on cherry-pickers, others in deep shadow next to them. The places where the cars had rammed the fences writhed with activity, EMTs and cops, stretchers and ambulances. It was chaos, all chaos, and I didn't belong in any of it.

A chorus of blaring car horns cut through the night and twanged the entire crowd's nerves, cops and protesters all turning to look up the road at the fleet barreling toward us: minivans with Muni logos, little electric Ubers, East Bay Municipal Utility District trucks, all packed in the kind of close formation you only got with vehicle-to-vehicle networking in self-driving cars, each vehicle separated by a precise, steady three inches of space on all sides. They raced down the street toward us, and people screamed and ran, smashing into each other; a couple of dumb and/or brave cops drew their guns and started firing at the engine blocks, intensifying the panic, and then—

—they braked.

The squeal of tires and the grinding of the engines wasn't as loud as the crashes had been, but they were somehow more jarring, asshole-puckering noises that every modern human knew meant *Get out of the way!* The cars may have been able to maneuver in lockstep, but they all had different amounts of tread and brake-pad wear—so when they all slammed on their brakes in unison, the tight formation turned into a cascading fender bender, and by the sounds of things some of those cars had tried to shift themselves into reverse when they realized they were about to crash—the tortured transmissions made a sound I can only describe as *eldritch*.

I had saved the night. No one knew it and if they did, they'd hate me for it, but I had rescued them all from a mass slaughter calculated to so paralyze everyone's minds with impotent terror that they would pay anything to anyone who could promise them relief. Instead of the freewheeling, law-skirting cowboys of Zyz, I'd delivered them to the cold and rational hands of Ilsa the She-Wolf and the mature and sober people of Xoth. I may even have put Zyz out of business, or, in the words of Carrie Johnstone herself, "neutralized" them as a threat.

I had done a good night's work. Tanisha would be okay, especially now that her high-priced lawyer could drive from one place to another without risking homicidal robo-cars. I checked my wallet. I had a thick wad of dollars, another thick wad of euros, and some very thin platinum credit cards.

Fuck all this noise: I was going to go to the Nikko hotel, and I was going to order room-service sushi, and pour every miniature bottle in the minibar into the ice bucket and chug it.

# CHAPTER 9

I'd apparently had the good sense to hang out the Do Not Disturb before passing out, because no one knocked on my room door and I was able to sleep in until twelve. The Nikko was built to cater to Asian businessmen rocking that crushing east–west transit arc, and it had first-rate blackout curtains. I brushed my teeth and then phoned down to room service for a bathing suit—it's a *good* hotel—and made my way to the pool to swim off the stupid succession of days and nights and booze and jetlag and violence and injury.

I had some good bruises and scratches that the pool water stung, but after a dozen laps my brain went to the swim-zone and my attention turned watery and I just sculled up and down, up and down, until my arms ached and my bruised knee throbbed, only stopping once my calves started cramping. Back in the room, I let the hot shower run just shy of scalding for so long that the mirrors were dripping with condensation, and when I squeaked out a clear patch with my palm, I saw that I'd turned the color of a jumbo shrimp.

I sat on the bedspread, damp and sweating, staring at my laptop, which was staring at me. I couldn't even remember if I'd transferred my nail polish/screw photos to my new phone. Any evil maids who'd taken advantage of my swim break could look forward to high-fives around the office that night.

It was too late for the Nikko's Japanese breakfast buffet, but room service sent up enough sushi to deplete a Pacific atoll and by the time I was done, I was feeling soft and satiated. Somewhere in my inbox would be terms of my new gig from Ilsa and Xoth, along with whatever duties they were expecting from me.

Mixed in with that business-as-usual, of course, would be bewildered messages from Marcus and Ange, and from Tanisha, assuming she'd been sprung. But the night's adventures had already faded like a hangover dream, a hazy mess that I'd automatically packaged up and put in their own tightly sealed compartment.

I'm good at waiting in hotel rooms, but with a comfortable future ahead of me and my hometown's familiar symphony of noises leaking through the windows from the streets far below, I found my feet itching for a walk.

Last night's clothes stank of sweat and were streaked with dirt and blood, but room service was happy to deliver a set of sweats with the hotel's spa logo on them. I turned my socks and underwear inside-out; there was a Gap on Union Square where I could buy some normcore generic clothing units. In the meantime, sweats were hardly too casual for the Tenderloin, where you could regularly find folks wandering around in their pajamas or even just underwear on a warm day.

At first glance, the Tenderloin was the same as it ever was. I passed an alley in which I saw someone shooting up heroin, afternoon sex workers soliciting outside flophouses, corner stores with old men stationed outside like statues, paper-bagged forties in hand; but gradually I started to register the changes: a fancy coffee shop that was tailor made for the Marcus Yallows of the world; a farm-to-table restaurant with a heavily scrawled-over menu under Plexiglas packed with young tech dudes with huge beards and shiny-haired tech women eating baby greens and chattering loud enough to be heard from the sidewalk.

San Francisco had moved on during my years away: my friends, my family, and my city—all transformed into something new and only vaguely familiar. Who would I have been if I'd stayed in the city? Would I have helped gentrify Oakland with a tiny apartment or a run-down house that I laboriously repainted on my evenings and weekends, when I wasn't grinding out code to increase ad-clicks? A decade ago, I'd been drunk on the power of technology to make a dent in the universe; I had sobered up in the intervening years, had turned my love into just a job, which is to say, I'd become an adult. Maybe if I'd stayed here, I could have remained a child in a city that just wanted everyone to play and have a good time (while increasing clicks on ads).

I could have remained my mother's daughter, seeing her for dinner once a week and talking on the phone on alternate days.

I went to the Gap and bought some normcore and left my tracksuit on a flophouse stoop. Someone would find a use for it. The street, I'm told, finds its own use for things.

By the time I had resolved to check out of the Nikko and find somewhere less haunted to camp out, I'd gone way past the checkout deadline and there was a red message light on the room phone that turned out to be the front desk telling me that "as a courtesy" they had billed my card for another night's stay. I decided I could live with another night of excellent room-service sushi.

I torrented a whole bingeable season of some HBO historical spy drama, which I figured would either be good for professional training or a giggle, plugged my laptop in by the bed, and changed into flannel pajama bottoms and an oversized tee from the Gap to start watching while I waited for my sushi.

The doorbell rang just after I had finished both tiny vodkas from the minibar and my stomach was growling. I cleared the litter of shopping bags and toiletry packaging off the desk to make room for the tray and opened the door, making a conscious effort to seem sober.

"There's space over—" is as far as I got before Carrie Johnstone stepped into the room and closed the door behind her.

"Hi there," she said, and bolted the door behind her.

Tanisha once saved my life.

I was never a great student, but my teachers knew I was too smart to flunk, so they put up with a lot of shit from me and still gave me C-minuses, which only encouraged me. I'd skipped a couple grades before getting to high school, so they could always chalk up my poor performance to my "immaturity" and "difficulty socializing."

Okay, forget the scare quotes. I *did* have difficulty socializing. In ninth grade, I was a twelve-year-old among fourteen-year-olds. They had pubic hair and tits and zits and height, and I was short and nondescript and shy and had buried the training bra my mother had insisted on at the bottom of my underwear drawer. I went into school traumatized by what would happen when the

other girls saw me while we changed for gym class; a month later I was traumatized by what *I* had seen and heard. We were only a couple of years apart,
but those years were epochal.

Inevitably, I tried to act "mature"—if it had been ten years earlier, I'd have
taken up smoking. Instead, I swore, I conspicuously drank coffee, I shoplifted
miniskirts and halter tops and changed into them in the school bathroom. I
tried to strike up conversations with the coolest, meanest girls, who recognized
that I wasn't significant enough to even bully, and ignored me.

End of tenth grade: I was standing alone by the portable classroom, trying to
look as tragic as possible, having just attempted a black eyeliner extravaganza I'd
been patiently reverse-engineering by sneaking looks at the other girls and then
trying to re-create what I saw in the bathroom mirror at home. I thought I'd finally gotten it right and had done my eyes in the bathroom before first bell. Now I
was performing "teenager," and really putting all the tragedy I could muster into it.

The senior who approached me out there was someone I'd seen around, but
I'd never learned his name. He was good-looking, tall, a kind of proto-hipster
with a lot of vintage denim and faded chambray shirts that gave him an urban
cowboy vibe. I liked his engineer boots, which were both worn and shined,
really completing the look. His eyes were big and soulful and brown, with little
laugh-lights that danced in them as he smiled at me.

"You okay?"

It took me a moment to realize he was talking to me, and another moment
to realize that he was commenting on my tragic performance. I swelled a little
at the success of my method acting. He was cute, if not exactly my type, and
he was old and mature and paying attention to me.

His name was Riley Turkle and he was a *great* listener, asking the kinds of
leading questions that opened me up all the way, so before the bell rang I'd
spilled half my life's secrets to him, and then arranged to meet him after the final bell to "hang out." He got me to hike up to Sutro Tower for the sunset, and
kept on with the questions, listening, drinking me in, hanging on my every
word, his attention like the searchlight beam lancing out of Alcatraz, hitting
me full force every time I snuck a glance at him. He bought me a burrito and
then saw me to my mom's door and even *shook my hand* instead of going in for
a sloppy California hug.

I floated up the stairs to my bedroom and put some Leonard Cohen on my CD player and got out my sketchbook and started doodling and daydreaming. I didn't go so far as to practice signing my name as "Mrs. Masha Turkle," but it definitely crossed my mind.

If this sounds stupid and sudden, just remember: I was *fourteen*. I was a raging ball of hormones and zits and moods. I had never had a romantic infatuation before and I didn't know what they were supposed to feel like. As far as I could tell, something *cosmic* had just happened to me, like reality turned 32.56 degrees north-northwest and given a hard shake. The world was not the same. Colors looked different. My skin *felt* different, tingly and weird in a way that I know now was *horniness* but then I had no words or concepts for.

Riley caught up with me the next morning as I was walking toward the school gate and said something like, "I was hoping I'd run into you," and I nearly melted down on the spot as blood ran into places it normally avoided, cheeks and ears and stomach and a spot a few inches south of my stomach.

He found me again on my free period, and at lunch, and I floated through the remaining periods until he found me again after last bell and brought me to his favorite graffiti alley and a skate park and a hot-dog cart on Market Street whose kielbasas he pronounced to be "magnificent" and I had no choice but to agree, never having had another one to compare it to.

Day three, he held my hand.

Day four, he kissed me as we went up the BART escalator.

Day five, Tanisha caught up with me on my corner, just as I was turning onto Geary. She fell in beside me.

Though we'd been friends years before, we'd drifted apart after middle school. I had taken some classes with Tanisha and been in a study group with her, but we weren't exactly friends in those days. But still, she was a familiar face. She'd been standing on the stoop of a shuttered clothing boutique, clearly waiting for me, but as familiar as she was, I was more surprised than freaked out.

"Uh, hi?"

"Hey, Masha. I need to talk to you."

"Oh."

"Can we walk this way?" She gestured uphill, a detour that would still get us to school, but without any main streets.

"I guess so?"

Once we'd turned off Geary again, she made a point of looking around, left and right and behind us, and I started to go from surprised to weirded.

"Everything okay?"

She didn't say anything. I snuck a look at her and saw that she was thinking hard, serious and frowny. Tanisha was always studious in school, one of the good girls who worked hard, but I'd never seen her with an expression like *that*. She sighed. Again.

"Riley Turkle is a rapist" is what she finally said.

I felt an icicle in my guts, but I kept walking, didn't miss a step.

"Did you hear what I said?"

"I heard you." My voice was smaller than I'd known it would be. My mind started to thaw, started to race, started to turn nasty: *jealous bitch, crazy ex-girlfriend, mind-fucker.* But even as I thought them, I was also thinking, *There's a certain internal consistency to this.* Some part of me had known all along that a handsome, older boy like Riley had no reason to go creepering around a young social outcast like me. No good reason. Not unless he had expended all his reputational capacity with the girls he *should* have been interested in. A part of me had been smart enough to look at the situation and think, *Well, this is a bit hard to explain, isn't it?*

But of course there was the part of me that wanted a different story: the story where a handsome prince looked beyond my weird face and my bad posture and my one tit bigger than the other and my zits and had seen his princess. When he kissed me, I'd felt like I was in a fairy-tale royal courtship. But fairy tales are not real.

"Okay, you heard me." She sighed. Again. "Look. I had a best friend in ninth grade, Sruthi Reddy. Riley came on to her like she was the only girl in the world, wrote her poems, sang her songs, carried her books. He talked her into sneaking out at night, her parents were strict, and took her to look at the stars. I got all of this in a play-by-play, of course, because she was my bestie, and so I knew something was up when she didn't call me after one of these nights. The night before he'd asked her to meet him at Sutro Tower to look at the full moon. He was going to get some weed, which Sruthi was excited about because it made her feel sophisticated.

"Sruthi didn't answer my calls or my texts, and when I called the landline at her house, I got the machine. I was worried, but it was a school day and I had band practice that night, and I sent her another text before bed, and she didn't answer that one, either.

"The next day, I left really early and I went to her house. I waited for her to come out the door, and waited, and waited and I was going to be late for school, so I rang the bell, and rang it, and I was about to go, but I thought I should ring it one more time and the door opened.

"She looked like a different person. Like her own ghost. One of her eyes was swollen shut, and her cheek was puffy, and she held one arm bent stiff in front of her, like it was about to fall off.

"As soon as she saw me, she made a mewing sound and tried to close the door. It was the most heartbreaking sound I'd ever heard, like she was too hurt to even cry out properly. I put out my hand so she'd have to close the door on my arm if she kept going and she jerked back like I was about to hit her and looked so scared and small it broke my heart. 'Sruthi, please, talk to me,' and she started to cry, quietly at first, but then she started sobbing and turned and ran away from the door. I let myself in, followed her cries up to her room, found her on her stomach on her bed, face in her pillow. I sat next to her, stroked her hair. When the cries let up a little, she told me.

"Riley Turkle is a rapist. They'd kissed and fooled around a little, but she wasn't ready to have sex and she'd told him so. They'd talked about it. He brought a condom along that night and was all like, 'I've planned our special night out together, baby, just relax and it'll be so good.'

"Sruthi loved Riley Turkle. He was the first boy who'd ever shown any interest in her. She'd never said no to him before, but she said no that night. She was loud and when he started grabbing at her, trying to take off her clothes, she pushed him and then she fought him. She yelled and screamed. He's a big guy, Riley Turkle. A big, rapey guy. Stronger than Sruthi. When he was done, he asked her if it was good for her and he told her he loved her and said he was so happy they'd taken such a big step together.

"Together!"

She'd stopped walking. I didn't want to, but I stopped too. I wanted to turn around and walk the other way. I wanted to tell her she was a liar. I wanted to go back in time ten minutes and put my fingers in my ears.

"They sent Sruthi away to school, a strict place where you're not allowed to use phones and they screen the letters you send out. Her parents were convinced that she'd done something wrong. They won't talk to me about her. I saw a For Sale sign on their lawn the last time I walked past their house."

I looked down. I was trying to find a compartment to put this in but it was too big for any of my compartments and it wouldn't fit. I'd build bigger compartments, later.

She sighed. A long pause. Another sigh. "Say something, okay?"

I shook my head. "What do you want me to do about it? You want me to get revenge for your friend?"

She was quiet for so long I looked up at her. She was jaw-open stunned.

"No!" she choked out at last. "I want to warn you so it doesn't happen to you."

*Oh.* "Oh." I realized she was trembling. "Thank you."

She let out a huge whoosh of breath. "I just don't want it to happen to anyone else."

"Thank you." I'd already said that, but it was all I had.

"Are you okay?"

I almost said I was, then I peeked inside my compartment. "No, not really." To my disgust, I started crying. I don't even know who I was crying for. Me? Sruthi? Both?

"Can I give you a hug?" Tanisha was a trailblazer in the whole consent movement. I nodded. She smelled of toothpaste. "Come on, I'll walk you to first period. We both have history."

The thought of going to school made me want to literally vomit. I tasted my breakfast burning up the back of my throat. The next time I saw Riley, I was going to break up with him, and when I did, he was going to demand to know why, and I'd either have to lie or tell the truth. I didn't know which would be worse.

"I'm going to go home," I said. "I'll call in and tell them I have cramps."

She nodded, her chin digging into my shoulder a little, then let go and looked into my eyes. "I don't think you should be alone right now. I know I wouldn't want to be. I saw how Riley got inside Sruthi's head. He's very good at being completely awful."

I didn't say anything. I'd gone to school with Tanisha for years but I don't think we'd spoken more than a couple of times. Was I really going to have her over to my house to hold my hand while I had a nervous breakdown?

Apparently.

Later that day, I played Harajuku Fun Madness for the first time, just the home version, solving online puzzles with Tanisha, keying off of each other, researching the fiendish riddles and drawing on our mutual deep knowledge of manga and anime, getting as far as we could without venturing out into the city to find physical clues (that would come later).

The next day, I took my ass to school, meeting Tanisha on my corner as arranged, and when Riley Turkle approached us at the gate, he got a funny look on his face when he saw Tanisha, and we both gave him our coolest looks. When he said my name, I stopped and looked him dead in the eye and told him if he ever spoke my name again I'd slap it the fuck out of his filthy mouth. He looked angry for a second and Tanisha closed ranks with me and we both stood up straight and dared him with our eyes. He wilted and slunk away and never spoke to either of us again, and both of us made it our mission from then on to talk to any girl we saw Riley Turkle speaking to, so that by the end of the year he would turn and run any time he saw me coming.

The next day, Tanisha introduced me to her best friend Becky and we formed an unstoppable Harajuku Fun Madness team.

The next day, I had a delayed meltdown about Riley Turkle, crying my face off in the girls' room next to the caf, imagining what might have happened, but for what Tanisha had done. I don't want to say that I'd have died if Riley Turkle had gotten a chance to rape me, but I'm 100 percent sure that Tanisha saved my life.

Carrie Johnstone didn't look so good, and she was still wearing the same clothes I'd seen her in the previous day (had it only been a day?). Judging from her crazy, glittering look, I'd bet good money she hadn't slept since the last time I'd seen her.

"Please cancel the room service, Masha. I don't want us to be interrupted while we talk."

Did she have a gun? It was hard enough to carry a sidearm when you flew all the time, the way Carrie Johnstone did, but when you crossed as many international borders as she did, it was impossible. California's ten-day waiting period meant she couldn't have just stopped at a gun shop on the way over and picked up a Glock. But maybe she didn't need to. Zyz maintained armories in many of the cities where it operated, especially pain-in-the-ass places like San Francisco. I decided I would assume she was fully armed and halfway out of her mind.

At least.

I picked up the desk phone and canceled the room service.

She picked her way to the desk chair like she was walking on a highwire and settled herself carefully into it.

"Masha—" she began, then stopped. She ran her fingers through her hair.

"Let me get you a glass of water?"

"A bottle, please. From the minibar." Because the tap was in the bathroom and I'd be out of her sight if I went to get her a glass from there. The water was the only thing in the minibar I *hadn't* drunk the night before. I gave her a bottle: Fiji, of course, because nothing connoted luxury like buying water from a conflict zone.

She unscrewed it and sucked back three-quarters of it in one go, then spilled the rest over her hands and palms, rubbing them together vigorously, up her wrists and forearms. Her filthy skin rinsed a little cleaner and the gray water ran into the gray carpet. She wiped her hands dry on the bedspread and then threw the empty plastic bottle over her shoulder.

"Masha, it could have been so good, do you understand that?"

Suddenly, I felt my disorientation recede. I knew how to deal with a depressive mother figure who felt that her best years were behind her and that I was somehow to blame. I had a *lot* of experience with that particular psychodrama.

"You'll do fine," I said. I got myself a water and sipped at it. My throat was very dry all of a sudden. "Don't catastrophize a minor setback."

Again, that glittering stare, purely unhinged. "It's not a minor setback, Masha. As I'm sure you understand, it's the end of Zyz. The end of something that a large number of powerful people put a lot of blood and treasure into. If we're lucky, someone will buy the company and break it up for parts. Someone like

*Xoth*." Her staring eyes were red-rimmed, wild. "They'll cream off the profit-able units and dump anything that competes with them."

She bunched her fists into the coverlet, squeezed rhythmically.

She closed her eyes, which was even scarier. "Masha, what are we going to do with you?"

If she were my actual mother, this is where I'd try to talk her down off the ledge. But she wasn't my mother. She was my abusive ex-boss. "You could get your ass out of my hotel room, for starters," I said. "You might be asking me for a job before you know it and you're not making much of an impression."

She actually smiled at that, but didn't open her eyes. "Masha, do you remember Costa Rica?"

Of course I remembered Costa Rica.

"Costa Rica was a cakewalk. I made sure it was. I talked down the people who wanted to make things much worse for you. Much worse. There's so much worse than Costa Rica."

Her voice held something I hadn't heard before, a thousand-mile sound of someone who'd seen and done things that I didn't want to think too hard about. I shuddered, glad her eyes were still closed.

I found my bravery. "Good thing Zyz is going down, then, huh? Sounds like it was enabling a lot of terrible people to do a lot of terrible things."

"If you think that they're going to forget what you did—" She opened her eyes. "You made a hell of a bed, Masha, and now you're going to lie in it."

"Carrie, what do you want from me? Why are you here?"

"I wanted to give you a chance. It's not too late. We know about Xoth's meeting with the city tomorrow, and we know you're going to be in it. You don't have to go, and if you do go, you don't have to say what Xoth wants you to say."

I was going to be in a meeting between Xoth and the city? Tomorrow? Glad someone decided to let me know. On the other hand, it was Ilsa's style, assuming that once you'd bought in, she could just maneuver you around on her chessboard without checking in with you. Carrie Johnstone's management style was half about making you want to help her out because she was your buddy, and half about scaring you because she was such a badass; Ilsa's management was a lot simpler: she was the boss and you did what she said. Very hierarchical. Very German. Once, I'd thought it refreshingly straightforward, free of the American pretense that we were all teammates.

I wondered how Ilsa would have gotten me back for the meeting if I'd boarded a plane to a Caribbean resort town after walking away from the demonstration—probably she'd have known as soon as I bought the ticket. Xoth provided a lot of anti-fraud services to the banking sector and it was an open secret that they could pull transaction data if they needed it. Zyz, too, of course, which would have been how Carrie Johnstone knew what hotel I was staying in.

Of course there'd be a meeting with the city. I was going back on the Xoth payroll. I'd have a new gig, doing the same kind of work I'd done in Slovstakia, and I could help out Tanisha and her friends on the side, just as I'd done with Kriztina. Because that had ended so well.

I'd already chosen my side.

"Carrie, I think you'd better leave now. Zyz is dead meat. You people committed murder with your car stunt. That's going to come out. You have no future. None. Get out of town. Get out of the country. Change your name. Get another passport from some Caribbean tax haven and start sending your résumé around to failed states. You guys lost, and you lost bad, and you lost because you fucked up, not because of anything Xoth or I did. Nothing I do is going to change history. Forensics are a thing. Someone is going to attribute those attacks, eventually, and then you all go down. The only question is when, not whether. Get the fuck out of here, you sad, failed, old woman, and go far, far away and never, ever talk to me again. Don't even think about me. Don't utter my fucking name. You created this situation, and the consequences from it are yours and yours alone to live with. If your sociopath asshole bosses are going to dart someone with shellfish toxin for fucking things up, it's not going to be me. As you know. Very well."

When this burst out of me, we'd both been hot. She'd been in a clenching, barely controlled rage, and I'd raged back, the rage bursting out of one of my many compartments, where I kept this sort of thing for tactical deployment.

But as I went on, we both changed. I went from hot to cold: cold and furious, knowing what my words were doing to her. I was all calculation as I slipped the knife in, knew what organs I was aiming for. "Sad" "failed" "old" "woman"—each cut as precise as surgery.

And I'd doused her fires, too. She, too, went from hot to cold, not the burning cold of fury, but the numb cold of defeat. A feeling I'd felt all too often, a feeling I could recognize. That sense of total, catastrophic failure had been my worst enemy on so many long nights, but now we were allies. I'd sacrificed something to it, put Carrie Johnstone on its altar, and bled her into its chalice.

I was done, and she was finished. She stood up, looking at me, assembling a fragile dignity out of pieced-together rags and pulling it around herself. She walked carefully and slowly out of the room, chin high, eyes fixed ahead of her. I stalked behind her, a step behind, breathing down her neck as she left, giving her a last memory to take with her for the long watches when she might consider revenge.

I was mightily tempted to kick her in the ass as she stepped out the door, but that would have been too much. I was proud of myself for making the grown-up choice to not kick her in the ass.

I kicked her in the ass. I planted my foot on her flat, wide ass in its dirty suit-skirt, right above the visible panty line on one of her sagging cheeks, and I shoved like I was kicking in a door, hurting my knee all over again, and she stumbled two steps, brought her hands up in time to cushion the blow as her face smashed into the corridor wall opposite, then sprawled onto the carpet.

I closed the door and locked it, then chained it. I wanted so badly to look out the spyhole to see if she was standing out there, but I didn't.

It was only once I'd sat numbly back down on the bed and was staring blankly at the wall over the desk that I remembered my fear that she had a gun. I guess she hadn't had one, because she would have blown my brains out if she had. It's what I would have done, if the roles had been reversed.

I thought about ordering room service, but my appetite had been replaced by a squirting, roiling gutful of acid.

Right up until that moment, some part of me, in some compartment, had been thinking about a triple-cross, refusing to help Xoth, refusing to keep silent for Zyz, marching to glory at the front of Tanisha's parade, with Marcus Yallow and even his girlie looking at me like I was a vengeful Valkyrie.

But after what had just happened, I was going to need a protector. Carrie Johnstone lived in a feudal world, where everyone had to align themselves with a lord for cover—even court sorcerers like me. I would have to become a creature of Xoth, to save myself from Zyz.

Somewhere, in a compartment, a small and stupid dream of doing something brave and foolish died.

I thought about calling Ilsa to get the details for this meeting, but I decided she could track me down and tell me about it if she wanted me there. It was undignified to go chasing after her.

Instead, I packed my bag, checked out, and got in an actual taxi to take me to my mom's house. The taxi was on general principle. I knew for a fact that Uber was leaky af and would sell my ride history to anyone and everyone. The taxi would take cash and didn't care if my phone was switched off for the ride.

Not having my phone on, though. There were a lot of compartments labeled "MOM," and without the soothing distraction of some kind of social-media feed or a cute video-loop or even just some angry headlines about the rotten world, I was left with nothing but myself in my skin and my head, staring out the taxi window at the familiar streets that were not familiar anymore. I'd spent so long staring at these places, out the windows of slow Muni buses, walking from one place to another, and I'd absorbed a kind of ambient, saturated knowledge of them. San Francisco was the only city in the world I'd known that way: no other place in the world had ever been sunk as deep into my psyche.

But San Francisco had changed. A lot. Goddamn how it had changed. So much *money*. Houses that had been semi-derelict student group houses or the peeling lair of some decrepit senior citizen who couldn't afford to keep up the paint job were now shiny and new, in painted lady finery, and anything that could be knocked down had been, and replaced by a high-rise. Old convenience stores with signs dating back to the 1950s were gone, replaced with the kind of coffee shops that I'd frequented in Shoreditch and Nolita and Yonghegong and Ružinov, high-end bicycle shops, boutiques, and very quiet restaurants.

Of course you can never go home again. But there I was, heading home, and the city of San Francisco was bludgeoning me with that fact. Was it just that I'd gotten older, or had my years away, becoming someone else, unmoored me from the possibility of ever belonging to a place the way that Marcus Yallow and Tanisha did—having those deep ties and that bone-deep, unconscious knowledge of the city and its places and people, a million faces seen a million times on a bus or a street corner, not friends or even acquaintances, but not strangers either?

As we got closer to the Richmond and my mother's house, a cold feeling took hold of me, the sense that I had made myself a stranger forever.

I paid the cabbie in cash, and picked up the backpack and shopping bags that were my only luggage at this point—everything else was at Tanisha's, and God knew where Tanisha was—and watched him drive away.

San Francisco was having one of those cold and foggy nights where the air isn't all that chilly, but the moisture gets right into your bones and the wind sucks the heat off your skin. I shivered on the sidewalk and looked at the house I had grown up in.

It was smaller than I remembered, its two stories modest compared to the grand painted ladies I'd driven past, and in the twilight its facade was more disreputable, faded and scuffed, than I recalled. The mailbox was stuffed with junk mail and the car in the driveway was the same old Corolla, now dotted with rust and sagging on its suspension. There was a light showing through the living-room blinds, and I stared intently at them, waiting for a shadow to cross the window. It was cold.

I let my feet walk their way up to the doorway, hearing each scuff of my new no-name running shoes on the paving stones. I watched my finger approach the bell and then push it. I listened to my breath coming in and out of my lungs as my heart went berserk.

At first, I couldn't hear anything from inside. Mom might be asleep on the sofa, or watching TV and thinking that it must be an ax-murderer or a Jehovah's Witness and wondering whether to chance it. I had a key ring with a key to this door, back in a storage locker in New Jersey that Xoth relocated all my things into when I took the Slovstakian assignment.

Then I heard her footstep, the sound of the squeaky tread third from the top step. The bow wave of air she displaced blew a little puff out from under the door and I smelled the unmistakable smell of home, and I had to put my hand on the door to steady myself.

Then she swung the door back and I looked at her and she looked at me, and oh my God she was *old*, small and hunched in a way that made her even smaller, and the wrinkles around her eyes, around her mouth, on her chest and neck and—

"Masha?"

"Hi, Mom." It was the best I could manage because I had just spent twenty-five minutes alone with my thoughts in a taxi without actually thinking about what I would say when I was standing before my aged and estranged mother again, because that's what compartments do to a girl.

"Masha?" she said again and put her hand up to her wrinkled chest. She was in a V-neck tee and track pants and bare feet and chipped toenails. Her fingernails were ragged and a few had been chewed, a filthy habit I thought she'd kicked.

"Hi, Mom," because it had worked so well the first time. I tried it with a grin this time. That did something, because she hugged me. And hugged me. And hugged me.

And you know what? I didn't mind at all. I really, actually liked it.

Mom asked me if I was well, she asked me if I was in trouble, she asked me if I'd eaten, in that order, and it was just like old times. She brought me biscuits and tea in a glass with a sugar cube and a chipped plate of lethally sweet jellied sugar "fruit slices" that I hadn't seen since Slovstakia and hadn't eaten since puberty and body-shame. They were delicious.

She sat at the other end of the sofa, sneaking disbelieving looks at me, frowning conspicuously at the bruises I'd picked up at the protests.

My tea was half-drunk before she ran out of patience. "Masha, what are you doing here?"

"You're not glad to have me?"

She gave me a no-bullshit stare: "Masha—"

Being home, on this sofa, the taste of dark tea and sweet lime jelly in my mouth, cracked open so many of my compartments, ones I'd sealed up so long ago that I'd forgotten what I'd kept inside them.

To my utter horror, I realized I was about to burst into tears. "Be right back," I managed to gasp out, before I leapt off the sofa and ran up the stairs to the bathroom, taking them two at a time, running past the family pictures that climbed the walls, familiar and strange and faded. I locked the bathroom door and stuffed my face into a towel, heaving out sobs that came from such a deep place that they hurt. Some distant part of me, a thousand miles away, observed the cries and diagnosed them as the noises that a sick or dying animal might make. Closer in, I was shaking, gasping, my diaphragm spasming so that I could barely draw air.

Of course my mother came and thumped on the door and then thundered on it. "Masha!" bursting urgently from her, the sound she'd made when I'd fallen down the stairs in fifth grade, flailing wildly to stop myself, picking up speed, smashing my head and then my face into the baseboard at the bottom, splitting my lip and chipping a tooth.

I swallowed and squeezed and clamped my jaws shut, but the tears wouldn't stop coming. I tried to shout, "I'm fine," but I couldn't. I wasn't. That distant observer was getting worried now. This was looking very bad.

I'd forgotten Mom knew the trick of shoving an unbent paperclip into the bathroom door's privacy lock to release it.

Her hand on my shoulder was another portal to a long-ago moment, another crowbar prying open some long-sealed boxes. Whatever was happening inside me, that familiar hand made it much worse.

Acid crawled up my throat, soured tea and fruit jellies. I swallowed it down. Mom's hand was moving on my back now, tracing a familiar circle.

I gulped, gasped, gulped. Got my diaphragm under control, then my lungs. My shakes subsided.

"I'm sorry, Mom."

"Don't be sorry." She was crying too. She was visibly terrified.

"No, really." I pulled myself together. Compartments slammed shut. "It's not fair to you, showing up after all this time, dumping this on you. Please, I'll be okay. You don't need to worry."

She made a face.

"Okay, of course you're going to worry. I've had a rough week. I lost a job, flew here, had some drama with my friends and my former employer—two former employers, actually—and then the employer who fired me hired me again as a contractor, so I'll be making more money. Really, I'm fine."

"Masha, you are not fine."

"No, honestly, it was just jetlag and stress and—"

"Listen to me, please. You are not fine." She stretched, groaned and held her back. "Come back to the living room, my body is too old for this."

Back on the sofa, she gripped my hand with a firmness that brooked no compromise.

"I don't want to talk about how long it's been since you visited or called or emailed. What I'm about to say has nothing to do with that. What I'm about to say, I'm saying because I'm your mother and no one else is going to say it to you.

"Masha, you are in trouble. I can see that. I don't know if it's a boy or this job or whatever. I know it because I've been in trouble. The situation with your father, my family, leaving them and coming here—there were times when it was—" She waved her hands. "It was desperate."

She was quiet for so long, staring a thousand miles away, and I was about to say something when she turned back to me, tears streaming down her face.

"I nearly gave you up, you know? When you were five or six. I was here, alone, there was nothing, no money, no one who could help me. You wanted so much, attention and clothes and feeding and lessons and being driven around to friends' houses for playdates, and I was so close to coming apart. My hair was falling out, Masha. I couldn't sleep, I'd get up once or twice in the night to be sick. I thought I had cancer, that you were going to be an orphan. I didn't have insurance, so I couldn't even go ask a doctor for a scan.

"I talked to a social worker, started doing the papers to give you up, surrender you for foster care. They sat on my end table for weeks, and every day I'd pick them up and get a pen and sit down at the kitchen table with them, then stand up and put them back beside the bed."

She looked away again, staring at the old Parks Service Muir Woods poster framed over the fireplace. "Then I filled it in."

I hadn't known any of this. I had vague memories of being six, still learning English, miserable all the time in my first-grade class where nothing made any sense and no one wanted to be my friend, showing up for school every day with weird food in my bag lunch—never enough of it—and being absolutely miserable all the time, fighting with my mother.

But I only remembered how I'd felt—I don't think I'd noticed how she'd felt. I couldn't imagine her giving me up for foster care. Whatever else you could say about my mother, her whole identity was wrapped up in this sentimental, crushing, overpowering Mama Bear routine that I'd spent my whole life trying to escape. It was impossible to even imagine her giving me up. It would be easier to picture her dancing in a strip club or running for Congress.

"Masha, I came *this close*." Another pause, so long this time that I snuck her a look to see if she was done. But she held up her hand to stop me, and opened and closed her mouth twice, three times, gasping, choking. "I was going to drop you off and go home and get into the bathtub and open my wrists. I took you to Walgreens on the way to the social services office and bought the razor blades, then I bought a BART ticket and we had gotten as far as the platform when I turned and really looked at you. You were so quiet, like you knew something terrible was about to happen. You were *never* quiet, especially in public." She smiled a faraway smile. "You had figured out that if you cried and begged in public you might get a chocolate bar." The smile vanished. "Not that day. Such big eyes you made at me. So quiet. A train pulled onto the platform and you put your hand in mine and said, 'Come on, Mama.'

"Your hand in mine, it pulled me back from the edge. I was ready to go over but instead, I was pulled back. By you." Another silence, this one even longer.

"Masha, you are on the edge. You don't need to tell me what put you there, but you can. But even if you don't want to talk, I want you to listen. You have a problem and you can't escape it. You have to face it. No matter where you go, your problem will go with you, because your problem is always *you*. My problem wasn't your stupid father. It wasn't my beautiful, stubborn daughter. You were my solution, not my problem. Other people are never the problem. Sometimes, though, they're the solution."

She took both of my hands. Hers were so wrinkled, so tiny, so frail. But they gripped fiercely. "I hope you have some people to solve your problems with, Masha. And if you don't, or even if you do, I will always be here for you, as long as I live. Not just because I'm your mother, but because I owe you this. Because you pulled me back."

She described it so vividly that it seemed now I remembered it, the Walgreens, the BART platform. But of course, she and I had been to the Walgreens hundreds—thousands—of times, and we'd waited on the BART platform together every day for years and years. Surely I was synthesizing the memory out of spare parts that had shook loose out of my compartments.

But I could see it, and my mother's hand putting the package of razor blades into her purse, the deep lines bracketing her mouth and the divot between her eyebrows that she got when she was suffering.

My mother and I had never spoken of suicide. It's not like I hadn't thought about it from time to time. Not killing myself, just not . . . being . . . anymore. Sometimes on long plane flights, the crazy ones with layovers in Dubai or Singapore between two or three ten-hour flights, I would get to the end of the flight and just want to be annihilated, make my mind shut up and just *stop*. When I thought about being dead, it was much the same thing, except that it wasn't boredom that was making me want to escape my own head—it was the inescapable logic of my terrible mistakes in the past had pushed me forward into more terrible mistakes, and more, and more, my future on rails I'd foolishly laid, stretching off to infinity—or to the end of my life.

Maybe it was "suicidal ideation," but I liked to think that it was less dramatic than that. I didn't want to buy razor blades and climb into a warm bath. I just wanted to go to bed and not wake up, or be killed instantly and painlessly by a massive stroke or heart attack. I just wanted it to end. I didn't necessarily want to end it.

"I think I should get some sleep." My voice was so tiny it was almost unrecognizable.

She looked at me for another uncomfortably long time. "That's a good idea, Kiska." Kitten. She hadn't called me that since I was in middle school.

Once I was under the covers, she came in and sat wordlessly beside me on the bed. She reached out to stroke my hair and I jolted at first, then I relaxed, completely, in a way I had forgotten how to do. She stayed beside me on the bed, stroking my hair, until I fell asleep. Maybe she kept it up after then.

When I woke up, the sun was bleeding around the blinds. It took me a moment to remember where I was (first thought: "This hotel is a *dump*"). I rubbed my eyes, and my sore knee, and then, as if on autopilot, immediately reached for my phone. I had eleven missed calls from a number in Germany and no messages.

My guts curdled. When I came back from the bathroom, I bolted the door and called Ilsa.

"You were sleeping?"

"Jetlag."

"Well, at least you'll be well rested. You have four hours. I believe you are at your mother's house? A car will come for you in two hours with your new colleagues. You can discuss strategy in the car. Can you be presentable? We can bring clothes for you."

"I'm a hacker. This is San Francisco. They'll want me to show up in a hoodie and jeans or they won't believe I'm any good."

She snorted very softly. "All the same, Masha, we like to project professionalism. I'll have them bring you something. You can change in the car."

Mom was in the living room when I slunk downstairs after a quick shower. She smiled sorrowfully at me and I gave her a hug that I put as much sincerity as I could muster into. "I'll be okay," I said, knowing it probably wasn't true and knowing that I wasn't saying it just to make her feel better—I was saying it because if she *did* feel better, she wouldn't insist on talking to me about this stuff anymore. "Thank you. I mean it, Mom." I probably did mean it.

She tried to feed me and I made up a brunch date with an imaginary high-school friend at a café around the corner that I used to like, hoping it was still there and that Mom wouldn't bust me for a stupid lie. She didn't, and I gave her another hug and escaped.

The café was still there, but the menu was different and three times more expensive than the last time. I ordered farm-to-table everything and a superfood smoothie made from pureed sunshine and virtue and took out my phone.

Only a few people had my number, but they'd all called it. Marcus Yallow, naturally. Then Ange, several times. And then Tanisha.

Apparently she was out of jail, then. That lawyer would want paying.

There were so many messages. Some of them were from Tanisha, in varying degrees of angry, worried, and exhausted. Then there was one saying she was taking over Marcus's phone, which was good opsec, if her own phone had done an extended stint in police custody. It was mighty generous of Marcus, though, of course, I'd bought him that phone.

I had less than two hours until the car would be by to pick me up and I'd disappear back into Xoth. I'd probably move into a corporate apartment—they kept some furnished units by the Kabuki Springs baths, I remembered—and there'd be a car at the start and end of the day to take me into the office, keeping me away from competitors and other adversaries who might want to bug me, mug me, or bribe me.

Tanisha was sprung, but my cushy, high-paid sentence was only just beginning. After today, calling my old friend would be a serious business, the kind of thing that might mean trouble for both of us. It was now or never.

"Hello?"

"Hi, Neesh. You okay?"

"Oh, shit. Hang on, let me get somewhere quiet."

I heard her walking out of a crowded room and onto a busy street, then onto a quieter one, like she'd ducked into an alley. I looked around the café at all the people not paying attention to me, threw two twenties on the table, and walked out myself, stepping into the doorway of a shuttered shoemaker's that had gone out of business so long ago that the brown paper taped over the window had sagged away, revealing the sad remnants of someone's family business—a litter of shoeshine stuff and a forlorn pile of toys.

"Are you okay?" She sounded tired.

"I asked you first."

She sighed. Again. "Not really."

"Yeah. Same."

"That lawyer, though. Thank you."

"Least I could do."

"You could have done less."

*I could have done more.* "I—" *just wanted to say goodbye.* "I've been worried about you."

"It wasn't good. But I hear it was worse where you were, out front."

"At least no one died, though."

"One guy died," she said.

"Oh."

"Where are you?"

"Near my mom's place."

"Are you gonna come and get your stuff from my place?"

That was convenient of her. "Can you hang on to it for a while? I've got a meeting today, then I'll know where I'm heading next."

"A meeting." It wasn't a question, but it demanded an answer.

"I, uh, got a new job."

A pause. "Do I want to know?"

"Probably not."

"Do you want to tell me?" That's why she was my friend.

"Yeah." My voice was tiny again. Where was it disappearing to?

"Shit. Today is busy, but tomorrow?"

"Probably too late. They're picking me up soon."

"Shit."

"It's okay."

"Naw. It's not. You're by your mom's? Lucky for you I'm on your side of the bridge. Twenty minutes."

I had been holding my breath. I let it out. "I'd really like that. Thank you."

"Mountain Lake Park?"

"Yeah." We used to trip balls there, staying out all night high on mushrooms, alternately shivering and dancing, laughing like hyenas the whole time.

"Twenty minutes." She was already shouting goodbye to someone as she hung up.

Neesh looked terrible, which made perfect sense, what with jail and all the traumatic news and cycling halfway across the city on a borrowed bike ("Fastest way to get here," she said, as she armed sweat off her shining forehead).

We found a bench and sat down and watched millionaires and future millionaires playing soccer in the park—young techbros in the peak of physical condition, not like the milk-white fatties and skeletons of my early days in the biz. These bros were crushing it 24/7 and that meant eating nothing but ketogenic slurry and running your ass around in shorts for hours every weekend in deadly serious competition in a park that had once been full of laughing Latinx kids horsing around. None of those kids could figure out how to get the park's booking app to show them slots as soon as they opened, but the bros all had sniper-bots that checked a hundred times a minute and grabbed every slot as soon as it opened.

"Tell me," she said as soon as the hug was out of the way.

"There's good news and bad news."

"Uh-oh."

"You'll like the good news. Zyz, the company that infected your phone, had you arrested, and hijacked every autonomous vehicle in the East Bay to terrorize the streets? They're going to lose their contract, pay big fines, and maybe, just *maybe*, some of them will go to jail."

She slow-clapped. "That is great news, Masha, and it just makes me wonder what the bad news is."

"Wait, I've got more good news." I could feel how lopsided my smile was. Tanisha and I didn't talk about my day job. "I'm the one who's going to dole out all this justice: it's my testimony that'll cost them the contract and get the ball rolling on an investigation. It's also going to kill their plans to roll this out in San Francisco."

"Yeah, that's also good news. I'm dying of suspense here about the bad news, Masha."

I took a deep breath. "They're going down because I'm going to work for my old bosses, Xoth, and I'm going to help them score the contract."

"Oh."

Some bros scored a goal on some other bros and were being noisily happy about it.

"Neesh?"

"Gimme a second, okay?" The game started up again, and the cheers gave way to tense competitive silence. "Masha, you said you wanted to talk to me, so now I'm going to talk." I felt like I was going to throw up. "My instinct here is to say to you, 'I love you, you're my sister and I'll stand by you, no matter what.'

"But." Sigh. Another one. "But, Masha." She bit her lip. "Masha, you do this, you go back to work for the same war criminals you were working for before? The ones that fucked up those people you were hanging with in Russia or wherever? You go help them work on doing the same thing to us, to me and my friends, to *your* friends, and—"

A couple more sighs.

I scrounged for some righteous indignation. "Tanisha, do you really think that's fair? Making me choose between our friendship and my career?"

She looked me dead in the eyes, calm and cold. "You're fucking right I do. Put it this way: Is it fair to ask *me* to be your friend when you're helping people who want to destroy me, destroy my friends, and destroy everything I care about in this world?"

I started to protest that this was just melodrama, but shit, it wasn't, was it? That's why I was talking to her, wasn't it? Because I needed someone to talk me out of what I was about to do?

"Look, Tanisha, if I don't help Xoth by attributing the attack to Zyz, then Zyz will probably keep their contract with Oakland and may even get that contract with San Francisco. You may think I'm selling out, but I'm making things better." I cringed at the whine in my voice. "You think things are bad now? How much worse will it be if the only people willing to work on these projects are the people with no morals at all?"

Without a moment's hesitation: "How much better will it be when everyone with any *morals* walks away from these evil fuckers and anyone who chooses to stay pays the price of being unwelcome in civilized society?"

You know, fair enough.

"Shit, Neesh, it's not fair." I thought about Carrie Johnstone sprawled on the hallway carpet of the Nikko. If Zyz survived this, she would do everything in her power to see to it that *I* didn't. I don't know for a fact that Carrie Johnstone ever personally killed another human being, but she certainly had no qualms about handing over that ax. She would happily spend the rest of her life with my blood staining her hands.

"What's not fair?"

"How is it my job to solve this for everyone else? I do what I can to make the world a better place. I know I could do more, but *everyone* could do more. Every time you chill at home with a stupid movie, you're not out organizing a protest, saving people's lives. Why does everyone else get to make the tradeoffs that keep them going and pay their bills, but my choices are everyone else's business?"

She rolled her eyes at me. "Masha, I'm not even gonna get mad at that, it's so foolish. You know better. Come on."

Yeah, dammit, I knew better.

She took my hands and made me look into her red-rimmed eyes. "Come on,

Masha. You know what's right and what's wrong. You want me to talk you out of this. You've spent *years* trying to get someone to talk you out of this. That's okay. We all need help from our friends, the people who love us. I love you, Masha. You're my sister. I'll always love you.

"It's *because* I love you that I'm not going to let you off the hook for this. I love you and I know you and I know how much you'll regret what you're doing someday. I'd rather hurt you a little by cutting you off than hurt you a lot by being complicit in your own ruin.

"Masha, I'm saying this to you as your sister, who loves you. You don't want to do this."

So many furious replies rose to my tongue, acid ready to spill over this paternalistic lecture and the incredible arrogance of her certainty that I, inside my own skin, did not know what was best for that skin.

"You sound like you've been rehearsing that, Tanisha."

"You know what? I have. I rehearsed it every single time I thought about what you were so busy doing. You ever think that the things you're building are going to be used on you someday? Not just brown people or poor people or strangers, but you and your mother and the people you love? That you might end up convincing yourself that you don't love anyone rather than admitting that you're doing the wrong thing? You want to end up living by yourself, a miserable old dragon sat on top of your hoard of blood money, trying to find something, anything, to distract you from the things you did and the people you did them to?"

"Tanisha—"

"Shut. Up. You're goddamned right I rehearsed this, Masha, because you appointed me your conscience and I have not done much of a job of it, girl. If there's one thing I've learned from hanging around with you all these years, it's that you're *special*. Not many people can do what you do. Maybe in twenty years, we'll have a whole generation of baby geniuses with your skills, but right now, when *you* don't do something, there's a good chance they won't be able to hire anyone else to do it. That means that *your choices mean something*.

"Now, I look at you and see your back stiffening and I know what you're thinking, you're all, 'Why the fuck is this my burden to carry? Let someone else save the world, I just wanna pay my bills.'

"But you need to flip your script. This is not a burden, it's a winning lottery ticket. Most of us are passengers of history, but every once in a while, if you're very lucky, lightning strikes and you get to drive. You got the wheel right now. Sure, it's an awesome responsibility, but awesome is awesome."

I smiled despite myself. "You are good at speechifying."

"I am." She didn't smile back. "Practice makes perfect. I'm an organizer, Masha. Speechifying comes with the territory. It's how people who didn't win the lottery try to get a chance to drive for a second or two."

"You're very persuasive." *I'll probably die if I take your advice. And there's a good chance it won't be a nice death.*

"Yeah. That also goes with the territory." She had a face on like a winged fury. I felt fiercely proud of her then, and horribly sad, because I knew I was going to disappoint her.

"You're not telling me something."

So much for my poker face. "That's true."

She softened, her eyes going gentle. "Come on, you can tell me. If there's one thing we know about each other, it's that we can keep each other's secrets."

In another world, I opened up to her. There wasn't a single reason not to. She really was as close to a sister as I was going to get in this world, someone who knew parts of me no one else knew. If there was anyone I could talk to about this . . .

"Neesh, I hear you. Thanks for the advice. It's good advice. I'm going to go and have a think about it. Seriously, thank you."

The winged fury was back. "Masha—"

I held up my hand. "It's okay," I said. "Really."

I couldn't go home and I didn't want to go back to the café. I walked the streets instead, limping until my knee limbered up, feeling Tanisha's eyes burning into my back until I turned the corner; not feeling really on my own until I'd turned a couple more corners and shoulder-checked that Tanisha wasn't behind me. I put my phone into airplane mode. I didn't want to talk to her or anyone else.

Growing up, my old neighborhood had been full of kids, young families, old retirees. Not anymore. I remembered reading that San Francisco had the lowest ratio of kids to adults of any major city in the USA, all the families

chased out of the city into the suburbs and past them—even Oakland was pretty light on kids, from what I'd seen.

I'd started as a fatherless refugee, and I'd somehow managed to get a top-notch education, a series of cushy jobs, a wallet full of platinum cards, and tax-free bank accounts in four countries. Admittedly, I'd done better than most of my peers, but look at Tanisha: a college degree, a job, an apartment, and enough time and security to have a second, all-devouring career as an activist. Look at Marcus fucking Yallow: married, with a down payment on a house courtesy of parents who sold up and left the Bay Area with a giant real-estate bubble payday (yes, I read his blog, and I'm not proud of it), half a college degree, a string of high-paid tech industry jobs, and now all the consulting work he could eat.

No one born today would have all that. San Francisco was a game of musical chairs where the music was speeding up and the chairs were being yanked away. It used to be an easy game, with so many chairs that there'd always be one for you provided you weren't choosy about which chair you got—now just *having* a chair marked you as a one-percenter.

San Francisco was—as always—ahead of the curve. But I'd seen this playing out in London and Berlin, Dubai and Hong Kong. The world was going through a phase-shift, what had been a smooth grade from poor to rich, with plenty in the middle, was becoming a cliff.

Working for Xoth would make me rich. Rich as hell, in fact. Of course, I'd be getting rich because I'd be helping people much richer than me hang on to their money and figure out who to arrest before the guillotines could be erected outside their walled estates.

I hadn't created this situation. Even with all I had done, I was still just a bit player on this huge board, and the game had been in motion long before I was born. Vast historic forces had brought this world into being, and I had to live in it with everyone else. If I took vows of poverty or swore myself to revolution, it wouldn't overturn the order. In a world of winners and losers, choosing the losing side wasn't going to help anyone, least of all myself. At least my comfortable couch in the outer halls of power afforded me enough slack to reach out and help a little, retail-style, one person at a time. And after all, that's the only way people came, one at a time, even in a big crowd. We were born as individuals,

and we died on our own, and even the tightest, best-coordinated group was just a bunch of singular individuals choosing to work together for a while.

All of this was self-serving, sure—it wasn't just ethical cover for an expedient way of keeping my skin intact, but also oiled with the most expensive lotions the world's luxury duty-free stores had to offer. But self-serving wasn't the same as wrong.

I had two hours before the Xoth car would meet me at my mom's house, and it was a thirty-minute walk, tops. So I turned uphill—there was always an uphill in San Francisco—and walked and walked until I found myself in a dog park of brown, dry grass, joggers in high-tech fabric, dried-up turds in baggies, stepped-in turds with long skid marks, and commanding views.

The people who jogged past me with their snuffling dogs were young and fit and beautiful, ten years younger than me, toned and leaving behind breezes smelling of clean sweat and good hair products. They were a far cry from the protesters outside the Oakland jail, and they were having a much better time. If the system—whatever that meant—could give these people a life like this, then maybe all those people hanging out with Tanisha needed to figure out how to be more like them.

This is how compartmentalization works, and of course I knew it. I was engaged in mental carpentry, building the boxes I'd put my feelings in. But compartmentalization is useful. What's wrong with being able to separate your feelings from the reality around you?

From up high, San Francisco was beautiful, all those low-slung white houses and the skyscrapers and bridges, the patches of green and the blue, blue sky. Every city was beautiful when you found the right place to stand. I was going to get me one of those.

# CHAPTER 10

The Xoth goons who picked me up for the ride to the City of San Francisco meeting were very respectable, for goons. Zyz liked guys who dressed in a lot of tactical gear, had shoulders that merged directly into their hairlines thanks to reverse-shrug marathons, and really enjoyed debating the relative merits of krav maga and Brazilian jujitsu. Xoth preferred a more upscale kind of merc, usually whip-thin South Africans with subtly elasticated denim jeans and fitted jackets with unobtrusive vents that let them do full gymnastic routines, squeaking over floors in leather shoes with grippy, oil-proof soles.

These two were polite to a fault, called me Ms. Maximow as they handed over a garment bag full of clothes, then got in the front seats and raised the partitions so I could wrestle myself into a white blouse and some kind of couture post-Chanel skirt-suit. The outside was conservative, lightly checked brown wool, while the lining was digital camo print on good silk, a sly little reminder that the person wearing it was a badass involved in serious security work.

After I had changed and stuffed my jeans and hoodie into the garment bag and transferred my money and cards to the soft buckskin attaché that came with the look, I wiggled my feet into a pair of matte-finish carmine flats that were a perfect fit—I remembered that Xoth had once issued me a pair of knee-high rain boots when I was doing a job in Hong Kong during a rainy season, a fancy gesture for which they'd had to requisition my size.

A quick hair brush, a touchup with some makeup that was still in its packaging, an awkward wrestle to roll on the unscented deodorant I hadn't noticed until after I'd put on my shirt, and I was a new woman, practically unrecognizable even to myself—except as a specimen of the type, having dealt with dozens of faceless women who looked just like me.

I lowered the partition, watched the guys in front flick their gaze to the rear-view to check me briefly, then return to scanning the foreground constantly and silently for threats. They did a wordless hand-jive for every pedestrian about to step off a curb, every car signaling a lane change. They almost always pointed the same way at the same time, making it seem like a party trick or a mentalist act.

"Is it at Civic Center?" All the municipal buildings were there. "Dogpatch?" Where SFPD HQ was.

They shook their heads. "Xoth offices. Financial District."

The last time I'd been to Xoth's San Francisco outpost, they'd been in the Outer Richmond, a scrappy little bureau with two harried full-timers who had been shipped over from the Dubai offices. Sounded like they'd moved up.

We ended up in the parking garage under a black glass office tower that I must have walked past a thousand times without seeing. Another goon—same South African accent, same tailor—was holding an elevator for us and we four ascended together. How terrifying this reassuring box of muscle would be if their job was to control me, rather than to protect me.

I was hustled into a boardroom. I'd been expecting to see Iron Mom from the blacked-out bus the night before, who I had tagged as "station chief." But instead, it was Ilsa, casually tapping at a laptop, a cup of coffee set neatly beside her.

She looked so fresh she might have just been unwrapped from her protective film. She'd caught a hellishly early flight from Europe.

"Good morning, Masha."

I nodded and slid into a chair by her side. The goons closed the door.

"What's the brief, then?" This woman and I were going to be welded together for the rest of my life, she was my new best friend, and possibly my only best friend from now on, but I didn't want to socialize with her. After all, the last time I'd seen her, she'd been firing my ass.

She took the measure of me in an instant. "The suit looks good," she said, and turned her laptop screen toward me and started briefing me on the parts of the pitch I'd be in charge of. It was clear that my job was to explain in the most technical and intimidating detail all the bad shit we'd caught Zyz at, and how they could verify the forensics and attribution, and then to answer questions with a minimum of emotion. We were Xoth, we were all business, we got the job done and didn't cowboy around.

She said it, I got it. I made sure to ask enough questions to prove that I'd paid attention.

When it was done her lid went down and she folded up her reading glasses and skewered me on a look. I met it.

"You're not hurt in any way?"

"Banged-up knee. I got lucky."

She shook her head. "This was extraordinarily foolish, even by Zyz standards. They're going to pay a real penalty for that. Thanks to you."

"Foolish? It was murderous. A war crime."

She rolled her eyes. "In my experience, very few things constitute a war crime. But it was murderous, yes. The body count was low."

"Lower than Slovstakia."

"Yes." She looked at me again. She never tried to disguise her age, wore it in a kind of mannish way, the way the old Borises in Slovstakia did. *I am very old, and that means I survived this long. Ask yourself: What must I have done for that to be true?*

"Was it 'foolish' when Litvinchuk did it?"

"Extremely foolish. That's why we canceled our arrangement with the state of Slovstakia. Xoth has standards."

"You canceled it?" I didn't know how much the contract was worth, but it was a big number. Big enough to cover the stupid money they'd paid me and the six other people on site, plus overheads—all that back-office support staff I used.

"We have standards."

"You sold them an exploit but you quit because they used it?"

"We didn't sell them that one. They bought it from a less-reliable vendor."

I took a moment to digest that. "Are you sure you're the one who fired them? Because it sounds like maybe they found another contractor—someone who could sell them the kinds of tools they were hoping for."

"You think they knew Xoth would refuse to help them kill people, so they found someone else?"

"Well, you do have 'very high ethical standards.'" I didn't put any spin on it at all. She pretended that I was serious.

"We do. That's what we sell. It's why we're about to win a very large piece of business today. I'm sure you think we succeed based on how powerful our tools are, that our engagements are with clients who don't care about the ethics behind our services, but you are mistaken. Good clients know that someday they will have to face the world and explain what and why they bought from us. Our tools are designed for clients who are concerned with the long-term future and its contingencies, including changes in the power structure in which they may be asked to account for their choices. That is a lesson of history that good clients have learned well."

Which was pretty rich, coming from a former Stasi colonel who became a millionaire executive by parlaying her experience spying on the most surveilled people in human history on behalf of history's most notorious surveillance bureaucracy into a career providing surveillance services to governments.

A smart woman would have just let this lie. I was trying to smarten up, but to be honest, I was struggling with it. "And Litvinchuk?"

"What about him?"

"Seems to me it would have been obvious from the first sales call that he wasn't the kind of guy who was thinking about what would happen when he got outed for buying surveillance gear from a foreign company. Pretty sure he was planning on jailing any journalist who tried publishing that, unless he was living in Venezuela with a giant suitcase full of cash by then."

"This is very amusing, Masha, but it is rather immature. We take numerous precautions to ensure that our products aren't misused, including some you aren't aware of. Please don't try to play gotcha with me. Life is too short for games."

Well, she sure told me.

Ilsa left me in the meeting room alone other than the caterers who bustled in and out with bowls of perfectly polished fruit and frosted jugs of ice water. An AV tech came in next and stepped through a slide deck that was a mix of the familiar (control screens for interception and analysis that I'd helped build) and things I'd never seen before (charts showing fantastic, bull-market upticks in arrests and public safety, combined with fall-off-a-cliff savings on policing budgets).

After that, I sat and twiddled my thumbs. I drank some of the ice-cold water from a tumbler with a thick bottom. I ate a perfect apple and put the core into the pristine, empty trash can. The unfamiliar clothes itched.

Finally, I got up. If anyone asked, I was looking for the bathroom.

I got as far as the reception desk before I encountered another person: one of the South Africans from the car ride detached himself from the wall where he'd been leaning without slouching and stepped smoothly into my path.

"Can I help you?" He had tobacco on his breath.

"Looking for the bathroom."

"Please wait in the boardroom and someone will come for you."

"Seriously?"

He just stared at me with those ice-blue eyes.

"You've got to be fucking kidding me." But I went back into the boardroom. My heart thudded. Not being able to go to the toilet on demand felt profoundly scary and demeaning. I didn't sit back down. Standing made me feel like I had more agency.

After a couple of minutes, the other South African came and escorted me out of the Xoth boardroom and to a shared ladies' room that his friend was already standing in front of. The guy guarding the ladies' room held up a hand and the one who was guarding me put his hand on my arm lightly, but coiled, like he could turn that into an iron grab if I made a run for it. I heard a toilet flush inside the ladies' room and water running, a dryer, and then a salary-lady—middle-aged, Asian, pale blouse and sensible skirt—stepped out. She did a shocked take when she saw the goons, then hurried in the opposite direction. Xoth weren't the easiest commercial real-estate neighbors, I guessed.

Once I was alone in the bathroom, I sat on the toilet for a while—nothing happened. Sometimes my bladder is more scared than the rest of me. I had been avoiding looking at my phone, but the reflex to check it from the privacy of the toilet stall proved too strong to resist. Anything to take my mind off the impending point of no return.

I was surprised to see that it was twenty minutes past the scheduled start of the meeting. That might explain why everyone seemed so on edge—the City of San Francisco was late.

The top bar of my phone was solid message notifications. I didn't want to hear from anyone.

I opened them anyway.

Ange wanted to know if I was okay. Tanisha had told her that she was worried about me but wouldn't say why.

Marcus . . .

Oh, Marcus.

> Don't be mad at Tanisha. I got her to tell me what was going on because believe it or not I'm your friend, and I care about you. I know you think you know what you're doing but everyone, all of us, we know that you're better than that. We're all better than that.

> We're coming to that meeting of yours and we're bringing friends.

A message from Tanisha, right after.

> Sorry, not sorry. I love you, but I'm not going to help you help them fight me. See you soon.

Well, fuck.

The South Africans were visibly anxious. One of them laid his hand on me, grabbing my bicep as I stepped out of the bathroom. I froze in my tracks.

"Release me. Now." I stared straight into his eyes, watery blue ice chips, eyelid twitching a little on one side. His grip was strong. I had no doubt at all that he could drop me, or make me come along, or hurt me in a thousand ways. But once that happened, there would be no pretense that I would end up being a Xoth contractor again. At best, I'd be someone they paid or frightened into silence.

"Come with us."

"I am not taking a single, solitary step while your hands are on me. You'll have to drag me. Let. Me. Go. Now. No more talking. Now. I do not consent to your touching me. Not now, and not ever."

I stared at him. His fingers tightened minutely, then his grip relaxed. I didn't smirk at him, though I wanted to. Instead, I said, "Come on, let's go." Let them know they'd been the ones wasting time with this macho bullshit.

One fell in behind me, and the handsy one got in front and we moved in tight formation back to the Xoth offices. The door was locked and handsy guy opened it with a fob. The receptionist wasn't at her post. The guy behind me made sure the door shut. They brought me to the boardroom.

Ilsa was sitting at her place, holding a sweating glass of water in one hand, stabbing at her phone with the other.

"Sit." Without looking up.

I sat.

"Go." She evidently meant the South Africans, because they left and she didn't complain.

More vicious tapping. Her knuckles were swollen. I'd always admired her fine, slender fingers, her young hands. Now they were old. She was old. She was a dinosaur, a relic of a bygone era of honorable spies and counterspies, when they poisoned each other or shot each other with guns hidden in ciga-rette cases. She was a living fossil, flopped up on the shore, trying to breathe air and grow legs as quickly as she could.

Her hands were so old. She needed me so badly.

"There are three to four thousand people downstairs. They're marching. They're holding signs in English and Slovstakian. They're chanting. About you."

"Well, that's not good." I reached for the water.

"Masha, it's not a time for joking."

I drank slowly. It gave me a moment to make sure all my compartments were securely sealed. All good. "It's not a time for anything, it seems. What do you want? I didn't ask them to come."

"Someone told them about this meeting. That much is clear from their communications. Was it you?"

"I told a friend. I asked her advice about whether to come today."

"And she told you to come?"

"No, she told me not to."

She fixed me on a glare that could have melted titanium.

"Do you think that perhaps she could be responsible for the current situation?"

I put my glass down. "That seems likely. I still didn't tell her to do this. Look, if you think that the City of San Francisco isn't going to be willing to do a deal with you if that deal attracts protests, you should be giving up right now. There are going to be protests. But remember when Oakland passed that amazing legislation requiring limits on surveillance tech rollouts in the city? There were *massive* protests when the council reversed that order a couple years later. They still reversed it, and it was a big payday for Zyz."

She set her phone down. "Until it wasn't. We had planned to use the autonomous vehicle breach to privately show that Zyz wasn't up to the job, get their contract voided so that we could step in. But your friend seems to have organized a demonstration whose public premise is that Zyz was responsible for the mayhem, and that stands to poison the well for anyone providing the kinds of services we offer to any government in the entire region."

I shrugged. "They're going to buy surveillance services. They need them. Their cops demand them. They can't build them on their own, because everyone with the chops to do that kind of work is earning so much working for you and Zyz and Palantir and the rest of the industry that they're not going to get any takers for a government salary. So eventually they're going to have to buy the expertise from a contractor like Xoth. If you want to be in the business of supplying anti-dissident tools to local governments and you're going to freak out every time some dissidents show up to object, maybe you're in the wrong line of work." Which was a weird thing to say, if I wanted to get work with Xoth. If I wanted them to defend me from Severe Haircut Lady and her vengeful army of out-of-work goons whose stock options I was going to help bottom out.

Which made me wonder whether I wanted to work for Xoth after all.

Which made me realize, I didn't.

Ilsa had dialed up the icy stare to liquid nitrogen. I won't lie, it scared me. She was a scary lady, and not simply because she was ruthless and connected—but because when you were on Ilsa's side, she took care of you and directed all that ruthless power at the people who wished you ill. I was scared of what she might do to me, but even scarier was everything I'd miss out on by breaking with her. I realized that this was the unnamed, compartmentalized sorrow I'd felt since the day she told me I was out at Xoth, and the source of secret, buoyant hope I'd felt since she'd brought me back in. As bad as it was to be on the team opposite Ilsa, it was very good to be on *her* team.

I thought about my mom, standing on the BART platform, razor blades in her bag. The strength of a small hand in hers. Her decision to tell me that story now, after I'd disappeared from her life for so long.

The thing is, I'd always known that compartments weren't a good thing. They were just the least terrible thing I had.

Technology debt is when you cheat a barely functional solution to an important problem early in the development cycle, telling yourself that you'll revisit your fugly hack later and put something real in its place. But you don't. So you're forever walking around with this lurking knowledge that you've built a fifty-story skyscraper full of people on top of foundations made out of whatever garbage you had lying around at the time. Technology debt eats away at you, keeps you up at night. The longer you carry the debt, the more interest you have to pay, as you write more code that depends on the eldritch topologies of your hacky module, all of which will break as soon as you fix the original problem. The most common solution to tech debt is defaulting: that is, the whole thing collapses (preferably after the coder responsible has left the company) and someone else has to rebuild in the rubble.

I had my own form of debt, coping-strategy debt, and my mom had given me a glimpse of what defaulting on that kind of debt looked like. Would Ilsa take my hand when the day came? Would anyone?

The thing about being a compartmentalizer is it makes you good at realistically assessing situations. Compartmentalizing isn't about kidding yourself: it's about knowing exactly how terrible things are, so you know whether or not to stuff it in a box and never look at it again.

I knew exactly how much debt I'd accumulated to date: all the friendships that had drifted away, all the people whose troubles I'd been implicated in, all the regrets I'd created for myself and tucked away to save myself from sleepless nights going over and over them.

"You know what?" I said. "I think that maybe this wasn't the right fit for me after all. Good luck with your meeting, Herthe, whenever you reschedule it."

The moment of panic in Ilsa's eyes was like watching a star being born. She knew that I was the kind of person who assuaged my guilt by making friends with the people I was supposed to be treating as my prey. She didn't think I was the kind of person who'd just *stop* doing things that made me feel guilty—not when there was a big paycheck to be had for selling out.

The panic flashed and flashed away. "Masha—"

I was already on my feet. "I'll return the clothes later, just email me with a drop-off address, okay?"

"Masha." Louder now. Angry. "Don't be ridiculous—"

I shrugged. "When the whole world is ridiculous, who am I to buck the trend?"

The guy who'd grabbed my arm was right outside the door. He reached for me and I stopped. "No, you don't touch me," I said, pitched for Ilsa to hear it. "You absolutely do not touch me."

We stood there for a moment. Behind me, I heard Ilsa let out a long sigh. "Let her go."

Three thousand people at, say, Civic Center or outside a big police station is a good-sized crowd. But when they're in front of an office tower in the Financial District, three thousand people look like a *million* people. There were so many cops and rent-a-cops in the lobby that at first I couldn't even see the protesters—just a corner of a sign (in Slovstakian!) peeking up over the shoulders of one of the SFPD bulls formed up before the elevator bank. One of the cops held his hand up: "Sorry, ma'am, this entrance is closed. I advise returning to your office until the crowd has dispersed."

I walked right past him. "They're with me," I said, and started shoulder-checking my way through the rent-a-cop lines. I think I must have genuinely shocked them, because they were slow off the mark, letting me get right up to the glass before one of them put a hand on my shoulder.

Tanisha was on the other side of the glass. We locked eyes. She took in the mall cop holding on to my shoulder, took in whatever my face was showing, came to a conclusion.

"That's her!" she shouted and thumped the glass so hard the mall cop flinched.

"THAT'S HER!" It was so loud that I heard it over the general muddle of crowd noise, through the glass.

In seconds everyone was thumping, fists hammering on the glass.

"LET HER GO!" Tanisha shouted, then again, as a chant, punctuated by thumps: "LET! HER! GO! LET! HER! GO!"

It was contagious: short, pithy, catchy. Had a call to action, even.

"LET! HER! GO!" Fists smashed into the glass, the voices roared.

"I'd do it," I said. "Otherwise it's going to get ugly."

The rent-a-cop looked over his shoulder at the SFPD officer on the back line, leading from the rear. The cop shrugged. It was clear he'd like to be anywhere except here.

"Am I under arrest?" I knew the script as well as anyone.

The mall cop was a middle-aged white guy, skinny, clean-shaven, with a look of grim determination bordering on terror. Seven-dollar haircut. He wasn't being paid enough for this.

He let me go and reached for the big green DOOR OPEN button on the wall. I stepped out of the building and into the crowd. Tanisha grabbed me in a hug so fierce she endangered a rib and the crowd roared. I found I was crying.

But only a little.

# CHAPTER 11

I ended up at Marcus and Ange's house, way out in the Outer Sunset, a cottage on a big lot that must have cost nearly a million bucks.

The Raspi Altair I'd given them as a wedding present was carefully centered on the coffee table, a gleaming monument.

I was staying on their sofa, which was, you know, awful and weird, but also—

No, actually, just awful and weird. Better than staying with my mom, which was not saying much. It took a hell of a long time to get from their place to Oakland, but I had made the trek three times in the two days since I'd been released, spending half my life on BART it seemed, and the other half at meetings that Tanisha's Black-Brown Alliance people were holding, organized by BOW, her Black Oakland Women group. I went out the morning after they sprung me and met with a grab-bag assortment of activist types, the BOW affinity group of young, serious black women, others old and young, male and female, some talking like socialists and some talking like Black Lives Matter activists and some talking like garden-variety crunchy-granola Bay Area liberals.

They all clearly looked up to Tanisha, and the fact that she vouched for me made them treat me without open hostility, which was about all I could hope for, given my checkered past.

Tanisha had me explain the kinds of work I'd done for Xoth in Slovstakia and what I knew about Zyz, the capabilities I knew about and the capabilities

I'd speculated on. Some of the attendees were cryptoparty organizers—they'd high-fived Marcus and hugged Ange—and they took a lot of notes. I imagined that all this would be finding its way into their wikis pretty soon.

Slovstakia kept coming up during the Q&A. It was clear that after the terror with the cars, everyone in town had suddenly developed a serious interest in the tiny Eastern Bloc backwater where the only other attack of this kind had taken place.

Mostly, though, we talked about countermeasures: What would work, what was safe? The problem was that they all wanted to carry phones because that was how they coordinated with each other, but they didn't want to have those phones used against them. I told them this was exactly what Zyz, Xoth, and everyone they hated and feared was banking on, and they told me that they knew that, but it wasn't like they were going to give up on using electronic communications to organize themselves. If their adversaries had digital communications and they had nothing but word of mouth, they would always be outmaneuvered.

I'd had so many conversations like this with Kriztina and her friends, and Slovstakia was in every second question, and from the questions I figured out that somehow these people had actually been talking to Kriztina and her friends, and they'd eked out some kind of working relationship, a one-for-all/all-for-one kind of thing where the people whose lives had been comprehensively turned upside down by Zyz and Xoth were going to speak their truth on behalf of the people whose lives were about to be turned upside down by Zyz and Xoth, who'd return the favor somehow, and they'd all honorably pledged themselves to the death of their mutual enemies.

A couple of days before, I'd have assumed that the whole thing was stupid, mice voting to bell the cats or ants pledging to defend their anthill from a bulldozer.

But now?

The second time I hauled ass across the bridge to meet with Tanisha and her pals was that night, when they packed a public forum on whether to allow a new high-rise development and got the meeting chair to agree to let them hijack to talk about the cars that had rampaged through the city. There were three councilors in attendance, and one of them beefed at the start, but when he saw that Ange was putting on her serious listening face and remembered that there was an election coming up, he sat back down again.

Tanisha's crew had queued up a blast of publicity for the livestream and got it trending, and some of those cryptoparty types had put together slides and quippy, sticky little descriptions of the different kinds of surveillance tech that they fired into the hashtag: your phone is being used to spy on you, your fridge and thermostat are getting fake software updates, your printer is scanning your network and exfiltrating your data, and, over and over again, *this is how we got to the murdering, marauding cars in our streets last night.*

Beside me, Tanisha kept up a whispered running commentary analyzing the various shades of green the three councilors were turning; two of them had voted to dismantle Oakland's police oversight rules, the third was the anointed successor of the guy who introduced the bill (that guy had finished his term and gone to work for Zyz as a consultant, talking to other city governments about why they should be buying stuff from Zyz and how to do so without triggering any kind of public comment process).

All three were up for reelection in a couple of months, and they were clearly doing the math. One of them was texting like crazy.

Then it was my turn to speak.

I had known it was coming, but I'd lost track of that fact. Now Marcus was hustling me to the front of the room, Ange one step behind him, and the front row was a firing squad of streaming phones, held aloft.

Right as I was looking down the barrel of all those camera lenses, a thought came to me: *I don't do this kind of thing.*

Sure, I'd given all kinds of boardroom presentations, even training sessions for big groups of hairy-knuckled Borises who needed to get up to speed on the surveillance gear I'd just installed.

But mostly I was a back-office kind of person. I've got plenty of glibness privilege one-on-one. But giving a *speech*? To a *group*? That's being *livestreamed*?

Shit.

"Hi—"

Not much of a start. Out of a compartment came a voice, corny af, but: *Speak your truth, Masha.* Corny, right?

"Hi."

An old white lady in the front row, tiny and frail in a Black Lives Matter tee and a knit beret, said, "Hello!" and gave me a sunny smile. Smartass. But it helped a little.

"Hi." Third time's the charm, and the audience laughed a little. With me, not at me. "Sorry, I don't do this a lot. Ever. Sorry. Hi." That got a laugh.

"What they just told you, it's all true. I know it's true because I work for Xoth. *Worked* for them, I mean. And Zyz. All over the world. Iraq. Mexico. USA. Uh, Slovstakia."

Fewer smiles now. Some scowls. "Yeah. I did. I worked here, in San Francisco, for DHS. After the bridge. The Bay Bridge. On Treasure Island." Grumbles. Someone in the audience distinctly said, "What the actual *fuck*?"

Flop sweat. My armpits wet. My back sticky. A single ticklish rivulet running down my back and investigating the crack of my ass. Why was I doing this again?

"Look, when the Bay Bridge blew up, I was scared. Angry. I wanted to help. I thought I could make a difference." Was that how it happened? Was there a time when I wanted to help someone, rather than just figuring out how to outsmart someone with my awesome technical prowess? There must have been.

"I was young and it was scary, really scary, and I had some technical know-how. It was amazing to be recruited to work there, to have access to all this data, all these systems, to know things other people didn't know and to have people paying attention to me, acknowledging that I had something to offer.

"And yeah, I started to figure out that the people I was matching wits with were just, you know, *people,* not monsters. Not even criminals. Calling them 'suspects' doesn't even make sense because the only reason anyone suspected them of anything is that they were trying to stop me from getting in their business. *I* don't like it when people get in my business. But by then—"

I stopped. The faces of the crowd were stony. The lenses of the cameras stared pitilessly. Suddenly the fact that this was being livestreamed felt a lot scarier.

"I—" I swallowed. "By then, it was who I was, part of my identity. The thing I was good at. I tried to help people on the other side, you know, when I could."

Stony. Mount Rushmore. Sweat.

"Ah—" How long had it been since I'd taken a breath? It had been a long

time. My chest was tight. I gasped. "You know what? It doesn't matter. I was on the wrong side. I know that now and I probably knew it then, to tell you the truth. Even when I was in Iraq, catching the kinds of monsters who used rape as a weapon, who killed kids, the people I was catching them *for* weren't any better. It was rare, fucking *rare* for me to hunt monsters on behalf of heroes. Sometimes, if I was lucky, I hunted monsters for other monsters, like in Iraq. Or like the Nazis I chased down in Slovstakia, because you know what, fuck those guys.

"Mostly, though, I hunted good guys on behalf of bad guys. That's the truth. I mean, I know there's nothing more stupid and American than dividing the world into good guys and bad guys, but the bad guys were *really* bad, because the people I worked for charged a *lot* and frankly most of the people who can afford that kind of thing are only able to get that kind of money in the first place by being absolute monsters. Sometimes the people I hunted were breaking the law, but they were laws enacted by monsters to keep their victims in line. It's true that the tools I built were useful for catching murderers and rapists and stuff, but only because they were useful for catching *everybody* and mostly who they caught were good guys whose only crime was wanting to get rid of bad guys.

"So I was on the wrong side. It paid well, I was able to talk myself into it, and that's that. But I'm not anymore. I'm done with it."

They stared.

"I have to tell you the truth. I think you're outgunned. I can show you how their spy shit works, and I can show you how to do spy shit of your own, but you're going to lose. They get paid a lot of money to spy on you and they use that money to pay people like me to pay *very, very* close attention to you. If you keep them from spying on you, they don't get paid. But neither do you. Not getting spied on is a serious job, a second job or maybe a third job, and it's unpaid work, and you're not very good at it. They need to use the money they get to find one tiny mistake you've made and then they get to crack your life wide open. You need to make zero mistakes in your unpaid second job. Third job. You are going to lose.

"And it's a team sport. When you get compromised, the bad guys don't just get to spy on *you,* they get to spy on everyone who communicates with you,

everyone who trusts you. The only way to stay safe is to not have any friends, and then, honestly, no one cares what you're going to do because there's only one of you."

This wasn't babbling, either. I was trying to speak my truth, and it turned out that *this* was my truth: you're all fucked. I'm fucked. It's fucked. I could see it on their faces now.

"I mean, by all means, do what you can to prevent casual, untargeted sur-veillance. If it's some ransomware creep trying to hit you and you've got better security than the next person on his list, he's gonna move along. But targeted surveillance? You're not good enough." I swallowed. "I'm not good enough either."

There was wetness on my face, which meant that I was crying but that fact seemed to come from a very long way away. Marcus was frowning so hard his face looked like a Greek tragedy mask. Tanisha was biting her lip like she wanted to stop me but didn't want to either.

Then there was a hand on my elbow and I turned. It was Ange, Marcus's gir-lie, my archrival, all of five-foot-nothing, curvy and blunt-bobbed, everything I wasn't. My first instinct was to pull away like she was about to kick my ass, because I was that keyed up and freaked out. But then I noticed her expression. She was looking at me with all this complicated stuff in her eyes: respect, con-cern, and yeah, *hope*. I could see what Marcus saw in Ange, her emotions right there on the surface, so powerful and genuine, unmissable and unmistakable. If you looked at her in a picture, which, yeah, I'd done from time to time, she was unexceptional. But in person, her face lit up like that, she was *gorgeous*.

She took my hand and squeezed it. Her fingers were small and warm, her palm slick. Her skin shone with sweat and exhaustion. She smiled at me and took the mic out of my other hand and kept hold of my hand as she brought it down to her mouth.

"She's right." The room's energy shifted to her and she seemed taller, some-how, standing so straight. "Everything Masha said is right. If all we have be-tween us and tyranny is cryptography and the internet, we're all dead. We should just surrender.

"But that's *not* all we have. Look, the cops have guns, and the way we keep them from shooting us isn't by buying body armor or driving around in tanks.

They have jails, and we don't stop them from locking us up by stockpiling dynamite.

"The way we stay free and safe and un-shot and all of that? Politics. Democracy. Holding them to account. It wasn't so many years ago that Oakland was the first major city to pass a law forcing the city to put every new piece of surveillance, every new database, up for public debate. You saw how hard the surveillance tech companies fought that, how much money they poured into getting it killed. They were *scared*. Because you know what's more powerful than all the crypto in the world? An accountable process. Politicians who answer to us, not the billion-dollar companies that hire them when they get out of office.

"Technology has its place. We can organize, securely, to a degree that the Black Panthers, the Free Speech Movement, the Yippies, the Wobblies, the Pink Panthers, the American Indian Movement, all those organizers and activists from this area, they couldn't have even *dreamed* of. We'd be idiots not to use those tools. But we'd be bigger idiots to *just* use those tools. The most important tool we have for curbing official abuses of power is consensual, legitimate, democratic government. That's what we have to use the tools *for*.

"I've known Masha here for a decade, and I've never doubted that she was a brilliant technologist. I mean, she was *definitely* worth every penny Xoth and Zyz paid her. But Masha"—and she turned to me, a gentle smile on her face—"you've never been very smart about politics. You've got tunnel vision, you think that if the tech doesn't solve the problem, it can't be solved.

"We *can* solve these problems, Masha. With your help, we can tool up to resist. When we resist we can organize. When we organize, we can *win*."

Her last sentence rang out in the silent school gymnasium. Her chest heaved a little and her eyes were bright. She meant every word and she made me want to believe it too. Maybe I did.

Marcus was looking at her with naked worship. I couldn't blame him. It's funny, I'd always thought of these people as suckers, sniffing their own farts and telling anyone who'd listen all about how good they smelled. But try as I might, dammit, Ange had made me a believer.

Tanisha gave her a long hug before taking the mic from her. She held the mic by her chin and sighed. Sighed again.

"We've been here before, people. Last time it was license-plate cameras and cell-phone trackers. Now it's cars being hijacked to target citizens in the streets. Last time, we had to convince people that there was an issue worth caring about. Now we have to convince them it's not too late to *do something about it*.

"Tomorrow we're going to have to show real numbers, national news numbers. You got someone you know who's always posting on Facebook about how fucked up this shit is, but who never gets their lazy ass off the sofa, you *get* them off that sofa. Go to their *house* and drag their ass out, and stop on the way to the march and you get five more friends. It's go time. Anyone tells you there's no point, you give them social proof, show them all the other people who are going to come, let them know they'll be the only ones at home in their track pants eating ice cream while the rest of us are out standing up for what's right."

She stared at them and her eyes blazed. I felt it, this pull, this sense of growing hope, even as a cynical voice was counting down all the myriad ways I could disrupt this group, neutralize its actions, shut it down.

Tanisha sighed. Again. Deep sounds, the sounds of someone getting ready to do something hard and real. Sighs that trembled inside me. I was crying. I turned away and wept into my sleeve like a baby. I must have been an awesome sight. I wondered if my mom was watching.

"Anyone got any questions? No? Good. You know what you have to do. Do it. See you tomorrow."

That was the second trip I made to Oakland.

I liked what you said," I said to Ange as we rode through the tunnel under the San Francisco Bay. There was a transit cop on our BART car, and he was making me nervous. Who knew what kinds of strings Xoth and Zyz were pulling? Every time I closed my eyes, I saw the murderous, unhinged glare of Carrie Johnstone, like a vulture about to tear my face off.

She reached out and squeezed my hand. "I liked what you said, too."

I felt a spurt of anger, felt my cheeks flush. "Bullshit." She didn't flinch. She radiated sincere warmth. "Come on, Ange. I blew it. I got up there and I babbled. I told them there was no hope. Basically, I told them to give up. Not even to try."

She glanced at Marcus. "You told them that technology wouldn't save their asses. That was something they needed to hear." Marcus smiled shyly at her and she took his hand, too. What a picture we must have been. We could have sung a couple of rousing choruses of "Kumbaya."

"Technology *won't* save their asses. We know that better than anyone. Technology is a tool that gives us the space to make political change. Politics are a tool we use to open the space for making better technology. It's like parallel parking: you go as far as you can in one direction, then back up and go as far as you can in the other. Use tech to make political achievements, use politics to improve tech. Back and forth." She swung our hands to match her words, like we were playing ring-around-the-rosy.

"You two—" She brought her hands together and made ours touch, and I felt a brief, electric crackle as my skin brushed Marcus's. "You have never really understood how technology works." Marcus started to sputter, but she rolled over him. "I mean, yeah, you know lots more about coding and crypto and algorithms than me, but when it comes to how technology really *works*—what it does in the world—you have never really grasped the way the system functions. You think that if technology makes something possible, it will happen automatically. You think if something can't be accomplished through technology, it's impossible. You've always missed the point: information doesn't want to be free—"

Marcus chimed in with the air of someone who'd had this discussion before. "But people do."

She smiled. "People do. People use technology to make themselves free, by using it to share and organize and connect. Freedom isn't something technology gives you, technology is something you use to get freedom."

We were quiet the rest of the way back to their house. I had never really had a real conversation with Ange. She'd always been Marcus's girlie, a rival who'd beat me before I'd even got started. I'd dismissed her as a technological lightweight—just like I'd dismissed Tanisha, if I were being honest with myself—she wasn't a coder and she wasn't a pen tester and she wasn't an engineer.

She smiled a sad little smile. "You should see the look on your face."

I couldn't help laughing. "Yeah. Well."

"You figured I was just some asshole who talked about technology because I couldn't make it, right?"

Yeah, she was smarter than I'd given her credit for. And that meant I was stupider than I'd suspected. "It's just—" I gave up.

"Both of you." She banged Marcus's and my hands together, hard enough to make my knuckles sting. "Look, if the people using all your fabulous technology don't get to have a seat at the table, then let's just give up now. People who live in cities have a legit interest in how the city works—it's not just architects and bricklayers who are qualified to talk about them."

Marcus was looking awfully pleased with himself, either because he was enjoying watching someone else squirm for a change, or because he was admiring his wife while she shone. Whatever.

I felt something loose and rattling inside me, something that had escaped from the crumbling remnants of my compartments. It threatened to come out as tears, but I blinked until they went away.

"That's really smart." I swallowed. "And I'm sorry I didn't figure it out for myself." Swallow. "A decade ago."

"Yeah," she said. "That might have really saved a lot of people a lot of pain."

"Maybe their lives." I meant it to come out as zero-fucks-given, but instead it came out in a whisper.

Ange looked me in the eyes. She let go of my hand and Marcus's and hugged me. I was stiff for just a moment, then I bent, putting my face on her shoulder. I didn't want to cry, and I wasn't sure why I was, but I was.

It wouldn't stop. There was a moment when it seemed like I was crying on my mother's shoulder, not Ange's. I couldn't even muster the emotional distance to note how weird and screwed up that was.

For her part, Ange just took it. Didn't seem to sweat the snot and tears on her shirt, stroked my back and hair like a pro. Like she knew the girl secrets of being a compassionate crying shoulder. Like she'd been in girl class on that day and I hadn't been. No one had ever cried on my shoulder like this, had they?

I was aware of Marcus getting up and going into the kitchen for a while, then coming back. I heard something getting set down on the coffee table and smelled coffee. Then he got up again and came back. More stuff on the table. When would the tears end? They seemed endless.

I forced myself to sit up and took the box of tissues Ange wordlessly passed me and wiped and blew and wiped and blew. She calmly sponged down her shoulder and gestured at the table set with two cups of coffee.

"It's decaf," she said. "You want it Irish, or just black? It'll be good either way. Marcus made the coffee." Marcus beamed. It was clear to me that I'd completely misunderstood the power dynamics in their relationship. I wondered if anyone would ever look that proud when I praised their coffee.

"Whiskey, please."

"Good choice," Ange said and opened the cabinet.

Boarding BART the next morning, wearing protest clothes looted from Marcus Yallow's closet—jeans, old leather jacket, worn tennis shoes with two pairs of socks so they'd fit—I looked around and realized that half the people on the platform were dressed for action. Some of them held hand-lettered signs—DHS OUT OF OAK, RESTORE THE FOURTH—all of them had the tense, intense vibe of Kriztina and her friends, and I pushed down an ache in my chest.

Marcus had brought a thermos of coffee (of course) and he poured out cups for me and Ange as the train dipped under the bay. I shivered despite the warm cup, thinking of the people who'd been trapped in the old tunnel when the bombs went off, then, back to today, remembering the cops who'd nabbed me in this tunnel. I'd always thought that someday I'd live in San Francisco again, but now I wondered if I would ever really feel comfortable here.

A bunch of kids—the same age I'd been when I started working for Carrie Johnstone, with half-shaved heads and gender-nonconforming wardrobes—were covertly vaping, which made Marcus tsk. But it was Ange who confronted them and quietly but firmly tore a strip out of them, about how bullshit it would be to get busted for something as ridiculous as public weed consumption when they were off to do something *really* important. Then she moved on to how fucked up it would be to get *other* people busted and keep them from the protests. The kids started off defiant, but quickly moved to shamefaced and pocketed their vapers, promising to dump them in the trash when we pulled into the station. Ange finished up by giving each of them a hug and telling them to stay safe.

"I'm starting to think you're the brains of the outfit," I said when she sat back down with us.

"You just figured that out?" Marcus said. "I'm a lucky guy." That didn't pang me at all, which was surprising and welcome.

I nodded. "You sure are."

It was so weird to be on this side of things. I could think of a million ways that I could have tracked us, from the IMSI catchers that I would have placed at all the BART exits for the first six stops on the Oakland side, to the long-retention video archives from the trains that I could run through facial recognition later, to the man-in-the-middled free wifi networks I could dot around the protest grounds, to the Bluetooth readers I'd use as backup to fingerprint anyone whose phone escaped the IMSI catchers. I'd buy, bully, or steal the turnstile data from BART, and inject fake-news alerts into the Amber Alert system telling people the protest had been canceled or moved somewhere else.

I'd never worked on the part of the business that outfitted and fielded provocateurs and infiltrators, but I'd provided intel to those folks, and it wouldn't be hard to figure out how to maximally disrupt the protest we were heading out to now, sowing confusion, cutting off key lines of communication, sending people the wrong way.

I couldn't shake off the sense of doom this gave me, the sense that we were walking into a trap. Ange noticed and gave my hand a squeeze. "Relax," she said. "We've done this a million times."

I remembered what she'd said the night before: we weren't trying to beat the system with superior technology, we were trying to use technology to open up a space to *change* the system. It didn't have to be perfect, it didn't have to keep everyone anonymous or impervious to snooping: it just had to work well enough to organize political change.

"Yeah, okay." We were on the Oakland side of the bay now, and every time we stopped, the car got more crowded, with more protesters. It was a Saturday and the crowd was swelling. "So many people."

"It was the cars," Ange said, and Marcus nodded. "What a fucking idiotic move that was. Maybe they thought that would make people desperate for more 'security,' but they were so wrong. The Bay Area's got a lot of techies, and once the story got out that the cars were actually a plot by Zyz to land a contract, it was easy for people to understand that and believe it. I've been watching on social; people are getting their lazy friends up off the couch, just like Tanisha said, getting them out in the streets. Zyz must have been pretty damn desperate to try that bullshit. It's one thing to torment those poor bastards in Slovstakia with killbots, Americans can forgive stuff that happens on the other side of the world, but trying it here? In the Bay Area? Nah."

I shook my head. "Are you sure? I mean, this is the kind of thing it's so easy to do disinfo for, blaming everyone until no one is sure who might have done it." Xoth made a tool for that, next-gen persona management with IP address randomization across a huge network of hacked devices that served as proxies and centaur capabilities that let a human come in and ride the disinfo bots whenever they detected an interesting conversation. I'd seen it deployed in Slovstakia and had spent hours playing "Bot or Not" with Kriztina and her friends, teaching them how to spot fakes and just how thoroughly outgunned they were on social.

Ange grinned. "Yeah, that disinfo stuff is getting old. We've had so much of it over the years here, especially about the Black-Brown Alliance. Thing is, there are so many ex-Googlers and other tech alumni who cashed out, and their fuck-you money means they have no reason to sell out, so when they say they've done the analysis and they think it's an inside job, people believe 'em. Attribution is hard, but it's not impossible, and 'cui bono' goes a long way."

Marcus rubbed his hands together like a chef about to carve a goose. "I remember when the disinformation campaigns first hit the net, and I thought, 'Oh shit, we made a monster,' like all these conspiracy theories and filter bubbles were unstoppable, and there was enough terrible stuff going on in the world that *anything* was believable. But it turns out that for most people, any stimulus eventually fades—no matter how difficult it is to ignore at the outset. I mean, some people will always be susceptible, the same way some people will always want to play *FarmVille* or go to Vegas and feed quarters into the slots. But for most people, disinfo just gets . . . boring."

Ange nodded along and the two of them were doing this adorable mind-meld thing that made me want to curl up in a corner somewhere. No one ever mind-melded with me. The people I spent all my time with were either trying to sabotage me and steal my job or were people that I was technically trying to put in jail. So I woke up my old self and pissed on their parade.

"Maybe that's true—though I'm here to tell you that sophisticates of the Bay Area or no, there's plenty of people who can get real worked up about a plausible scare story. But that's not the whole point of disinfo anyway: the point of fake news isn't just to make it so that no one can tell what's true, it's to make it so that no one *cares* anymore, so that when you try to get all your friends to go out and march about something that they should already be thinking about, they're all like, 'Eh, is that even *real?*' Your enemies don't need people to disagree with you, they just need people not to *care.*"

Marcus and Ange gave that enough thought that I felt weirdly guilty, like maybe I'd convinced them that it was all hopeless. Because to tell you the truth, I was hoping that they'd convince me that it *wasn't* hopeless, the way Ange had done earlier.

"Good thing they did something so incredibly, flamboyantly stupid, then," Ange said. "People might not have cared about surveillance checkpoints and racial profiling, but turning the streets of Oakland into a killing field full of murderous self-driving cars turns out to be a real attention-getter."

And there it was, the nugget of hope I'd been looking for, a reminder that my old bosses weren't invincible supervillains, just garden-variety dumdums, no smarter than me. They had more money and more resources, but they were motivated by idiotic, petty revenge, ego, promotion-seeking, and other easily pushed buttons. Carrie Johnstone's murderous eyes didn't scare me anymore—it was comforting, a reminder that she was a broken person whose specific character flaws made her surprisingly easy to push around.

"You are a smart lady." I turned to Marcus. "You *are* an incredibly lucky boy." I meant both.

Marcus looked embarrassed, but Ange just quietly owned it.

I have been around a *lot* of protests, especially if you include protests that I've watched through CCTV and drone feeds as I helped coordinate responses. There are many different kinds of protests, and most of them are a kind of dutiful exercise, whose participants seem to be saying, *We know this is terrible and we know we can't stop it and we know you all will never care about it, but we're not about to let it go by without doing* something, *even if we know it's useless.*

But every now and again, you get the kind of protest that feels like something vast and unsuspected, waking from slumber. It's something about how the people look at each other as they're converging on the site, like, *Can you believe there are this many of us? I thought I was the only one!* They're people who thought they were heading to the first kind of protest, the dutiful exercise, only to discover that they were part of a vast movement. Oksana once described it to me as being like the first time she went to a gay bar, the realization that she wasn't alone, she wasn't a weird outlier, she was part of a movement.

This was the second kind. The escalator up from the BART platform was thronged, the stairs were jammed, the line for the turnstiles filled the whole upstairs. People looked around, laughed at one another's signs, paired phones with each other by touching them together for some kind of cryptographic messaging something-or-other.

We took the next flight of stairs in the press of bodies, and it wasn't just BO and patchouli I was smelling in the crowd of bodies. The cool air from the street above pushed down and mingled with the excitement pheromones all around me and filled me with a crazy, irrational sense of promise. We were thronging, we were numerous, we were invincible.

I mean, we were *not* invincible. I could name several ways in which we could be quite handily crushed, but the crisp air and the warm bodies and the excited buzz, it was *incredible.* I looked around and recognized the expression on the faces around me, an expression I'd seen in the Bltz central square and one that I felt on my own face.

I'd felt this excitement before. Every time, some part of me had known that there would be a time, in the very near future, when I would have to reconcile working to destroy that thing I'd been so excited to be a part of. I'd developed a reflex: when I felt a moment's hope that *this time,* something would change, I crammed that hope into a compartment and triple-locked it, and told myself not to be a sucker.

I felt the reflex. I ignored the reflex. It felt . . . *scary.* But good.

We slowed near the top of the stairs, to a crawl, and as we got close to the top, I saw a way. The crowd had filled the street so tightly that there was nowhere to

ATTACK SURFACE ··· 333

go. It was inching its way toward the Oakland Super Fusion Center, but there were so many of us that it could barely move—like grains of sand trapped in the pinch of an hourglass.

"Holy shit," Marcus said beside me. Around us, people laughed.

There were drones overhead; some were police drones, some were civilian drones, some were press, and some were police pretending to be civilian or press. I could tell the police ones by the little dirtboxes on their bellies, fake flying cell-phone towers sucking up the identities of every phone within range; some had nozzles for spraying pepper spray. At least, I hoped that was pepper spray, and I hoped those were cop drones. If there was anything scarier than participating in a civic disturbance with police gas-drones buzzing overhead, it was participating in a civic disturbance haunted by overhead gas-drones operated by anonymous parties unknown.

Some of the civilian drones were harriers, deliberately locking onto the cop drones and obstructing their path, triggering their collision-avoidance and making them swerve and buck, consuming battery. That was a new one on me. Must be a Bay Area thing, some machine-learning kids with too much time on their hands, training a classifier to identify and chase cop drones. I saw a couple of collisions and near-collisions and heard a lot of shouting as the drones conducted their aerial warfare overhead. Nothing fell out of the sky . . . yet.

"Shit's getting real," Marcus sang.

"Don't be an ass, darling," Ange said cheerfully and dragged me through the crowd.

Someone was speechifying; we were still half a block from the front of the Super Fusion Center and stuck in a crowd so thick I had to wait for someone else to exhale before I could inhale, but they were doing that thing again with their phones, holding them up and having them all magically sync up, each one a speaker and in phase with the rest. I supposed the mics had to be in play, listening to the neighbors and figuring out how far along they were and matching up to keep from creating weird dopplers and echoes.

"We *had* a rule that our city couldn't buy surveillance without telling us about it first. Not even *asking* us about it, just *telling* us about it. Telling us what they were buying, how they were using it, how they were paying for it.

"That rule got killed. The surveillance companies couldn't tolerate even that little bit of transparency. They bought our city councilors, who promised us they had it under control. *Do things look like they're under control?*

"We need to take our city back. Take it back from gentrifiers who kick us out of our homes. Take it back from politicians who want to 'boost property values' even though that means raising the rent. Take it back from cops who beat and kill with impunity. Take it back from private spies who help them in their never-ending mission to neutralize anyone who can stand up to them, something they started doing with the Black Panthers and never stopped doing.

"They told us that if we trusted them, everything would be okay. *Everything is not okay.* The evil, dystopian shit they spend our money on when no one's looking is *not okay*. Being spied on all the time is *not okay*. Being judged by black-box algorithms that decide who is guilty and who isn't is *not okay*. Having our personal lives invaded, our facial expressions analyzed, our browsing habits correlated with our shopping habits with our BART rides is *not okay*. No one would vote for that shit, never, and that's why they have to keep it a secret. I promise you, it's not a secret because they know you'll be delighted by it and they don't want to *ruin the surprise.*" The crowd, tightly wound, ducking drones, surrounded by phalanxes of cops, exploded in laughter. It was a good line, sure, but everything else made it better, a vent for all that pent-up steam.

We were getting closer to the stage now, and the crowd vibe was twanging like a guitar string, thrumming deep in my belly and the soles of my feet.

Over hundreds of phone speakers, the person speaking sighed. Sighed again. It was Tanisha.

Then we could see her, standing on a security bollard, steadied by people around her, holding her legs—women from BOW. She was only a dot, so far away, but even from this distance her bearing was awesome, regal, despite (or maybe because of) the precariousness of her perch.

"Our city sold us out. But it's still our city. Oakland is *ours,* not the cops', not the private mercenaries', not the property speculators'. The *reason* for cities is *people*. We are the people of Oakland, and we, the people, will not give our city up. No way."

She was killing it, all right. Like a radiant, avenging angel, so far away, but drawing every eye to her. My friend, my stupid, funny, weird friend. I'd loaned her my makeup, borrowed her T-shirts, talked boys and parents with her. When I'd moved away, I'd thought that I was escaping to better things in a bigger world. Tanisha was always my hometown friend with unambitious, hometown aspirations.

Holy shit was I wrong.

Letting hope out of its compartment felt good. It let me recognize truths about my friends that I'd deliberately kept hidden.

Letting hope out of its compartment felt *terrible*. It made me confront all the evil I'd done and let others do thanks to my self-deception.

The guy who went for her was indistinct from my distance, but he was big and fast. The clothes were pure gray-man, athletic wear, like a bro coming from the gym or a dog walk, his face half-shadowed by an Oakland Athletics cap. I spotted him when he was still a couple of paces away, visible at first as a bow wave in the crowd as he shoved his way through by force. His hand stretched up and out and I made out the waggling end of a telescoping baton. I'd seen what someone who knew what he was doing could do with one of those—what he could do to knees, or elbows, or the bridge of a nose, or teeth, or the soft spot at your temple.

I screamed a useless warning and tried to shove my way forward, but the crowd wasn't budging. They had nowhere to budge. Marcus and Ange were calling my name, people were cursing me, and I was pushing, pushing, going nowhere. Meanwhile, the man behind Tanisha was getting closer. Tanisha's voice was coming out of all those speakers on all those phones:

"—they see how many of you came here today, they're not gonna have a choice, they're gonna *have* to listen. All this time, they thought that we would get tired, that we'd get discouraged, but they had it all wrong. You step on us, we don't learn to be meek, we learn to be—"

He grabbed her so fast that she had no idea what was coming and then she was over his shoulder. This made no sense. How the hell was he going to get away with Tanisha over his shoulder in that crowd, in broad daylight, with all those cameras on him?

Two of the BOW women who'd been steadying Tanisha on the bollard went for him and the telescoping baton flicked, one-two, fast as that, and they both went down. He moved faster now, kicking out at anyone who got in his way, and I could see another bow wave moving through the crowd, toward him, a flying wedge of riot cops in full gear, shields out, batons flashing. If they'd come out like that before Tanisha got snatched, they'd have met heavy resistance. Now the crowd was aiming its attention in two directions at once, getting in its own way. Even from where I was standing, I could see the panic swirling: people falling, bumping into each other. People taking head-knocks. Some of the protesters were wearing helmets now, pushing back, getting in the cops' way, but they went down under the batons, then were passed, limp and bloody, through the cops' wedge.

"Fuck!" Marcus shouted. He was beside me, and then Ange was beside me too, and we were our own wedge, moving through the crowd. Ange was good at it, touching shoulders, smiling, thanking people, but insistent, small and unstoppable as a tugboat, the point of our wedge. We were moving *toward* the police line, the violence, Tanisha, and none of us had to say a word.

I'd seen this, seen this in the square in Slovstakia, the people who would run *toward,* not away, and it had seemed suicidal. Now, with hope out of its compartment, it seemed like the only choice.

We weren't the only ones who felt this way. People had masked up, bike helmets buckled over face kerchiefs, protest signs ripped from sticks that turned out to be stouter than the general-issue splintery garden stake. It should have been scary, but it felt *amazing.* All the sickening hopelessness I'd felt watching Tanisha get snatched turned to vengeful fury. I discovered I was yelling. I wasn't the only one. I discovered I didn't want to stop. Hope is a powerful thing.

Choppers now, joining the drones, and chaotic movement and shoving, a mist on my face and then water slick underfoot and I realized they were using hoses, and I didn't give a shit. I bulled my way into the people fleeing the hoses, linking arms with Marcus and Ange, and we pivoted to flank the direction of the water. It was slow going, but there was a tide pushing behind us, and some of the people fleeing the hoses turned around when they met our line, joining us. When people fell, they were swiftly helped back onto their feet.

Suddenly we were on the front line, facing the water cannons, and they weren't just riot-shielded hoses: the cannons were being fired from slits in a high, moving wall, maybe twenty feet tall, with some kind of earth-moving

machine behind it. The wall was like a tall, straight snow-plow blade, mounted on bulky, protruding armatures, painted police blue and emblazoned with OPD and a police star. Peeking above it, a glassed-in driver's box, a grim-faced cop driving it forward like a farmer high atop a tracker. Peeking beneath it, booted feet, as cops advanced from behind the blade. The hoses played over the crowd, picking off people on the edges, knocking them on their asses or into the people behind them. Whoever was operating those hoses was enjoying himself, letting the fallen people almost back on their feet, before hitting them with the jet again and knocking them over. One guy got hit in the ass as he was crouching on all fours, struggling, and then he came back up with blood streaming from his face—maybe he'd lost his front teeth, or broken his nose. It was slapstick for dictators.

We were in the middle of the front line, still pivoting to flank the slow-moving siege engine, and the spray kept nailing us as the gunner swung the cannon from side to side. We kept our arms firmly linked and our combined weight and the people behind us kept us from going down. We marched on.

I don't know what I expected. Would we reach the moving wall and climb its sheer surface? Would we stream around its edges and take on the riot cops behind it with our bare hands or perhaps the little clubs the Black Bloc had smuggled in as sign sticks?

In retrospect: I didn't expect anything. I wasn't thinking. I was acting. My friend had been taken, but I was with comrades, and we were moving to the place where she had been last seen. We had a unity of purpose and it was transmitted through the lock of our arms, the tromp of our feet. I'd never felt anything like it before. Watching from my screens, I'd thought I'd understood what people in moments like this were feeling. I hadn't understood a thing.

We marched on. My knee groaned beneath me, but I didn't hear a thing.

The moving wall advanced. We advanced at an angle, still trying to get around it, slipping when the water hit us. Some people had goggles, for gas, I supposed, but it helped when the water was on them. The drones buzzed low. One got hit by a stream of water and it spun out, smashed itself to pieces on the ground.

The others all knew chants that I didn't know: "If we don't get it/Shut it down" "Whose streets? Our streets!" and one I'd heard in half a dozen languages: "The people! United! Will never be defeated!"

Everyone I'd ever heard chanting that had been defeated. They'd had hope. They'd kept chanting. I chanted it. Hope fluttered like a banner.

Out on the front line, I had lost all sense of how many people were still in the game, but when I managed to look behind me I was stunned. Watching as the people around me got picked off, I'd had the sense that we were down to a few, crazy, doomed marchers. Not that that was going to stop me, obviously, but I was sure we were down to the dregs.

Instead, I discovered that I was on the forefront of an endless, rolling wave of people. The people who'd turned and run? They'd turned back around. They were at our back, so thick that I didn't think I could have stopped and retreated if I'd wanted to. I didn't want to. I wasn't going to.

Maybe we wouldn't be defeated.

We were close enough to count the rivets on the steel wall's face when it finally ground to a halt. The hose swung back and forth, dry-firing, the wide bore of the nozzles staring blindly at us. I flinched when one passed me, and I wasn't the only one. They sputtered a little, and I realized they were empty. This was the moving wall's grand public debut and the cannoneers had squandered their ammo, firing before they could see the whites of our eyes.

Our pace quickened.

The cops who stepped out from behind the blade were meant to be terrifying, masked and booted and shielded, cans of pepper spray on their belts, but the force of our numbers robbed them of all power to frighten. If they started swinging, they'd go down under our mass in seconds. The riot truck started to reverse and the cops scrambled to retreat with it. The distant sirens and helicopter roar from overhead reminded us that there were reinforcements on the way, but all that did was make me want to move faster, before they arrived.

A compartment was rattling in the back of my mind: snatching Tanisha wasn't an accident. Doing it in front of all these people wasn't an accident. They knew they would get this: they had their giant anti-riot killdozer standing by, just out of sight.

That morning, the Super Fusion Center and its contractors were facing an extinction-level event, thanks to Zyz's idiotic, ham-fisted stunt with the cars. Xoth was smarter than Zyz, much smarter. They had discipline.

This was a disciplined provocation. If we rushed the cops—*when* we rushed the cops—it would flip the script, make the case for surveillance. The cops may not have realized it, the protesters certainly didn't, but we were all about to hand Xoth tens of millions of dollars in contracts, and a reference-customer they could use to sell their services to every other city in America. Hell, the world.

I skidded to a halt, and the crowd behind me pushed me on. I had to stop them.

S it down," I shouted to Ange. "We have to sit down."

Ange looked at me like she couldn't understand what I was saying.

"We have to stop this. We have to sit down. They're trying to provoke us into a riot."

Ange shook her head, looked at me, shook her head.

"We have to stop!"

She looked at Marcus, then at me. A moment before, her eyes had been alive with purpose, making her look like a vengeful fury. Now she looked confused, and a little scared. She stumbled and we held her up.

"It's a setup!" I shouted.

We slowed and the crowd pushed us from behind. Now I was stumbling, and in danger of going down.

Ange shouted, "On three, then," and I realized she believed me. "One! Two!" We sat.

The first thing that happened is that I got kicked in the back and the head about six times in as many seconds, as the people behind us tripped and stumbled. A few sprawled ahead of us, and that slowed everything down, as people stopped to help them up and we grabbed them and dragged them back down, shouting, "Sit down, sit down, it's a setup!"

If we hadn't been at the front, there was no chance it would have worked. But we had caused a huge pileup and it was getting bigger by the second. The people behind us were still crushing us, kicking us, unable to stop in time, but the rate was slowing. Enough people had sat down that some of the protesters who went past them doubled back to find out what was going on—and the isolated few who kept going quickly realized that they were on their own and they, too, stopped.

It became a chant: "Sit down! Sit down! It's a setup!" I had never been much of a chanter, but I found myself screaming it as loud as I could, keeping time.

All around us, people sat.

# CHAPTER 12

We weren't on the front line anymore: from where we sat, we were looking over the heads of row after row of sitting people who'd overshot us, knee-to-knee and hip-to-hip in the courtyard ahead of the Super Fusion Center. The engine roar of the running crowd had slowed to a rumbling idle as people talked to each other in hushed tones. Every now and again a group of people would bubble up and start to stalk toward the police line, but others still on the ground grabbed their legs and told them to sit down, sit down.

The cops looked as confused as we were. I can only imagine what must have been going through their heads: a minute before they were about to be human sacrifices, overrun specifically to create a provocation that would justify an all-out retaliation. Now they were facing thousands—many thousands—of people on the ground, sitting, talking. The overhead helicopters drowned out the drones' mosquito whines, and they struggled to station-keep against the rotor wash.

The cops looked at each other, smacked their clubs against their palms, raised their visors and rubbed their sweating faces. The siren noises grew louder and switched off as the reinforcements arrived. Some of the cops pressed hands to their ears, listening intently to their radios.

The police reinforcements marched in rows like an infantry on parade, in greens instead of blues, carrying shields and garlanded with huge bouquets of zip-tie cuffs. It quickly became apparent that there was nowhere for them to go—they filled in all the space between the police lines and the sitting protesters and still they poured in, trampling on protesters (accidentally at first, then less so), and still they came. I could see the cops' mouths moving and their hands pressed to their earpieces as they tried to sort out the mess, and still they came.

Around us, people shuffled in tighter, going from knee-to-knee to overlapping knees, and it occurred to me that the tighter we got, the harder it would be to disperse us: as close as we were now, it would be pretty much impossible for anyone not on the edges to get up and leave.

I must have laughed, because Ange asked me what was so funny and when I explained it to her, she laughed too, and then so did the people around us. It was a brittle laugh, not humorous in the least, but it was a much-needed release.

Now that we were catching our breath, Tanisha was back in my thoughts. Getting her bailed out the first time had been a major operation. At least I had a lawyer on call. I pulled out my phone and quickly powered it up, sticking my hand over my other ear to shut out the rising noise of the people all around me. The call took forever to connect. Maybe it was all the phone surveillance, or just all the other people taking a breather and calling friends they'd lost in the chaos. Using a phone in the midst of a protest, in the unseen presence of so many surveillance devices, felt *wrong*.

"Are you okay?" She sounded businesslike, exactly as you'd hope your lawyer would sound in a tight spot.

"I'm okay, are you okay?"

She snorted. "I'm working on things."

"Things?!"

"The police have Tanisha in custody, but I'm on it."

"You're on it?"

"I'm on it. I have backup, too. But Masha, are you in any distress? Because this really demands my full attention."

"Is Tanisha all right?"

"She is, for the moment. I'd like it to stay that way, so Masha—"

"Fine, fine, but Aino—"

"Look, Masha, I have to go. The standoff is about to break."

"Standoff?"

"I'll call back." And she was gone.

Marcus was frowning in concern. "Is everything okay? What standoff?"

And I explained, my voice almost a whisper in his ear. Everything seemed very fragile right then.

Minutes. Hours. My legs and knees ached from sitting and I was on my third and last phone battery: those IMSI catchers weren't just a grotesque privacy invasion; they were also murder on your phone's power consumption, as it connected and disconnected from the fake towers over and over again. The paralegal had called and told us they were on top of things. Marcus was busy giving press interviews to reporters who had his number on speed dial. Of course.

Ange kept getting into these intense conversations with the other organizers by phone, talking in these oblique terms that skirted admitting any kind of culpability for any illegal stuff that might happen next, talking with the curious tones of someone who knew other people were listening in.

Once upon a time, I would have been doing the listening. Now I was sidelined, watching other people's jittery, breathless livestreams from elsewhere in the crowd.

Then my phone rang, at last.

"Finally!"

"Yes, finally."

My stomach did a slow roll. That wasn't Aino's voice, it was Carrie Johnstone's.

Instinctively, I cupped my hand over the receiver. "Spoofing caller ID is a little amateur hour, isn't it?"

"Masha?" Tanisha sounded angry and scared, then cut off. Carrie Johnstone got back on the line. "Yes, that's pretty amateur. Not the sort of thing I need to resort to. I'll meet you at the Super Fusion Center doors in ten minutes."

"There's no way I can get through this crowd."

"You'll find a way."

She was right. I found a way.

In Slovstakia, the senior ministers all got these black, shining Mercedes vans that they practically lived out of; the drivers would run errands for them and wait while they had long meals or visited their girlfriends. I'd spent a lot of

times in those vans, along with Ilsa, giving live demos of our tech as we inter-
dicted the street protests, sucking up protesters' data from their phones and
running real-time threat-assessment monitors of social media that matched
people's online identities to the messages they were sending and then pinpointed their locations and mapped their social graph. It was super-impressive-
looking, the kind of thing you wanted to shout "enhance, enhance" at (or stand
up and salute).

In America, they did things differently. They liked designated "mobile command posts": armored buses filled with monitors and mini-fridges and equipment lockers.

Zyz's MCP was a lot plusher than the Xoth bus I'd been on outside police
HQ, all leather captain's chairs and stainless-steel surfaces—the kind of thing
you'd make to impress someone with purchasing power.

Carrie Johnstone had one large Starbucks and two large goons, and in the
detention cell at the back of the bus—a heavy wire cage with fold-down shut-
ters to shield the vehicle's legit passengers from spitting, shouting, shit-flinging,
and other prisoner shenanigans—she had Tanisha, who was looking pissed
and scared, sitting up as straight as she could with her hands cuffed behind her
back. I locked eyes with her for one second on my way in, then looked away. I
needed to get my head in the game.

Carrie Johnstone had cleaned up a lot since I'd last seen her, found a smart
suit to wear, done her makeup, brushed her hair. Her eyes, though: still pure
unhinged vengeance.

I stood and looked at her, poker-facing it, waiting for her to make a move.

She pointed at the chair. I sat, taking my time, not breaking eye contact.

"Masha." She gave the pause a long time to hang out there in the bus. Power
move. "I have prepared a forensic dossier detailing your investigation into this
week's unfortunate vehicular incidents. You will sign it, present it at a meeting
tomorrow. It identifies Xoth as the responsible party, and justifies this iden-
tification by discussing the proprietary elements of Xoth's incursion systems,
which you have personal knowledge of. This is structured to take advantage of
California's whistleblower laws, and will be copied to the Securities Exchange
Commission. You will be eligible for a cash reward, should this lead to a criminal conviction. Of course, you will be able to retain this award."

I wished I'd kicked her harder.

"We are of the opinion that, given your friend's organizing role in this violent"—Johnstone smiled a very thin, very small smile—"civil disturbance, a grand jury might indict her for fomenting political violence." She looked at Tanisha, who was watching with narrow-eyed contempt. "That is, *terrorism*."

Carrie Johnstone had a way of saying *terrorism* that made it sound like *Christmas morning*, a long-awaited moment of thrilling bounty, sumptuous meals, and vicious fighting around the table. I poker-faced it.

"Yeah, and then I tell everyone that we had this conversation, and Zyz will look even less trustworthy than it does now. Carrie, you need some game theory."

She shook her head, just a tiny amount. She was enjoying this. So. Much. I put my fear in a compartment. I let the hope out.

"We have the evidence we need to bring down the world on everyone you love and care about, Masha. If Zyz ceases to do business tomorrow, there will be several of its senior operational staff who will make it their job to see to it that your mother pays a price. That your friend Marcus pays a price. That your friend Ange pays a price. That your friend Tanisha over there pays a price. If you think we can't make that happen, you weren't paying attention."

"I can take care of myself," Tanisha said.

"They can take care of themselves." Not my mother, though. And Tanisha—there were a lot of people on her side, but there were some very powerful people who'd be happy to show up in public as the enemy of the lawless rabble. And there were lots of old white people in the Bay Area who would throw their support behind anyone who would assure them that all the powers of the fully functioning Death Star/Police State would be appropriately turned toward ensuring that brown and black people were kept under constant watch, under constant threat.

Carrie Johnstone acted as if she hadn't heard me. "It's actually a win-win for me, to be honest. You don't cooperate, fine, then Zyz goes down and I end up cherry-picking the best people and picking up their old clients, and get to enjoy watching my less resilient colleagues make a point of destroying everything you love and care about in every country and city you've ever lived. And if you *do* cooperate—which, frankly, I don't think you will—well, then we get to rescue this contract and I get to hum along, and *you* get to spend all your days and years to come waiting for the other shoe to drop. My other shoe to drop." Her eyes were terrible. "See? A win-win."

I insisted on reading through the full report before I put my name to it. It was only ten pages long, and it oscillated between impossible-to-understand flow diagrams that supposedly documented the way that the city's cars had been hijacked; and detailed, baffling explanations of why this proved that the whole thing had been masterminded by Xoth in a bid to steal the San Francisco contract from Zyz. The report gave the whole thing a catchy name: "a Pied Piper gambit," which was halfway clever enough that I smirked when I saw it.

Carrie Johnstone looked over my shoulder. "My idea." Pride in her voice.

I finished the report, drew a deep breath.

"No." I stood up, keeping my eyes on hers.

Behind me, Tanisha hissed, "*Yes.*"

She stood too. Her goons half stepped toward me. "It's not going to go easy for you, you know." She was good at doing the Voice, high school principal meets Darth Vader. It went straight past my higher faculties and twanged my parasympathetic nervous system. I squared up.

"Goodbye, Carrie."

She nodded at the goons and they shifted to block my way, filling the narrow space of the battle-bus aisle. One of them reached for me and—

The thump on the bus door couldn't have been better timed. I looked at Carrie Johnstone.

"It's for you."

The goons glanced back to her for guidance, and Carrie Johnstone made an impatient gesture that sent them skittering back to starting positions, behind her. She stood and smoothed her jacket and walked past me to the door, slapped the button that made it sigh open just as the thumping, now a steady rhythmic pounding, was reaching a crescendo.

Behind the door were two uniformed Oakland Police Department patrolmen, a guy with the air of a detective, and another guy, gray and suited, whose whole look screamed "decision-maker." With him: Ilsa, She-Wolf of the etc., etc.

Carrie and Ilsa must have met somewhere down the line: the industry just isn't that big and they'd both been there when it was being born—when you could hold a trade show in an airport Hilton ballroom instead of a major city's convention center.

But the look that passed between them when their eyes met was much more complicated and aggressive than I'd have predicted. Think animals: birds with their feathers out, cats with their backs up, dogs with their necks ruffled. Everyone caught it and edged back—goons, cops, decision-makers. It wasn't like anything I'd ever felt. Impossible to describe. Impossible to forget.

"Please step out of there," Ilsa said, her accent faint but hard-edged.

Carrie Johnstone's hand twitched over the door button, but she didn't slap it and slam the door in Ilsa's face. She breathed instead, a slow and measured in-out. "No."

"Yes," Ilsa said, and the cops moved past her onto the bus's bottom step.

In the end, Carrie Johnstone and her goons left under their own steam, Carrie preserving her all-important dignity by stepping off with stiff back and neck, nose up, before the cops could drag them off. Ilsa poker-faced her better than I ever could as she stalked off with the decision-maker and the detective, her goons trailing behind her like baby ducks. Tanisha was still back in the mobile command post. I tried not to think about her just then. I needed to be in the moment. I could go back for her after.

"Our bus is over here," Ilsa said crisply, and led me around a corner to, yes, the bus I'd encountered the section chief in, a thousand years ago.

"What are we doing here?" I asked her, as soon as the door was closed behind us, the OPD wingmen on the other side.

"We're revisiting," she said. "Masha, did you think we would give up just because you had a tantrum? The reality is this: you're not stupid, and only a stupid person would refuse to cooperate."

"You're right. I'm not stupid. I'm smart enough to know that you have precisely nothing. Zyz is finished, but can Xoth get the contract without my testimony? Or, put it this way, can Xoth get the contract if I'm testifying *against* it? Telling everyone that *your* escaped zero-day was Zyz's secret weapon? Herthe, I don't work for you, and I'm *not going to* work for you." I could see the words land. She knew it was true, and that I didn't care what she did to me, that I could not be commanded and would never be commanded again. She went from icy to furious.

Before Ilsa could reply, her phone rang. She closed her mouth, whirled around, and clamped it to her head: "*Hallo.*"

She shook as she listened, and looked away from me. The mask was slipping and there she was, just another terrified, sadistic, terrible actor. Better than Carrie Johnstone—but only at hiding her emotions.

Once I'd had mentors, women I'd looked up to. Monsters who showed me the monster I could be, if I worked hard at it. Now, I had friends. Not monsters and not golden heroes. Just civilians, with deep reserves of bravery and principle. People who made a dent in the universe without having to become monsters. Could that be me?

Ilsa put her hand over her mouth and whispered urgently into the phone. She got as far away from me as she could. Whisper whisper. Click.

When she turned around, she looked twenty years older. She was gray. No, *ashen*. Her ramrod posture was gone, and she slumped, round-shouldered and old, like my mother.

"Go," she said. Even on that one syllable, her voice trembled. She opened the door.

# CHAPTER 13

The government of Slovstakia fell a few minutes after midnight, local time, but nobody noticed for some hours—not even the soldiers defending the presidential palace.

Oh, everyone saw the new president's helicopter lift off and scream east—it eventually landed in Baku, where the Azeri ruling family met him with champagne and blini—but it was just one of many choppers circling the endless protests at the time.

Everyone in the square was on a list of some kind or another. The Slovstakian secret police knew their names and their social graph. They had intercepted their communications and sown discontent within their ranks with provocateurs and false flags.

Every one of them had a friend or a loved one in prison or in a grave. Some of those graves were unmarked. They had been spied on with their own phones. They had been chased through their own streets by their own cars. They had been blackmailed into spying on their own loved ones, forced underground, forced into exile.

The privacy tools I'd helped them learn to use hadn't made them impervious to any of that. But it had made them *resistant*. It had introduced friction into the self-running, turnkey systems of automated control and oppression. It meant that the fastest and nimblest of the people of Slovstakia could outrun the killer robots chasing them down the wires and through the streets—for a while.

They used that time well.

The blood in the streets kept them from wavering. For once, the radicals of Slovstakia were able to resist the offers of the elites: the relentless power of the Slovstakian elites failed to co-opt the new political leaders, a succession of looter presidents who used bribes and favors to win the loyal cooperation of the country's richest men and the most powerful generals. The demonstrations, once seen as proof that some people were too foolish to know when to leave well enough alone, became proof that other people felt the same truth in their hearts: that the situation was too rotten to stand, that a better world might be around the corner.

Litvinchuk had thought that painting the streets of Slovstakia with blood would make people afraid to walk them. Instead it cost him his job. When his far-right successor took his place, everyone had stayed noisy, stayed in the streets. Eventually, the new man's helicopter, too, disappeared over the horizon.

The news traveled fast. Someone in the cabinet told someone in the military told someone in the police told someone in the infiltrators told a protester and then the message raced from person to person, phone to phone. Inevitably, many people had caught videos of the helicopter liftoff without knowing precisely what they'd recorded, and these were posted and shared and then—

It ended.

A policeman walked off the job, quietly. He put down his shield and billy club, took off his helmet and mask, set them by his feet, and walked off the line. The cops around him called to him, but he gave no sign that he heard, and then the protesters in the square cheered and jeered as they closed ranks, kicking his abandoned gear behind the line. Colorful Revolutionaries lobbed volleys of glitter: red, green, blue, smashing into the face of the palace, drawing cheers.

Another cop walked away. Another.

Then one turned and ran. The police line was getting *awfully* thin. Seconds later, it dissolved as the remaining officers realized that they were practically alone up there—just a few seconds before the crowd realized the same thing. They were jeered and chased as they ran, and one of them got a thrown bottle in the back of the head, falling face-first into the cobbles before being hauled back to his feet and dragged away by a friend, momentarily flashing his bloody, terrified face at the crowd.

The blood brought the crowd up short. Someone made to throw another bottle, only to have the person behind him pluck it out of his hand and drop it to the ground, where it shattered.

The sound broke the spell. Suddenly, people were hugging each other, whooping, tossing their hats into the air, spontaneously kissing. A group of young teens raced to the palace steps and vaulted them, climbing the riot fencing like monkeys, swinging from rail to rail, showing off their parkour moves, then they were over the fence and yanking open the palace doors.

A pair of surprised soldiers stood there—they hadn't gotten the memo—then they looked out at the crowd, who'd moved forward to grab the riot fence with many hands, shaking and lifting it, attacking it with bolt-cutters and ropes. The soldiers had grabbed for the guns slung around their necks, but now their eyes widened and they disappeared into the palace together.

The fences came down and the crowd poured into the palace.

It was surreal: the lavish furnishings (so much gilt!); the oil paintings of the last president and his family still hanging; the hunting trophies; the wall of color-coordinated book spines (glued over blocks of Styrofoam, as it turned out—no books required!); the giant TVs opposite each of the toilets; the kitchens (three!); the rec room with its leather-topped pool table, massage chairs, and putting green; the back yard with its exotic animal menagerie, topiary, and Grecian marbles. And amid it all, the signs of panic: half-empty Mexican amphetamine packets, drifts of microwave pizza boxes, cigarette-butt-filled half-empty Jack Daniels and VSOP Cognac bottles, a pile of bloody Kleenexes and a worktop covered in white, powdery residue.

The protesters toured the palace in shocked silence, punctuated only by the occasional bark of laughter or exclamation of surprise when a new excess was discovered. A locked, armored basement door was broken down, to reveal an armory lined with assault rifles with all the trimmings, every scope and mall-ninja suppressor known to man. This created a *lot* of excitement, so when another locked door was discovered hidden behind another fake wall of books, everyone crowded in to watch the battering ram team go to work on it.

It turned out to be full of servers.

Kriztina's team turned the basement study attached to the clandestine data-center into a war room, stationing Oksana as gatekeeper at the doorway to explain what was going on to the curious and recruit those with serious IT skillz to assist in the effort.

The presidential off-the-books IT team was definitely not the A-team: IT talent is scarce and even a big budget only goes so far when you're trying to recruit people who could easily walk into jobs with name-brand Silicon Valley companies with billions in offshore accounts and bustling, sleek-officed campuses filled with smart, attractive people who don't fantasize about cutting off their enemies' fingers one knuckle at a time.

So the A-team was off drinking bulletproof coffee in Mountain View and the B-team was building liquidity-provision algorithms in the City of London and the C-team was working for US military contractors and the D-team was working for the US military and the E-team was doing startups and the F-team was writing cryptojacking scripts and injecting them into ad networks and so on.

The Z-team who'd worked for the Slovstakian presidents? They didn't even know well enough to encrypt their hard drives.

When Kriztina's friends yanked out the servers' drives and connected them to their laptops, they found themselves drowning in information. The president had much better accountants than IT staff, the kind of people who keep meticulous records, including PowerPoint decks carefully explaining how they were routing the president's money through a New Zealand numbered company and then through a Wyoming LLC and then through a Scottish limited partnership and then through another LLC in Nevis, with the money coming to rest in the form of luxury flats in Phnom Penh and Hong Kong—where the real-estate markets burned so hot that an empty apartment was a safe deposit box in the sky, convertible to cash in twenty-four hours flat thanks to a waiting list of buyers who needed somewhere to stash the money *they'd* looted from their *own* countries.

mething big is happening.

a?"

said, and then frowned. "She *was* there, inside a police

one second ago." She swung her head around, craning her

up to see over the milling police hats. "*Shit.*"

worn that I had no more juice in the tank for panic or dis-

I was, heart thudding, palms sweaty. A low-flying helicopter

then rose up, sirens wailed, people shouted, and I stared at Aino.

nisha. She had one job, and she'd—

!" she shouted and took off. "Senator!"

ed him, polished politician type, better suit than the city officials,

aircut, as he caught sight of Aino McCulloch bearing down on him,

iling behind her like a naval mine. For a second he looked like he was

to head in the opposite direction, but then he pasted on a gleaming

te smile. "Aino, are you all right?"

that
cluding
a show of fc

What's more,
the Stanford- and
the Slovstakian state, a
tures, which created irrefu
Slovstakian state, and the bloo

The president's palace had its o
data-centers in both Russia and Latvi
was only a matter of minutes before every
in a massive document dump. The hashtag w

flinch
brane, be
to the Oaklan
Aino regained
about Tanisha when
like his ass was on fire. S
"Hey, where's Tanish
"There," the lawyer
van, right there, like
neck and jumping
I would have
tress, but there
buzzed us and
She'd lost T
"Senato
I spott
better h
me tra
goin
wh

I spotted Aino in the milling crowd of cops and city
lice lines. From behind, the cops' killdozer was every
was when it was bearing down on you, a futuristic horror t
mayhem and dystopia. How the hell did you go through the pr
one of those? I mean, what responsible grown-up looked at the glossy
for that thing and then signed the purchase order? It was like a Tonka t
sadistic assholes.

I made my way over to her, limping on my freshly aching knee. "I have *no*
idea what's going on, but *something* is going on."

Aino seemed even more dazed than I was, and took a worryingly long moment to focus on me and figure out what I'd just said. "Masha?"

"Shit. My psycho ex-boss from Zyz nabbed Tanisha, then used her to lure
me in, and she was getting ready to shred me and spit out the pieces, and then
I got rescued by my other psycho ex-boss from Xoth—" I told it as quickly as
I could, while the cops surged around us, and it took everything I had not to

# CHAPTER 14

Marcus had basically shit himself as soon as he caught sight of Carrie Johnstone. She'd PTSDed him that hard, and when he saw her beckoning to me from the door of her mobile command post, he'd whimpered and taken three involuntary steps backward. He'd have kept going except that Ange was right there with him, keeping pace, and she grabbed him and dragged him back.

"We're not going in," she said. "But Masha needs us."

They'd prowled around the bus, trying to catch a glimpse of us through the darkened windows, and then they saw Ilsa and her flying wedge of cops head for the doorway and start pounding it with the butt of a nightstick.

"That's what's-her-name, isn't it? Masha's boss from Xoth?" Marcus whispered.

"Masha calls her 'Ilsa,' but that's not her real name. She's an ex-spook. Stasi. East Germany."

Marcus shuddered. He knew plenty about the Stasi's reputation, it was his personal horror narrative. The guy was a walking encyclopedia of historical and contemporary torture and surveillance tactics. Don't get him started on the Khmer Rouge.

They watched us move from Zyz's bus to Xoth's, following at a distance, but stopped when they spotted Aino, poking at her phone and looking worried and pissed off. They watched her watching the police van, then, recognizing Tanisha's distinctive silhouette through the van's darkened windows, they switched to watching that van, and then, when Carrie Johnstone arrived at the van with a couple uniformed cops and climbed into the front compartment with them just before it drove off, Marcus took off after it while Ange started blasting out texts.

Marcus streaked past the clustered cops, and while the first two he passed decided they had more important things to worry about, inevitably one of them told him to stop—when he didn't, then *all of them* decided that they had better take an interest, and that's when Marcus caught up with the van that Tanisha was in and threw himself in front of it.

The ensuing melee, in which Marcus was thrown to the ground and piled onto by no fewer than ten cops, hit sixteen times with nightsticks, pepper-sprayed and then tazed, ensured that the van wasn't going to go anywhere. The last thing Marcus saw before his eyes swelled shut was Carrie Johnstone, furiously stalking toward him.

It's easy to think of that guy as being a grandstanding doofus, but give him credit: he had run directly *toward* a vehicle bearing Carrie Johnstone, amid heavily armed cops, many of whom recognized her as a surveillance contractor up their chain of command. She was his greatest fear, the face he saw when he bolted upright out of nightmares, and he ran straight for her.

He did it for Tanisha, who he barely knew, but whose cause he believed in. Marcus Yallow did something truly brave that day, and took a beating for it. Long after the bruises healed, he was still seeing a shrink.

A nge had spent her hours sitting on the ground setting up distribution lists for mass texts, all triggered by shortcuts she had programmed into her phone. When the time came, it took her less than a minute to reach sixty-three of her most trusted allies in the movement, including Black-Brown Alliance network organizers with their own distribution lists. Even before she put her phone back in her pocket, it was buzzing with replies; she could hear the sound of people already moving behind her as she rushed toward Marcus.

She reached him just as Carrie Johnstone was bending over him, in a power-stance that was nevertheless way overbalanced, her weight far forward, her wide-planted stance locking her knees, so that when Ange barreled into her from behind, she went headfirst over Marcus, straight into the sidewalk, breaking her fall with her outflung hands and skinning her palms but sparing her skull.

Ange, right behind her, landed on top of Marcus, torquing his shoulders and forcing the bones of his bound wrists beneath his body into the cement. She scrambled to her feet just as the cops closed in on her.

She held her hands up and waited to be tackled, but at that precise moment, at least five hundred protesters surrounded her, the cops, Carrie Johnstone, the van with Tanisha, and Marcus's prone, groaning form.

There was a moment of silence, everyone staring at everyone else, like, *Shit, what the fuck do we do now?* Carrie Johnstone got up on all fours, then to her feet, and eyefucked everyone within her field of vision, before heading back to the van that held Tanisha.

"Tanisha's in there!" Ange shouted, and just like that, a dozen protesters blocked Carrie Johnstone's way. A couple of cops took a step toward Ange, then stopped. Carrie might be in their chain of command, somewhere, but who the hell was she, really, and what did she have to do with this prisoner who had made such trouble for everyone? Watching their streets torn up by haywire hacked cars had shaken them, left them furious and untrusting of these outsiders whose status was always shrouded in tedious and insulting mystery.

The cops turned back to Marcus, and Ange, beside him, and Ange was definitely someone they knew how to deal with: protester, sign, backpack: *Attack*.

Within seconds, Ange found herself on the ground beside Marcus, facedown, a cop three times her size yanking up her arm as he looped her hand through one plastic cuff, then bound her other hand with its free end. The protesters shouted and recorded video and jostled, but none of them stepped forward to intervene as the cops read Ange her rights.

That's when I got there with Aino and the state senator, and the senator grabbed a lieutenant who grabbed a sergeant who started shouting into his radio.

I was there when they sprung Tanisha and Ange from jail. Aino had managed to get them into the same cell and they'd forcefully demanded that they get a simultaneous release. With a press conference. Where they could denounce Oakland PD, Xoth, and Zyz.

Tanisha was sprung first, and the first person she saw was Aino, and the second person was me, but the third person was Salima from the Black-Brown Alliance, and as soon as Tanisha was done hugging me, she was busy mind-melding with Salima, figuring out how they could get some kind of media for the cause, given that no one had delivered her fucking press conference. She gave me one last solemn look as she stepped out into the Oakland night.

Then came Ange. The cops who flanked her were as tall as she was short, making her seem even smaller than usual, but her posture was regal and she walked tall, defiance embodied. I heard Marcus suck in his breath and realized I'd done it too. Of course he loved her. Who wouldn't love her?

She gave him an all-out hug that lasted and lasted, his face in her hair, the two of them breathing slowly together as they squeezed each other. And then, she hugged *me*, every bit as tight, and for a moment, I felt like I was part of something much bigger than myself, something I could believe in.

When Ange finally broke off the hug—much later than I would have—she held me at arm's length for a moment, and I saw there were tears standing in her eyes, brimming them. One slipped down her cheek.

"Thank you, Masha," she said.

"For what?"

Ange laughed, then realized I wasn't kidding. "*Masha.*" So much weird inflection on that word.

"What?"

"You made a good choice."

The words hit me right in the gut. I made a good choice? All my life, I'd made choices that weren't *bad,* but they sure weren't *good.* They were, at best, *expedient.* Had I finally made a *good* choice?

Ange and Marcus offered me another night on their sofa. I said no. They walked off in the direction of BART. They wouldn't let me pay for an Uber. Aino shook my hand in a way that made it clear that I'd be getting a bill and got in her car. Then it was just me.

I pulled out my phone to tap up a rideshare and saw I had a message. From Mom, texting to ask when I was coming home, and then again to say whenever I came home, it would be fine, she didn't want to nag.

Better be getting home, then.

# EPILOGUE

Ange's hug was every bit as warm as I remembered. She'd stood as soon as I entered the café and beamed at me as I threaded my way through the tables, then gathered me into an embrace that went on about twice as long as I was strictly comfortable with.

Once we'd ordered our keto smoothies—it was that kind of place—and ritually sealed our phones in mesh-lined baggies, Ange gave me a long, soulful stare.

"Are you thriving?"

What a thing to ask. "I guess."

"Because you should be. You're a brilliant, principled, strong, beautiful woman. You deserve to thrive."

*Deserve.* People. "Thank you."

She grabbed my hands across the table and squeezed them. "Masha. I'm not fucking around here. I know what you've done. I know who you are. You're not worse than me. You're not worse than Marcus, God knows."

"Sure." I was regretting this coffee date.

"Fuck, come *on,* Masha. Look, you've made some shitty choices. Choices that I never would have made and that hurt people. You can't ever undo or make up for those choices. They're permanently written in the unalterable log of your life. You've also made some *really good* choices, that were braver and more principled than I would have ever made. There are people you've hurt who may never forgive you, sure, but that's true of everyone. It's sure as shit true of me. And there are people who owe you their lives, their freedom, and more, because you did things that no one forced you to do, no one paid you to do, no one even *asked* you to do, that you did because it was the right thing to do.

"Masha, I get the feeling from you that you think life is like a double-entry bookkeeping system, where the debts go on one side and the assets go on the other and you need the assets to exceed the debts or you go bankrupt. That is not how it works. That's why all the good things you've done have not made you feel any better: you keep waiting for the good deeds to cancel out the bad and since that never happens, you feel like you're drowning in ethical debt. You will never pay off your debts, Masha, because the past is unalterable.

"Someday, you will figure out that the reason you feel so bad is that you're trying to make up for things you can never make up for."

My pulse thudded and my palms slicked. I wanted to leave. I wanted to shout at her. I put the feelings in a compartment and calmed myself. From another compartment, a muffled voice explained calmly that if mere words were able to elicit such a strong flight response from me, they were probably true.

But I didn't know what to say. If I couldn't make up for the mistakes I'd made, then what could I do about them? Nothing, it seemed.

"Masha, I get the feeling that you think you and I are rivals, but I don't know what we're supposed to be rivals *for*. Glory? Justice? *Marcus?*" She snorted. "Come on, I love the guy, but if I have to worry about him running off with another woman then what's the point?

"We're not rivals, Masha. We're on the same team. Or, at least, I'm on *your* team. Plenty of people are, but you don't seem to know that. So know it. Team Masha is alive and growing. You need anything, you just ask."

She wouldn't let me pay the bill. She hugged me again when she left.

I waited until my mother was at work to go through the things she'd carefully stored in my room. I got a little tearful, but also a little angry. So much of this stuff was just *garbage* but because she'd saved it for a decade, it had acquired a penumbra of precious antiquity, like Duchamp's urinal: once you treated something like it was worth keeping, it *was*.

I was ruthless. I opened a can of Marie Kondo on that shit and filled bag after bag, until I was down to one small banker's box containing a few journals, a box of photos I'd send out for scanning, and a small packet of handwritten letters, mostly from camp friends. I TaskRabbited it to the dump before my mother came home, presenting her with a fait accompli and a roast chicken and sweet potato dinner that I'd actually cooked (the secret is to rub baking soda and salt into the chicken skin to crisp it up, then stuff the cavity with something to keep it moist, like a quartered lemon and a quartered onion), along with a bottle of really good Mendocino Pinot Gris that always made me nostalgic for drinking out of my friends' parents wine stash when we were teenagers.

Mom greeted the meal with delighted and appropriate suspicion and demanded to know what the occasion was. I told her that she was absolutely right, there was an occasion, and it's that I was going back on the road, back to Europe. And also: that I'd finally sorted out my room.

It made her tearful and angry and, worst of all, *motherly*, concerned about my mental health, and exacting promises that I'd find a therapist. I made her promise the same thing and told her to send me the bill. She got briefly distraught upon the revelation of my razing of the Shrine to Teenaged Masha, and then she ate chicken with me and drank wine and got sloppy and funny and told dirty jokes she knew from Russia and I told her ones I'd heard in Iraq and Slovstakia—sex is universal, but dirty jokes are *not*—and we laughed and stayed up late and then she said she'd do the dishes and I said that I'd let her and I went to bed in my empty room with its bare walls and my packed suitcase at its foot, and the single box of heirlooms packed up and ready to be shipped to me whenever I landed somewhere that I was going to stay in.

Tanisha met me on the way to the Oakland airport, waiting at the bottom of the escalator at Coliseum BART, holding a brown paper sack. "Coffees and empanadas. Better than anything they'll serve you at the airport and it means we can go hang out at the park instead of some café."

We found a dry spot overlooking the marshy wetlands on the shore of the

San Leandro Bay, where the grasses rustled and the wind whipped little white-caps up on the water like meringue peaks.

"See?" she said around a mouthful of empanada.

"Yeah." They were really seriously delicious. The white noise and irregular, peaceful flashes of white on blue soothed me.

"Yeah." She sighed. Again. "You okay, Masha?"

I swallowed. "I'll be fine."

"That's not what I asked."

"You're very sharp."

"That's not an answer."

I took another bite, giving myself time to think. There weren't many people on Earth who had permission to chase me around the conversational ring-a-rosy like this, but Tanisha was one of them. "I'm going to be okay. I'm probably more okay than I've been in a long time. But yeah, I'm not okay."

She nodded. "You're coping, but you've got a lot to cope with. Is that it?"

"Yeah." I swallowed again. The words didn't want to come out. "Neesh, for a long time, I didn't look too hard at who I was and what I was doing. It was like . . . have you ever spilled food on your favorite shirt and then you just don't want to look down and see how bad the stain is?"

"Yeah. Or this—" She pointed to a scar on the tip of her index finger. "Sliced it open cutting an avocado. California battle scar. I held it under the tap for like ten minutes because I just didn't want to see how deep I'd gone. Needed three stitches. It was deep, but until I looked, I barely felt it."

"That's it. I spent a lot of time carefully not thinking about certain parts of my life, parts that I spent like, eight or ten hours a day on. And now . . ."

"You're thinking about them?"

"As much as I can. It's hard. Neesh, I made a lot of shitty decisions. I think—" I suddenly couldn't speak, my throat closed. I swallowed some more. "I think the reason—" It came out in a croak. "The reason I drifted away from you, from my mom, from everyone here, it was that every time I talked to you, I remembered who I had been, and that reminded me of who I was, and then it was like I was looking at that cut, seeing that it went all the way to the bone."

Tanisha didn't look for words to say. She just hugged me, long and hard, and didn't let go when I tried to pull away, which was awkward, but then I surrendered to it and it was so, so good. That feeling lasted all the way to Seattle, but by the time I changed planes for Berlin, it was gone. It was a long flight.

Settling in in Berlin was a long and tedious process that usefully occupied a lot of my time, between Ikea and paperwork and bank accounts and all the rest of it. I plugged into the expat community pretty painlessly, going to late-night Kreuzberg booze-ups that hopped from big beer halls to small bars to tiny speakeasies to someone's living room before I bike-shared home, my hair and clothes stinking of cigarette smoke, and me too tired and too semi-drunk to have to think much before sleep overtook me.

Then Kriztina showed up on my doorstep one day at noon and rang my buzzer until I got out of bed and went downstairs to look through the peephole (I'd disconnected the intercom camera and screen by physically detaching the wire because I don't *do* networked microphones in my living room) and saw her shining elvin face bulging through the fisheye. She'd mermaided her hair, all kinds of purples and pinks and shaved-up undercut sides, and looked as cute and Berlin-y as you could ask for, like a tourist bureau postcard.

I unbolted the door and submitted to the obligatory hug and two-cheek kiss.

"It's good to see you too, Masha."

She looked both younger (her haircut, her clothes) and older (her eyes) than she had in Slovstakia. She was so young. That was something I'd conveniently not thought much about when I'd been in Slovstakia. It wasn't just the hair that made her look younger, though: in Slovstakia, she'd always had the brooding air of someone embroiled in a life-or-death struggle (duh) whereas now she looked like your basic Kreuzberg hipster, the kind of person you'd find discussing blockchain and Know Your Customer rules in a speakeasy while chain-smoking Turkish cigarettes.

"Kriztina?"

"It's me!" That giggle. How had I forgotten that giggle? The smile, too, was much younger. Carefree, even. I also smiled.

"Okay, come in. You could have given me a heart attack, you know. I'm an old lady."

She giggled again and walked on my heels all the way up the stairs to my place, then I made tea and Kriztina plated biscuits and I cleared junk off of two chairs and kicked my dirty laundry into a corner and we hunkered down to marvel at each other.

"The new government is a disaster," Kriztina said. "The centrists seized power, and now they're calling for 'reconciliation' and no 'blame game.' They want to let Litvinchuk slip away with all the money he stole, want to let his collaborators off the hook. Worse, they've let the Nazis help them form a coalition."

"What?" Slovstakia's white nationalists were the only people Kriztina hated more than Litvinchuk and his cronies, even though they'd been useful idiot shock troops for brawling with the palace guards.

"Oh yeah, sure. The coalition government includes assholes who say that they want to protect their 'white, Christian identity.' They're very respectable, not skinheads, no tattoos, but they wank themselves to sleep at night by fantasizing about gas chambers. Fuckers."

"What a disaster."

She looked uncomfortable.

"There's something else, isn't there?" She was never very good at poker-facing.

"Shit. Fine. I've been watching these Nazis. Someone has to."

"Watching how?" But I already knew.

"With your things. You know, the ones Litvinchuk used to use to spy on us. We caught the intelligence service network administrators trying to wipe the servers, told them we'd let them go if they gave us the root passwords. So now I'm inside it and I've got everything the Nazis say and do, everywhere they go. I can listen in on their phones, even when they think they're turned off; I can see their message traffic before it gets encrypted and the incoming messages after they get decrypted. I know where they are and where they go. I can track every communication between the street-fighting thugs and their friends in suits in parliament. I *own* them."

I carefully kept my expression neutral. "You do."

"Yes!" She grinned like a wolf. "I do. It's fucking *amazing*."

"It is."

I didn't manage to keep the danger out of my voice, but Kriztina had so much excited momentum she couldn't put on the brakes. "But, Masha, it's only the start. There's so much there I can't figure out how to use, the automated tracking and logging, the automated power-structure analysis. It's complicated and there's no online documentation, of course."

"Of course." I felt like I was turning to stone.

"So that's why we need *you*." To fire. "We need you to come to Slovstakia, to help us." To ice. "With your help—"

"Kriztina." My facial mask must have slipped because Kriztina was looking worried.

"We can unravel them. More than that, we can unravel their friends, the Nazis they're networking with in other countries, the ones who are funding them, the cryptocurrency wallets they're using—"

"*Kriztina.*"

I put down my teacup and stared at her. She finally noticed my expression.

"What?" She stared at me. "Oh. Oh, Masha, come *on*. They're Nazis, they want to *exterminate us*. They don't deserve your mercy."

"Kriztina. I don't have an ounce of mercy for those Nazi dogfuckers. But you of all people should understand the importance of eliminating surveillance on Slovstakia's network. You should be burning everything in that datacenter to the ground and replacing it with all-new gear, instituting random hardware audits with a CT scanner to look for hardware implants. You should be plugging every hole you can think of and you should never stop looking for more."

She shook her head vigorously, glared at me. "Pretty words and fine ideas. But I have a real problem, not a theoretical one. Real, actual Nazis in my country, and they could very well take over my government."

"And if they do? They'll have all that surveillance technology and they'll be in charge of deciding who to aim it at. Jesus fucking Christ, Kriztina, you *know* this. Any weapon you don't know how to use belongs to your enemy."

She stuck her lip out like a toddler. "I know how to use it."

"Which is why you've come to me to ask for help."

She got to her feet. "Fuck this." She turned to go, then whirled around and stared at me. Her eyes were so *old*. "Funny how you finally found some principles, long after they can do any of us any fucking good." She literally spit on my floor, which was the most post-Soviet thing you could imagine, and then stormed out.

I listened to her stalk down the stairs, listened to my door slam. I went to the window and watched her charge blindly down the Berlin sidewalk. "It's okay," I said to the empty room. "I'm a tough piece of old shoe leather. Been called worse things by better people, et cetera, et cetera. Besides, Kriztina's earned it. Watched people she loved get their heads split open. Been held at the tender mercy of torturers and thugs. She gets to be a dick sometimes."

I felt like I could cry. I didn't. I would reserve my sobs for a later day, a worse trauma. I did.

Ange's phone rang and rang. It hadn't been a good night for me. One of those nights where the theater of the mind replays a greatest-hits highlight reel of my humiliations and regrets, jolting me awake with fresh, shameful shots of adrenaline when a new memory dragged itself center stage. There weren't many people I could call about that kind of thing. In truth, there weren't *any* people I could call about that kind of thing. Add to that the fact that it was 3 a.m., which was late even by Berlin's standards, ruling out the majority of people I saw on a daily basis.

Ange had said I could call her anytime. It took me a lot of dithering to get up the nerve to actually do it. Six p.m. in San Francisco, before dinner, after work. Best time to call, really. And she had said I could call.

I'd been reading (okay, skimming) books (okay, articles) about self-care, and the best advice I'd read was to stop imagining that other people were more judgmental than you. If Ange called me at 6 p.m. to say she needed someone to talk with, would I be pissed off? No, I'd be fine with that. Maybe a little honored, even. Ange was cool.

I wasn't cool. But Cool Ange would be okay with that. I dialed her. Then: ring, ring, ring.

I was tapping to disconnect before her voicemail picked up (I got pissed every time I got left a voicemail, and so I assumed everyone else would prefer that I not leave them a voicemail either, and I had a high degree of confidence in the validity of this assumption) when the phone picked up.

"Ange Carvelli's phone." Marcus sounded out of breath.

"Marcus?"

"Who's this?"

Shit. I hadn't wanted to talk to him. Shoulda hung up. Now I couldn't. I'd left the caller ID unmasked so that Ange would see the German number and figure out it was me. "Hi, Marcus. It's Masha."

Just one instant of extra time slipped past before he said, "Wow, Masha! Uh, great to hear from you. Everything okay?"

"Oh yeah, everything is fine. I was just, ah, calling to check in with Ange. Is she okay?"

"Fine. Just left her phone at home while she went for a walk in the park. We've been experimenting with mindful device use." Thankfully, the line quality was poor enough that he didn't hear my eyes rolling so hard they fell out of my face and bounced all over the old wooden floors of my Berlin flat.

"All right. Just tell her I called."

"Do you want her to call you back?"

"No, it's okay. I'll probably be going to bed soon."

"Wait, are you in Berlin? Shit, it's like, two a.m. there!"

"Three a.m."

"It's three a.m. there! You sure you're okay?"

"I'm sure. Just working on West Coast time for a while," I lied, fluently. "Contract job."

"Oh. Okay, I'll tell her you called."

"Tell her I'll email."

"I'll tell her."

"Thanks."

I was about to hang up—

"Masha—"

"Yes?"

"Are you *sure* everything is okay? I don't want to be pushy or anything, but . . . look, I know about just *some* of the things you've been through, and if it was me, I wouldn't be okay. I've been through a few things, and I'm *not* okay."

I was about to blow him off, but I hadn't been maintaining my compartments and they were all a little leaky. "It's not okay, yeah. But that's okay, if you know what I mean."

He laughed. "I actually totally do."

"I suppose you must." I liked his laugh.

"Masha, if you want to talk about anything, seriously, I'm here. We've had some weird times together, but I consider you my friend, even my good friend, and whenever you need me, I'm here. Seriously. Night or day."

Fuck. I hated crying. I held the phone away from my mouth and sucked in some air and tried to get my breathing under control. I was partially successful. My "Thanks" came out in a broken squeak.

"Masha?"

"I'm okay. Really. I got to go."

"You can talk to me, really."

"No, it's okay."

"You keep saying that. Is it really okay?"

Fuck. "Fuck."

"Come on."

So I told him. About Kriztina and her Nazi problem and her spying and the fight. I hadn't spoken to Kriztina since, and our last conversation kept going around and around in my head.

"Man. That's—man. What a mess."

"Thing is, I'm pretty sure I can get in and shut it all down. No one ever double-checked my work and so I always left myself a login. It's plausibly deniable, the default password for an old testing account that's not in the docs."

A long pause.

"But you wouldn't do that, would you?" He sounded cautious, nervous even.

"Well, obviously I haven't. But why wouldn't I? It's not like Kriztina is likely to ever be my friend again."

"Because she's fighting Nazis, Masha."

Something in my stomach went sour and cold. "Marcus, you're saying you think it's okay for them to be surveilling the whole country—"

"But they're not. They're just surveilling Nazis."

"By scooping up *the whole country's* communications, Marcus. And even if that's okay with you, what about when those Nazis win the next election and *they* get to use all that shit on everyone?"

"But they won't win the election if Kriztina is inside their loop, right?"

I wanted to throw the phone.

"Yeah, if they're perfect, if the Nazis don't cheat. And then they have to perfect and never face cheaters or internal coups, forever. Jesus, Marcus, a you seriously arguing *for* mass surveillance?"

He shot back, "Are you seriously arguing *against it*?" so quickly that (afte the fact) I realized that I'd lanced him in a soft spot. At the time, it just pisse me off.

"Yeah, Marcus, I am. I'm perfectly aware of the irony of this. Are you? I'll tell you one thing, Marcus Yallow, I know exactly how easy it is to talk yourself into that kind of move, how easy it is to convince yourself that you're doing the right thing. I know *exactly* how easy it is to convince yourself that every problem with mass surveillance can be fixed with *more* surveillance. Do you know? Have you ever been there?"

"You're telling me that because you've engaged in surveillance, you're entitled to an opinion that I'm not entitled to, because I've only ever been a subject of surveillance?"

"That is exactly what I'm saying, Marcus. Do you seriously disagree?"

And then he stopped. I rewound the conversation, the fast slide from his sympathetic tone to an accusing one, and how furious that had made me. We had gotten right under each other's fingernails, in record time.

But he was stepping back, cooling down, thinking through. Like a man who'd been married to a strong woman who wouldn't take any shit off of him and expected better than a gunfight every time they disagreed.

"No. No, I don't disagree."

Oh, shit. "Thank you."

"So what are you going to do?"

"What I have to."

We said some other things, and then he said, "If you ever need to talk—" which was his way of letting me get off the phone and onto my laptop.

> You fucking traitor. The message came in on my phone from a number I'd never seen before, a burner. Registered in Slovstakia. I had a pretty good idea who it was from, though.

And then I fell asleep. It was surprisingly easy.

# AFTERWORD

## BY RON DEIBERT, CITIZEN LAB

When Cory Doctorow asked me to write an afterword for his new science fiction novel, I was both delighted and honored to do so. Although I have never met Cory in person, he is a legend in the world of digital media. For well over a decade, I have followed and admired Cory's many trenchant essays about topics ranging from the excessive limitations of digital rights management to mass surveillance. Cory's approach to these topics, and his open-source, Creative Commons, hacktivist-focused philosophy lines up squarely with my own and so, well, I count myself a fan.

But it wasn't until I opened up his manuscript for *Attack Surface* that it dawned on me why Cory had asked me, specifically, to be one of the people to undertake this honor of writing an afterword.

As the founder and director of the University of Toronto's Citizen Lab, I and my dedicated team of hacker/researchers have spent the last twenty years probing beneath the surface of the digital ecosystem that surrounds us. We've turned the academic world of peer-reviewed, evidence-based research into a kind of counterintelligence for civil society and human rights. It's been said we run a "tight ship" (thanks for that, Cory); believe me when I say we *must* in order to take on the adversaries we do and still live to talk about it.

We've reverse engineered apps to uncover hidden algorithms of censorship and surveillance. We discovered surveillance backdoors in the Chinese version of Skype. We've brought to light Iranian, Russian, Chinese, Egyptian, Turkish, Mexican, Ethiopian, Syrian, and numerous other nation-states' hack jobs targeting journalists, human-rights defenders, and even international investigators into mass disappearances.

Using a variety of network measurement techniques, we have scanned billions of internet-connected devices to look for telltale fingerprints we have associated with commercial surveillance gear. Thanks to these wide-area mapping methods, we pinpointed the use of Sandvine/Procera Networks' deep packet inspection (DPI) devices as they were being used to deliver nation-state malware in Turkey and Syria, and to covertly raise money through affiliate ads and cryptocurrency mining in Egypt.

Armed with two weeks' worth of data shared with us by WhatsApp—whose messaging application was exploited by the Israeli-based spyware firm NSO Group—we identified and then notified more than one hundred unwitting civil society victims whose phones had been hacked and who were being spied on by government black operations. Some of these victims whose devices were popped were tracked by Rwandan death squads.

Our research has exposed Saudi espionage against journalists and dissidents which was, in turn, linked to the gruesome execution of the late *Washington Post* journalist Jamal Khashoggi. Thanks to that work, researchers at my lab were themselves targeted by ex-Mossad agents working for a private Israeli intelligence company called Black Cube. Working with a team of journalists and outfitted with our own hidden microphones and pinhole cameras, we were able to expose this subterfuge through a carefully orchestrated counterintelligence sting of our own. (Two can play that game, Black Cube!)

So you may empathize that as I became engrossed in *Attack Surface,* I found myself feeling as though I was looking through a portal into a kind of queer parallel universe of the world we at Citizen Lab inhabit. Zero-days for the Tor network; Regexps through stolen police SMS data dumps; Facebook-enabled uprisings in post-Soviet spaces; IMSI-catcher countermeasures; even phones infected with "malformed WhatsApp messages" (something that hits very close to home). The characters and settings all seemed like desaturated Instagram pics of people I have worked with or places I have been—as when undertaking high-risk, in-country technical tests from dilapidated hotel rooms in zones of conflict or authoritarian regimes.

As I read I became more inspired, more appreciative of the hacktivist culture with which I had (perhaps) grown a little too familiar. I was reminded of what got me into this business in the first place: a deeply rooted desire to question authority (I blame the leather-strap-wielding nuns in my Catholic elementary school for that); to not take the technical systems that surround us for granted; to lift the lid on the internet; to expose despots, dictators, and others who commit abuses of power regardless of the risks; and above all else, to approach the surveillance capitalism environment in which we are drowning with an ethic of relentless curiosity and experimentation.

Some science fiction is meant to alert us to possible worlds we may come to inhabit if we continue unreflectively on our current path of technological development. Think of the awesome risks of genetic engineering as displayed in H. G. Wells's brilliant and very disturbing *The Island of Dr. Moreau*.

For his part, Cory sees his science fiction as an allegory of our (oftentimes dark) technologically mediated world. *Attack Surface* certainly fits the bill.

I hope you will be inspired by this book in the same way I have. I hope, like me, it encourages you to question the technologies that you depend on, that you carry with you wherever you go. Like Masha, I hope you find a way to turn them to your advantage by knowing them from the inside out in the way she does.

Above all, I hope you become inspired to use them to create a better world than the one in which we now live.

Ron Deibert
Professor of Political Science and Director of the
Citizen Lab at the University of Toronto

# AFTERWORD

## BY RUNA SANDVIK

My job is to enable and empower journalists to do their work securely—to communicate with sources, research sensitive stories, and publish hard-hitting news. When I was growing up in Oslo, Norway, I wanted to study law and support families in child custody cases. I didn't think I'd become a vocal defender of press freedom, end-to-end encryption, and online anonymity.

I got my first computer when I was fifteen years old. It was an HP Compaq with a 4 GB hard drive and Windows Millenium Edition. I replaced the operating system with Slackware a year or two later, followed by Red Hat and Debian. I remember a fascination with learning how to do things I wasn't supposed to do. And I loved the puzzles, the challenges, and the never-ending stream of things to dig into. I still do.

I first heard about the Tor Project in 2009. I thought it was interesting that one could use technology to be anonymous online. I wanted to understand how the system worked. I read about the software, the servers run by volunteers, and attacks against the Tor network. It was only later, and gradually, that I recognized how crucial Tor is for different communities. Enabling ordinary people to circumvent censorship, access blocked sites, and express themselves online.

When I support journalists with practical security, I focus on three things: the steps they can take given their starting point, the time they can dedicate to learning new tools and workflows, and the context that they work in. Sandboxes, air-gapped devices, and burner phones do have a place in a journalist's toolkit. But for digital security to be a part of the journalistic process, our guidance must be easy to follow. Looking for a place to start? Try this:

Secure your online accounts with two-factor authentication. This prevents unauthorized parties from gaining access—even if they have your password. Check out Google's Advanced Protection Program for extra features.

Review third-party apps and integrations linked to your accounts. Only keep the apps and integrations that you know you'll want to use moving forward. Don't need the meme generator you set up five years ago? Disable it or close it down.

Use a password manager to create and store unique passwords for your accounts. This will help you avoid reusing passwords across sites. This, in turn, will make it more difficult for someone to log in to your accounts even if they have one of your passwords.

Keep your devices secure by installing the most recent software updates. These updates include fixes for security issues, as well as new features and emojis. Enable automatic updates on your laptops and phones, if you haven't done so already.

Email and direct messages are convenient ways to interact with people. But what you send and receive is often stored by default and visible to the platform providers. Instead, try using Signal, WhatsApp, or Facebook Messenger's "Secret Conversations" feature.

Practical security means balancing staying safe and taking actions to move forward. In my work, I often collaborate with journalists to find secure ways to achieve their goals—whether they're going on a high-risk trip to Syria or setting up a Twitter account for the first time. I wouldn't want anyone to throw out all electronics and go live in the forest. I want us to enjoy a social, connected life while understanding what that means for us and the people we are close to.

A security engineer friend of mine says that "everybody deserves good security." This principle does not limit itself to corporate accounts, systems, or devices, nor to standard working hours. Tanisha doesn't stop being an activist when she's not attending Alliance meetings. Cory doesn't stop being an author when he's not writing. We must focus on securing identities, not only the role someone plays between the hours of nine and five.

"Just don't do it" is the phrase that continues to fail us when it comes to se-curity awareness training. Every day, we make trade-offs in exchange for solu-tions that enhance our lifestyle. Google tracks your location but helps you get to your meeting on time. Amazon tracks your likes and dislikes but provides you with personalized recommendations. Some period trackers share data with third-parties but help you keep up with your flow and cycle.

It's not realistic or fair to tell people that if they want to be more secure, they should avoid doing common things, like clicking on links, using public wireless networks, and posting on Facebook. That would be like telling people not to send nudes. It doesn't work. And there's nothing inherently wrong with these things, either. People want to make connections, share ideas, and take part in global conversations. In an ideal world, they would do so securely by default.

But that's in an ideal world, and we don't live in that world. Unfortunately, lawmakers argue that a secure, networked future requires surveillance, cen-sorship, and back doors. Where law enforcement agencies repeatedly say that online anonymity is a threat to their ability to solve cases. Where politicians demand that tech companies break encryption for everyone in an effort to fight terror, drugs, and online child predation.

What's also unfortunate is that people lose sight of what end-to-end encryp-tion affords us. Room to explore, space to be ourselves, and protection for our online life. I'm grateful to those who advocate for anonymity, despite receiving threats online. There is a need to balance online privacy, everyday security, and the ability to solve crime. But not at the cost of individuality, freedom, and self-expression.

Authorities will, from time to time, talk about needing a back door to see what people are doing online. And in doing so, asserting that it's possible to have one just for the "good guys." I can assure you this does not exist. And even if it did, who would decide who the "good guys" are? Who would decide what's right or wrong, what's acceptable or not, what should be available or censored?

Don't accept the solutions proposed by the authorities if they don't have data to back them up. Whether it's back doors, unlimited data retention, or enhanced surveillance, demand to know how effective today's measures are. What's working, what's not, and how new solutions will change things. Make sure you understand the negative impact—the cost—that new solutions have on our lives. Only then can we start to make better choices for ourselves and our collective future.

The front pages of newspapers tell stories of courageous acts by ordinary people. People like you and me making the difficult decision to speak up. About surveillance, election interference, harassment, climate change, the global spread of a new virus. This book is a powerful reminder that you, like Masha, can choose how you live your life. How you use your skills, knowledge, and time. I encourage you to look at how you spend your days and see what you find.

What will you stand for?

# AUTHOR'S NOTE

When I started working in technology, I was a technological optimist: that is to say, I believed that, with the right technology, we could create a kind of demimonde that lived alongside mundane reality, out of reach and out of sight of temporal authorities.

Then, as I got more experience and watched people suffer stinging defeats while trying this maneuver, I thought that perhaps technology could be a force multiplier for the powerless, a sling for the world's Davids to use on the world's Goliaths.

This, too, turned out to be a dead end. Technology *could* topple Goliaths, but they wouldn't stay down. You might be able to dump docs on a corrupt military contractor or publish a video of a despicable mayor shouting racist things and smoking crack (you can take the boy out of Toronto, but you'll never take the Toronto out of the boy—I love ya, YYZ, you're the city that never sleeps . . . in). But then the FBI would flip your Anonymous coconspirators and get you sentenced to jail for sixty-three months (free Barrett Brown), or even thirty-five years (free Chelsea Manning!).

Today, I remain a technological optimist—but a realistic one.

Technology *can* build cryptographically secured fortresses that can shelter you from the authorities . . . just not indefinitely. Even if your ciphers are secure, your movement isn't, because your human network has to be perfect in its operational security to remain intact, while the authorities only need to find a single slipup to roll you all up.

Technology *can* be a force multiplier, for the powerful and powerless alike. But the use of technology by the powerless is more salient than when it is wielded by the powerful, because giving power to the powerless is a change in *kind,* while increasing the power of the already powerful is merely a change in *degree*. But that temporary power boost will be denatured by the powerful as quickly as they can manage it, so the advantage is not enough to make lasting structural changes.

To make lasting structural changes, *you need to use technology to change politics*.

In other words: technology is a tool for social change because it can temporarily shelter you from the all-seeing eye of a corrupt state, and because it can temporarily give you a force multiplier to take on the powerful—and what you need to do during that temporary, technologically dependent window is *reform your society* so that your government is just and responsive and transparent.

Technology cannot substitute for a just society, but it *can* help you create that society.

As this book is going to press, the world is riven by authoritarian politics, supercharged by technological surveillance and influence campaigns. We stand at the brink of a permanent environmental cataclysm that threatens our very species. We have never, ever needed shelter and force multipliers more than we do today.

To the technologists reading this book: your employers need you more than you need them. You don't get massages and free kombucha because your employers are swell fellows, you get them because they're terrified that you will go and work for someone else. You have power. You can use it. Tech workers at giant and small tech companies are unionizing and demanding that their employers confront their role in the climate emergency, the inhumane treatment of prisoners and migrants, their labor inequities, and their contributions to harassment and disinformation campaigns. You are not alone in wondering whether your work is a force for good in the world, nor in desiring to make it so. Organizations like Tech Solidarity are standing by to help you organize to make your work a force for good.

To the users of technology reading this book: it doesn't have to be this way. No one came down off a mountain with two stone tablets reading "Thou shalt stop rotating thine logfiles and instead mine them for actionable market intelligence." Social networks can connect you with your friends and people who share your principles and interests without commodifying those relationships or ginning up conflicts in order to increase pageviews. There is nothing about providing a well-designed phone or computer or car or tractor that necessitates that you be barred from installing a competitor's apps or getting it serviced by a third party.

Technology does not have to be extraction's handmaiden, nor surveillance's constant companion. These are decisions that named individuals—billionaires, mostly—took for their own purposes, and then they argued that there was no alternative. There is an alternative. You have the right to technological self-determination. If the companies that dominate the marketplace and the politicians who do not lift a finger to stop them refuse to give you that self-determination, then they must be stopped. Not through individual action, but through collective action, organized through the internet and projected into the real world through regulation and prosecutions.

This is a book about how people rationalize their way into doing things that they are ashamed of, and how they can be brought back from the brink. I wrote it because I am as guilty as you are of that kind of rationalization, and it's only by confronting it that we can overcome it.

I had some fantastic help in writing this book. First, I had the support of my family, especially my parents, Gord and Roz, and my wife, Alice, and our daughter, Poesy. My agents, Russ Galen and Ann Behar, are indispensable: supportive, shrewd, responsive—pit bulls when fighting for you and cheerleaders in between. My editor Patrick Nielsen Hayden and the people of Tor—Molly McGhee, Sarah Reidy, Alexis Saarela, Fritz Foy, Lucille Rettino—and the Tor alums—notably Patty Garcia and Dot Lin—made this book and the ones that came before it possible.

Juliet Ulman's editorial help with this book was indispensable. She showed me how to cut forty thousand words out of it! Thanks to Juliet, and to Scott Westerfeld and Justine Larbalestier for introducing me to her.

Michael Marshall Smith was good enough to let me borrow his swearing for the "Fuck right off and keep fucking off" soliloquy. Smith is a brilliant writer, but he's also an unsuspected grandmaster of profanity.

In the twelve years since I published *Little Brother,* I have had occasion to meet people who work in the tech industry—security researchers, cyberlawyers, software developers, network administrators, tech ethicists, activists—who came to the field after reading that book and its sequel, *Homeland.* I never know quite what to say when you folks introduce yourselves, and the truth is, it's because the pride and delight I feel when this happens is so huge and all-encompassing that I can barely choke out a response.

So for the record, let me say this: To everyone who credits my books with getting them interested in technology as a force for good, *thank you*. Not for flattering me with your praise, but for getting involved in a field where that kind of thoughtful, combative, sensitive, ethical posture is needed more than ever.

My sincere thanks also to my EFF colleagues past and present, and to our allies at other organizations, from the Free Software Foundation to EDRi to Fight for the Future to Creative Commons to the Internet Archive to Wikimedia to Mozilla and so, so many more.

Thanks, finally, to the people who promoted *Little Brother* and got it into so many greedy young hands—Neil Gaiman, to be certain, but also the librarians, teachers, and mentors who did so much for me and my books over the years.

Folks, it's 2020. The world is on fire. The web is five giant services filled with screenshots of the other four.* Present-day wealth concentration makes the Gilded Age look like a socialist paradise. We can do better. We will do better. We are an amazing thing, we humans, and we have done amazing things. We will do more amazing things together, and we'll need a free, fair, and open internet to coordinate us while we do them.

We fight on.

---

* Hat tip to Tom Eastman (@tveastman)

# ABOUT THE AUTHOR

CORY DOCTOROW is a regular contributor to *The Guardian, Locus,* and many other publications. His award-winning novel *Little Brother* was a *New York Times* bestseller, as was its sequel, *Homeland*. His 2019 novella collection *Radicalized* is one of five finalists for this year's CBC "Canada Reads" program. Born and raised in Canada, he lives with his family in Los Angeles.